AKUR

A SCI-FI ALIEN REBEL ROMANCE

THE RESTITUTION
BOOK 3

A. G. WILDE

PETRONIE
PUBLISHING

AKUR

They thought they could break her. They were wrong.

Captured by the dying Tasqal empire, Constance faces a fate worse than death. But they didn't count on Akur—the rebel warrior who'd rather die than fail, and who's determined to tear their world apart to save her.

Stranded on a planet that shouldn't exist and hunted by an enemy that will stop at nothing, Constance and Akur uncover a devastating secret: the Tasqals' plans reach farther—and darker—than anyone imagined.

Every choice brings them closer to answers...and closer to doom. Trust is their only weapon, and love? A weakness they can't afford. With countless worlds hanging in the balance, failure isn't an option **—not when the cost is annihilation.**

BEFORE YOU READ!

If you're picking up this book right after reading *V'Alen*, you can skip this part.

If not, I recommend going back to *Ajos* (or even starting with my series *Captured by Aliens - Xul*). As the plot is an overarching one, some things will be easier to understand if you read that book first. For those who don't want to go back, or are new to this series or my work, here's a brief rundown of what's happened before.

MASSIVE SPOILERS AHEAD

In books 1-5 of *Captured by Aliens*, we met five couples. Five human females and five alien rebel heroes who rescue them from the High Tasqals—a race of overgrown toad-like beings who are dying from some incurable disease that makes it impossible for them to reproduce on their own.

And who better to fill that gap than lovely humans. (I mean, you already know it. We're just too awesome for our own good.)

At the end of that series, we find out there are more humans trapped in a stasis hold somewhere and our rebels make an oath to rescue them.

Then comes the book, *Ajos*.
A rebel fighter who helps open the stasis hold, he falls for Kerena, a female who was trapped inside it.
Ajos takes Kerena with him on what should have been a safe-enough mission, but nothing goes to plan. Kerena is kidnapped by a plant. Yes, you read that right.
While imprisoned by this flora, she discovers the plant reacts to human blood.
It turns out, the compound created when this plant reacts with human blood is key to healing the very beings who abducted her: the Tasqals. (Boo, right?)

But more important is a device Kerena and Ajos discover during their mission: a glowing orb. They have no idea what it's capable of, but the High Tasqals are desperate to retrieve it.

This leads us to *V'Alen*.
A cybernetic being, V'Alen, and Alaina—the human who made him feel—embark on a mission to protect the orb. They hide it away to ensure its energy signature can no longer be detected by the Tasqals. During their journey, they discover two opposing compounds derived from the one Kerena found: one that could cure the Tasqals... and one that could annihilate them.

And now we come to *Akur*. Happening alongside *V'Alen*, his story is integral in helping us navigate this war.

If you're still with me and any of that made sense—buckle up and keep reading!

I hope you enjoy!

 AG

1

Akur

Star date: *Three cycles ago*

The gravity beam sliced through the chaos like a blade of pure light, and everything went silent.

Akur's ears rang from the explosion that had just rocked the Restitution's base. Lifeblood trickled down his forehead, mixing with the sweat and grime of battle. Through the smoke, he glimpsed the massive Tasqal ship hovering above—its hull a nightmare of dark metal and pulsing energy nodes.

Time slowed. "Qrak." It all but stopped.

Another boom rocked the area, and everything nearby—everything including him and the human he was carrying in his arms—vibrated with a hum that went straight down to his very cells. The ground beneath his feet crackled with building energy, making his nefre pulse in warning. That sixth sense all Shum'ai warriors possessed was screaming danger.

Gravity beam. They needed to run.

But he couldn't move.

The beam was already active.

Distantly, he heard bodies fall. Heard them break. Rebels who had fought alongside him for many moons. Brothers he'd trained with, bled with, survived with—now scattered like nothing across their once thriving base.

The war they'd known was coming had finally arrived. The Tasqals had launched an all-out attack...but the Restitution hadn't been ready.

"Hold on!" The command came from his comrade nearby. V'Alen fell to the ground, his cybernetic suit lighting up as he braced hard over the human he was protecting, and everything snapped back into place.

In a single click, time sped up once more.

Air rushed into his lungs as the particles around him began rising. And the light, that qrakking beam that had illuminated them just moments before, suddenly became like a living thing.

Gravity ceased to exist.

The human he'd been taking to safety was no longer in his arms. She floated out of them even as he tried to hold on. His digits barely brushed her arm as the beam lifted them both—suspended in a moment of weightlessness. A moment of terrible inevitability.

They were taking her. The Tasqals. They hadn't only come for the new weapon hidden here on the Restitution's base—that mysterious orb no one understood. They'd come for these females, too.

Grabbing the female's arm, he held on with everything he had. Muscles straining, tendons pulled taut, his digits locked with hers while his other claw gripped the broken edge of a building.

But the gravity beam was a merciless thing—a column of light that defied Shum'ai strength, defied even his determination. The ground beneath him was breaking apart under the pull, his entire body a living anchor fighting against an impossible force.

But the beam was an unrelenting foe.

"Kon-stahns!!"

Kon...stahns. That was her name? It floated on the energy-infused air, a strained cry that came from the lips of the human V'Alen braced over. But Kon-stahns didn't respond. Instead, her gaze locked with his. Those strangely bright eyes—so blue they were almost white—held the quiet horror of someone watching their death approach. She scrambled to grab hold of the one thing anchoring her to the ground.

Him.

But it wasn't enough.

His hold on her didn't fail, but something else did. The piece of building he was gripping suddenly crumbled. In a moment of suspended time, he was floating with the human upward, his body frozen as if tied by invisible threads that prevented him from doing a thing.

His gaze flicked to the massive ship pulling them into itself before his focus shifted back to the human floating upside down just above him. There was nothing to grab, nothing to brace against. Just empty air and that strong pull upward. And like entering the maw of some beast while completely paralyzed, there was nothing he could do.

His greatest fear had come true.

So long wanting to end this war...but rendered completely help-less when it mattered most.

The moment the beam deposited them into the damned vessel was the exact moment the Tasqals' minions, the Hedgeruds, descended. There was no time to think. He was grasping his blade before the thought even reached his mind. With a roar, it slid through flesh, taking one guard down. But there were too many. And the human...

She was gone.

"Kon-stahns!"

As more of the reptilian Hedgeruds converged, he spotted brown strands. Saw as the Hedgeruds dragged the human away with two others of her kind. Her blue-white eyes met his one final time, not with the terror he expected, but with something far more devastating.

Resignation.

It was a look that had him momentarily frozen. Enough for a

Hedgerud to find an opening, a boot coming straight to his face as they kicked him backward.

That look in the human's eyes was the last thing he saw before he was tumbling backward into thin air.

Frozen, he was wide-eyed as he fell. Wide-eyed and momentarily frozen. Because that look...

Kon-stahns had looked at him as if she expected him to fail.

As if she knew he would.

There was no gravity beam this time. Just plain old gravity and a distinctly clear view of the massive ship as he fell from it. Impact with the ground below felt like it destroyed every cell inside him. Breath left his lungs. His bones felt shattered. And yet he could only focus on that ship, watching as the vessel began moving.

Hands—metal, familiar—hauled him from the ground. Through the ringing in his ears, he heard V'Alen's voice over the cacophony of destruction. The base was falling apart around them. Blaster rounds tore through buildings, their heat so intense it melted the reinforced walls into slag. The air itself seemed to burn with each explosion, thick with the stench of scorched metal and burning flesh.

Through his blurred vision, he saw rebels running, falling, *dying*. Some were crushed beneath collapsing structures; others cut down by Hedgerud forces that kept materializing from the smoke. More Tasqal ships passed overhead, carving through what remained of their defenses. More screams. More death.

So...after all these moons...this was how it ended?

Qrak that.

He tried to rise. All that happened was his limbs refused to cooperate.

As if far away and not right beside him, he heard V'Alen talking to the human he'd managed to keep grounded, her voice trembling as she worried about the one he'd lost. Kon-stahns. Meanwhile, somewhere in the chaos, medical teams were risking Hedgerud attacks by dragging the wounded to safety, their tunics stained with the multi-colored blood of different species. The Restitution had been more than just a rebellion—it had been home to warriors from across the stars.

Now they were all falling together.

"Go," he ground out. V'Alen needed to go. Needed to take the human he was protecting before she was lost like the one he'd been trying to hold on to. Needed to get to that orb hidden somewhere on the base. The one these jekins had come for. V'Alen had to make sure this scum didn't reach that orb first. And as for the humans that were just taken...

He would just have to deal with that himself.

Through the smoke, he glimpsed another building collapse, burying both rebels and Hedgeruds beneath its weight.

Move. They needed to move.

One moment, he was hauling himself away from where he'd fallen from that ship, the ground beneath his feet trembling with each new blast. The next, he was in the lift that led down to the bunkers, leaving behind a world on fire. The last thing he saw before the doors closed was a squad of rebels making their last stand, their weapons blazing against an enemy that kept coming, wave after merciless wave.

Reality swam and faded. Everything blurred into a haze of pain and motion. The lift carried him down into the safety of the bunker. V'Alen was there one moment, and the next, he was gone—likely to secure the weapon. Or perhaps it hadn't been a single moment at all. Now there were other voices—broken, haunted things. The few survivors. A handful of humans with wide, haunted stares. Rebels with missing limbs and burned flesh. He heard the medic's clipped tones. Felt the burning rush of infusions as they tried to knit his battered body back together.

But he couldn't escape it—that stench from above still clung to his skin. The scent of smoking ruins and broken bodies. The smell of *defeat*. Of everything they'd built reduced to ash. The remnants of everything they'd fought for, years of sacrifice gone in moments.

And that darned ship.

He needed to go after it.

It wasn't over yet.

He couldn't let it end like this.

Staggering off the medical table despite the medic's protests, he headed for the dock. His boots left smears of lifeblood on the floor. His? Someone else's? He didn't know.

He needed a ship. Any ship. The Tasqals wouldn't get away with this. They wouldn't get to write this rebellion out of history like all the others.

And he almost made it to a ship. Through the haze of pain, he barely made out the curved horns of the male that now blocked his path. Even in the dim emergency lighting, the fresh wounds across E'lot's chest gleamed wet and raw.

Thank the stars. He was alive. One of the Restitution's best fighters, still standing. He could barely grunt a breath of relief. At least not all was lost. Some rebels remained. Not everyone was dead. Not yet.

"Move."

"Get back to the bunker, Akur."

"The Tasqals..." He breathed. "They have humans. I saw the ship. I have to—"

"You can't go." E'lot made himself bigger. "You're in no shape to go alone."

"Try to stop me," he grunted, brushing past the large male as he staggered toward a small shuttle. It was a little thing, barely worthy of taking into deep space, scorched and dented from debris—but there was no other option. It was either that or give up.

He was Shum'ai. He was built to persevere.

Weakness was not an option. Not when their enemies thought they'd won. Not when they needed to show that this rebellion wouldn't die so easily.

And not when the haunting gaze of that bright-eyed female still scorched his memory. That quiet acceptance in her eyes had cut deeper than any weapon could, and he'd be damned if he'd prove her right.

Throwing the shuttle doors open, he glanced over his shoulder, vision waning as he looked back at the large male. E'lot stood there, covered in scars and fresh wounds, but with his chin tilted high.

Qrak. He wasn't going to let him go alone, was he.

"Are you coming or not?"

E'lot huffed a breath through his nostrils, the septum ring he wore swaying with the motion, before he stepped forward. In his eyes burned the same fury, the same refusal to let this be the end.

~

Star date: *Present time*

AKUR'S CLAWS curled into fists, his knuckles blanching pale teal as he fought the urge to slam them into the console before him. Beside him, E'lot asked something. A question he barely heard, but one that manifested like a whisper ricocheting in his head, anyway.

What if they didn't find the humans?

The ship that took them could be anywhere across the stars by now.

But he couldn't accept that. *Wouldn't* accept it. There had to be *some* sign of them, some trail to follow across this endless void. There was no other option.

Otherwise... Otherwise, he'd have to face the destruction left behind.

He'd have to face their loss.

His *failure*.

His claws dug into his palms, breaking the skin. Lifeblood swelled, but he barely felt the sting. His mouth curled in irritation instead.

"We've been searching for long, Akur." There was a tinge of resignation in Elot's voice. "We don't know where to look."

He was right. Their chances of finding the Tasqal ship were dismally low.

Perfectly healed now, he was thinking straight. That didn't change the fact that he wasn't turning back. But the void was vast, and the Tasqals cunning.

They had better weapons. A faster ship. Even with a damaged vessel, they were better off than the shuttle he and E'lot were using to chase after them. Not to mention that the Tasqals also had more resources—and a terrifying new warp technology neither of them understood.

"Perhaps we should return," E'lot continued. "Help any survivors..."

Silence enveloped their little shuttle.

There was nothing left to return to. Both of them knew that. The Restitution's base was a place that only now existed in their memories.

The qrakking Tasqals and their allies. *The Council's wrath on them all.*

They couldn't go back. Accepting defeat felt like betrayal. His pride refused to let him. But they'd searched every outpost and space station in every direction and found *nothing*. No ion trails. No whispers of that ship or the human captives trapped on it. It was as if the ship with the females had simply...vanished.

His gaze slid to E'lot sitting over at the secondary controls. They stared at each other, golden eyes meeting brown, a silent battle of wills. When Akur didn't respond, E'lot released a breath of hot air through his nose.

The humans were out there, lost among the stars. And it was up to him and E'lot to find them. There was no one else.

There was no one left.

"We'll find them," he grated. And they would. They'd find them before the Tasqals could use them for whatever purpose they intended. Because he wasn't going to sacrifice everything only to end up losing in the end.

The Tasqals had finally revealed their weakness—their obsession with both the "orb" weapon and these humans from a distant world. The Restitution had possessed both. Now, retrieving those humans was the only way to deny their enemy what they needed most.

But...that wasn't the only reason for his stubbornness, was it...

She was out there. Kon-stahns. The one that had looked at him like he'd failed. The shame ate at him like acid. He was Akur the Undefeated. And she was just another human. Someone else he had to rescue.

Yet...

Akur frowned, staring out the viewscreen.

Yet he remembered her face. Those bright eyes. Couldn't get past that final look she gave him.

And that's probably why he wanted to get her back so badly.

Flexing his bloodied hand, he fought to still the tremor that went through it. Just thinking about the state of everything he left behind made the nefre running along his nape writhe and pulse with agitation.

They had to find that ship.

"There's still nothing on the scans," E'lot's grim voice broke through his thoughts once again, causing his gaze to refocus on the viewscreen. Out there, the endless void stared back at him. Cold, empty, and lifeless, just like the organ that should be beating at the center of his chest.

"Keep looking," he growled. "They couldn't have just disappeared."

But...they might have. That new tech the Tasqals had—the one that allowed them to warp right into the Restitution's base, past all their defenses—that technology meant anything was possible.

Staring blindly at the console before him, his claws spasmed again, desperate for an enemy to tear into. There had to be *something* he could still do. Somewhere he could channel this simmering rage and guilt into action.

"They must have gone into hyperspace." E'lot glanced his way.

Akur kept his gaze on the viewscreen because E'lot's suggestion was a possibility he refused to consider. If that ship had managed to jump, any chance of ever finding the qrakking scum was gone.

"V'Alen damaged the engines," he said instead.

"And if that didn't slow them down?"

But E'lot's logic only stoked his anger.

Releasing a breath, Akur closed his eyes for a moment, but those anger management classes the Council had forced him to take were obviously useless.

Without a word, he slammed a fist into the control panel before him, momentarily causing the buttons to blink in staggered confusion as his command went unrecognized. Pain shot up the wound in his palm, and he welcomed the sting.

E'lot glanced his way before a breath heaved in his chest once more. Running a hand over his curved horns, the ring in his nose jangled once more as he exhaled and stood.

"If we can't find them..." There was an edge to E'lot's tone as he stood there, facing the rear of the ship. It was a note he hadn't ever heard in the warrior's voice before. One etched with doubt. Defeat. Was he giving up, too?

A growl rumbled in Akur's chest. "We *will* find them."

Them. *Her.* He had to believe that or spiral into the same despair he was sensing in E'lot's tone. The Restitution was gone, but they were still alive. *That had to mean something.* The urge to see every last Tasqal die at the tips of his claws was all that was keeping him focused on this desperate journey.

"We should stop at the next station." E'lot rolled his shoulders. "Regroup. Find what's left of the rest of us. Make a plan." E'lot was right, but his words fell like sharp knives.

Lips curled, Akur pulled his attention from the viewscreen and looked up at his comrade. "Why come along if you think our chances so dim?"

E'lot's eyes narrowed only slightly before he rolled his huge shoulders again, bones cracking and muscles rippling. E'lot was one of the few warriors that could match him in a fight. But no aggression came from his comrade. There was no pushback. Not right now. "I wasn't going to let you come out here to die alone."

As E'lot's heavy footsteps faded as he headed to the rear of the ship, guilt tweaked Akur's conscience. *He was not the only one who had lost everything.*

Subtly, Akur rubbed the nefre at his nape, trying to ease the strange tingling within it. "We'll find them." But he wasn't sure E'lot even heard. Wasn't sure he even said it loud enough. Because...what if he was wrong? What if he was stubbornly trying to deny the fact this was, indeed, the end?

What if even the humans knew it? What if that look in that female's eyes...what if even Kon-stahns knew?

Qrakking crukks.

His nefre pulsed again, and he brushed a palm over it roughly, annoyed at the insistent pulses going through it. Eyes on the void, he willed something to happen. Anything.

The answer was there; he simply had to find it. Even if he had to search through every star chart, trajectory, and smuggler's route in the quadrant, he'd find them. The Restitution couldn't end like this. On such a pitiful note. Not after all these orbits. He would tear apart the whole qrakking universe if he had to.

It was the only purpose he had left.

And that's when he saw it. A blip on the screen. A single flash of fine light in a sea of nothing. He stiffened in his seat, staring at the spot where the blip had occurred. There was nothing there now. Almost as if it didn't happen. But he knew he saw it. A spark of hope in a sea of darkness.

His nefre pulsed as he leaned closer to the screen, staring at the coordinates as they generated before him. He felt his mouth curl, a snarl rising on his lips.

It was them. He was sure of it.

A long shot, but they had nothing else to go on.

And this time, he wouldn't fail.

2

Constance

GULPING, Constance fought to maintain her steady breaths as she opened one eye. Gator-guards were moving outside the cell. Her jaw still ached from where one of them had punched her days ago.

Back then, she'd been so pumped with adrenaline and fear, that the pain had felt like nothing. But now it ached like a bitch. Her jaw was swollen, probably black and blue, but at least she still had all her teeth.

Opening her mouth as wide as she could, she rolled her jaw and stretched the aching muscles, forcing blood to flow as she kept her eyes on the guards. None seemed to notice she wasn't unconscious. They'd stopped paying attention to her and the other two women imprisoned in the cell ages ago.

And that was a blessing.

The ship shuddered, the deck plates vibrating beneath her, but not enough to cause alarm. Because for the entirety of their journey to *wherever* the ship had been shuddering. Something was definitely wrong with it. She didn't know much about spaceship engines or mechanics—being a therapist didn't exactly lend itself to aerospace engineering in between counseling sessions and paperwork. Just a few months ago, her biggest concerns had been growing her practice and helping her clients.

Now here she was, on a damaged spaceship light years from home with walking alligator guards intent on her demise. It was still so unreal, like a bizarre dream she kept expecting to wake up from. But the constant tremors of the struggling engines kept reminding her this was anything but a dream.

Turns out waking up on an alien planet after being forced into cryogenic sleep wasn't the nightmare. It was the terror of being abducted *again*.

So much death, and for what? The Restitution was destroyed, countless lives lost, and just to retrieve—squinting in the dim light, she turned her head slowly, eyes landing on the others with her—*two* other humans? Unless there were other captives somewhere else, surely this was a failed mission.

Her gaze locked with the woman across from her. Meredith, she'd said her name was. She was lying on the floor in a similar position, sharp gaze pointed at the guards, her chest rising and falling with heavy breaths.

Meredith was ready. And so was she.

They were to pretend to sleep or act like they were still unconscious. Lull the guards into a state of complacency and then take hold of the ship. Somehow.

It wasn't a solid plan. About as solid as the shifting deck plates beneath them. But it was something.

She clung fiercely to that thought. There *had* to be hope. She just needed to survive long enough to find it. Because they were on their own. No one was coming to save them.

Everyone else was dead.

"The citadel is in the next quadrant." The words of a gator-guard reached her ears.

Constance stiffened. There wasn't enough time.

Daring to peek at where the guards were stationed outside the cell, her eyes landed on the one that spoke. He was larger than the other. Obviously older and more experienced, judging from the battle scars on his scaly skin. The other was younger-looking. Thinner. Possibly new. Or maybe that was just her hoping. Praying on his inexperience.

"Prepare for arrival," the guard continued before turning and heading down the corridor. "Get the *jekins* ready."

Now?

Constance swallowed hard and dipped her head once more. The alarm in her eyes reflected that in Meredith's. Giving the other woman a slight signal with a dip of her chin, she watched as Meredith mimicked the action. Meredith was more than ready.

Eyes sliding to the only other female in the cell, worry tickled the edges of Constance's senses.

Even in the dim light, the woman was hard to see. Dark hair hung over her head, concealing her features, and she sat with her legs drawn up to her chest. The woman seemed frail, as if she hadn't been eating since waking up from cryo. But none of that was why the worry was now crawling up her spine. For she knew this woman. Had seen her from those very early days after they'd all been rescued from the cryo hold.

She was the one that didn't speak. The one who had been awake during the entire journey from Earth to the stars. Locked in stasis but completely conscious. And she didn't need her psychology degree to tell her the woman's mind was still processing that trauma.

Had she even been listening while they'd whispered this very shaky plan? Did she even care?

She couldn't see the woman's eyes, but she was sure they were open. Staring dead ahead like they usually did. No recognition. No awareness.

She wasn't living here in the present. Wherever she was, it was far away from here.

Fuck. That was just going to make this a lot trickier.

Gulping, Constance's gaze flew back to Meredith's. She gave her another slight nod of the chin and readied herself. As soon as the opportunity provided itself, they would take it.

For a few moments, nothing happened, and she wondered if the rookie was going to follow his orders or not. But when he finally moved toward the cell, she knew it was time.

And he was alone.

Even better.

It was obvious they didn't think humans would give any trouble. To them, humans were only good for one thing. A gross underestimation. Because if the Tasqals wanted humans so badly, they should have researched and learned one thing about humanity:

Humans didn't know when to give up.

Tensing, every muscle coiled itself tight as the lone gator-guard approached. This was it—possibly their only chance. One quadrant remained. They were almost at their destination. And if she had it her way, they would never get there.

The gator-guard stopped in front of the energy barrier, peering in, and she had to force herself to remain still, feigning unconsciousness. With a snort, yellow eyes glowing, the guard tapped something on his wrist, and the barrier dissolved.

"Wake up, pitiful creatures," he growled. "You jekins expect me to carry you?"

Her pulse roared in her ears as he stepped into the cell. Just a little closer...

He stopped just inside, claws hanging loosely as he peered down at them, so arrogantly certain they were helpless. And she continued pretending to be...until he reached for her.

It must have been a reflex because her hand closed around his scaly wrist so quickly, her eyes widened in surprise.

"Trauma's a bitch that way," she frowned at her hand before meeting the yellow eyes staring down at her. "It sticks around."

This was it. Time to get out of this mess. She could do this.

The gator-guard growled. A low hiss that traveled through his gut and up his frame. But she held on, jaw set.

"The last time one of you fuckers reached for me in my sleep, I got punched in the face," she grated out. "Not this time."

As the gator-guard growled again, glare filled with poison at the fact she dared touch him, he reached for her with his other claw, and she suddenly moved. Ruse over.

Releasing his wrist, she rolled out of the way, his claw missing her by mere inches. Only his heightened growl and hiss told her he was getting pissed by the second. But he wouldn't get to reach for her again.

In the corner of her eye, Meredith hurtled from the floor, slamming her entire body into the guard's massive frame. Not expecting the sudden torpedo of human female, his reaction was too slow. Definitely a rookie. He stumbled back with a harsh grunt, crashing into the corridor wall. Not part of the plan, but this was their chance.

Rising, terror surging through her veins, she pulled her attention from Meredith's distraction and raced to the third prisoner—the broken, silent woman huddled, still unmoving in the corner. Not even reacting to the desperate bid for escape occurring right in front of her.

"Come on! We have to move!" Even shaking her, the woman didn't lift her head. There was no spark of recognition in her vacant eyes. Damnit!

A deep thud yanked Constance's attention back just as the gator-guard let out a roar.

"Qrakking annoying jekinnnsssss!" The gator-guard had thrown Meredith off him and now advanced on her, lips peeled back from rows of sharp teeth, jagged in his long snout. The only mercy was that even with his roar, there were no footfalls of other guards coming to his aid. Some god was showing them grace, but they still needed to take that bitch out.

Meredith grunted and struggled to her feet. "Constance, hurry!" Blood, scarlet against her clothes, spilled from the deep gash the guard's claws had torn across her midsection.

They were running out of time. Gritting her teeth, Constance grabbed the unresponsive woman and hauled her to her feet. "I'm not leaving you here," she ground out. They just had to make it to the corridor. Had to escape. And they needed a weapon. Anything. Her eyes landed on a metal rod leaning against the wall. *There.*

Hauling the female with her, Constance stepped outside the barriers of the cell, her gaze fixed on the guard. He was still focused on Meredith. Good. Now, the rod. She gently lowered the unresponsive woman to the floor, then snatched the metal rod from against the wall. One end was clearly the handle, a button set into its surface. She pressed hard, and the thing zinged to life with so much energy she felt the current go up her arm, the hairs rising off her head as if attracted to a lightning call.

At the sound of the weapon being charged, the gator-guard halted, claw pausing mid-air from where he was about to rend Meredith. Yellow eyes looked over his shoulder as his long snout turned.

His reptilian gaze locked with hers, and a fierce swell of triumph surged through Constance's veins. The hulking guard didn't get to act, didn't get to roar out a challenge or attack before she charged, forgetting all else except this single purpose.

She saw the moment of confusion swarm in those alien eyes, the split second where he thought to dodge her reckless attack. In that suspended heartbeat, she wondered if he would evade her in time. If she had just made a fatal mistake.

But a raw-throated scream of pure rage sounded from behind the guard, and in that same breath, Meredith braced against the wall, using one leg to deliver a powerful kick to the center of the guard's belly.

The force of the blow was enough to make him stagger, unable to shift out of Constance's path in time. Teeth grit, she lowered her shoulder and slammed the rod into him with every shred of strength left in her battered body.

The sizzle was almost as great as the shudders that wracked his frame. Vicious eyes filled with anger locked with hers, and Constance stared into them, not letting go of the rod.

As he hit the floor with a meaty thud, dead or dying, she allowed the weapon to hang loose in her fingers. Heavy breaths made her chest heave as her gaze locked with Meredith's. They were both breathing hard. Both staring at each other wide-eyed.

They'd done it. This first step, at least.

"You ok?" Stupid question. Meredith was obviously not okay.

"Could be better, but I'm breathing." Meredith braved a smile, but she wrapped an arm around her belly, the stain of red there seeming brighter than ever.

The corridor remained empty. Against all odds, they were still alone.

Now for the next impossible step—finding a way off this ship. Turning, her gaze fell on the silent woman. She was still standing in the same position. Unmoving.

How would they escape with only one of them at fighting strength, one unresponsive, and who knew how many more enemies? But she couldn't think about that. The odds didn't matter.

"Let's move."

Meredith nodded.

No other guards had come yet to investigate the commotion. But they couldn't let the silence quell them into the same complacency that brought that rookie guard down.

They weren't safe, not by a long shot. Wordlessly, they moved down the dim corridor, supporting the unresponsive third captive between them. Her vacant eyes still stared straight ahead, seeing nothing.

Constance had no idea where they were going, just away from the cell. Each step ratcheted her fear up another notch, but she clenched her jaw and pushed on.

Where were the other guards? Maybe most of them were killed when they attacked the Restitution's base. That's probably the only reason they had a chance now. She could only hope.

As they turned a corner, she spotted a door left partially open, pale light streaming through the crack. Holding her breath, her gaze met Meredith's. They had to check it out.

"I'll go," Meredith whispered, and for a second, she wondered where this woman was drawing her bravery from. She was already bleeding, no doubt badly hurt.

"No," she blocked Meredith with an arm. "*I'll go.*"

Leaving them pressed against the side of the corridor, she crept forward, holding her breath as she strained her ears for any sound.

Nothing.

This was too good to be true.

She was right at the door when she paused, gripping the shock rod and lifting it before her as she used a foot to slide the door open wider.

It was a control room, and there was no one inside.

Jerking her chin, she beckoned Meredith over as she entered.

Gently, they lowered the silent woman to the floor just inside the doorway before closing the door behind them. Constance sagged against it for a moment, pulse thundering in her ears.

Catching her breath, she took in the space. It was cramped, filled with panels of blinking lights and strange symbols. Consoles and monitors lined every surface, displaying incomprehensible readouts. She swallowed hard.

"Any chance you can fly an alien spaceship?" Her gaze slid to Meredith's, whose eyes were busy roving over the controls.

Meredith let out a weak, rasping chuckle, then winced as the motion aggravated her injuries. "Sure, just let me check the manual first."

But this must be a secondary control room. No way this was the bridge for the vessel she'd seen from the ground. The ship they were on was a colossal beast.

"Maybe this room controls communications?" Meredith whispered, clearly thinking the same thing. "Do you think we could send a message?"

Constance bit her lip. It was a good plan. If they didn't make it farther than this, a distress signal would be their best bet. But neither of them could read the alien symbols. The translators embedded behind their ears didn't work with text.

Shaking her head, she locked eyes with Meredith. "We should keep moving." Something tightened in her gut. They shouldn't have stopped. "We can't do anything here."

Meredith nodded, wincing as she reached for the unresponsive female. They both had their arms supporting the woman when a roar echoed far down the corridor behind the door. *Find them!*

"Oh shit," Meredith whispered, one leg buckling as she gripped her belly and winced.

No. No. No, no, no. They needed more time.

Her heart skipped a beat as her gaze shot behind her. There was no exit in here. Only the single door they'd entered through. Unless she could turn the consoles at their backs into turrets, they were sitting ducks.

"Shit." Supporting the unresponsive woman, she hurried back to the door, but the footfalls that echoed down the hall stopped her in her tracks. Her heart seized as she glanced back at Meredith. What now?

Meredith grunted and nodded sharply. They'd known it wouldn't be easy. Far from a stroll in the park. Getting off this ship was going to be a test for their very survival. If they wanted freedom, they'd have to fight.

Constance nodded back, hand tightening on the shock rod still in her grasp just as the door slid open. Two hulking gator-guards crammed into the doorway, yellow eyes glowing.

"Found them," one spoke into a communicator on his arm.

"Qrakking pests," the other hissed.

"Back off." Constance's jaw clenched as she took a step back, forcing Meredith and the other woman to step back with her. "Stay the fuck away from us!"

The guard grunted, a snarl on his lips revealing darkened teeth. "Risky, little jekin..." He hissed. "Where we come from, females know when to remain quiet."

The other grunted. "They will be quiet soon enough."

She didn't know why. Why the rage swelling within her suddenly peaked like a rising inferno swelling to the head of a volcano.

"You know what?" She spoke through gritted teeth. "I'm so damn *tired* of you pieces of *filth*."

That set them off. Her heart stuttered for a single second as the gator-guards lunged. She only saw a blur as Meredith dove behind a console, pulling the other woman with her. Constance's arms tightened as she fired up the shock rod again. Electricity zinged as the cramped space descended into chaos, the guards taking no care as they launched themselves on top of the equipment, claws extended, dirty, and still stained with blood from their last victims.

A deafening alarm blared as both guards focused on her, or rather, on the weapon in her hand. It was the only thing keeping them from grabbing her immediately.

Swinging the rod, she kept one guard at arm's length as the other lunged for her. With everything she had in her, she brought the rod down on his arm. It sizzled, and he roared in pain or maybe anger. She wasn't quite sure, and she didn't get a chance to find out.

He didn't retreat, even as his blackened flesh smoked. If anything, the shock enraged him further.

"Get the other two," he growled. "I'll take care of this one."

A massive fist caught her shoulder, and she hit the floor hard, breath bursting from her lungs.

The rod spun from her grip, and she rolled to grab hold of it again just as a clawed foot stomped down, talons gouging the metal flooring between her fingers and the weapon she so desperately needed to grasp. In her periphery, Meredith grappled with the second guard, trying her best to shield the unresponsive woman.

When a thick claw closed around her throat, it brought her right back to the start of this nightmare. When she'd woken up on the Restitution base in the middle of the night to her roommate's scream and a claw around her throat just like this one. The woman's name had been Alaina...and she was probably dead, too.

Something hurt deep inside, clenching and seizing. Alaina and all the others, too. Even that cocky idiot that had come to save her that night. Akur or whatever his name was. They were all dead. Just like she would be if she didn't find a way out of this somehow.

As the guard slammed her into the wall, agony exploded through her side. She slid down the moment he released her, dazed, as the gator loomed over her.

"Enough!" a voice bellowed from the door. Another gator-guard, even bigger than these two, stood at the entrance. He stalked in, pushing his comrades out of the way.

Reaching down, he grabbed her by the throat, and through the corner of her eye, she could see the other guard doing the same to Meredith. "Do you realize where you are, *fools*?"

Constance blinked, the pain shooting through her side, making it a little hard to think. But he wasn't speaking to her. He was speaking to the guard who'd been ready to smash her head in.

Through the pain, she took in the destroyed room.

The lead gator-guard gestured at a sparking console, shouting something so gutturally she almost didn't catch it.

"You idiots blasted a signal!" he growled.

Raw fury twisted the guard's reptilian features as he stalked forward, not caring that he was simply carrying her along. Her body swayed, dizziness threatening as her gaze flicked to Meredith at the same moment that the other guard pulled her along. Alarm went through her as she saw the other woman on the floor. Hair still falling over her face, she sat unmoving. And even when the remaining guard grabbed hold of her, she didn't react.

This was it? Their bid for freedom had failed so quickly?

Desperate, she reached for Meredith. She didn't know why. She didn't know this woman. They hadn't been friends back on Earth. They weren't family. Before these assholes abducted them, they'd been strangers. They were simply both thrust into this nightmare because some egotistic aliens had taken them from their home. But Meredith was human and the closest thing she had to anyone.

For a moment, they managed to grab hold of each other, both hanging on to that one grasp of each other's fingertips as if they were each other's lifeline. Her hands grew moist from the blood coating Meredith's fingers, and her heart ached even more. She wasn't sure Meredith would make it. Swallowing hard, she could see the woman fighting away the tears and the fear—a look that was probably mirrored in her own eyes.

They had only that one moment before they were wrenched apart.

"What are you doing?!" She heard herself shout the words. Heard herself speak but didn't recognize her own voice. Raw rage and fury did that. "Have you no conscience?! Can't you see what your masters are doing is wrong?!"

No answer. If anything, the lead gator-guard tightened his claw on her, breaking her skin.

"Meredith!"

It was all she could do as the guards marched them through corridor after corridor until she lost any sense of direction. When they stepped into a wide open space, her heart dropped through a pit in her gut.

Separate crafts waited in the launch bay. And as they pushed Meredith into one craft, then the silent woman in another, only one thing was clear. It was over.

"Foolish qrakking pilkras," the lead gator-guard growled as he got in and slammed the door of the craft shut. "Blasting an unencrypted signal. If we anger the masters or injure these hideous jekins, we don't get all the credits for this job!"

Gulping hard, she sat upright on the seat behind the pilot; eyes focused on the little viewport as dread filled her. This was it. She could try to strangle him now. Wrap her arms around his neck and use all her strength to—

She hardly saw it coming. Just saw the moment he turned, those horrid cold eyes finding her as if he could read her mind. The prick of the small device as it sunk into her neck had her freezing, wide eyes shifting to the thick, scaly arm that had moved too fast for her to even respond.

He'd...he'd injected her with something. He'd—

She reached for the spot as her vision blurred and her head swayed.

No. This can't—

Her head swayed again.

No. She needed to remain conscious. Couldn't fall asleep. Not now.

"Qrakking signal must have been like a beacon." She heard the reptilian grumble as the little ship they were on shook and swayed before stabilizing. It took her a moment to realize they were floating above the deck now. They were going to fly.

Her head fell back against the seat as automatic restraints strapped her in, her gaze focusing on what she could see of the viewport even as she fought to remain awake. But she was weak. Oh, so weak.

The gator-guard kept grumbling about the signal, his anger and annoyance evident. It made her giggle.

Wait. That giggle felt good. The tension in her muscles was seeping away like it was just a figment of her imagination.

She felt good. Better than she'd felt in years.

This wasn't so bad after all. The pain in her jaw and the other injuries she'd sustained suddenly didn't exist. Being abducted was so bad, was it? She felt like she could stand in a flower garden and dance. Another giggle went through her throat as the guard grumbled some more.

Why was he so worked up, anyway? Whatever communication was sent didn't matter. Survival was dim—and that was hilarious!

Only a fool would see a ship like this and come to rescue them, guns blazing.

3

Akur

"Get the blasters." Akur sat up straighter in the seat.

It had been just a blip, but he was following the coordinates. Something was there. Something big.

"What did you find?" From the back of the ship, E'lot lifted his head from where it had hung between his claws.

Akur's brows furrowed as the message from that one transmission came up on screen. It made no sense. Just a bunch of tones and pauses that were either some kind of code...or a mistake.

He stared at the message, his nefre pulsing so hard he had the urge to reach back and rip it from his spine.

He had a good feeling about this. For the first time since they embarked on this journey, there was a thrill deep within his gut.

It was the ship they wanted. He just knew it.

Rising, he was walking to the back of the ship where the weapons were stashed before E'lot could ask another question.

Grabbing a blaster from the wall, he tested the weight. A growl rumbled in his throat, one that almost sounded like a groan of pleasure just feeling the heft of the thing. Killing something with this would feel good. So qrakking good.

When he glanced over his shoulder, he realized E'lot was at the control panel now, eyes on the spatial chart. He hadn't even heard him move, but that's why he was one of the Restitution's best. Both of them. And if they were all that was left of the rebel forces, then by all the gods, they were going to make it count.

Grabbing another blaster, he strode up beside E'lot, his own blaster rifle slung at his hip now, ready to be unleashed. At his back, his twin blades burned with insistence, ready to be bathed in blood.

The display showed them closing in rapidly on the signal's origin point.

"Whatever it is, it's in orbit around..." E'lot frowned, scrutinizing the information coming up before them. "...*something.*" Without looking, he accepted the blaster thrust toward him, checking the charge level as he continued analyzing their approach vector.

They'd trained and fought side by side for so long that they could anticipate each other's moves instinctively on a mission. Two parts of a lethally effective whole. And this could be their most important mission yet. This was the moment Akur had thirsted for across all those empty cycles of pursuit.

He'd failed before. He would not do so again. This time, he was taking that human back. And the other females, too.

"Approaching target," E'lot reported before standing at his full height. His jaw was set, eyes hard as the ship phased into normal velocity.

Akur held his breath, his entire being freezing as he stared at the sight before him.

It *was* them.

"Qrak," E'lot murmured, a note of disbelief in his voice. "You did it. You found them."

The Tasqal mother ship loomed ahead. But that wasn't what had them both frozen, both staring at the sight before them.

"That's a planet," E'lot said. "But it's not on any spatial chart." His gaze shifted to Akur. "I would know. I've been studying every inch of the charts since we left on this mission."

"I know."

The silence in their shuttle remained now unbroken as they stared at the huge planet in the distance.

"This is it, isn't it," E'lot finally said. A statement, not a question. "The Tasqal base. The one the Restitution could never find."

His comrade's words floated heavily in the air, almost feeling like they were swallowing the surrounding oxygen. He didn't dare answer. The enormity of this find was too much. Could they truly have been so lucky?

But the planet before them technically didn't exist. Just like all the other impossibilities, this planet was an anomaly.

It had to be it.

The High Tasqals' base was before them.

A dream of the Restitution for so many eons. To find it. Destroy it. *End this*. They needed a whole host of fighters and ships to flood the surface and finish this war once and for all. But instead of an army of rebels ready to rain vengeance, there was only an old shuttle and two rebels who didn't know when to give up.

The planet before them seemed to pulse with an energy that defied the void of space around it. And the Tasqal mother ship they'd been chasing hovered like a sentinel, guarding the secrets of this hidden world.

He finally broke the silence, his voice barely more than a whisper. "If the Tasqals have managed to hide an entire planet, who knows what defenses they have in place."

"Aye. So, what's the plan?" E'lot grabbed his spear from where it was secured on the wall of the ship, his eyes still on the enemy vessel ahead, and that was when it became clear. They had no real plan. Not for this.

It was all instinct. Find the vessel. Rescue the females. And kill as many qrakking Tasqal minions as possible in the process. But this was so much bigger than they first realized. They were at the nest of the enemy. The place they'd searched for across many orbits. It was an opportunity they couldn't let pass. No matter what.

"Even if we cloak," E'lot said, hand tightening on his spear, "they'll spot us soon. We can't hide."

"So we don't." Akur's brows tightened as he stared at the planet. The readings on the screen showed that whatever was on the surface wasn't an arid desert filled with nothingness. There was life down there. Civilization. A host of his enemies all in one place. "We go in close. Take out their side cannon and find a way onto that ship."

"Get the humans before they reach the surface?"

"Affirmative. And then return to what's left of the base. Gather as many of us as we can..."

E'lot's gaze shifted to him, and the silence grew loud again because they both knew neither of them would be making it out of this alive. They could save the humans. But themselves...probably not.

"We wear the suits." He was moving even before E'lot's surprised grunt reached his ears.

"That is unwise," his comrade said. "Those suits offer little protection—"

"There is no other option." He was already by a pack, releasing the suit held within it before E'lot could finish. But he knew his friend was right. Again. If things went wrong with the suit, the wearer would be left to the mercy of the void. The suits were built for maintenance. Not for anything else. They offered protection from the void, protection from extreme temperature changes, but they weren't combat suits. If things went wrong, the being protected inside could easily perish.

But he wasn't any being. He was Akur. And he was Shum'ai. That had to count for something.

"Even you, with your regeneration, Akur, you can't survive—"

"I *must*." Suit on, he turned to face E'lot again, staring at him through the transparent visor of the helmet now on his head. "Change of plans. You stay here."

"*What?*"

Attaching his communicator, he made sure his blades were still strapped to his back and the blaster to his side. "Be my eyes."

"Like qrak I will." E'lot's nostrils flared as he took a step forward. "You cannot mean to enter that ship alone."

Akur paused, staring at his friend for a few moments. "There are only two of us, brother. If anything happens, someone must relay a message back to the others—if any remain. Someone must let them know these coordinates. Someone must keep the Restitution alive."

"I will not allow you to sacrifice—"

"It is not your decision."

That was it. E'lot's mouth slammed shut, his jaw ticking because he knew the words left unsaid. They locked gazes, an eternity of their missions together playing in front of his eyes. He loved this male as much as he loved his womb-mate. They'd fought and laughed together. And this may be their last foray.

One of them had to do this, and he was the only one that had a trick up his sleeve.

E'lot's shoulders sagged. "May the gods guide you, warrior. May the souls of our fallen brothers fight by your side."

His chest tightened. This was goodbye. He stared at E'lot. With a salute and a nod to his comrade, Akur headed to the exit bay. "See you soon, brother."

It was a grunt, E'lot's response, but it was enough.

As the ship ejected him into the void, his body spun with weightlessness for a moment before he righted himself, using the thrusters attached to the pack on his back to face the colossal ship before him.

Hopefully, he was small enough not to tip off the scanners. They might expect a ship heading toward them, but not a single being.

"E'lot, do you read?" The connection warbled in his ear, and there was no response. The big ship before them was causing some interference. The same interference that had hidden them from sight for so long. The fact a blip occurred that led him straight to them was nothing but a miracle. With the sight of that planet now in the distance, he was convinced the transmission that led him here had been a mistake.

"E'lot, if you can hear me, fall back. No matter what happens, do not come in range. Not yet."

Thrusters at his back firing, he shot toward the monstrosity before him. Pure black metal, blending into the void itself. How many civilizations fell to afford the Tasqals the resources to build such a thing?

As he shot toward it, his entire frame stiffened as he blinked. Was the vessel...was it moving? Qrak. It was slowly turning away from the planet before them. His whole being froze even as the thrusters shot him forward.

Had he miscalculated? Was this not their destination? It *had* to be. An uncharted planet. Signs of life on the surface. This *had* to be it.

His life organ stuttered as he reduced the thrusters, his body hanging in the weightlessness of the void as he stared at the massive vessel turning in front of him.

He should return to E'lot. Plan. No. Too slow. But that didn't feel like the right course of action. Not now. He had to get on that ship. Find the humans and somehow get off without getting them all killed. *Now or never.* He turned, about to engage his propulsion, when movement caught his eye.

Something suddenly shot from the enormous ship before them.

No, not some*thing*. Some *things*. Shuttles. Three of them.

"What in the gods of Tonvuhiri..."

He watched the shuttles shoot toward the surface, his nefre pulsing at the back of his neck with each moment that passed.

Those shuttles were small. Possibly holding one, maximum two, beings each. How many females had been taken? Apart from the female they'd stolen from his arms, he'd seen only two others. There could have been more. And he couldn't allow the Tasqals to get hold of a single one.

Qef. He had to decide. And he had to make it fast.

A glance over his shoulder and he saw E'lot was angling their shuttle toward the enemy ship that was leaving. He probably expected him to return to the vessel so they could pursue the big ship. That was the logical thing to do. But none of this felt logical.

There was a yellow planet beneath them that shouldn't exist and three shuttles heading toward it. Something stopped him from returning to the shuttle with E'lot. Something pushed him in the other direction. He made the decision, knowing E'lot would understand. Knowing that, just like those other times, he didn't have to explain every single detail to his comrade. E'lot would know what to do.

Angling his thrusters, he shot toward the disappearing shuttles, the planet beneath them looming like a great big yellow ball. He didn't even look behind him. Couldn't. If he was wrong, that meant he was chasing useless Hedgeruds into the unknown while the females he was after were still on that big ship. He could only hope that if his luck ran out now, E'lot had a better chance tracking the females down.

"Qrak." He was about to do something reckless. Something completely stupid. The shuttles before him shot down to the surface in straight lines, cutting a path toward the planet's surface. Following them was beyond risky. The maintenance suit wasn't meant for this. The turbulent atmosphere and crushing pressure would tear the fibers apart. But he had no choice. Gritting his teeth, he angled his head down and punched the thrusters to maximum.

In the grand scheme of things, he was so small that whoever was piloting those shuttles probably couldn't see him. Not yet. He put all faith in that assumption as the planet before him grew so large it was all he could see.

The buffeting started immediately as he plunged into the dense yellow haze. A low tone blared in the suit, a warning spreading across the transparent visor before him. He ignored it. Ignored the heat he could feel as he plunged into the atmosphere. Ignored the fact it felt like his organs were simultaneously being pulled from within him, even as they were being crushed into a tight ball.

For a moment, all he could see was the haze before him as he fell blindly to a surface that could hold countless unknown evils.

Fluid pressed into his eyes, making them bulge as he forced himself to squint through the visor, trying to glimpse the shuttles.

Nothing. They'd be traveling faster than he was, probably slowing down only upon entry. He didn't have that luxury. He had to find one, or he was going to shoot right past them.

His jaw ached as he grit his teeth so hard they could shatter under the pressure. He was heating up. Could feel the change in temperature even beneath the fibers that should block such changes. The fall was too much for the suit. The built-in temperature regulation was struggling to keep up with the searing heat outside. This wasn't good. The heat could either kill him or send him into a mating frenzy. He could almost laugh—the idea of killing Hedgeruds while pumped up on the need to mate was almost comical—but this was no laughing matter. There were already too many things against him. He'd thought the suit would last a little longer, but he could already feel his skin starting to cook within the confines of the fibers.

"Just a bit more." He clenched his teeth, willing himself to push past the pain as he plummeted, his velocity increasing with every passing click. Every muscle screamed in protest. He was dying, his cells trying their best to rebuild even as they were destroyed by the pressure of the fall. For a moment, it became too much. Roaring behind the visor, he pulled on images of what he left behind. Of the base. His fallen brothers. The civilians they were to protect. He let the loss of their lives fuel the rage simmering within him as he fought against the pain.

"Qraaaaakkkkk!!!" But he refused to relent.

Suddenly, a flicker of movement caught his eye—a brief flash of dark metal piercing through the swirling clouds. The shuttles! He was close. So tantalizingly close. If he could just reach them before—

A shrill alarm replaced the other droning one, piercing through the din of rushing wind behind his helmet. The suit's integrity was failing, the fibers straining and splitting under the immense stress. He had a few clicks, maybe less, before it gave out entirely.

But he caught sight of the target. He could see it fully now. The shuttle. Even its occupant. Twisting himself, he angled his fall toward the vessel.

It tore at him. The wind. The heat. The pressure.

He fought against it anyway.

"Filthy Hedgerud," he snarled, just as he reached alongside the vessel and locked eyes with the Hedgerud at the controls. Surprised, slitted yellow pits widened on his golden ones.

His vision tunneled, the edges going black as he poured every last ounce of his strength into one final, all-or-nothing lunge. His arms stretched out, straining, grasping for the shuttle. Just a little more, a little farther...

The moment he touched it was the moment some sort of energy surged within him. Hope. With a grunt, he held on, his other arm straining to grab hold. The fact they were going in the same direction helped. He managed to grab on, hauling himself up over the transparent dome that held the passengers. One Hedgerud guard...and one human.

Clenching his jaw, he growled against the pain that shot through his senses as he stared at the female tucked behind the Hedgerud guard. It was her. The one that had looked at him with such resignation it seared his soul.

Kon-stahns.

He'd found her. His instincts had not failed him. The humans were in these vessels, and this one was...*smiling*?

His eyes narrowed on the human as her shoulders shook the moment her eyes locked with his. She looked battered. A nasty bruise on her jaw, claw marks on her neck, but she laughed anyway. One of her small hands rose as she pointed at him before she grabbed her midsection, and a fit of laughter shook her frame.

He was staring at her, forgetting all about the Hedgerud, when the shuttle suddenly swerved and half his body flailed in the air, only one arm keeping him locked on the vessel itself.

"Qrak!"

The Hedgerud was trying to shake him off.

Not going to happen.

He was this close now; he wasn't going to let go. Nothing, not even the fall itself threatening to tear him apart, was going to make him lose hold.

With a grunt, he swung his body back, attaching himself to the falling shuttle again. If the female wasn't inside, he'd have taken out his blades and wreaked havoc on the thing, taking it down with him on top and the Hedgerud stuck inside. But he couldn't. The human was in there, and he was here for her. That's the only reason the fool before him was still alive.

The Hedgerud inside snarled, and Akur felt his lips twist in a wicked grin.

"Surprise, you ugly pillar." He stared at his enemy, glaring at him, but that was not enough. He needed to take control of the shuttle. He could already see the surface below. Could already feel the air against his back and other sections of his body where his suit had failed. He couldn't allow himself to land like this.

"*What are you doing here?*" The words came across his visor, and for a moment, he didn't understand what they meant or where they came from. Not until his gaze shifted to the female tucked behind the bulky Hedgerud. Right. This suit was engineered for maintenance, allowing for communication relay even if verbal communication failed. The human was speaking, and his suit was picking it up. He saw her laugh again, and despite the pressure on his frame, he tilted his head, staring at her.

"*You look funny.*" The words wrote themselves out on his screen again, just as others joined. "*A Shum'ai. Yes. From the Restitution. I'm sure of it.*" A pause. "*Filthy rebels. If the masters hear of this—No, I do not know how he found us here. He will die before he reaches the surface. I will make sure of it.*"

The latter was obviously from the Hedgerud, and his gaze locked on the reptilian again.

"Try me." Reaching back, he wrestled a blade free, the wind ripping at it, a wild thing fighting to escape his grasp. At that exact moment, the Hedgerud snarled and swung the ship, making it swerve.

"FUHK!" The human expletive seemed apt as his body swung in the opposite direction. Like a flag flailing in the wind, he hung on for dear life.

"*Wheeee!*" The female's glee translated into words across his screen once more. "*Do it again!*"

She was happy? Not even the Hedgeruds themselves were happy to be in each other's presence. This wasn't the same female he'd had hold of before that beam caught them both. Something was wrong with her. He'd deal with that later.

With a grunt, he swung the arm with the blade toward the ship. The first attempt failed, simply skating off the dark metal. As the haze of clouds dissipated and the surface below came into full view, his nefre pulsed with insistence on his nape. He was in danger. He needed to secure himself, or he'd be thrown off before the shuttle stabilized.

With another grunt and a swing of his arm, he plunged the sword into a groove of the ship. He could see the red warning light that lit the interior. Almost hear the female's awe as she giggled again.

"*Oooh, is this a disco?*"

"*Silence, foolish jerkin!*" A pause. "*No, you fools! Hold your fire! You will hit us, too!*"

In his periphery, he saw the other two shuttles swerve and come up on either side. Two Hedgerud pilots. He couldn't see the passengers, but no doubt there were human females tucked behind them, too.

Three against one. The odds weren't good. But that's what made it exhilarating. With a grunt, he climbed higher, tightening his hold on the blade. It was the only anchor point he had. The surface was close enough that he could see details of buildings. Rivers. Trees. Hover vehicles.

They were nearing fast. And behind them, a shadow.

"*What the qrak is that?!*" Glancing up, he saw what the Hedgerud was referring to, and for a moment, a grunt of respect almost made him smile.

The little shuttle he and E'lot used to chase after these excrement holes was in pursuit. E'lot hadn't gone after the big ship after all. Must have followed when he'd seen the reckless turn of events.

Qrakking, E'lot. But he should have known his comrade wouldn't let him die so easily.

"Blast it down!"

His nefre pulsed as he saw a stream of laser light erupt from the surface. The three enemy shuttles broke formation, swerving out of the way at the last second. But E'lot swerved, too. It was a near miss, but unlike the fresh new shuttles of their enemies, his evasion put him off course. At this rate, before he managed to realign, they would reach the surface.

Qrak.

"Split up and take that one out. I'll deal with this pest here."

Akur's lips pulled back in a snarl as he stared at the Hedgerud before him. The one giving the orders. Sure enough, the other two shuttles headed in separate directions, and he could only pray that E'lot knew what to do.

He did. Just as usual, it was as if E'lot read his mind. E'lot swerved, choosing a shuttle and following it. Good. Divide and conquer. If anything happened to him, they still could save even one human. That had to be good enough.

Hanging on tight to the handle of his blade, he swung his other arm to his hip, hoping the tethering line was still there and not ripped off by his entry into the atmosphere. The gods must be on his side because it was. It took just a few seconds to grab the line, swing it around himself, and secure the other end to the hilt of his blade. Just as the shuttle suddenly dipped and swerved, going upside down.

Akur grunted as his body swung. But the tether held, barely. The ground was rushing up to meet them at an alarming rate.

Inside the shuttle, he could almost hear the female's whoop of exhilaration. *"This is better than a rollercoaster! Hey, lizard man! Do a loop-de-loop!"*

"I said silence, jekin! This is no game!"

Jekin, huh? Akur grunted, still holding on. Jekin was a word used for the lowest of things. He couldn't imagine what the Hedgeruds would have done to those humans if their masters hadn't needed them so badly.

"Aww, you're no fun," the human's words continued to translate across his screen. As the shuttle swerved again, flipping itself right-side-up, he swung himself so he could glare at the Hedgerud guard, whose eyes widened as they locked on him again. And so did the human's. *"Hey, rebel dude! You're still alive! I remember you!"*

His lips curled in confusion as his gaze shifted to the female.

"You know...you're not so bad looking when you snarl like that. Gives big badass vibes. When we land, can I get a ride on your shoulders? I bet the view is amazing from up there!"

"Silence!"

Akur's gaze shifted back to the Hedgerud, who was absolutely backed up with excrement. His panicked orders to the other shuttle pilots confirmed his rank. A general. Akur's lips curled into a predatory grin. Oh, he would *relish* killing this one.

"No! Don't fire! The fool damaged our stabilization, but I'll take the shuttle down. Land in District Six."

The vessel swerved again as the Hedgerud gave his commands, and Akur glared at the beast before him. It was clear he was trying to shake him off, but there was nothing else either of them could do. He could only hold on—

The shuddering was what made him look down just as they zoomed past a towering building. And then another. And another. The shuttle was coming in hot, as if the Hedgerud inside had little control, swerving dangerously close to the structures of the city beneath them.

"Bracing for impact!" The Hedgerud's panicked shout scrolled across his screen.

That's all the warning he got before the shuttle cleared the city and slammed into the ground. A mountain of sand shot high as the shuttle rose before slamming down again.

"Oooh, I love this part!" The female's words lit up his visor just as his body whipped back and forth like a lifeless toy, his entire frame slamming repeatedly into the shuttle's hull. Pain exploded through him with each impact, his vision flickering as he looked up to see the

utter excitement reflected in the female's face through the dome that still protected her.

She was still breathing. That's all that mattered.

Finally, mercifully, the shuttle ground to a halt, half-buried in the side of a building. Smoke poured from its crumpled side, sparks dancing across the buckled metal.

For a moment, he hung limply there, every part of him screaming in agony. His suit was in tatters, barely threads holding together across his back. But he was breathing. Somehow.

A groan from inside the shuttle drew his attention. The Hedgerud was stirring, clearly dazed but still a threat. And Kon-stahns...

"Let's do that again!" He could hear her voice now. Her actual voice. There was a breach in the vessel. But that didn't matter. They were on land. He needed to get up.

Gritting his teeth, Akur pulled himself up on his elbows. He had to get in there, had to secure the human before the Hedgerud recovered.

"Hang on, rebel dude!" Kon-stahns called out. "I'll come to you!"

Before he could even process what she meant, the shuttle's hatch popped open, and Kon-stahns came tumbling out, giggling all the way. She rolled to a stop right before him, those bright blue eyes of hers staring up at him.

"Tada!" She struck a pose as if expecting applause. "Whoo, that was one heck of a ride. What's next, boss man?"

Maybe it was her eyes. Maybe it was the fact he didn't expect this...this jovial demeanor. He'd expected the same resignation and maybe the same despair as the last time he'd seen her. Maybe it was because this was so unexpected, or because some part of him didn't think he'd find her at all. Or maybe it was the fact his body was at the point of breaking that his instincts were dulled. Yes, maybe it was all that which caused him to not notice they weren't alone as he stared into those blue eyes twinkling with happiness that seemed so misplaced, but so...right. So...good.

That's why the surroundings faded. Why he didn't see the

Hedgerud in the vessel beneath them wasn't the only threat in the vicinity.

He could only stare at her.

"I've found you, Kon-stahns." His gaze shifted from her blue-white eyes to the soft filaments that crowned her head. "Female of ice and fire."

She giggled, those twinkling eyes regarding him and nothing else.

Curses. She was completely out of it. Meanwhile, he felt like an insect stuck to the behind of a frazzled floop. He needed to get her out of this place and back to safety, find E'lot, and—

"*There he is!*" It was the shout that finally made the surroundings come back into focus. Akur lifted his head.

"Qraaak."

The female lifted her head, too. "Uh-oh!"

"*Halt!*"

Yeah...he needed to get them some cover...if they survived the next few clicks, that was.

4

Akur

AKUR STIFFENED, shifting his body so he was braced over the soft, pale female. She blinked, looking up at him with a laugh in those big blue eyes. Completely unaware of the surrounding danger.

Struggling to keep his balance, he barely moved as the dust cleared and the landscape around them came into view. Through the haze, he glimpsed towering white spires that pierced the tan sky. He'd only seen buildings like those in certain other places— worlds the Tasqals had taken as their own. Majestic white buildings that served as their lodging. So at odds with the breeding grounds they stood over. But even with that similarity, this place was different.

Bigger. Grander.

This wasn't just some wild, uncharted breeding ground he and E'lot had somehow discovered. No. This was the Tasqal base. The enormity of this one section alone told him so. It was a place no rebel had ever found, let alone infiltrated...until now.

The gleaming white structures stretched as far as his eyes could see. Even the ground beneath them seemed to pulse with a thick energy that felt like it was trying to leech from his skin. As if the entire planet were alive with the Tasqals' influence.

But there were no Tasqals in sight. Just their lackeys—Hedgeruds. About seven of them. All armed, ready to attack.

Beneath him, the female twisted, rising on the back of her arms before laughter bubbled from her throat. "Looks like some Ninja Turtles shit."

He could feel when the Hedgeruds' focus shifted from him to her. Feel their hungry gazes. It made his nefre pulse, sending awareness skittering across his spine, and he crouched lower, some part of him wanting to hide the vulnerable female from their searching eyes.

"Mm," she tilted her head, looking up at him. "You're warm, but tut tut tut." She waggled a digit at him. "You're not getting into my pants so easily, big guy."

Another giggle bubbled from her throat the moment his brow tightened at her words. The pain shooting through his entire frame was nothing compared to his confusion.

Qrak. This human was going to be the death of him. The nickname "big guy" made him pause, though, his mind flashing to their first chaotic meeting just turns ago. When he'd grabbed her from her lodging, intent on getting her to that bunker. Before that gravity beam had caught them. He still remembered how she'd decked him—right before using that same term of endearment. He wasn't entirely convinced it was a compliment. She had a tendency to combine violence with casual familiarity.

"What are you waiting for?! Get the filthy rebel!"

He didn't know which of the Hedgeruds uttered the command. Didn't care. There was no time to think. Praying his legs worked, he put all his energy into them as he rolled off the shuttle with the female pressed to his side. The landing was rough. He almost planted on his face, but he fought for balance, dragging her up with him. Three Hedgeruds circled them, crouching low. The bloodlust in their gazes evident.

They wanted to see him bleed.

Ha. The feeling was mutual.

Staking his sword into the ground, he reached up and flung the helmet from his head, spitting out a mouthful of lifeblood that had risen in his throat.

"Ooh," Kon-stahns' voice took on a deeper note as she looked up at him. "You know, for an alien dude with green skin, you're not half bad."

"I am not green." He tried not to consider what her tone meant. Despite the trouble surrounding them, it sent a bolt of *something* straight to his groin. She was out of her mind.

"After this, you owe me a favor," he growled, reaching for his blade once more. He'd have to fight one-handed. No big deal. He could fight these fools with his eyes closed.

"Strange way to ask for a blowjob, but alright." Kon-stahns giggled, her shoulders heaving in an easy shrug.

"A *what*?" His gaze barely shifted to her before a roar came from his left. Twisting with her in his arms, he let out a roar of his own even as his body protested the strain. Come on. *Regenerate.* Years of training kicked in anyway, his muscles moving from pure memory as his blade spun in his grasp, cutting down the Hedgerud that had charged.

Kon-stahns giggled. "Better take it. It's your one free pass."

Akur pushed her words from his mind because nothing she was saying was making sense. Flexing his arm, he brought his blade up again as one part of his enemy fell one way, and the other half went in the opposite direction.

"Just like old times," he rumbled, watching the blood run down the blade as movement in his periphery made him turn. Clutching the female tight around her midsection, he ducked, swinging her as he did, the momentum of her body bringing him down low.

"Whee!"

The blade that had tried to slice him in two skimmed just over his nose. His gaze locked with the Hedgerud that had attacked, a moment passing between them as he thrust his own weapon upward.

"That must hurt. Hope you didn't want younglings."

Blood gushed through the Hedgerud's open maw.

Kon-stahns giggled, waggling a digit at the Hedgerud as he fell to his knees. She didn't even seem to care about the lifeblood that splattered her. "Naughty! No babies for you!"

He could hardly catch a breath before another attacked. Two more fell as he clutched the female to himself and ran—more like stumbled—away from the damaged shuttle and death at their back.

Find somewhere to hide. Have to find somewhere safe.

Wherever he looked, more and more Hedgeruds were appearing. Some kind of alert must have been sent out, and they were all converging on this single location. Qrak!

"Filthy rebel!" It was a roar as the Hedgerud charged. His body felt like it was going to lock up again, but he couldn't let it. Spinning, he swung Kon-stahns out of the Hedgerud's path, one arm still gripping her and the other flipping the blade in his grasp before he buried it to the hilt into the charging Hedgerud. This one stopped in his tracks, but it was too late. His momentum already impaled him on the weapon. Slitted yellow eyes met his own as the Hedgerud choked on his own internal fluids.

"Surprised?" Akur couldn't help but taunt, even as his own body staggered with the effort to keep the female at his side while bracing against the sudden deadweight of the Hedgerud on his blade. "I had these specially made to pierce right through Hedgerud armor."

With a kick, he dislodged the vermin before he lifted the female and headed toward the nearest building. He needed to get them some cover and walls, even those made by his enemies, would provide some defense. He needed to get her to safety. He needed to not fail—

"Hey, big guy," Kon-stahns whispered, her breath tickling his neck where his skin was exposed.

"Fine, female," he grumbled, gripping her tighter as he hobbled forward. "I accept...your pass of freedom...for this job of blows." Two more Hedgeruds got cut down as he made his way. He just needed to get to that building. Put some distance between himself and the constant attacks. He only needed a few minutes. He'd regenerate. He would.

"A hedgehog or whatever you call them is coming behind us." Kon-stahns giggled again, a snort echoing in her nose. "Hedgehog."

He turned just in time to see the pilot of the downed shuttle stagger from the vessel. He'd hoped the brute had died. Was that too much to ask?

He'd have continued on, ignored the idiot if he didn't see the Hedgerud lift a blaster. Even with the distance between them, he recognized the model. It's one he'd seen used before.

Oh, qrak. Had they given up on that whole thing of wanting the human alive? Because that weapon was definitely going to harm her. Probably even kill her.

As the brute engaged the weapon, a bright beam of energy hurtled towards them. This wasn't one he could deflect or take in the back and hope for the best. Those blasters were charged for elimination on contact. They'd fry his cells. Even he couldn't regenerate such damage. And he had her. Kon-stahns. The human couldn't regenerate at all.

The warrior in him took over, pulling Kon-stahns close as he dove to the side, narrowly avoiding the searing heat of the blast. They tumbled to the ground, his body protesting enough for him to see stars. They landed next to the unmoving form of a downed Hedgerud. The beast's body partially blocked them from a shower of blaster shots coming their way, each one singeing flesh and dissolving bone.

This would only buy them a few moments at best.

"Stay down," he growled, pushing himself up on one knee to scan the area. Hedgeruds were advancing on all sides. Only the towering building that loomed behind them offered any refuge. If they could just make it inside...

"Hey, I wanna play too." Delicate hands reached for the blaster still attached to his hip.

He looked down at the female beneath him, unconvinced. But did he have a choice? Negative.

Metal sang against metal as he yanked the second blade from his back, crossing it with the first just as a Hedgerud's weapon slammed down. The impact jarred his arms, the qeffer's strength nearly driving him to the ground. But his blades held.

Out of the corner of his eye, he saw Kon-stahns lift the blaster from his hip.

"How does this even work?" She was grinning with her tongue out, clenched between her teeth in an act that looked painful. The blast that released from the barrel went right through the skull of the Hedgerud bearing down on him.

He stopped breathing as he watched the male fall.

"Surprise, mother-fuhker!" Kon-stahns cheered.

"That could have been me." He looked back at her.

She shrugged, a grin on her face that made her look more mischievous than harmless now. "I have good aim."

As if that was the end of that, she activated the weapon again, releasing more charges at the rising number of Hedgeruds coming their way. Her aim was terrible. Miraculously, some got hit. Others dove for cover. But there were too many. They couldn't win like this.

More blaster fire came at them, some hitting the sand far too close to the human for his liking.

It was two against too many, and when he glanced behind them, unease crept up his spine. More were closing in from behind the building, too.

"Don't hit the human, you fools!" One of them shouted. "We need it alive! Tear the Shum'ai limb from limb if you want, but the human must remain intact!"

Sheathing one blade, he gripped the female again, throwing her over his shoulder in a move that almost made his knees buckle. Almost. He wasn't about to kneel before these vermin. He stumbled, but that didn't stop him from throwing his body forward into a charging Hedgerud. This one fought back, his blade slicing across the muscles in Akur's chest. Lifeblood soaked the ground, but eh, a little lifeblood was nothing. He'd lost more than that the moment the Tasqals had arrived on his planet.

"Try again, *scum*." His mouth filled with lifeblood, too, and he spat it out as he thrust his blade forward, rending the Hedgerud in their way. That one went down, but another took his place. Retreat was slow.

"Mint Man!" Kon-stahns yelled. "Little help?"

Glancing over his shoulder, he only had a moment to catch the eyes of the shuttle pilot as he dropped the blaster and took out another weapon Akur couldn't recognize. Whatever it was, they were too far away now. Certainly, whatever it was—

And that's when he heard the zing.

It was a sound he'd heard before. A sound other rebels had told him about. A weapon the Hedgeruds had used on his brothers time and time again.

There was little time to release the female. Little time to push her out of the way before he saw the fiery sparks of the shock rod appear before him. Coming from above, the wielder launched himself from the very building he was heading toward.

No.

The yellow eyes of the Hedgerud almost seemed to pulse with pleasure as the rod connected with his chest.

Sparks flew. The whole world lit up, his cells being fried even as they fought to rebuild. With a grunt, he gripped the charged end, watching his skin turn black as his life essence depleted. But he wasn't ready to die. Not yet.

He had a human to save.

But not much of him was left. He could feel it in the way his vision was tunneling. In how he couldn't push the rod back from where it was being pressed into him.

"Female," he grunted. Even the lifeblood in his mouth seemed to fry and dry up. "Run. *Hide.*"

"Fat chance." The female giggled. He was seeing black. Darkness was encroaching, but he still saw the flash of her brown hair as she rose, firing the blaster with zero accuracy but still managing to hit some of the scum. It was wild fire. Blaster shots wove through the air, heating it. Scorching it. One Hedgerud went down, clutching his throat.

The female was fighting. The least he could do was survive long enough to get her through this first test.

Gritting his teeth, his muscles bunched and trembled as he swung his blade. Sparks flew as it connected with the shock rod, the wielder releasing a growl of rage as he managed to dislodge the weapon from his skin. Electricity ran up his arm, and his muscles spasmed some more, but he pushed through it.

Can't die now.

Can't fail now.

"He's cornered!" One of the Hedgeruds shouted. More of them were pouring in from all sides. He would have laughed if his throat didn't feel like it'd been fried. They didn't care about the human firing crazily at them. They only cared about him, and as soon as he was taken care of, they'd converge on her.

He wasn't going to let that happen.

Kon-stahns' back pressed against his as they faced outward, surrounded. "Any bright ideas, big guy?"

"Working on it." His voice sounded like gravel, and he couldn't see. Shadows. They were all shadows now. The converging Hedgeruds were wisps coming to take him to oblivion.

It was practice and skill. Revolutions of battle that took over. His blade sang through the air, taking down two more Hedgeruds, but for every one that fell, three more appeared. Their window of escape was shrinking fast.

And that's when he saw it—or, at least, he thought he saw something. High in the towering building before them. White robes blowing in the wind. Anger swelled deep inside him, and he growled, swinging his blade once again.

It was one of them. The scourge that descended on his planet and so many others. The ones who took the females. Who raped. Killed. Destroyed entire civilizations. They were the reason so many were fleeing, seeking safety. They were the reason the Restitution began.

Above, way up in that building above them, was a High Tasqal.

He would live only to spite the qeffer and make him bleed, too.

But fate and desire were two separate things.

He saw the shadow in his vision move before he felt the pain in his side. A Hedgerud had made it past his swinging blade, his lack of focus...*his weakness.*

This wasn't the grand battle he'd imagined. This wasn't retribution. And the human... Qrak. He was failing her again.

Another blow, and this time, lifeblood spurted from his lips the same moment it gushed from his side.

"Mint Man!" Darkness fell, his vision blew, only the words of the human as she gripped his arm coming through. "Come on, dude. Don't—You can't—" He could feel her gripping his arm, trying to keep him on his feet. His knees buckled anyway, and they both went down.

"I have failed, female." Gravel and coal. His voice was barely recognizable. "Forgive me!"

He could feel the soft palms of her human hand. Felt the way she gripped him. He could almost hear the anxiety in her voice.

"No!" Her hands trembled. "I don't know why this was all like a comedy before, but this shit isn't funny anymore."

Ah. So whatever they'd injected her with was finally wearing off. Bliss inducer, perhaps.

He almost wished that wasn't the case. Wished she wasn't aware of everything. She would see him fall. Would remember how he failed her. And what's worse, unlike when he'd failed her before, that resignation that had swallowed her was gone.

She was feeling it all now, and it tore at him more than the fact he could feel his cells expiring.

When the ground beneath them trembled, he thought it was his failing body. Death was supposed to be quick. Not prolonged. This was more painful than the wounds themselves.

"Big guy, what are you doing?"

He was dimly aware the Hedgeruds were no longer attacking. He'd fallen; the threat was neutralized. There was no reason for them to charge, so they let the female kneel by his side, gripping him even as he fought to rise to his knees.

But the shaking didn't stop.

The air itself seemed to vibrate, humming with energy that made his nefre pulse with insistence.

Heat.

The air was heating.

Something was about to happen. And it wasn't the tremors of death reaching him.

That strange tech Tasqals possessed. They were using it again.

"Hold on!" With the last bit of his energy, he pulled the female against him, his body encompassing hers as the ground gave way beneath them. But instead of falling, they were enveloped in heat that was searing.

It could be his imagination. His vision was still barely there. That didn't stop his stomach from lurching as reality bent around them. For a moment, they were everywhere and nowhere at once.

Then darkness. Cool, damp air replaced the heat.

Dimly, he was aware of Kon-stahns. She wasn't moving. And this darkness, this space...they weren't in the heat of battle anymore.

Maybe he died. But wasn't death supposed to feel...better?

Or maybe the entire world went silent because they had no chance now.

His body collapsed, the softness of the female beneath him cushioning his fall. She still wasn't moving. He'd failed her.

Again.

But then he heard a sound. Felt slight movement.

Kon-stahns coughed, and it was the sweetest sound he'd ever heard.

"What...what just happened?"

5

Constance

THE WORLD CAME BACK in fragments, like shards of a broken mirror piecing themselves together. Each shard brought with it another sensation—the damp chill in the air, the weight pressing down on her chest, and the absolute darkness surrounding them.

Constance coughed, her lungs burning as she drew in stale, musty air. "What...what just happened?" Did she get knocked out? Where the hell were they?

No answer came. Only the echo of dripping water somewhere in the distance and her own ragged breathing. Those were the only two sounds that broke the silence. The weight on her chest didn't move. Didn't respond.

"Rebel guy?" Her voice cracked. The fog in her mind was lifting, replaced by a clarity that felt like ice water in her veins. "Big guy?"

Still nothing.

Reality crashed over her like a tidal wave. The battle. The gator-guards. The rebel's blood spraying through the air. Her hands trembled as she pressed them against his shoulder, trying to shift his massive frame.

"Come on, you overgrown mint candy. Get up. We have to get out of here." Heck, she didn't even know his name. Never talked to him back on the Restitution base. Never really got close to him until that night when the entire camp...oh god, the entire camp was gone. And he...*what was he doing here*?

When he still didn't move, panic threatened to close up her throat as she wedged her arms under his shoulders and pushed with everything she had. His body rolled slightly to the side, enough for her to wiggle free. The ground beneath her was rough stone, uneven and cold against her palms as she scrambled to her knees.

"Where are we? How...how did we get here?" Her whisper sounded loud in the darkness, and that only made the hairs along the back of her neck rise as if in warning. Where the hell were they? Her eyes strained against the darkness, but she could barely make out a thing. The air felt close, confined. Underground, maybe? But they'd been in the middle of the street moments ago. A street that had tall white buildings that looked so surreal...

And the rebel. Gods, it felt like a dream, but it must have been real. That gator-guard pushing her in that shuttle and injecting her with...*something*. And then seeing the tall teal alien free-falling toward their ship. It seemed impossible, but it wasn't. It hadn't been a dream because he was *right here*. And if everything that happened out there was real...there was no way he was still alive.

"Shit," she breathed. "Oh, shit."

Her hands shook, grasping bits of loose stone underneath her fingertips. A laugh threatened to rise, but she wasn't sure if it was because of the drugs or just pure anxiety. She was pretty sure the alien was dead. And the other women? She didn't know where Meredith and that silent woman were now.

"Oh, shit." In the dark, her eyes slowly adjusted. She could barely make out the alien's still form beside her, and her heart cracked where it had risen at the center of her throat. What this alien did— however he'd transported them from the center of that fight—was the only reason she wasn't kneeling in front of one of those High Tasqals right now. The only reason she wasn't being forced to bow before those deceased toad-like creatures.

She wasn't a fool. She owed him her life, and she knew it. But the worst thing was, she couldn't even thank him for what he did. He wasn't moving, and the weight of that—the weight of it all—felt almost too heavy to bear.

What now? She couldn't leave him here. She couldn't just abandon him to find a way out. Not after what he'd done to save her. At the very least, he deserved to not have his body left rotting in... wherever this was.

"Shit," she muttered again.

That's when she heard it. A faint sound that whispered across the stillness—the barely audible sound of a soft breath, labored and wet.

Her heart stopped. "Big guy?"

Reaching out in the dark, her fingers trembled as they closed on his chest. Hard, the muscles felt like stone under her palm, but even with the chill stiffening her fingers, she felt the slight rise and fall.

He was breathing.

"Oh God." A breath of relief shuddered through her, followed swiftly by anger that had no fire. "You stupid, stubborn..." A sob made her choke as trembling hands ran over what she could feel of his body, trying to map it as she assessed the damage. Her fingers came away sticky and warm. She lifted them in the dark, unable to see the blood that no doubt stained her hands red. "You fool." Her hands trembled, a strained laugh that sounded more like a sob leaving her throat. "What kind of idiot dives into a horde of monsters to save someone they barely know?"

But the alien didn't respond. Probably couldn't. She was trying to remain positive, but the amount of wetness that came away on her hand could only mean one thing. He was alive, but barely so.

It was too dark for her to see the extent of his injuries, but she could feel them. Deep gashes in his side, charred flesh that crumbled under her touch. The metallic scent of blood that filled her nostrils. Her stomach turned, a wave of nausea rising at the unseen extent of the damage beneath her fingertips. It was more horrifying than anything she could imagine.

But the fact he was breathing meant he was still fighting. And that meant she'd fight with him, too.

"Don't you dare die on me." She gripped the alien's shoulders, staring down at where his face must be. The voice that left her lips was firmer, surer than she felt. But by God, she wouldn't let him die. Fuck that.

Mind set, a sort of wild determination gripped her, burning through her veins like the heat emanating from the alien's skin. She yanked at her blouse, gripping one end with her teeth as she pulled hard, tearing a strip of fabric. Beneath her, the alien released another breath, followed by a low groan, and she ripped the fabric harder.

"We're going to get you patched up, and then we're going to find a way out of this hole and back to the Restitution." She ripped another piece of her blouse, so hard her jaw hurt. "I promise you that."

The material was thin, but it would have to do. She wrapped the largest piece around him, struggling in the dark to get the fabric under and around him as she pulled it tight against the worst of the wounds she could find with her fingers. His skin was so hot, she was sure he was running a fever. But that had to be a good sign. It meant he was still fighting to stay alive.

"I have no idea where you came from." She ripped another piece of fabric. "I still think I imagined it. You were...I saw you falling through *space*." Her words tumbled out between hitched breaths as she worked. "If that didn't kill you, I'll be damned if we let this take you out."

He needed to make it.

Right now, he was her only hope, and it seemed she was his.

Her hands moved as fast as she could make them, binding the makeshift bandages as tight as she dared. "You want to be a hero? Then stay alive, dammit. We're not out of this shit yet."

God. Why was she saying all this? The nerves? The anxiety? The fact she was stuck on an alien planet with nothing but enemies all around them? If the teal alien hadn't come, she'd have been alone.

And she was thankful that he was here. Some selfish part of her was happy he'd come, even though he had to risk his life to make it so. What did that say about her?

The only part of her blouse left was a short scrap that barely covered her breasts. She didn't know if all the binding was even helping. Even with her eyes adjusted to the dark, she could still barely see a thing. For all she knew, her efforts were doing jack squat.

Swallowing hard, her fingers trembled again as she stretched them over the alien's chest, documenting the rest of his injuries. There were other deep wounds, some that she missed. Fuck, he was charred and fried. Stabbed and clawed. How was he still breathing?

All she was wearing were pants made of the same thin material as her blouse. It took a lot of effort to bite into the material at her legs, but she made two holes, tugging at them until she turned the pants into shorts. With the free fabric, she balled it into her fist before pressing the wad against the remaining wounds she could find. It was all she could do, and she was very aware it wasn't enough.

"Come on," she whispered. "You can't die here. You—"

The words stopped in her throat, her entire body stilling as a loud screeching sound echoed through the still air. In the dark, Constance's head snapped toward the sound, her heart beating hard in her chest as her ears perked.

That wasn't the sound of the wind.

They weren't alone.

It was a chasm of darkness all around her. If she was at the edge of a cliff, she wouldn't know. And that meant that whatever made that sound would be hidden by the darkness, too.

Seconds turned into minutes where she didn't breathe, eyes wide in the dark as she stared in the direction the sound came from. But it didn't repeat. Whatever it was, it was either gone, or it was still somewhere out there, lurking.

Swallowing hard, she forced herself to focus on the alien before her. Using the wad of cloth she'd ripped from her clothes, she pressed it against the largest unwrapped wound she could find. "Now would be a really good time for you to do that magic thing you did and teleport us out of here," she whispered. But that wasn't going to happen. For all she knew, he wasn't going to ever move again.

"Come on, Constance. What would he do?"

She closed her eyes and forced herself to breathe slowly. What *would* he do? This teal alien was a warrior. One of the best. She knew that, because when the gator-guards descended on the Restitution, he was there. He and a cyborg guy had saved her and her roommate, Alaina. He'd moved with lethal precision and he'd saved her life. Just like he'd saved her life again here.

If he wasn't injured, he'd take his swords, and he'd find a way out of this. He'd fight his way through. Swallowing hard, her hands moved over him again, and she tried not to focus on the damage she could feel. The charred skin, the ripped flesh. "Come on, big guy. Was it some kind of device? The thing you used to get us out of there?" Her hands ran down his legs, pressing against his trousers as she tried to find whatever thing he'd used to teleport them. If she could just find it, she could figure out how to get it to work again, maybe. It was the best idea she had now. "Maybe something I could use?"

Her fingers continued moving as she searched his pants. They closed around a definite bulge at the apex of his thighs that made her stop short, a moment before she jerked her hands away. Fuck. Of course, he had a dick. He was a man. A *male*, rather.

"Sorry," she muttered. "If you're hiding some kind of magic stick, it's definitely not that, I'm sure." But she couldn't find anything on him. Nothing except his two large blades, which almost cut her, and his blaster that she'd been carrying.

"Fuck." Her voice caught as her hand brushed his chest again. Was his breathing more shallow?

"No, no, no." She leaned down, pressing her ear to his chest. The heartbeat she found was thready and weak. "Don't you dare die."

But he was still burning up.

She needed to help him.

Head tilting, she looked over her shoulder into the darkness. There was still that sound of dripping water off in the distance. Shit.

Trembling, she reached for the alien's sword. It was heavier than it had looked when he'd been wielding it just moments before. Gripping the hilt in her hand, she released a shuddering breath.

"Alright." She shifted from his side while remaining on her knees. "Here's what's going to happen." She had to force steel into her voice, even as it wavered. Because what she was about to do went against all the instructions her inner Constance was screaming. "You're going to keep breathing. That's your only job right now. Just keep breathing, and I'll...I'll figure something out."

Fuck. She was really going to do this.

Crawling on all fours, she used one hand to map the way before her. It was slow going. The soft clang of the sword in her palm every time it hit the stone seeming to crack the silence like an alarm. The tunnel—she was almost certain it was a tunnel now—seemed to stretch endlessly. But that sound of dripping water was getting louder.

God, please let it be water. *Clean* water.

When the air moved slightly to her right, Constance paused. Tongue like a ball in her throat, she stretched her arm right. There was an intersection here, and the tunnel curved slightly. Ahead, the air movement grew stronger. Somewhere around that bend, there had to be an exit. Or at least another tunnel. Something that might lead them to safety, or help, or...

She'd rather not think about it. For now, she'd think about the most immediate catastrophe—the alien bleeding to death somewhere in the tunnel behind her.

Off to her left was the pitter-patter of water she'd heard. She headed that way.

Making a note of the turn, she moved as quickly as she dared. It took several minutes, her breath sounding like echoes as she moved quietly. She could hear the water more loudly now, but it felt like it was taking forever to get there.

Feel. Move. Crawl. *Focus on the sound. Not on the fact you can't see a thing. Not on the fact you have no idea where you are.*

She could hear the pitter-patter louder now, as if it was right in front of her. But when she stretched her hand there, she came upon nothing.

But it had to be here. Where was it?

Crawling forward, her palms almost slipped against the wet stone. The water! Blindingly feeling in the dark, she followed the moisture, her palms moving over the stone until she was following the water up the wall. There, the drops began to hit her skin.

She could almost rejoice. She'd done it! She'd found it! But now for the test.

Bringing her hand to her mouth, she took a tentative taste, bracing for the worst. If this was some kind of sewage, she was prepared to cut her tongue out—

But it was water. Clean water. At least, it tasted that way. She'd just have to trust she'd found a busted pipe in what she was realizing must be the city's underground. These tunnels must stretch wide and far. Somehow, the teal rebel had transported them to this location, but it was only a matter of time before the gator-guards thought to look for them here. Until then, they had to get teal guy better and find a way off this planet.

Tucking the hilt of his sword under her arm, she washed her hands before cupping them underneath the leak. It wasn't effective, but it was the best she could do. When her hands were full, she turned around and counted her steps back.

It took much longer to find the alien again. At one moment, she wondered if she'd lost him, took a turn she didn't realize, but when her shoes hit against his boots and shock almost made her lose the water she'd so carefully carried, she released a breath of relief instead.

Falling to her knees, she crawled over the alien, finding his lips with the back of her hand. They wouldn't budge. He wasn't opening his mouth.

Shit.

The water trembled in her cupped palms, precious drops already escaping between her fingers. She couldn't waste a single moment, but she also couldn't lose what little she'd gathered. She needed him to open his mouth, and she needed him to swallow.

Leaning closer, she tried to gauge his position by touch alone. She could barely make out his features in the dark, but she thought his face was turned slightly to the side based on where his breaths hit her cheek.

His breathing had grown more labored in her absence; each inhale a painful rasp that made her wince. She needed to get the water into him, and she only had one idea.

"Don't you dare read anything into this." She didn't know why she even bothered speaking. She doubted he could hear her. "This is purely survival. Like in those wilderness shows where they have to... never mind. Just don't die on me."

Carefully, so carefully, she lowered her face until her lips found his. They were warm, just like the rest of him, and barely parted. The sensation made her pause. Made her almost change her mind. But she had no other choice.

Using the gentlest pressure she could manage, she pushed against his lips with her own, trying to create enough of an opening.

His lips remained stubbornly closed.

"Come on." It was a plea. "Work with me here. You need water. You need to heal. You need to *live*, you stupid, brave fool."

She tried again, this time using her teeth to catch his upper lips and pulling ever so slightly. A tremble went through her that she ignored. He tasted exactly like he looked. Like mint in chocolate. An inappropriate thought for one of the most inappropriate things she'd ever done. Pressing her eyes closed, she worked her lips against his, nudging, teasing until finally—there—the smallest gap. It would have to be enough.

Moving with painful slowness, she positioned her hands above the opening she'd created and let the water trickle down, drop by precious drop. Most had been lost on the journey back. Only a few drops made it into his mouth.

There was a weak cough, then the blessed sound of swallowing.

"That's it," she whispered, relief making her voice shake. "Just like that. Stay with me, Mint Man. Stay with me."

Gripping his sword once more, she turned to face the darkness once again. The water was working, and that meant she needed more.

He was still fighting. Still holding on.

And as long as he was fighting, so would she.

6

Akur

Pain. Everywhere.

Was death not supposed to be peace? It wasn't. The gods of Tonvuhiri lied.

He tried to groan, but all that happened was a strained sound in his throat.

If he wasn't dead, then by some miracle, he lived, and he wasn't sure which was worse. He couldn't move. Still couldn't see.

No. Wait. He *could* see. But darkness surrounded him so thickly, it was as if no light had graced this space in eons.

The human. Where was she?

Kon-stahns. Qrak. They've probably taken her already. Left him here thinking he was dead. And he couldn't even move. The most he could do was ball his claws into fists.

There was cold, uneven stone beneath him. The chill of it seeped into his back, but he welcomed it against his burning skin. Because he *was* burning up, and that was a problem. One he'd have to deal with later, if he even managed to rise from this.

Some sound in the darkness made him freeze. It was faint, but he hadn't spent most of his life in constant survival to think he imagined such a thing. On instinct, his arm flexed, reaching for his blades, but all that happened was his muscles refused to work. His arms remained dead at his sides.

Qrakking crukks. It would have been better if he hadn't survived this. To die now while aware of everything but unable to move was torture from the devils of the Vuhiri.

The sound came again. Closer this time. Enough that he could hear the constant soft rhythm. There was something in this darkness with him. A Hedgerud? No. They didn't move so quietly, and why would they need to? If they put him here in this place, they wouldn't need to creep around.

Again, he tried to reach for his blade, but his arms didn't move. He was stuck. Vulnerable. A feeling he'd never encountered before, but one he despised immediately.

It was the shape he saw first, barely discernible in the shadows. A figure that became clearer as it came closer. Something, or rather someone, he didn't expect to see. *Her*. The female. The human. Konstahns was here.

She stepped closer, slowly, carefully, soft words whispering from her lips as she neared. She was counting.

"Three hundred nineteen." She slowed down even more. "Three hundred twenty." She was right at his feet now. There, she paused. Stretching one leg in his direction. That single leg seemed to test the air, seemed to search for something, and his gaze moved over her bare skin. Visibility wasn't great, but he could still see her garments were ripped. Or more like torn. Her bare leg stretched out, still searching. Only stopping when her foot met one of his boots. Then and only then did she release a breath. She kneeled then, and he wondered what the qrak she was doing. All this, this entire situation, was simply unbelievable.

She was here, which meant the Hedgeruds hadn't taken her away. And if they hadn't, then where were they? More importantly, how did they get here?

He watched as the human crawled over him, her hands cupped

together as she swayed on her knees with the shuffling movements she made to push herself forward. She was carrying something. Water, judging from the droplets that escaped her palms to fall on his chest.

They heated. Felt like they evaporated with the warmth emanating from his being. A warmth that shouldn't be there. A warmth that—

Qrak. He couldn't think about that. The human was climbing over him, her thick thighs pressing against his chest now. Sweet pain. It distracted from the searing heat and his throbbing wounds.

A deep breath left the human's frame as she leaned forward. At first, he thought she was leaning forward so she could see him. Humans didn't seem to see well in the dark, and this darkness was oppressive. But if she was leaning closer to see him, why did her eyes flutter closed?

Kon-stahns?

But he couldn't speak.

When her lips met his, he expected her to pull back. He'd seen his comrades with their human mates. Seen them do the mouth-touching. It was never done with anyone else. It was only between mates. Even his brother, Ajos, did not allow his human mate to do this greeting with anyone else. Once they touched mouths, it often resulted in them heading to their private quarters. It was a human mating signal. He was sure of it. And this female...this female was touching her mouth to his.

Surely, it was a mistake. Surely—

When her lips fitted against his upper one, gently nudging his mouth open, the entire universe stopped moving. His nefre pulsed, a low thrum against the back of his neck, an awareness that had nothing to do with the pain wracking his frame. The warmth already building within him intensified, pooling low in his gut. Spreading outward like a wildfire.

No.

Not *that*. Not yet. Not here.

Fighting the heat coursing through him, he tried to ignore what the female was doing. She didn't know. She didn't know that he wasn't only dying, that he was coming alive in a process that couldn't —*shouldn't*—be happening. That this heat, the one warming the very air around them, was a sure marker that even if they made it out of this alive, he was well and royally qeffed.

But one problem at a time.

The female must think his teeth clenched for some other reason, because she grunted against his lips.

"Come on." It was almost like a plea. "There's not much water left." She nudged him with those soft lips again. "*Please*, big guy."

She was begging him. Begging him to respond to her mouth mating?

... Well...this was a turn of events even he who was ready for anything could not have expected.

He couldn't respond, couldn't speak, his body still locked in the aftermath of the shock-rod and whatever the qrak had happened afterward. But the softness of her lips, the gentle pressure as she moved against him, sparked a response he couldn't suppress. He unclenched his teeth. Allowed her soft lips to pry open his. Tried to ignore the flood of sensations that threatened to overwhelm him from this unexpected intimacy.

There was a tenderness in her touch, a vulnerability that both intrigued and confused him.

"Good," she whispered, pulling back slightly, and qrak, didn't he want to posture at that simple praise.

What was he? Some kind of simple male?

She tasted sweet, and despite the pain going through him, despite that this was not the place to indulge in such things, he wanted more. The fever just underneath his skin made everything too intense, too real. Made him hyperaware of every point of contact between them— her thighs, even the brush of her long filaments against his jaw.

So many sols chasing after that ship. So many sols of hopelessness. The last thing he'd imagined was a human's lips pressing against his. Maybe he really was dead, and this was all a strange afterlife where nothing made sense.

She pulled back slightly, just enough to whisper something he couldn't quite catch, before something cool dripped against his lips. Water.

It was like a splash of cold reality.

Water?

Ah, yes.

He was being subjected to forced hydration. He swallowed, the realization that she wasn't, in fact, ravishing him settling with a dull thud of disappointment.

He might as well go on and die now.

"Stay with me," she murmured. "Just keep fighting."

Alright, fine. He wouldn't die.

He'd growl, but she was still so close, he didn't want to startle her.

That, and the starving male in him didn't want her to leave so quickly.

So he lay there as she emptied the water she carried in her hands before her shoulders slumped, and she released a slow breath. Her head tilted as she looked around, eyes wide, and yet it seemed she still couldn't see a thing. Her throat moved when she finally stopped looking around and turned back to face him. He blinked, expecting her to realize he was staring right back at her, but there was no recognition.

Instead, she shifted from over him, the sweet pressure of her thighs disappearing as her palms moved down his chest instead. Only then did he realize he'd been bandaged. Strips of garments tied around his frame.

This female...she hadn't just given him water. She'd been caring for him all this time? For how long?

And where the qrak were they?

As her soft hands moved over his chest, her breathing short and labored, he squeezed his eyes tight, focusing on the sounds of those breaths and not the heat rising within him. E'lot had been right. He shouldn't have left the shuttle wearing just a maintenance suit as protection. He'd trusted his regeneration a little too much. Maybe he'd been laughing in the face of death a little too much, too.

The heat from entry into this world. The heat from the shock rod. And the heat from the moment before they appeared in this place. It was all bad. All completely bad timing. Even dying, his body was taking that heat to mean one thing.

He'd thought that when his brother had gone into the mating frenzy on accident that it had been a once-in-a-lifetime occurrence. Shum'ai don't just go into heat at slight temperature changes. That would be stupid. But he'd had three separate intense encounters. Three encounters that might have started a chain of events that he wished didn't exist.

Because if he was going into heat, they were doomed. Him and the human. And that meant he had to get her out of this place, off this planet, and take down the Tasqals all before that happened.

So when the female eased off him, when her softness disappeared, he kept his eyes closed. Fighting not the pain of his injuries, not the torture, but the heat.

She was gone for long minutes, all while he remained unable to move.

When she returned, he heard her counting again. "Three hundred twenty."

Smart little fighter. She used the numbers to find him again. To kneel over him once more. And this time, when her lips met his, he kept his eyes closed.

He let her lips tease his.

Qrak. This was going to be the hardest mission he'd ever had to do.

7

Constance

A SOUND CUT through the darkness. A wet, rattling breath, followed by a single word spoken in a voice like gravel.

"Female…"

Constance spun so fast she nearly lost her balance. He was awake?

She didn't wait for a response, already running toward the sound. Her foot caught on his boots and she stumbled, the water cupped in her hands falling between them.

"Oh, shit."

There was a chuckle, or something like it. He sounded horrible, but the alien was alive. It worked. All those trips just trying to get him hydrated worked!

"I'm here." She crawled over him, careful not to rest her weight on any part of his wounded frame. Her hands found his chest in the dark before reaching up to his jaw. He must be looking right at her, judging from the position of his head. He was awake. She couldn't believe it. His heart still beat, but each breath sounded like it was being torn from his lungs. "I'm right here. You're going to be alright."

He was still burning up. So much so she was pretty sure his temperature had increased more than before. Contrary to what she'd been thinking, maybe it wasn't a good sign after all. The last thing she wanted was for him to have a seizure or something. Little drops of water wouldn't help with that.

"The wall," he rasped. "Please help me...to the wall."

His voice was different from what she remembered—rougher, strained, but still carrying that otherworldly resonance that marked him as not-human. She nodded before remembering he could probably see her perfectly well in this darkness while she was practically blind.

"Okay. Just...let me figure this out." She ran her hands carefully along his frame, trying to determine the best way to move him without aggravating his wounds. "Can you move at all?"

A grunt that might have been affirmative. She felt his muscles tense under her touch, a slight tremor running through him. The heat radiating from his skin was alarming—no one should be able to survive a fever this high.

"I'm going to get behind you. Support your shoulders." She worked her way around, hands never losing contact with him. The darkness was absolute, but she'd memorized his position through what must have been hours of tending to him. "Tell me if anything hurts too much."

Another sound, this one definitely amusement. "Everything...hurts."

Her own body ached. Tiredness had transformed to weariness. She could hardly move. Felt like she would collapse at any moment.

But she wasn't back on Earth where she could just fall into bed and call for takeaway on a lazy night in. She was on an alien planet in some part of the universe humans didn't know about. And she was surrounded by aliens who wanted to use her for things she didn't want to even imagine.

So the tiredness, this weariness, it would have to wait.

She'd collapse when she was dead. Right now, she was going to help this alien get back on his feet.

"More than it already does, then." She positioned herself behind his head, legs spread to brace herself. The uneven stone pressed hard into her ass and her thighs, making her wince. But she pushed the discomfort away. "Ready?"

His only response was to try to push himself up. She slid her arms under his shoulders, pulling upward as carefully as she could. The noise he made—somewhere between a growl and a hiss—made her pause, but he didn't tell her to stop.

Too tough to give up.

At least they were on the same page.

The movement was agonizingly slow. Every inch gained seemed to cost him, his breathing becoming more labored, the heat from his body intensifying. She could feel the tremors running through his massive frame as muscles fought against whatever was still affecting him.

"Almost there," she encouraged, though they'd barely gotten him a few inches off the ground. But he was their only hope. Fight as she might, draw bravery as she might, she was no match for what awaited them outside these tunnels.

The thought made her swallow hard. She was a liability. He would do well to abandon her here. After all, this whole rescue attempt was a suicide mission. If he forgot about her, he had a better chance of making it out of this alive.

Shit.

She bit her bottom lip, worrying it between her teeth, happy he wasn't facing her at this moment to see the fear flashing in her eyes.

She had to help him. But she also had to ensure he didn't leave her here. And that meant becoming invaluable to him. Whatever it took, she was making it out of this place alive.

It was a promise.

Grunting, she braced against him, but his weight was substantial. "Fucking hell."

Despite the pain wracking his frame, the alien managed to make a sound—something between a wheeze and a chuckle. "First...mouth mating ritual."

What?

His words made no sense.

And then they did.

Her eyes widened in the dark. Oh God. Oh God, no. He was conscious when she kissed him?

"Promises of jobs of blows and...and now the hells of mating." His voice was strained, but carried a hint of dry humor. "You humans are...very confusing."

She almost dropped him in surprise. "What?"

"I'd rather the hells of mating, with gratitude. If I am to die here, female, I can think of no better way to go." He tried to push himself up, but his muscles trembled and he failed. "Qrak," he cursed. "Never thought I'd ever say this, but I haven't the energy to mate."

What the—

She got the idea he tilted his head slightly as if to look at her, and she stared open-mouthed at where his head was. "I didn't say anything about mating."

He grunted.

"It was just an expression. And the water thing...the kiss wasn't...I was only trying to..."

God, she was a therapist, but if she survived this, she was pretty sure she was going to need to go in for some therapy herself.

"Explain later," the alien grunted. "Wall first."

She nodded, grateful the darkness was hiding her cheeks because she was pretty sure they'd gone red. "Right. Wall first."

When they finally got him somewhat upright, she had to pause, her arms shaking from the effort. He was pressed against her. Slumped back against her chest from the simple fact she'd been too weak to shift from under his falling weight. At the very least, the position forced her to rest.

Every breath he took, she could feel against her chest. His head fell back, too, to rest against her shoulder. The position brought home just how large he was compared to her. Even sitting, he dwarfed her frame.

"Rest," she whispered. "Just for a moment."

He grunted again.

For a moment, there was silence. Silence and darkness. Silence, darkness, and heat.

He was scorching hot.

"You feel...good," he suddenly rumbled. "Maybe I do have enough energy for the hells of mating after all. Though, with me, it will be no hell at all. Only what you call 'heaven'."

Her brows dived as she pushed against his shoulder. "Get off me."

She only knew he laughed because she felt how the mirth moved through his frame.

"Do not fear, female. I only make light of this situation."

Constance released a slow breath. "Well, I don't think you should be making jokes. For a good while there, I thought you were dead."

"I might as well be."

His sudden words, said so matter-of-factly, caught her off guard.

"But I won't," he continued. "You are still here. You are alive. I must get you home safely."

Home. A place she didn't even know anymore. Where was home?

He relaxed more against her, and she hadn't the energy to push him off or slide from under him. He still needed more energy, but at least he was awake. That was moving in the right direction.

"You found me," she whispered after a few moments. "You...you found us."

The alien grunted. "Don't rejoice. I nearly didn't."

But he did. "How did you even find us? I thought...I didn't think anyone was coming. Are there more rebels out there? Will there be a counterattack?" She kept her voice low, still aware the darkness could be hiding any number of things. The screeching sound she'd heard long before hadn't returned, but that didn't mean they were in the clear. It didn't mean they were alone.

"There is no one."

Her breath stopped in her nose, halted neither in her lungs nor outside of her. "What...what do you mean?"

But he didn't say anything else, and frankly, she was too afraid to ask.

There was no one else?

The last she saw of the Restitution's base had been death and destruction. Before that beam took her, the entire base had looked like a war zone—and her side had been losing. But even though she'd lost hope that they were coming to save her, she guessed a part of her had still wished some of them had survived.

But he said there was no one.

He was the only part of the resistance that was left?

His breathing was ragged, each exhale burning against her skin where he tilted his head against her shoulder. She could feel his pulse racing, feel the way his muscles spasmed as they tried to respond to commands.

"Gratitude," he rumbled.

She hummed a tone in her throat. "For what?"

Heavy breaths were all that came from him, and he breathed deep and long.

"You braved this oppressive darkness." He said after a few moments. "You are a courageous one, female of fire."

She didn't know how to respond. Thinking about it now, she'd crawled through pitch-black cold darkness to get the water. She wasn't scared of the dark, but what she did was nothing compared to diving after a ship in space.

After what felt like an eternity, he managed to speak again. "Left...pocket."

For a moment, she didn't realize what he meant, but then it clicked that he was giving her a command. She shifted, trying to maintain her grip while reaching around him. Her fingers found the pocket he mentioned, feeling something smooth and flat within. She hadn't felt that when she'd been looking for his teleportation device. When she pulled it out, his hand covered hers, the heat within them warding away the chill as he guided her fingers to what felt like a tiny depression. A button.

The sudden flare of light made her eyes water. It wasn't bright—just a soft, bluish glow emanating from the device in their hands—but after so long in complete darkness, it felt blinding.

As her vision adjusted, she finally got her first proper look at their surroundings. She was right about them being in a tunnel. It was about as wide as a subway tunnel, the walls rough-hewn from solid rock. The ceiling arched overhead, disappearing into shadows beyond the reach of their small light. For as far as the light reached in both directions, the tunnel stretched on.

"Hmm." It was a grunt. As if the alien was surprised to see where they were.

"Think you can do your magic and get us out of here again?"

"You speak of this 'magic' as if it is a weapon I wield." His head tilted as he looked one way down the tunnel, then the next. "I had no part in transporting us to this place."

"What do you mean you had no part?" She shifted, adjusting her grip to better support him. "We were above ground, fighting those assholes, and then we were here. If you didn't do it, *who did*?"

He was quiet for a long moment, his breathing still labored, and she didn't like it. It made her anxiety go up a notch. Made the chances of their survival seem to waver and fade.

"Unknown. But..." He paused, seeming to gather strength. "Not good."

Great. If he hadn't transported them here, and the Restitution was gone...

"It had to be them. The gator-guards. They put us down here for a reason." Her head snapped up as her eyes scanned the length of tunnel she could see. Suddenly, the absence of that screeching sound was even more notable. Where was the thing that made that sound? Was it waiting? Watching them?

"Possible." The alien's muscles tensed under her hands. "Or worse."

Note to self: if she wanted positivity, she probably shouldn't turn to him for it.

"Worse?" She didn't want to ask, but she needed all the information she could get. "What could be worse than our enemies?"

He made that sound again—the one that wasn't quite a laugh.

"Many things. But I am here now. You need not worry." Then, so low, she almost didn't hear him. "You are far too precious."

She frowned at him, her gaze skipping over the side profile of his face.

His skin was still darker than its usual vibrant teal, but she was pretty sure the color was slowly coming back. She stared at him, noting the two narrow furrows that gave definition to his skull, his humanoid features with their distinct 'alienness'. Like the way he had no hair, not even eyebrows. Or the way his shoulders sloped dramatically, displaying corded flesh that was pure muscle. He only had three thick fingers on each hand, and from what she could see of his feet and the strange way his boots were made, they looked to be digitigrade.

But it was his condition that drew her attention and made her breath catch. The makeshift bandages were saturated with what looked like black oil in the soft light, but it was his blood. So much, so thick, it looked dark against the brown fibers. The wounds beneath were brutal. Burn marks from the shock rod created patterns across his exposed skin, and deep gashes were already forming scabs all over him. The skin around the injuries was mottled with colors she didn't have names for, patterns shifting beneath the surface like oil on water.

And yet, even in the few minutes that had passed since the light source activated, he looked to be improving. It shouldn't be possible, but even his breaths were evening out. He was adjusting to the trauma, probably even healing, faster than any human could.

"You're healing," she breathed, her voice barely over a whisper.

He made a sound that might have been agreement. "Not...fast enough." His free hand moved to one of the deeper wounds, fingers pressing against the strange discoloration. "You tended to me with your garments."

She didn't answer. Didn't have to.

"Why?"

But that question felt like it came out of the blue. Why? Why did she help him? She thought it was obvious. She'd thought he was going to die if she didn't help. And, more than that, she was the reason he was here. He came after her and the others. He tried to save them. That meant he was worth saving, too.

"I didn't want you to die."

He released a grunt, and she was sure she saw his lips twist into a wry sort of grin.

With another grunt, he eased off her a little, enough for her gaze to fall on his back. There were more injuries there. Deep welts that were scabbing over. But what grabbed her attention almost immediately was the fin-like structure that ran from his nape to disappear into his spine.

It was red. An angry red. It looked like a warning sign.

"Mint...rebel guy...your neck. It's red."

He froze. Went so still it was clear he stopped even breathing.

He shifted away from her then, so suddenly that she gasped. Gone was the wounded creature she'd been supporting. In his place was something entirely different—predatory, powerful, otherworldly. She couldn't see the fin structure now because he turned it away from her. All she could stare at were his eyes. They caught the light. Reflected it like a cat's now. And they were staring right back at her.

She swallowed hard, instinct suddenly screaming at her to back away. This wasn't some injured soldier anymore—this was an apex predator from a world she couldn't even imagine, and she'd gone and stepped on a landmine. Suddenly, everything about him radiated danger. From the way he was looking at her to the way he was so impossibly still despite his injuries.

It was then that she realized the absence of the warmth. The heat radiating from him was gone. While he'd been leaning against her, his fever had been keeping her warm and, despite how wrong it was, she hadn't realized she'd been comforted by it till now.

But he didn't look like a male dying of a fever. This was...this was something else.

"What did you call me?" he finally said, golden eyes still piercing into her soul.

Constance blinked. "Um..." Her eyelids fluttered a few more times, her brain trying hard to catch up. "I don't know your name."

He released another grunt, but his face was unreadable. He wasn't even pretending to smile.

"It is Akur."

Akur. A name she didn't expect, but one that suited him perfectly, nonetheless.

"I'm Constance."

"I know your name."

She swallowed hard.

What had she done wrong? Had mentioning the red fin really been such an offense?

His head turned slightly, the soft light casting strange shadows across his features. "We need to move. It is not safe here."

She blinked at him, but it was like he'd suddenly transformed. He was all business now, and she supposed that was alright. This wasn't a five-star hotel where they had an unlimited stay. They needed to escape. Get the hell out of here.

"Right. Any idea which direction?"

The alien—Akur's—eyes narrowed as he studied both directions. "Right. Slope...slightly upward. Surface closer."

Wow. Damn. It took her crawling on hands and knees to even figure out that there was an exit somewhere close, and he discovered that in a matter of seconds? How?

He was already shifting upward, trying to stand. Guess they were moving.

"Right it is then." She braced herself. "Ready when you are."

Akur grunted and rose, stumbling slightly. She reached for him, but all he did was jerk away. She frowned. Well then, he can piss off if he's suddenly going to be a dick.

Scowling at him now, she watched as he reached for his sword that she'd been carrying for protection. That only left the blaster she'd been wielding in the fight above ground. It was a few feet away on the stone floor. She'd all but forgotten about it.

Limping, her muscles ached as she reached for it. By the time she turned back around, the alien was standing straight. His movements were more fluid now, controlled. And frankly, a bit freaky with how quickly he was recovering.

Meanwhile, she felt like roadkill.

Without a word, he turned and began walking, the glow of the light source moving with him. It only took a moment for her gaze to skip around the tunnel before she looked up into the cavernous darkness above them. With the light quickly receding, it was like the dark had mutated and was trying to swallow her whole. Her body jerked into action. Guess that was her cue to follow the alien.

Hurrying after him, he was already a few strides ahead, moving down the tunnel with steps that were becoming steadier with each passing moment. The soft light cast their shadows long against the walls, making them look like monstrous creatures following alongside them. Constance put more energy in her steps, making sure there was hardly a breath between her and the alien in front.

This would be scary if she wasn't already crippled by fear. That meant it was past scary. She was frickin' terrified. If she could tell her friends back on Earth about all this, she'd say it was something out of a nightm—

She almost ran into the alien's back. The same moment that the light suddenly went out.

"Shit. Did you run out of batter—"

Her voice stopped in her throat when Akur's palm slammed against her mouth—or more like her face. His palm was so large it was almost like he was trying to suffocate her, and she was mildly aware that he'd shot his arm back to do it.

The scent of blood on his palm filled her nostrils. But he wasn't trying to stop her from breathing. He was silencing her with the universal signal to shut the fuck up. And she'd be damned if she was going to be a fool and argue about it.

So she kept her mouth shut, frowning into the darkness, wondering if he'd heard something that—

But then she didn't have to wonder. Because she heard it, too. The scratching.

Her body went still.

It was the same scratching sound she'd heard before. The one she'd wanted to forget about as if it'd never happened. She wished she could, but there was no way to forget about it now.

This time, the scratching sound wasn't just coming from one direction. It was coming from everywhere—ahead of them, behind them...above them. Her head tilted back slowly, her face shifting under the weight of Akur's hand as her eyes widened in the pitch black.

The scratching sound echoed off the tunnel walls; it was impossible to pinpoint the source, and it was impossible to ignore.

Akur went rigid beside her. "I knew this was too easy," he said under his breath.

Too easy?

Clearly, they had a different interpretation of difficulty.

"What?" Clutching the blaster in both hands, she wished she could see something, even though the thought of actually seeing something appear from the darkness made her quake inside. "What is it?"

Her voice was mumbled, words fading into his hot skin.

She felt him turn. Felt his warmth envelop her even as the scratching sound grew so loud it sent a chill straight through to her soul.

"How fast can you run?" he spoke so quietly she barely heard him.

The scratching grew louder. Closer. Something skittered across the wall above, sending small rocks pattering around them.

The alien's palm left her face, and he gripped her shoulders instead.

"Listen, human. You're going to turn around, and you're going to run."

"Wh-what are they?"

He didn't answer. Instead, his heat became almost scorching as he pressed his face into hers, forehead to forehead. Their breaths mingled. Hers frantic and uneven, his steady and measured.

"You don't want to know. Now run. And whatever you do, don't stop running until you no longer hear a sound."

He released her so suddenly that she almost stumbled. When she reached out, he was gone.

"Akur!"

"Run, human!" It was a command this time, and only a moment before a sound came from the darkness that made her blood run cold. It was a low, wet chittering that spoke of teeth and hunger and crawling things that should stay buried.

As Akur's roar echoed through the tunnel, followed by a deafening screech that made her teeth vibrate, Constance raised the blaster and took off running. Whatever was in that darkness with them, she wasn't going to make it easy for them to catch her.

She just hoped she was running toward safety and not straight into their nest.

8

Constance

RUN.

Faster.

She pushed her feet to do what her mind told them to, but it was hard. Not even adrenaline could counter the complete weariness or the fact her body had been through so much.

And yet she tried. Her feet pounded against the tunnel floor as she ran, each breath burning in her lungs. The darkness pressed in around her like a living thing. Suffocating. Unholy.

Behind her, the screeching sound and Akur's roar had devolved into sounds of battle that echoed off the stone wall—the clash of metal, inhuman screeches, and Akur's deep-throated roars that sounded more animal than sentient.

He was fighting the things, whatever they were, even as he chased after her. He was keeping them back so she could find a way to safety.

But the creatures' chittering grew closer, then farther, then closer again. She couldn't tell if they were gaining on her or if the tunnel's acoustics were playing tricks on her mind. Couldn't tell if she was heading toward more danger or away from it. And when her muscles screamed for rest, she forced herself to keep moving. Thin leather shoes beating against hard stone.

The command Akur had given her rang in her ears: "*Run, and don't stop until you can't hear anything.*" Run. All she had to do was run.

A rush of air swept past her face, carrying with it a stench like rotting meat and stagnant water. Something massive moved in the darkness beside her. Before she could react, a form brushed against her arm—smooth and cold and *wrong*. It felt like touching wet leather stretched over something gelatinous, with ridges and protrusions that caught at her skin. The texture alone made her stomach heave.

She screamed, stumbling sideways as razor-sharp edges—claws or teeth or both—raked across her upper arm. The pain was immediate and intense, but the adrenaline coursing through her system pushed it to the background. All that mattered was running, staying ahead of whatever horrors lurked in the darkness.

Behind her, Akur's footsteps thundered closer. She could hear his labored breathing, punctuated by grunts of exertion as he fought. The screech of his blades cutting through something solid made her flinch. Whatever had touched her let out a wet, gurgling shriek that echoed off the walls.

"Keep running, human!" his voice boomed through the tunnel even as she heard him grunt in pain, followed by another inhuman screech.

The darkness was now a physical thing. Like a dark force she had to push through. The walls themselves felt like they were closing in, and her heart dropped when she realized that was exactly what was happening. The tunnel was getting narrower. She didn't know if that was a good thing or—well, just another sign that this was the worst lucid nightmare she'd ever had.

Pushing her legs faster, she didn't even wince when her shoulder slammed into the wall at her side. Adjusting herself slightly, she kept going, even as something skittered across the ceiling above her. She could hear the click-click-click of what had to be claws on stone. The sound surrounded her now—ahead, behind, above. How many were there?

"Akur?!"

A particularly loud clash of metal on something hard came from behind her, followed by Akur's pained shout. She wanted to look back, wanted to make sure he was still fighting, still alive. But looking back meant slowing down, and slowing down meant death. Death in the dark when she couldn't see anything, anyway.

The tunnel floor began sloping upward, making each step harder. Her legs burned with the effort, and her lungs were working overtime. How long had she been running? It felt like hours, but it couldn't have been more than a minute.

Suddenly, the tunnel opened up into what felt like a larger space. Her footsteps echoed differently, and the air moved in a way that suggested multiple paths. An intersection? She slowed just enough to think. To feel the flow of air blowing from her left to her right. There were multiple paths here. Which way?

Another screech sounded behind her, closer now. Too close. She picked the right tunnel on instinct and pushed herself to run faster.

"Turning right!" Fuck. She hoped he heard her. Hoped he followed.

The scratching sounds were all around her now, loud and a constant background noise that made her skin crawl.

He'd told her to run. Maybe these things would give up. Maybe this was their only choice. He obviously knew what they were and she could only imagine. She could still hear him fighting. His roars. His grunts. Akur hadn't taken the turn. He was still in the main tunnel. Still fighting. But then she heard it—a grunt of pain that sounded different from his battle cries.

They'd gotten him. She was sure of it.

Constance skidded to a stop, her shoes scraping against the stone floor. Something big brushed against her and, on instinct, she lashed out. The butt of the weapon she was holding hit something fleshy yet hard and a resulting screech nearly burst her eardrums.

Run. His command echoed in her mind: *don't stop running until you no longer hear a sound.*

But as something else hit her again, this time from behind and she stumbled forward, she heard the alien's pained grunt once more. The sound of his blades clashing came through, too. He was still fighting. That was clear. But something was wrong.

If she kept on running, there was no doubt in her mind that she'd be leaving him behind. Injured. Alone with those things...

"Fuck it," she muttered.

This was madness. Her only combat experience involved mediating arguments over gluten-free muffins. She had no business marching back into a fight with literal monsters. Yet, she was turning around anyway.

"Don't you fucking die!" Rushing back the way she'd come, she raised the blaster, aimed over her head, and fired. The energy burst lit up the tunnel for a split second, and in that brief flash of light, she saw she'd made it to the intersection again.

And she saw them, too.

The creatures.

Her blood turned to ice in her veins.

They clung to the walls and ceiling like massive insects, but they were nothing like any insect she'd ever seen. Their bodies were thick and fleshy, covered in that same wet, leathery skin she'd felt earlier. Naked mole rats. That's what they looked like—if those Earth creatures had an extra set of limbs that ended in hooked claws that dug into the stone. Their heads were eyeless, dominated by gaping maws for protruding saw-like teeth. As they moved, their bodies seemed to ripple and flow in a sort of movement that didn't seem right. Wrong. Just so *wrong.*

And Akur—she saw him too, down on one knee, twin blades flashing as he fought off three of the creatures at once. The red fin at the back of his neck seemed like a beacon in that blaster flare. Almost as angry as the fresh wounds on his arms and chest, blood oozing from deep gashes.

In the darkness that followed the flash, the creatures' chittering grew louder, more excited. They knew she had stopped running. Knew she had turned back.

Constance raised the blaster again, this time aiming at the nearest monster she'd seen. They wanted to hunt? Fine. Let them hunt someone who could shoot back.

She didn't know what the hell she was doing. Before this day, she'd never fired a gun in her life. But suddenly, it felt like second nature.

Maybe it was fear. More likely, it was rage. Rage at the fact she didn't ask for any of this. Rage that her life had been ripped apart by a set of selfish beings that destroyed *everything*.

She squeezed the trigger, and the tunnel lit up again with the energy blast. This time, she was ready for what she'd see. The creature she'd aimed at screeched as the shot caught it in the side, its flesh sizzling with an acrid stench that made her gag. But it didn't fall. Instead, it twisted in a way that shouldn't have been possible, its body contorting as it redirected itself toward her.

"I told you to run!" Akur's voice carried over the din of battle, strained with effort and what might have been pain.

"Yeah, well, I'm not good at following orders!" She fired again, this time aiming for what she thought was the creature's head. The blast illuminated its grotesque features for a split second before connecting. The monster's flesh seemed to absorb the energy for a moment before bubbling and bursting. It fell from the wall with a wet splat.

But there were more. So many more.

In the strobing light of her blaster fire, she could see them flowing down from above like the walls were made of flesh, their movements both fluid and jerky at the same time. Each flash revealed them in different positions, like a horrific stop-motion film. And each time the blaster fire lit up the space, she was greeted with one undeniable sight.

They weren't paying attention to Akur anymore. She understood now why he'd told her to run. Why he'd been content with her abandoning him. These creatures, whatever they were, focused on the threat first. Because each shot of her blaster revealed one thing: *she was the target now.*

They were converging on her, no longer focusing on the alien, but on her instead.

Shit.

She stepped back, continuing to press the trigger on a gun that was quickly heating up with the extended fire. There was no use trying to aim, but she kept the muzzle pointed high. Underneath the shower of her retreat, each flash showed the alien getting to his feet. Of his blades being drawn. He looked haggard, badly beaten with little time to recover, but he was swinging still. And as the blaster stalled, the final shot being eaten by the darkness, as those creatures converged, she heard her name on the alien's lips like a battle cry she didn't know she needed to hear.

"Constance!"

Run. She needed to run.

Blindly, she spun, but something hit her from below the knee. She stumbled.

It was like falling off a precipice, losing her balance in that darkness. The world tilted, and the ground seemed at once close and far too far away at the same time. There was the sickening sensation of the creature that made her trip. The pain in her shoulder as teeth dug in. And her name.

"Constance!"

He was still fighting. And maybe, maybe, she needed to hear that. To hear him grunt. To hear the creatures screech as he fought to get to her.

Maybe it's the reason she snapped out of the pain of the fall as her body slammed into flesh and stone. Maybe it's why she found the strength to pull her arms back. To slam the butt of the weapon into the creature beneath her.

The creature shrieked, another high-pitched sound swallowed by the echoing darkness. Constance thrashed, her limbs flailing, driven by pure, unadulterated terror and a need to get out of this. The blaster, now a uselessly hot weight, slipped from her numb fingers and clattered against the unseen floor. She couldn't see, couldn't think, only feel—the sharp pain in her shoulder, the weight of the creature now pinning her down, the rough texture of the tunnel floor against her cheek.

"Constance!" He was still trying to get to her.

"Forget about me! Just kill them!"

Blindly, she bucked and writhed, her movements frantic and uncoordinated. She kicked out, her shoes connecting with something solid. Another shriek, closer this time, followed by a wet, gurgling sound. She didn't know if she'd hurt it, or if it was just the sound of its breath, hot and rank against her ear.

But she could feel them. All around her now. Their bodies moving against hers.

Pure instinct took over. She swung her fist, a wild, desperate punch that connected with something soft and yielding. A wet, squelching sound. The creature fell back, disoriented, or at least she thought it did.

It could have been her imagination when the darkness moved, but reflex took over. She was a cornered animal, fighting for its life. She slammed her forehead forward, her head connecting with what must be one of the creatures' snouts. Bone slammed against bone and hot pain shot through her skull. The creature screeched. Deafening. But the sound was punctuated by another sound, deeper, more guttural. "Human!"

His voice ignited something within her. A spark of defiance. She wasn't going to die down here. Not like this.

She pulled her arms back, her elbows scraping against the rough stone, and slammed them into the flesh she felt moving at her sides. A grunt. A shift in weight. She used the momentary reprieve to wrench her shoulder free, a searing jolt of pain shooting up her arm. But she was free.

She rolled, blindly searching for a weapon, any weapon. Her fingers brushed against something smooth and hard. The blaster! It was cool again. No time to fire, she gripped it like it was a lifeline and swung it like a club, the hard carbon cracking against something solid.

More screeches filled the tunnel, the sound amplified by the stone walls until it felt like it was coming from inside her skull. When her finger found the trigger and pressed down, she caught glimpses of Akur through the darkness and blaster fire. For a moment, time stood still.

He was magnificent. A reaper. An ender. His blades were a blur of motion, cutting through the creatures with precise, deadly efficiency. But for every one he cut down, two more seemed to take its place.

Something warm ran down her arm as she fired the blaster again, and she grunted, pushing through the pain. The creature must have cut deeper than she thought, but there was no time to check how bad it was.

A particularly loud shriek made her spin toward the intersection she'd just left. More were coming. The scratching sound of their claws on stone grew louder, and in the next flash of blaster fire, she saw them pouring forward like a nightmare made flesh.

"Akur! More. More are coming!!" She could only hope that he wasn't too wounded for them to make it out of this alive.

She felt rather than saw him shift his stance. He'd reached her side, adjusting himself to fight back-to-back with her. His flesh like burning coal against her spine.

"This position is not defensible," he growled, voice rough with exertion. "We need to move."

"Yeah?" she panted. "Got any bright ideas?" She fired at another creature, catching it in what passed for its chest. The thing barely slowed down.

"Keep moving. You lead. I follow."

"Never thought I'd hear such words from the mouth of a warrior like you," she panted.

"Survival requires...flexibility. And a certain...trust. I find I trust you, Constance, female of fire."

Trust. He trusted her.

Well, she trusted him, too. It was only him and her in this hell.

Another creature lunged from the darkness and Akur's blade took its head off in one clean sweep, but not before its claws caught him across the chest. He grunted, but it sounded almost like an unamused laugh.

"You okay?" She fired three more shots into the darkness, the flashes revealing a whole wave of creatures heading their way.

"Irrelevant." His voice was tight. "We need to move. Follow them."

"What? *Follow* them?"

It was then that she realized the movement of the creatures had changed. Instead of converging on them since they were standing targets, most of the creatures were heading past them like a wave.

They weren't trying to kill them anymore. They were...they were moving like they were running away from something. What could be worse than—

Just then, echoing down the tunnel, came a new sound. Not the screeching of the creatures, but something else. Something mechanical.

"That's not...that's not good news, is it."

"Negative," Akur said at her back. "You decide, female. Run, or stand and fight. I, for one, am committed to doing the latter."

Constance tilted her head to look back at him. Her crown barely reached the center of his back, and she wished there was some light so she could see him. His expression, at least. Because he *had* to be joking.

"Are you *insane*? Do you have a death wish?"

He didn't answer. All he did was grunt as she heard him slice through one creature that came towards them.

The mechanical sound grew louder—a rhythmic thumping that seemed to shake dust from the tunnel ceiling. In the next flash of blaster fire, Constance saw something reflect the light. Something metallic.

Sounds echoed down the tunnel. Words. Words in voices she wished she'd never hear again.

The gator-guards. They were coming.

"Well," she managed between breaths, "at least we know which way is out."

Around them, the creatures' chittering rose to a fever pitch as the sound of machinery grew closer. They were caught in the middle, running out of options and running out of space.

Constance looked down at the blaster. There was a power bar, and if she was reading it right, there was less than half of the power remaining.

They were in trouble. Deep trouble.

"Ready, rebel?"

"Just say the word."

He was ready to fight, that was clear. He was brave. A sort of bravery that made her lean against him. Made her respect him.

He was brave...and maybe she was a coward.

"Run today. Live to fight tomorrow."

Jaw set, she reached back and grabbed the alien's arm right before she took off in the sea of creatures. She'd be damned if she was going to die in this tunnel, torn apart by monsters or gunned down by their captors. They just needed a plan.

She just hoped they could come up with one before they ran out of tunnel.

9

Constance

RUNNING in total darkness meant relying on instinct and prayer. Constance's fingers remained locked around Akur's arm as they fled, their footsteps drowned out by the cacophony of mechanical sounds and creatures shrieking around them.

She was either going to piss herself out of fear or her heart was going to give out. "For someone who prefers to stand and fight, you run remarkably well," she panted.

"For a non-violent human, you fight remarkably well," he countered behind her, his voice almost lost to the sounds around them.

"Hey, I'm not non-violent." She almost stumbled as one of the creature's thick bodies slammed into her from the left. She was supported immediately as Akur came up beside her. A moment later, she heard a squelch as his blade found its mark. "Just...selectively violent."

She was sure he laughed. A deep, rich sound that shouldn't reach her ears so easily with the surrounding chaos.

The tunnel seemed endless. Endless darkness. Still so thick she couldn't see. Only when Akur adjusted his stride, his body slightly ahead of hers as he led them now, did she realize he could definitely see much better than she could. Adjusting his grasp, he turned his hand so he was gripping hers instead.

A glance over her shoulder and she couldn't see the pursuing vehicle. But she could hear it. See a light far off piercing the darkness. They were coming.

"Any chance these things are running toward something pleasant? Like a nice underground spa?"

Akur's grunt might have been amusement or pain. "Your ability to joke while fleeing death is...concerning."

"My therapist would have a field day with this. Oh wait, that's me."

The mechanical sounds grew louder, accompanied by shouted orders that echoed off the walls. They came down the tunnel as if the fiends were right behind them. Had the gator-guards spotted them already?

As if reading her mind, Akur answered. "They know we're down here. They haven't spotted us yet. These creatures are giving us cover."

Constance swallowed hard. Nice, and what would happen when the creatures fled into whatever hole they came out of in the first place? They'd be left running in the open like ducks. "What are these things, anyway?"

"Tunnel dwellers. Ancient. Hungry." He grunted, tugging her along. "Less talking. More running."

She wanted to argue that talking helped her cope with terror, but she saved her breath. The tunnel curved sharply left, then right. The floor became treacherous—slick in some places, uneven in others. She stumbled once, but Akur's steady grip kept her upright.

"Careful," he growled. "I would love to, but I cannot carry you. Not yet."

Right. He was barely alive. Not that she wanted him to carry her. She was barely making it, but she could do so on her own two feet.

"Wouldn't dream of asking." But she squeezed his hand in silent thanks.

The sounds behind them changed—metal striking stone, followed by inhuman shrieks cut short by weapon fire.

"They're killing them." She looked back the way they'd come, hardly able to see a thing except for the light from the vehicle illuminating behind a bend.

"Good. Let them fight each other."

But even as he spoke, more creatures poured past them, forcing them closer to the wall. The tunnel was getting narrower; the ceiling lower. She was even sure Akur was ducking his head from how he moved.

"This is bad," she whispered.

Akur grunted, a sound she assumed was the affirmative. "The creatures know these tunnels. They're leading us somewhere."

"Yeah, to dinner. Us being the main course." She wanted to fire again, but she was sure if she did, it would be like sending a flare, telling the gator-guards exactly where they were. "We need another option."

"I am open to suggestions." Was that actual humor in his voice?

As they rounded another bend, the airflow changed immediately, and her heart sank.

"We have a choice to make. The tunnel divides. There are three paths ahead."

And, from the feel of it, the creatures were pouring into the rightmost tunnel like water going down a drain.

"Left," she decided instantly.

"Why?"

"Because they're going right, and I don't trust the middle path. It's too obvious."

Another sound that might have been a laugh rumbled through his chest. "Your logic is…"

"Brilliant? Strategic?"

"Human."

She was going to take that as a compliment. "Yeah, well, following monster swarms isn't usually the best survival strategy."

"Better than capture." A grunt as he presumably cut down

another creature that slammed into him hard enough that he was thrust back against her. "Unless you prefer fighting those brutes head-on?"

The mechanical thumping grew louder, the gator-guards' shouted commands bouncing off the walls even clearer. They were gaining on them.

"Neither option sounds great."

She thought he'd follow his instinct. Head after the flood of creatures going right. But he did the opposite. He went left.

"Hurry, they're getting closer." She tried to pick up the pace, but her legs felt like lead.

"Your powers of observation continue to impress." Despite his words, there was no mockery in his tone—only strain and something else she couldn't quite identify.

The left tunnel proved to be a mistake. After only a dozen meters, it narrowed dramatically. Akur had to run partially sideways to fit through, his massive frame scraping both walls.

"This may have been a tactical error," he rumbled.

"You think?" The words came out sharper than intended. "Sorry, near-death experiences make me snippy."

The tunnel narrowed further.

"We appear to be out of options," Akur said, but his voice was oddly calm.

"That's twice now you've been ready to die in these tunnels. I'm starting to think you're not very pragmatic."

"I would take them all down." His body shifted, and maybe he was looking back at her. "But I have you. I will not risk your life for just a few kills."

His words made her lids flicker. "You're not fighting because of *me*?"

Akur's grip tightened on her wrist. "You are more important than you realize, little human. I am fighting...*for* you."

His words held a lot more than she could process. What's worse, it felt like they were running from the inevitable. No matter what, how did they get out of this?

"You shouldn't have come." Her breaths felt hot as they pressed through the narrowing tunnel. "You're only here because you followed me."

"So I did." Those three words carried a weight she wasn't ready to examine.

Behind them, the sounds of battle grew fainter, but the mechanical thumping of the guards' equipment could still be heard. New fear unlocked.

"They really want us back," she panted.

"You sound surprised."

"Well, yeah. I mean, I'm just a human. There's nothing special about me. And you're..."

"A rebel? A warrior? A thorn in their side?"

"I was going to say a pain in the ass, but those work, too."

Another of those rumbling almost-laughs, cut short by a grunt of pain. She'd almost forgotten that just hours before, he was near death. They needed to find a spot to hide. To rest. To recoup.

She wasn't sure that would happen. The tunnel was getting even narrower; the walls pressing in on both sides. Her chest felt tight—whether from exertion or claustrophobia, she couldn't tell.

"We need to turn back," Akur said suddenly. "This path is a dead end."

"How can you tell?"

"The air. It is stagnant ahead."

He stopped moving, but hope made her squeeze past him in the tight space. Even when she took a few steps forward, one hand outstretched to guide her, he didn't let go of the other. For about twelve feet, she paced before her outstretched hand met solid stone. He was right—the tunnel ended in a blank wall.

"No," she whispered. Her hand traveled over the rock face, searching for an opening that wasn't there. "No. There must be something."

Behind them, the mechanical sounds grew louder. Light flickered at the edge of her vision—they were close enough now that she could see the shadows of their pursuers stretching along the tunnel walls.

"Stay behind me."

Her gaze flicked to the alien, and her breath caught. With the gator-guards' light, the darkness was not as absolute as before. She could see her companion now. See the blood. The gashes in his flesh. See the way he was standing tall despite all that. Guarding her. Something deep inside her constricted at the sight.

"No. In this narrow space? We'd be target practice." She spun around, staring at the dark wall before them as if hope would open a door. "This is my fault. I chose this tunnel."

"Yes." He released her now, the heat of his grasp disappearing as he grabbed both his swords. Turning from her, he faced the tunnel, almost completely blocking her from view. "You did."

"Thanks for the comfort."

"I don't offer comfort. I offer truth." He shifted slightly, a stance that told her he was ready for business. "But I followed you, anyway."

The simple statement hit her hard. He was right. He'd followed her. Trusted her. And she'd led them into a trap.

This was the end.

When the wall behind her shifted, she didn't first notice. But then, when it happened again, it was distinct enough for her to feel. A definite movement in the stone she was pressing against. Before she could process what was happening, the wall moved, and something grabbed her arm—a hand that felt wrong. Rough. Bumpy. Moist. She glimpsed white fabric, a flutter of robes, and then she was being pulled backward through an opening that hadn't been there seconds before.

"Akur!" Eyes wide, his name left her lips on instinct as she stretched for him. And he was there. He moved quicker than he should be able to, grabbing her outstretched arm as she was yanked through the hole, taking him with her. The force of it sent them both tumbling, their bodies twisting in the darkness as they fell. Her stomach lurched at the sensation of emptiness beneath them, the ground disappearing as they plummeted. They hit hard—first her, then him on top of her with a grunt that knocked the air from both their lungs.

10

Constance

SHE EXPECTED it to hurt more, but the pain didn't come. Because somehow, this big lump of an alien had wrapped his arms around her, protecting her spine and head.

Why the hell did this keep happening? Where were they now? Before she could process what had happened, there was a grinding sound of stone on stone above them and then silence. The alien molerats' screeches became muffled, distant. The sound of the machines, too.

The transition was jarring—one moment, they were in a dead-end tunnel with guards bearing down on them, the next, they were... somewhere else. Somewhere darker, if that was possible. The air was different here, too—cooler, damper, with an organic smell she couldn't quite place.

Constance groaned. "What just happened?" She was still pressed against Akur's chest, hardly able to see a thing.

"We were rescued." His voice didn't hide his suspicion. "Or captured. Again."

"By whom? I felt...thought I saw..." She trailed off, unsure of what she'd seen or felt.

"Keep moving," a voice whispered from the darkness ahead—rough, sexless, impossible to place. "Quickly now."

Akur stood, taking her with him with an ease that shouldn't be possible. The moment they were upright, his entire body went rigid. The growl that tore from his throat was unlike anything she'd heard from him before—deep, animalistic, filled with such pure hatred, it made shivers go down her spine.

His hand found her waist, pushing her firmly behind him even as his other arm raised what had to be his sword. The tension in his muscles spoke of barely restrained violence—as if it was taking every bit of energy within him not to tear whatever was before them apart.

"*You*." His single utterance sounded corrosive. Enough to make her suddenly grateful for the barrier his body provided between her and whatever could make him sound like that. His hand on her waist tightened to an almost painful degree, as if he feared someone might try to tear her away.

"There is no time for old grievances," the voice said from the shadows. "We cannot tarry here. The guards will find this chamber soon."

She couldn't tell what species it was. The translator behind her ear made it so she understood what was said, but the voice itself...she couldn't pinpoint it. This stranger before them wasn't anyone she knew.

That was obviously not the case for Akur. His growl deepened. Every hair along her arms stood on end. "*You dare speak to me about time?*" The words came out mangled, as if each one had to fight past his hatred to emerge. "After what you—"

"The human will not survive what comes next, Shum'ai," the voice cut in, still maddeningly neutral. "Neither will you. Not in your condition."

Constance felt Akur's muscles bunch. The scrape of his blade against stone told her he'd shifted into an attack stance. But something was off about his movement.

"Akur?" she whispered, pressing her forehead against his spine. His skin burned so hot it felt like pressing her head against an oven.

A wet cough escaped him, and something warm spattered her hand where it rested against his side. Blood. Fresh blood.

"Your wounds are great," the voice observed almost clinically. "Even a Shum'ai has his limits."

Akur stiffened, but his blade didn't waver. "Better death than cower before the likes of you."

Shifting slightly so she could look around the tall alien guarding her from the threat, Constance's jaw clenched. She couldn't see shit. Blast these damn human eyes. But whoever it was had taken them out of immediate danger. That had to mean something. Right?

"Follow me," the voice said.

"By the gods, I would rather die."

And she knew he meant it with every fiber of his being. After all, he'd been trying to die this entire time, it seemed.

Pressing her forehead to his back, she felt every labored breath. "We should follow them," she whispered. "Whoever they are, if they wanted us dead, they wouldn't have pulled us through that wall."

The sounds behind the wall grew louder. Dust or small pieces of stone rained down. They were running out of time.

"Your human speaks sense," the voice said. Was there a note of approval there? "They really are intelligent beings, aren't they." That was said with the sort of tone that gave her the distinct impression she was being observed. "The choice is simple: Trust me for the next few hors, or die here now."

"*Trust* you?" Akur's laugh was awful—raw and filled with something that sounded like madness. "After what your kind has done?"

"I promise you, Shum'ai. If I wished your demise, I would not have to hide in the bowels of the city waiting for the opportune moment to crush you beneath my heel." The voice remained maddeningly calm. "I ask your trust because this time, our interests align. Or do you think it a coincidence that I am here, in these tunnels, at this precise moment?"

Something in those words made Akur go very still. The trembling in his muscles stopped. When he spoke again, his voice had changed —become harder, more controlled. "You knew we would come this way."

"I knew there was a possibility." A whisper of movement in the darkness. "I knew what they would do if they caught you. Both of you. Hiding you in the tunnels was only temporary. I cannot use that method again."

Wait...what?

"So it was you..." Akur finally said. His words felt so sharp, so heavy they could cut iron.

There was silence again. "I have already said too much."

The sounds behind the wall grew louder.

"Your lifeblood seeps, Shum'ai, and you are starting your heat," the voice continued. "If you truly want to save this human...follow me."

Heat?

As if to emphasize the stranger's point, the heat coming from Akur felt even hotter than before, as if his fever, or whatever it was, had gone up by several degrees.

This...stranger. Who were they? If she'd learned anything through her counseling sessions, it was that you shouldn't go trusting voices that spoke to you from the darkness.

But they didn't exactly have any cards to play here. Just the sound of those guards approaching on the other side of the wall was making her fear ratchet up to alarming levels.

"I know I don't have the best judgment—" she whispered into Akur's back.

"Your judgment has been demonstrably poor."

She would have choked on a laugh if her heart wasn't beating so hard. More muffled voices came from the other side of the wall.

"We don't have much of a choice," she hissed.

"We always have a choice," Akur growled, shifting his weight to block more of her from the dark shadows that held the stranger. The muscles in his back tightened as if he were about to launch himself forward at any moment.

More muffled sounds filtered through the wall, closer now. The stranger made a soft clicking sound. "Your trust or your lives, Shum'ai. Choose quickly."

Akur grunted, his back becoming so hard it was like solid rock. His breathing changed, too, becoming deeper, more controlled. The low rumble in his chest told her exactly how much he trusted this situation: not at all. A lump formed in her throat.

Instincts said they had no choice, and she'd already given her opinion. She couldn't see what he could. Part of her was too afraid to ask. Now it was Akur's turn to decide which path they took.

As the sounds on the other side of the wall grew louder, Akur's growl cut off abruptly. His muscles bunched, then released with a sharp exhale. Wordlessly, he moved forward with her still tucked behind him, following their mysterious rescuer down what felt like an even narrower tunnel.

The passage twisted and turned; the floor sloping gradually downward. Water dripped somewhere nearby, creating a constant background patter that made it hard to tell if there was anyone following in the darkness behind them.

"Almost there," the voice said from ahead.

"Where is 'there' exactly?" Her question received no answer, and Akur, Akur was rigid where he reached back and pressed her into his spine, completely alert and ready. She still had the blaster in one hand. She was ready, too.

They walked for what felt like extended minutes; the tunnel growing progressively damper. Sometimes, she was sure her alien friend almost stumbled and not from almost falling over something.

"How badly are you hurt?" she whispered low. It felt like a stupid question. If he were human, she wouldn't have asked. But he'd almost died several times now, and he was still standing straight. He was like some sort of Superman or something.

"Badly enough."

"That's not an answer."

"It's the only one you're getting." His pride was bleeding as much as his wounds. This thick-skulled mountain of an alien. But his hand briefly tightened where he was reaching back to maintain her presence behind him.

She wanted to argue, but this wasn't the place to discuss their weaknesses. Not with an unseen stranger—she'd decide later if they were friend or foe—leading them into the heart of the unknown.

When Akur paused, she did too, at his back. There was a sound of metal groaning, then a rush of stale air as something opened ahead of them. Despite every instinct screaming at her that this was a trap, she followed Akur's lead as he moved forward, still keeping her tucked behind him.

The space they entered felt vast yet close, the air different from the damp tunnel—cleaner. Akur remained just over the threshold.

"You would think me a fool to enter this place with you," he rumbled.

A strange sound filled the darkness—a pop, and then others, like bubbles popping in a witch's brew. Laughter. A type of laughter she'd never heard before. "If you wish to return to the tunnels, you are welcome to try your luck with the guards." Their guide's voice held an edge of...what was that? Amusement? "But I think we both know why you followed me this far."

Impossibly, Akur stiffened further. If he were a rod, he'd break with the tension. His grip on her tightened. "We are not your pawns." His voice was so dangerously soft, the words seemed even more threatening. "Choose your next words carefully. They may be your last."

There was the distinct sound of his blade flipping, so sharp it sounded like it cut the air.

Did the hidden figure gulp? It sounded like they did.

"Threaten me if you must," the voice said. "I cannot say it is undeserved." What now? Something shifted in the darkness. "Wait here. I will direct the guards away and return shortly."

The air moved as Akur stepped across the threshold. For just a moment, Constance felt something cold brush against her arm. It was soft. So soft. Like silk. A sensation so at odds with whatever she was expecting that she jumped. For a split second, she thought she saw a flash of white in the unending dark.

When the metal door slammed shut, she jumped again. Something knotted and clenched inside her stomach.

They were alone.

11

Constance

SHE STEPPED from behind Akur at the same moment that he swayed.
Without thinking, she wrapped an arm around his waist, trying to
support him. His skin burned against hers. "Who was that? Could
you see them?"

"You don't want to know, sweet thing."

Her eyes fluttered at the term of endearment. "Lean on me," she
whispered. "I won't tell anyone you needed help from a human."

He tensed before grunting a laugh. "I get the impression your
secret-keeping skills are questionable at best."

"Hey, I can keep secrets. I'm a therapist, remember?"

"You mentioned it. Once or twice."

"Well, it's kind of important to my identity." She shifted slightly,
adjusting to his weight. "Like being a warrior is to yours."

He was quiet for a long moment. "A warrior would not be here,"
he finally said. "Accepting aid from—" He broke off with a growl, his
muscles tensing beneath her hands. "This goes against everything I
trained to be."

Before she could respond to that surprisingly vulnerable statement, there was a click and dim lights flickered to life around them. The room was smaller than she'd initially thought, with rough stone walls and what looked like medical items, food, and other things arranged on a table at the center. There was no sign of their mysterious guide.

And the door they'd come through was sealed tight—no handle, no control panel, no visible way to open it from their side.

They were trapped. Again.

Constance looked up at Akur, really seeing him clearly for the first time since the battle began. His injuries were exactly as she'd feared. He looked as if he'd been through the wringer. How was he even speaking, let alone standing? But it was the look in his eyes that caught her attention—pain, yes, but also something else. Something that made her breath catch in her throat.

"Well," she said, trying to keep her voice light, "at least we're not dead yet."

"Yet," he agreed, but his eyes didn't leave her face. "You should have kept running."

"Yeah, well." She gave him a small smile. "I wasn't going to leave you; let you die in a swarm of monster mole rats."

"You should have listened."

"And you shouldn't have come." She frowned at him. "You came alone to take on an entire army by yourself?" She paused, studying him. She couldn't think of one good reason why he'd done it. "What were you thinking?"

He shrugged. "I'm stubborn."

"Well," she followed him to the ground as he lowered himself, "so am I."

"So I've noticed." His lips twitched. "Human."

"Warrior," she countered, and felt him chuckle despite his injuries.

There was a sound at the door that made them both stiffen. A narrow panel opened, and she found herself looking into impossibly dark eyes.

Dark eyes that haunted her nightmares. Eyes she'd seen in holo-images of the beings that had destroyed *everything*. It felt like her blood stopped running as she went rigid. It was a High Tasqal. The architect of all this death and destruction was right here.

Her heart gave a big, frightened wallop as she lifted the blaster in both her hands. Those dark eyes didn't even flinch.

"Akur!"

"At ease, human," the Tasqal said. Even her breath stilled. That voice... It was the same voice as the mysterious stranger who had been helping them. Her heart gave another thud. The being that assisted them had been a High Tasqal?!

"Akur?" A question now, her voice wavering as she kept the blaster aimed at the door. She wanted him to tell her she was wrong. That this was some trick of the light, some misunderstanding. But his silence told her everything.

The piece of shit that had started this was pretending to help them?! Playing some sick game while they stumbled through the dark? Her stomach rolled as puzzle pieces clicked into place: the mysterious rescues, the convenient escapes, the way they'd found just the right tunnel...

They hadn't been rescued. They'd been herded. Like cattle. Sheep.

The room suddenly felt too small, the walls pressing in. Her breath came in quick gasps as she looked frantically around the sealed chamber. No exits. No escape routes. They'd walked right into the heart of the enemy's lair, following their tormentor straight to the slaughterhouse.

Now she understood Akur's initial rage. His distrust. The way he'd nearly attacked at just the sound of that voice. He'd known. He'd recognized what they were dealing with. And he'd had to swallow his hatred just to keep them alive.

"The guards will not check here," the Tasqal continued.

She couldn't believe it. Glancing down at Akur, she noticed his brows were drawn tight, and that he was staring down at the ground between his feet. One fist clenched and unclenched over the hilt of his sword. This was killing him—having to sit here, wounded, while their enemy stood before them.

Her finger tightened on the trigger. The logical part of her brain knew the blaster wouldn't do much damage—there was just a small slit in the door, and her aim wasn't that good. But she wanted to wipe that calm certainty from the Tasqal's voice. Wanted to make it feel just a fraction of the pain it had caused.

Her hands shook with the effort of restraining herself. "You..." The word came out as barely more than a whisper. "You did this. All of it. The attacks, the base. *You took me from my planet.*" Her voice broke as faces flashed through her mind: the family she'd left on Earth; the humans she'd met in this nightmare. All the rebels. And the last images she saw of the Restitution's base.

Battered. Bloodied. Burnt.

Destroyed.

"*You did this.*" Her hands shook. "And now you're what? Playing games? Pretending to help while you lead us deeper into your trap?" Each word felt like it was being torn from her chest, years of carefully maintained professional distance crumbling in the face of this creature's calm regard.

The Tasqal didn't even blink. "I have a proposition."

Its voice was eerily gentle, almost kind, and that made it so much worse. These were the beings that had slaughtered entire civilizations, and now one was offering help like some benevolent savior. She felt sick.

"I cannot guarantee your safety, Shum'ai. We have no need for you. But the human...the human has a better chance." Those dark eyes shifted from Akur to her, and she felt rather than heard Akur growl again.

"Leave the human here and come with me."

A laugh barked from Akur's chest. "Try again."

"It is not a trick," the Tasqal said. "On Tasqal honor—"

"Your *honor*? What honor do your kin have?" To her surprise, the Tasqal looked away.

"Not much," it said after a few moments. "There is not much I can do. But I can save you, Shum'ai. Potentially."

So they were doing this. Bargaining with the enemy. There was no other choice. At any given moment, they had to make decisions based on the current circumstances—and the circumstances now involved making a deal with the literal devil.

"There is only space for one," the Tasqal continued.

"Space for one?" She kept her blaster trained on the fiend. She'd seen holo-images of the species, but seeing one up close, even if it was just its eyes, was terrifying. "Space for one *where*?"

"A shuttle. We are sending it for a supply run. The Shum'ai can sneak on board...if he comes with me."

"Forget it." Akur's deep voice rumbled at her back, and she stretched out her hand to stop him.

"And why can't I go with him?"

The Tasqal's dark eyes felt like they were leeching over her skin as it looked at her. Even the dim light didn't hide that fact.

"The vessel flies on pre-programmed directives. It will collect supplies at a station in the outer reaches," the Tasqal continued, its focus never leaving her face. "The autopilot docks at Station 459. To reach the internal airlock undetected..." It paused, and she could have sworn there was a slight change in its voice. Weariness. "You need to traverse the external hull. Exposure to the void. A Shum'ai's biology can withstand the void for the required time. Humans cannot."

Her breath paused. It was the first real chance of escape since their capture, dangling right in front of them. "Why should we trust you? You're the reason we're here."

The Tasqal didn't blink. Through the narrow slit in the door, he stared right through her. "I am not my people," was all he finally said.

Swallowing hard, she turned away from him. The hair along her back stood on end the moment she did. Some sixth sense made her very aware the fiend still had its eyes on her.

Closing her eyes, she tried to focus. Her mind raced through the implications. No doubt Akur's physiology differed from any other being she'd ever encountered. Back on the Restitution's base, she'd been sure he'd died when the ship took her away. And then again here, he'd dived after her ship in the upper atmosphere and made it out alive.

He could heal quicker than anything she'd ever encountered before.

Her gaze slid to him where he'd propped himself against the table.

The look in his eyes made her pause. Restrained rage. Restrained bloodlust. He looked like a man that could kill. Would kill. Right now.

But, if she was to believe this creature, there might be a way out for him.

It wasn't her decision. It was his. The Tasqals didn't want the rebels. They wanted people like her. They wanted humans.

She moved to kneel before him. Setting the blaster down, she took his large hand between both of hers. His skin was still fever-hot against her palms, and she could feel the tension thrumming through him.

"This is your chance," she whispered, trying to keep her voice steady. "If you believe him, you should take it."

His fingers tightened around hers almost painfully, bloodstained but strong. "No."

"Listen to me," she pressed on, leaning closer. "You're injured. You need treatment. If he's telling the truth, this might be our only opportunity to get you out of here."

"*Our?*" His voice dropped to a dangerous rumble. That moment in the tunnel, when he'd suddenly turned on her and she'd become aware of just how dangerous he was, it was here again. And yet, she didn't want to run away. "You mean *my* opportunity."

"Yes." She squeezed his hand, glancing away now. The murderous look in his eyes, even if it wasn't meant for her, was making her survival instincts rise. "*Your* opportunity. Take it. Get to safety. Recover your strength. Don't throw away this chance because of—" Her throat became tight. "Forget about—"

The movement was so fast she barely registered it. One moment she was kneeling before him, the next her back hit the cold floor with enough force to drive the air from her lungs. Akur's hand wrapped around her neck, not quite crushing but inexorable, pinning her beneath him. His face hovered inches from hers, golden eyes blazing with an intensity that made her breath catch.

"*Forget about you*?" he growled, low and dangerous. "Is that what you were going to say, human?"

She tried to swallow but couldn't quite manage it with his grip on her throat. "Be reasonable—"

"Reasonable?" His laugh was harsh. "Like you were reasonable in the tunnel when I told you to run? When you disobeyed my order and turned back to help *me*? Or reasonable when you crawled on hands and knees through darkness just to bring me water so I could heal?" His fingers flexed against her skin.

"This is different," she whispered, though her conviction wavered at the raw emotion in his eyes.

"*No*." He leaned closer until she could feel the heat radiating from his body, until his breath ghosted across her lips. "It is *exactly* the same. You're trying to sacrifice yourself."

"I am trying to *save you*! These creatures, they're doing all this just to get us humans. They destroyed an entire base, Akur! They killed everyone! I'm only trying to save you! You don't have to d—" Tears welled in her eyes. "You don't have to die, too."

Ever since she'd been pulled into that ship, she'd hidden away from it all. But this was the truth. All the death. So much death. All those beings she'd walked alongside on that base. Dead. Dead because this species was obsessed with hers.

Nobody else had to die.

"I'm just. Trying. To save you." A tear ran down, one she couldn't stop, and with that single tear, it felt like all the rest threatened to fall.

"And who will save *you*?" His voice dropped even lower, becoming something intimate and fierce. "Who will stand between you and them once I'm gone? Who will ensure you survive until I can return?" He dropped his sword, and his free hand came up to trace her jaw, the gesture at odds with the steel in his tone. "Or do you think I could live with myself, knowing I abandoned you here?"

What? What was he talking about? Was his sense of duty so strong that he would sacrifice himself for a stranger? It must be. She already knew he was insane. He dove through space to save her. If that's not insanity, then she didn't know what was.

"You don't even know me! You don't have to care. Just forget about me."

He pressed her harder into the floor the moment she uttered the words, his entire body pressing into hers, filling her with his heat. "*No.*"

"Fuck! You stupid stubborn—"

She was sure he grunted out a laugh.

"I will not let them win. I pledged it. You will leave here alive, even if I have to die to make it happen."

"Don't you *dare!*" She twisted beneath him, anger and fear and grief tangling into something wild in her chest. Her fist connected with his injured side, and she felt him flinch. "Don't you dare make promises like that!"

She struck again, knowing she was hurting him, hating herself for it even as she couldn't stop. The pressure of the past days—the deaths, the terror, the guilt—it all came pouring out in a flood she couldn't contain. Meredith was gone. Probably dead. That silent woman. All the other humans she'd met in this living nightmare.

"You don't get to die for me!" Another hit, weaker this time, the jolt causing pain to shoot through even her wounds. "I won't let you! I won't—"

His hand shot out, catching both her wrists and pinning them above her head. The movement pressed him fully against her, and she could feel the rapid rise and fall of his chest, the tremor in his muscles from pain or restraint, or both.

"Stop." His voice was rough, strained. "You'll tear my wounds."

"Good!" She bucked against his hold, trying to break free. "Maybe then you'll listen to reason and save yourself!"

"There is no reason to abandon you." His grip tightened as she struggled. "There is no honor in running while you face death alone."

"Fuck honor!" She nearly spat the word. "What does honor matter when you're dead? When everyone is dead?" Her voice cracked. "Just go. Please. Please, just go. It's me they want. This whole time, it's just been about us humans."

"*No.*" The word rumbled through his chest and into hers.

"*Why?*" She thrashed against him again, tears flowing freely now. "Why are you so damn *stubborn*? Why won't you—"

His mouth crashed down on hers, swallowing her words in a kiss that burned like wildfire. There was nothing gentle about it—all heat and desperation and something darker, something that tasted like possession. His hand remained locked around her wrists, but his other slid into her hair, holding her steady as he devoured her protests.

She gasped against his lips, and he took advantage, deepening the kiss until she could barely remember why she'd been fighting him. It was a strange meeting of their mouths, as if he wasn't quite sure what he was doing but wanted to devour her now that he'd caught a taste. His tongue swept against hers, and she felt the last of her resistance crumbling. She arched into him, no longer trying to push him away but to get closer, closer. This was fire. This was heat. This was life.

When he finally broke away, they were both breathing hard. His golden eyes had gone molten, boring into hers with an intensity that made her shiver.

"I will not go," he said, voice raw. "I will not leave. Not while you draw breath. Accept it, or we can continue this argument until the stars burn out." His thumb brushed across her lower lip, still tingling from his kiss. "But know that my answer will not change."

The Tasqal cleared its throat softly, reminding them of his presence. "The offer stands for only moments longer."

In a blur of movement, the blaster was in Akur's hands and a shot burned through the air. The panel in the door slid shut a split second before the energy beam scorched the metal where the Tasqal had been moments before.

Akur snarled, not taking his eyes off her face. "I made a vow on Tonvuhiri. I will not run away."

Tears pricked at her eyes. "Stubborn warrior."

"Foolish human." His grip gentled, becoming more caress than restraint.

The panel slid open just long enough for the Tasqal's dark eyes to meet hers, a silent farewell—or perhaps a threat. Then, with a quiet click, the door sealed shut, the opportunity vanishing with him.

Only then did Akur release her. He rose, took his warmth, and staggered away, stumbling almost as if blind to land on the other side of the room.

Her chest heaved as she watched him go, one hand rising to brush against her lips. The taste of him lingered—heat and desperation. He didn't owe her a thing, and yet he wasn't going to leave her. He was going to fight for her, even if it meant his death.

And the realization of his vulnerability, of the sacrifice he was willing to make, pierced through her anger and fear, leaving only a raw ache in its place.

12

Akur

THE WOUNDS. They were much. And he was healing.

He was healing too quickly.

There was only one reason he allowed himself to get hit and clawed in that tunnel. Only one reason every wound that made him bleed gave him some satisfaction rather than annoyance.

The pain was the only thing keeping his hold on reality.

Pressing the back of his head against the cold stone wall, he remained still. The cold stone felt good. Drew some of the heat away from him, but not nearly enough. His gaze fell on the human on the other side of the room and he pressed his eyes closed.

Shouldn't look at her or he'd probably find himself across the room once more, demanding more than a pressing together of mouths.

A breath and he tried to ground himself through the waves of heat coursing through his being. But every breath brought her scent to him. She smelled of fear, determination, and something else that made his lifeblood surge.

And this was why the wounds helped. Pain was clarity. Pain was control. But even that anchor was slipping.

He shouldn't have touched her. Shouldn't have pressed his mouth to hers in that foreign gesture. But when she'd started striking him, demanding he leave her behind, something inside him had snapped. The need to silence her protests, to make her understand, had overwhelmed his reason.

Now her taste lingered on his tongue, sweet and addictive. Wrong. So wrong. His people didn't exchange fluids this way. The intimacy of it should have revolted him. Instead, his body hummed with the memory, craving more.

No wonder his brother, Ajos, was so addicted to his human mate. Only a taste of this stubborn little thing in his presence, and it was already all he could think about.

Painfully, his shaft pulsed in its pouch. Qrak. It pulsed so hard it made him tense, his digits digging into the stone floor beneath him. It was one thing to be stranded on a world filled only with one's enemies. But to simultaneously be going through a heat that shouldn't be happening was a different kind of torture.

"Are you alright?" Her voice was soft, concerned. "Well, I know you aren't alright. Maybe there's...maybe there's something here that can help you."

He could almost laugh. The only thing that could help him now was something he was sure she wouldn't want to give. At least she didn't understand what was happening. Her ignorance saved him some shame. Even with the Tasqal mentioning it so carelessly, the human still didn't understand. That he was going into heat, and that when a Shum'ai male experienced such a thing, all focus turned to relieving the ache.

His nefre burned, the usually pale flesh now surely a blazing crimson that would betray his condition to any of his kind. But she was human. She didn't know. She saw his burning flesh and his shame had surged. But humans knew nothing of his species' biology, their cycles, their drives. The fact he, a warrior, the male that had come to save her, was being brought down by something as simple as his cock was laughable.

Of all the times he'd dreamt of taking the Tasqals down, he'd never imagined he'd have to do it like this. Hot and hungry and wanting nothing more than to forget they existed so he could focus on the female in his presence instead.

"There's medical stuff here." She was still moving around. He could hear her. Even then, he still refused to open his eyes. "Even though this doesn't look like a place these things would usually be in." She hummed in her throat. "I think that Tasqal put them here. I think he prepared for our arrival." He could hear faint shuffling as she sorted through what she found. "Some gauze...and I think this might be antiseptic..."

"I require nothing," he managed through clenched teeth. The effort of maintaining control made his head pound. Back in the tunnel, it had been easier. Death was right in front of them at every turn. This sudden lull wasn't helping. The warmth was everywhere, seeping into his bones, awakening things that should have remained dormant for years yet. Wrong timing. Wrong place. Wrong female.

He heard when she took a step toward him, the sound making him jerk back so violently he nearly lost his balance. "Stay back," he growled. The concerned look in her eyes only made it worse. His people fought during these times. They didn't offer comfort. They didn't show kindness.

"You're burning up," she said, and he could see her mind working, trying to make sense of his condition through her limited under-standing. "Some kind of fever?"

If only it were that simple. His muscles spasmed, and he had to fight to keep from doubling over. The heat was building, clouding his thoughts, making it harder to remember why he shouldn't just—no. He would not think like that. He was a warrior, trained since he was a youngling to control his urges, to channel his strength.

But none of that training had prepared him for this.

None of his training had prepared him for *her*. A female who would fight as hard as he did...and for *him*. No female had ever shown him such kindness. Ever.

"Leave," he commanded, but his voice shook. "Go back to your side."

She didn't leave. *Of course, she didn't leave.* The stubborn female never did what was best for her own safety.

"You saved my life back there," she whispered. "At least let me try to help you now."

A laugh tore from his throat. It was harsh. Bitter. The exact sort of sound that should make her run away. She didn't.

"Help me?" She didn't know what she was offering. The very thought of her trying to "help" sent another wave of heat through his frame, making his vision blur at the edges. His pouch ached, and he knew if he didn't get her away from him soon—

"Fine."

What?

She moved away, and something in his chest cracked. Growling at himself, he turned away from her as she headed back toward the table. Closing his eyes once more, he shut her out.

"Fine." The word came out rougher than intended. He needed distance. Space. But in this sealed chamber, there was nowhere to go.

"You're a terrible liar." More shuffling. She was touching other things there. Things that scum left here for them. He hardly had the energy to consider *why*. Didn't want to focus on his greatest shame yet—the fact he was relying on that fiend.

May his ancestors forgive him.

"I do not lie," he growled, eyes still closed.

"Ah, but you do." She released a laugh that sounded tired. "I've had enough people sitting across from me, lying to my face, some of them not even knowing it."

He growled, loud enough for her to hear. "Do not therapy me. I am not one of your weak human clients."

The sounds stopped. She probably paused in her perusal of the items to look his way. He refused to open his eyes.

"There's nothing weak about seeking therapy."

He released a breath, adjusting himself so he was leaning back against the stone again, but he still kept his eyes closed. "I know. I follow a very effective form of therapy."

She scoffed, and he popped an eye open. He shouldn't have. There was a smile on her face and even with the dirt smeared across her face and the bits of dust and rock in her hair, the human looked...beautiful.

He slammed his eyes shut again.

"Let me guess. Brooding in the dark while plotting the demise of every Tasqal in existence? Because that's super healthy."

"It is. I feel flooded with life when their lifeblood is dripping from my blades."

She scoffed again, but said nothing else. He popped an eye open once more to find her bringing something that looked like a meal bar close to her nose. She sniffed it and put it down.

"Akur..."

His pouch spasmed at the sound of his name on her lips and he groaned. When she looked over at him, he didn't bother to hide the severe frown on his brow as he glared at her. The maddening female didn't even pause.

"What happened back at the base? Why did you come alone?"

He closed his eyes, focusing on steady breaths. "There was no time for a coordinated response. Not many...not many of us were left alive."

There was a moment of pause and he thought that was the end of it. That she wouldn't unknowingly torture him with her voice anymore. He wasn't so lucky.

"Any..." She cleared her throat. "Any humans survived?"

He looked at her now, and the mirth that had graced her features was gone. She wasn't facing him. Wasn't even looking his way. She stood there, half clothed in those ripped garments she'd torn just to save him. Her filaments a tangle of chaos on her head. Lifeblood on her arm...

Lifeblood? She was hurt. And he was the pilkra that didn't even realize. Too caught up in his failings.

"You're bleeding."

Her gaze snapped to him. "So are you. I don't see you complaining."

"This isn't a competition, female."

"Yeah, well, tell that to yourself."

He pressed his lips together.

"Were there any other humans."

He could hear it in her voice. See it in the way she stood. Ah. This was something he knew well. Something he'd had to come to terms with a long time ago. Something that almost killed his brother. Almost took away the one kin he had left in this universe.

Guilt.

The guilt of still breathing when others had to fall.

It was the reason he fought. The only reason he hadn't given up yet. He survived for a reason. The least he could do was make sure the Tasqals paid the price of the torture that was his existence.

"Yes," he answered. The female's throat moved.

"And the rebels?"

"Not many."

"But surely—"

"They fought. *We* fought." The memory of the chaos flooded back. "Many tried. The Tasqal ships appeared from nowhere, using some kind of warp technology we'd never encountered. By the time the alarm sounded..." He clenched his fists against the stone. "Well, you remember. You were awake by then. I found you after V'Alen called me."

"V'Alen. He's the...the robot. The cyborg."

A wry smile stretched his lips. If anything, this conversation was helping distract him a little. He'd humor her some more. "He is much more than that. He is our most powerful weapon. He alone could end this war."

Her gaze snapped to his. "If that's the case, why didn't he fight?"

He released a breath. "If it was so simple, the Tasqals would all be dead. V'Alen is on a different mission now."

"Finding the other humans?"

"No. He went after something else. Something possibly more important."

Her throat moved, and she watched him for a few moments. Enough that he could feel the heated lifeblood moving in his veins. So he kept on talking.

"When the Hedgeruds came, they weren't interested in fighting. Only extraction. They targeted the human quarters first."

"Do you know what happened to Meredith?" she whispered. "The other woman who was with me on that ship?"

"I don't know." And that uncertainty gnawed at him. "Everything happened too fast. When I realized they had taken you..." He trailed off, unwilling to admit how the thought of her in their hands had driven him to recklessness.

"So you just...what? Jumped in a ship and followed? And then jumped again into the void of space when you saw my shuttle heading to this planet?"

"Essentially." He shifted, trying to find a position that didn't make him solely aware of the pressure behind his pouch. "Though 'jumped' is perhaps too elegant a term for what actually occurred."

She made a sound between a laugh and a sob. "You're insane. You know that, right? Completely insane."

"So I've been told." His lips twitched despite everything. "Mainly by you."

"Because it's true!" He heard her pacing now, energy crackling in her movements. "And what about the Tasqal who brought us here? Why would one of them help us?"

That question had been burning in his mind as well. "There are Tasqals and High Tasqals. They are hierarchical, absolutely loyal to their collective. For one to act independently..." He shook his head, an ache going through his skull that had nothing to do with any wound. "It's highly suspicious."

"Unless things aren't as unified as they appear?" She sounded hopeful. "Maybe there are factions we don't know about. Internal conflicts."

"Possible." He settled back, closing his eyes. "Hiding in dark holes isn't exactly their style." He looked around the room. There were several things that pointed to the fact this hole of a room was hardly, if ever, used. There was dust and dirt. The air itself was stale. "They pretend to be pristine despite being diseased. Grand gestures for all to see. This…"

"Isn't like them at all," she finished for him.

"Affirmative, little human." He winced and saw movement in the corner of his eye as she started toward him. He didn't mean to bare his teeth in a growl. He did anyway. She stopped and folded her arms, glaring back at him.

"He left supplies." She was still glaring at him. "He knew we were hurt. Somehow he'd been tracking us."

He snarled some more. Because she was right.

"He's smart." She swallowed hard now and turned away, running her hand along one arm as she nursed the other. "He could be leading others here, too."

She was right about that as well. But unlike her, he knew more about this scourge than she did. "I have been fighting this war for a long time, human."

"Kon-stahns."

"What?"

"Kon-stahns. Stop calling me 'human'."

He stared at her, and before he could stop himself, he scoffed. "You call me 'mint man'. Whatever that means."

"I didn't know your name. But I know it now and you know mine. If we're going to die together, we should at least call each other by name. It's the least respect we can give each other."

His eyes narrowed slightly. He hated that she was right. As a matter of fact, he was starting to hate everything surrounding her. It was making him ache. And he didn't ache. Stupid qrakking heat.

"Kon-stahns." He hated how good her name sounded. "The Tasqal don't…" He had to pause, gathering his thoughts through the haze. "They don't consider comfort. Specimens are kept in stasis or secured for immediate…study. This…" he gestured at their surroundings, "this shows consideration for basic needs." His gaze met hers. "He means to keep us here."

She stopped rubbing her arm. "Why? The gator-guards were following us. He could have simply let them take us."

Another spasm rocked through him, and he dug his digits deeper into the stone. "Could still be a trap. More elaborate than their usual methods, but—"

"But what would be the point?" She turned to face him, and he could see the analyst in her taking over, piecing together the puzzle. When he didn't answer, she pressed on. "He's hiding us. Not just from the other Tasqals, but from the gator-guards, too. And he's provided everything we'd need to..." her voice faltered slightly, "to survive for a while. Including medical supplies that seem specifically chosen for your condition."

"What do you mean?" His gaze shifted to the items on the table, watching as she picked up some things.

"I'm wounded, but not horribly," she glanced over at him, "thanks to you. I'm sure half of this isn't for me. There's gauze and some tubes of stuff." She lifted a few and one caught his eye. Made him freeze.

Metcer cells.

The realization hit him through the haze of heat. The Tasqal had left metcer cells? Where did that fiend even get them from? Those cells were the only thing that could tame his heat. Bring him back to his former self without the worry of his cock extruding and demanding sating. Why? Why would a Tasqal do that?

Why not leave him weak and tormented? It would be easier to take the human away then.

"I mean, what are these things?" She picked up some more vials, her brow furrowing in confusion.

"You cannot therapy this, female—" She glared at him. "Konstahns." Qrak. "The Tasqals cannot be read. They are unpredictable. The only thing one can predict with those *scum*..." He stared back at her now. "Is their obsession with your kind."

Silence descended between them.

"They want you. More than they've wanted anything else. I can only guess why."

Her throat moved again. "Why? Why do you think…"

He studied her for a few moments. She really didn't know? He supposed she wouldn't. Her world was far away from this part of the galaxy. No one in the Restitution understood how the Tasqals even found her planet. And she'd been locked in stasis for much of the war. She didn't know how the Tasqals fought to retrieve the first five humans…or how many more they killed.

"Because," he finally said, not quite sure if he should speak the words so clearly. If he should let her know. Not sure how she would take it. "Your species holds the key to their survival."

13

Constance

THE STUBBORN ALIEN was still refusing help. He remained in the corner, glaring at her. And it might be the light, but she swore that red tinge from that fin at the back of his neck was spreading across his skin.

He was in heat. She'd heard the Tasqal say it and even though she didn't trust the fiend, every second that passed she believed what he'd said was true. And Akur seemed intent on not telling her about it. He didn't want her to help.

And...

And he'd kissed her.

She watched him now through the corner of her eye as she made use of the medical supplies the Tasqal had left. Cleaning and bandaging the wound on her shoulder, she'd taken the time to clean and put ointment on the other scratches and scrapes along her sides as well.

There was running water from a small spout in the corner and she made use of it, too. Washing her face. Her hands. Cleaning the blood, grime and what else from her skin. When she finished, she watched as Akur silently did the same. The heaviness of his silence weighing between them.

Fine. If he didn't want to talk about it, then that was fine.

Her movements were slow. Maybe it was the biting cold in this room or just the tiredness. She was so very tired. Weary. She needed rest. But she wasn't going to close her eyes. Adjusting herself on the stool by the table, she checked for any other wounds she might have missed, ever aware of the Shum'ai across the room. His last few words echoed in her head, despite that he remained silent.

Your species holds the key to their survival.

Those words; they meant more than he knew. Felt like they were important in some other way than just a grim proclamation or her role in this intergalactic war.

When she picked up one of the little vials of medicine the Tasqal had left and brought it close to her face, she heard the alien shift. She could see him sit up straighter in her peripheral vision.

An idea occurred, one she acted on immediately, pretending that the little vial slipped from her hand and she caught it before it hit the table. The way he jerked confirmed her suspicions. The vials, whatever was in them, he wanted them.

"You're sure you're alright?" She said, choosing to stare at the vial as she held it up to the light and turned it over.

"Fine." His voice was so rough now, as if he was experiencing intense pain or torment.

She smiled. "That's probably for the best, then. We should throw these away. Who knows what that Tasqal put in them." She tapped her fingers on the table before gathering the vials. There were three.

"No!" He'd eased off the wall now, golden eyes wide. "Give them to me."

She finally looked at him. "You want them? I thought you were fine."

He bared his teeth at her, and her lips twisted into a smile. "I need them."

She set the vials down one by one on the table, watching the contents swirl in the light. "Okay." She shrugged. "Come get them then."

Her gaze pierced his, watching as he hesitated. He looked like he was in so much pain he couldn't move, but she doubted it was as simple as that. Doubted that was the reason he'd planted himself across the room and hadn't moved since he'd pressed her into the floor and kissed her in a way she wished she could forget. In a way no man had ever kissed her before.

"Throw them to me."

She blinked at him, feigning incompetence. "Me? No way. I have horrible aim. If you really want them, just come and get them rather than risk me throwing them into the wall."

His eyes narrowed slightly, and he huffed out a breath.

Yes, she was right. That red tinge was even under the skin at his shoulders.

"I can bring them to you." She began easing off the stool.

"No!"

Ah, so there it was. It wasn't that he couldn't get them. His problem wasn't his wounds. His problem was *her*.

He didn't want to be close to her.

Why.

She eased back on the stool, studying him. His injuries were healing. She could see that like some slow motion playback. Every time she looked at him, he looked better.

And yet he winced with each little movement he made.

His eyes locked onto the vials again, and she could see the internal struggle playing across his features. The way his digits flexed against the stone, how his chest rose and fell with carefully measured breaths.

"You're afraid," she breathed. "Not of me, but of yourself." When he didn't respond, only stared into her soul, she pressed on. "Whatever is happening to you, these help control it, don't they?"

A low growl rumbled from his chest. "You are trying to therapy me, human. Stop. You understand nothing."

"Then help me understand." She rolled one vial between her

fingers, watching his gaze track the movement. "Because right now, you're acting like I'm some kind of threat, when we both know that makes no sense. You've saved my life multiple times now. Saved my life in those tunnels. We fought off those creatures together. But suddenly you can't even come within ten feet of me?"

"The Tasqal," he ground out, "is playing games. Trying to—" He cut himself off with another growl, pressing back harder against the wall.

She set the vial down carefully. "Maybe he is. But right now, you're suffering. And these?" She gestured to the vials. "These could help you. Couldn't they."

His growl cut her off, deeper this time, more primal. "You do not understand what those vials truly mean. What accepting them would mean."

She studied him, noting how his claws scraped against the stone wall, how his breathing had grown more labored. How he refused to look at her directly.

"Then explain it to me," she whispered. "Because from where I'm sitting, you're in pain. And I have something that could help. Isn't that simple?"

"Nothing about this is simple." His voice was strained. "I cannot accept—"

She leaned forward on the stool. "You cannot accept it because you're suspicious it might be poison...or because you'd be accepting something from the enemy."

His golden eyes flashed. "Stop trying to understand. Stop trying to help. You cannot help."

"Why not?" She stood slowly, and he pressed himself harder against the wall. "Because you don't trust me? After everything we've been through?" It almost hurt, his rejection. No. It *did* hurt, and she didn't understand why. "Because I'm *human*?"

She felt his heat even before she saw him move. Even before she was whisked off her feet and her back was pressed into the wall on the other side of the room. Akur moved like something unreal. Just a blur of heat and muscle, and suddenly he was pressing her into the wall. Her breath stopped in her lungs. She was suspended off her feet, just his fist around her neck and another hot, so very hot, hand supporting her up underneath her rump.

Every breath brought in the scent of him, like spices filling her airway.

"Akur." She swallowed hard. It wasn't a plea. Even in this position of his complete dominance over her, she wasn't afraid. She was... shit...fear was definitely not present here.

"Akur," she repeated his name, searching his golden pits as they bored into hers.

His heat was all-encompassing. Chasing away the frigidity of the room like a blast furnace, leaving her flushed and breathless.

"You cannot help," he snarled, lips mere centimeters away from hers. "This isn't something you can fix."

"I know you're in heat."

The air seemed to still.

"I know it's why you're acting like this." She searched his gaze. "Is it dangerous?"

He laughed, harsh and hollow, his breath brushing against her lips. "Yes. But not to me."

Dangerous to her. She wasn't a fool. The unsaid was obvious.

"It doesn't matter," he breathed, and for a moment, as his body pressed against hers, he closed his eyes.

"It *does* matter." Her words made his eyes snap back open. "If something's wrong with you—"

"Nothing is wrong with me." The words came out as a snarl. "I am what I am. What I've always been. A weapon. A warrior. Nothing more."

"Liar." She didn't know him. Hadn't been around him long enough to. They were strangers, thrown together by circumstance. But logic had long since abandoned ship. Something in his touch, in the intensity of his gaze, resonated deep within her, sparking a recognition that defied reason. It was as if some part of her, some hidden, instinctual part, already knew him, knew the heart of the warrior beneath the alien exterior.

He pushed her harder against the stone, his teeth bared as he tilted her head back to reveal her neck. He dipped his lips there, a breath easing from his mouth as it whispered across her skin.

"You cannot help me...because you are something I must protect. Not something I should harm." He inhaled deeply before he lifted his head, molten gaze meeting hers. "Because...Constance...you are different."

She searched his gaze, every breath still pulling him in. "What makes you think you will harm me?"

He stiffened. Didn't answer for the longest while. The only movement was the sensation of his hand kneading the flesh at her ass. She didn't even think he was aware he was doing it. And she could focus on nothing else.

"You have no idea what I am capable of."

As suddenly as he'd come upon her, the hand at her neck disappeared. Akur set her down.

Reaching back, he grabbed the vials, popped the lid off one, and downed the contents in one swoop.

As his chest heaved, those intense eyes meeting hers again, the door mechanism clicked.

They were no longer alone.

14

Constance

THE DOOR swung open with a metallic groan that sent ice through Constance's veins. She stepped back instinctively as the Tasqal emerged, its massive frame filling the entire doorway like a nightmarish sentinel. The flowing white robes it wore seemed to absorb the dim light, creating an otherworldly silhouette that made her heart slam against her ribs.

Those black holes it had for eyes found her immediately, and time seemed to slow down. She'd seen images of the Tasqals before, heard whispered descriptions from other humans who'd survived encounters, but nothing had prepared her for the reality. The creature before her was both more and less than she'd imagined—more terrifying in its alien intelligence, less like the mindless monster of her fears.

Before she could draw another breath, Akur moved. The transformation was breathtaking—one moment he was beside her, radiating that impossible heat, the next he had the Tasqal pinned against the door with fluid grace that belied his injuries. The door slammed shut with a resounding bang as Akur's blade pressed into the creature's throat, drawing a thin line of dark fluid.

"At ease, Shum'ai." The Tasqal's voice was surprisingly calm, but those eyes never left hers. Something about that unwavering gaze made her skin crawl. "Have you not yet concluded that I am not here to harm you?"

She couldn't look away from those eyes. It was like staring into wells of liquid darkness. They were unnervingly intelligent, reminding her of dissections she'd done in biology class, the way a cow's eyes had stared up at her from the steel table. But where those had held a sort of peaceful emptiness, these eyes contained calculations upon calculations, wheels turning within wheels.

The Tasqal was humanoid in basic form, standing upright on two powerful legs barely visible beneath its robes. But its face—God, its face was pure nightmare fuel. Underneath the hood of the robe it wore was a wide and flat face like a toad's, with a lipless mouth that seemed frozen in a perpetual sneer. Its skin was a mottled dark green with patches of brown, covered in what looked like pulsating boils. Each one glistened with yellowish fluid that made her stomach churn. The sight was both repulsive and strangely hypnotic, like watching a slow-motion explosion of something foul.

"Give me one reason," Akur growled, his voice thick with centuries of hatred, "why I should not end your miserable existence right here."

The Tasqal didn't struggle against the blade at its throat. Didn't show an ounce of fear. Instead, it regarded Akur with an unsettling calm that made her awareness increase. Something was wrong here. Every instinct she'd honed through years of reading people was screaming that this wasn't how a captive should act.

"Because what I have to tell you, Shum'ai," the Tasqal said, each word precise and measured, "will change everything you think you know about your purpose here."

"Pretty words from a desperate creature." Akur pressed his blade deeper, drawing more of that dark blood. "Your kind has stolen mors from their younglings, turned living worlds to ash. Every breath you draw is an insult to the dead."

The Tasqal remained perfectly still. She was sure its mouth twitched. Sure there was a ghost of a smile there. "That, Shum'ai, is precisely why I am here."

She took a step forward before she could stop herself, drawn by something in the creature's tone. "What do you mean?"

"Stay back," Akur snarled, not taking his eyes off the Tasqal. His voice dropped low, dangerous. "They're dying. Their own biology turning against them. And in their desperation, they've only grown more cruel. Stealing females from world after world, forcing themselves—" His blade drew more of that thick dark blood as he forced it deeper. "You've brought nothing but death to the galaxy."

For several heartbeats, the Tasqal said nothing. The only sound in the room was Akur's labored breathing and the subtle drip of dark fluid down its throat. Then, "You are right, Akur the Undefeated."

Akur went rigid, his lips pulling back in a snarl that revealed teeth meant for tearing. The use of this title seemed to enrage him further, and Constance could feel the heat rolling off him like an invisible torrent, almost like an indication of his anger.

The Tasqal's gaze shifted to her then, his focus seeming to strip away her defenses layer by layer. "I do not deserve his mercy, but I plead with your human sensibilities. Listen to what I have to say."

"Don't let him into your mind, Constance." Akur's voice was rough with barely contained violence. "They are manipulators. Masters of twisting truth until you question your own reality."

She'd spent years learning to read people, to see past their masks and defenses to the truth beneath. But this creature...this being that had orchestrated the destruction of countless worlds...everything about it felt wrong. Because she was trying to apply human psychology to something that had evolved along completely different lines.

Taking a careful step forward, she placed her hand on Akur's arm. His muscles were coiled tight like steel cables beneath her touch, thrumming, ready to react. This close, the Tasqal's presence was overwhelming. She didn't step back.

"Maybe we should hear what he has to say." The words felt like betrayal in her mouth, but they needed information. Needed to understand why they were here, what this creature wanted from them.

Akur's growl vibrated through her palm where it rested against his skin.

"You can kill him after," she added softly.

For a moment that stretched like eternity, she thought Akur would ignore her completely. Then he released the Tasqal—letting it drop like a bag of trash—before stalking behind her. His footsteps were heavy, each one like a drumbeat, the only other sound in the room apart from her pulse roaring in her ears.

The Tasqal rose, adjusting its flowing garments with meticulous care. The gesture was so oddly human that it made her skin crawl again.

"Why are you here?" She crossed her arms and refused to rub the tiny hairs along them that stood on end. She was good at this. She'd catch every detail—the way the Tasqal smoothed its robes, the subtle twitch in its left eyelid, the almost imperceptible way it kept track of Akur pacing behind her. This creature, for all its alienness, still gave off tells. "Why did you bring us here, and what do you plan to do with us?"

"What do I plan to do with you?" For the first time, the Tasqal's voice changed. It wasn't subtle either. It became something darker, something more honest. "I planned...to kill you."

The temperature in the room seemed to plummet. Even Akur's burning heat couldn't ward off the chill that settled in her bones. His pacing stopped abruptly, and she could hear his fingers clenching and unclenching on the hilt of his blade.

"Not you, Shum'ai." The Tasqal's eyes flicked to Akur briefly. "The Hedgeruds would have taken care of you aboveground."

Constance's throat went dry. Her heart seemed to stutter in her chest as the implications sank in. "But me. You planned to kill *me*."

"Yesss," the Tasqal hissed, but there was something almost like regret in that alien voice. Or maybe she was imagining it.

Her arms tightened across her chest, heart still hammering against her ribs. "You'd take me from my planet, put me in stasis, risk everything to capture us again...just to kill me?" Her eyes narrowed as she studied the creature before her, looking for any crack in its composure. "Even for you monsters, that seems excessive."

The Tasqal blinked—a horrifyingly slow motion where its entire eyes disappeared beneath folds of skin before emerging again.

"He means he planned to kill you in the way they kill all the females they take." Akur's voice was lethal silk behind her. "By disease. Inescapable once they seed you with their young." The raw hatred in his tone made her shudder, images of other women's fates flashing through her mind.

The Tasqal made that unsettling sound again, like bubbles popping in its throat. "Even you, Shum'ai, are wrong."

"Wrong?" Constance forced the word past the knot of fear in her throat. "Wrong how? Isn't that what you do?" Her voice rose, months of suppressed terror and rage bubbling to the surface. "Isn't that why you brought me and the other women here? To br—" The word stuck like poison in her mouth. She swallowed hard and tried again. "To breed us?" The thought alone made her stomach heave.

The Tasqal seemed to stand taller, looking down at her with an intensity that made her want to step back, to run, to hide. But she held her ground. When it spoke again, its voice dropped to barely above a whisper, as if it was sharing some dark secret.

"What if I told you there was something far worse for you than being bred?" Those membrane-covered eyes seemed to glow in the dim light. "Something that could tear apart the very fabric of existence?"

Akur raised his blade again. "Stop speaking in riddles, scum."

"Not riddles," the Tasqal replied. "Truth. We have...come upon interesting technology. Technology that can bend the fabric of the void. Take us to worlds unknown. Transport beings across space..." It paused, those black eyes seeming to expand. "...and time."

Akur's breath hissed between his teeth as he resumed his pacing. The sound of his footsteps was even harder now, echoing off the stone walls.

Something wasn't right. Her instincts were giving her mixed signals. The Tasqal was like a serpent—deadly, yes, but not striking. Not yet. He was dissecting her piece by piece, but the malice she expected...wasn't there.

"We found something," the Tasqal continued, taking another step closer. It was barely a foot closer, but Akur's blade shot past her shoulder, the tip reaching the center of the Tasqal's throat with deadly precision. The creature stopped moving but continued speaking as if the blade wasn't there at all. "Deep in the void of the empty. A Vikteki vessel, preserved in the cold darkness for eons."

"The Vikteki?" Akur's grip on his sword tightened until she could hear the leather wrapping creak. "They vanished long ago. Their technology was destroyed."

The Tasqal's lips curved in that unsettling almost-smile again. "I see you have not heard from your ally yet. The Kyron you call V'Alen."

Akur went rigid beside her, the heat rolling off him intensifying until she could barely breathe. The Tasqal was referring to the cyborg and Alaina. What did they have to do with this?

"Yes," the Tasqal continued, smile widening unnaturally. "He and the human he claimed still live. And they have something of ours. They have the orb."

She glanced up at Akur. His jaw was locked like a steel trap.

She forced her expression to remain neutral, every instinct screaming that this was a game of strategy where showing too much could be fatal. Each word felt like a chess piece being moved across a board she couldn't fully see.

She was happy her voice remained steady. "What about this orb?"

"Yesss, the orb," the Tasqal's voice took on an almost reverent quality. "Technology not even as powerful as that orb led us to *your* world." It paused, those black eyes boring into her soul. "To humans. My people want it back."

"Do you really think we will just hand it over to you?" She met that alien gaze, though her heart threatened to burst from her chest. "Do you really think we'll barter our lives for it?"

The sound of bubbles popping in the Tasqal's throat as it laughed made her go still. Even with Akur's blade still at its throat, it showed no fear. The creature's confidence terrified her more than any threat could have.

"Why did you choose us?" The question burst from her before she could stop it. "Why humans?"

"Because you are the key." The Tasqal's voice grew softer now, almost intimate. As if it was stating something she should have already known. And she did, because not long before, Akur had said those same words. "Your species...you carry something in your makeup. Something we have searched for. And we found it after so very long."

The way it said those words sent ice through her veins. There was weight there, meaning she couldn't quite grasp.

Akur snarled, his patience waning. "More lies. You seek only to use them as you have used others. As breeding stock for your dying race."

"Perhaps..." the Tasqal's shoulders moved like it shrugged. "But we only found them because of that Vikteki vessel. It had records... information left behind of the Vikteki seeding worlds. Of our ancestors being placed on a minor planet dubbed HREX4X1." Its lips curved as its gaze landed on her once more. "You call it Earth."

Constance's breath caught. "What do you mean?"

"I mean," the Tasqal took another step forward, deliberately pressing into the blade at its throat, "that when we found your species, we weren't seeking your wombs. We were seeking a cure."

She stepped forward, too, anger rising hot and wild in her chest. Her lips pulled back in a snarl that matched Akur's. "Then why didn't you take your cure and *leave*?"

The Tasqal released a breath that smelled antiseptic despite its decaying skin. "*There was no cure.* Our ancestors have not evolved. They *devolved*. They became...stunted. Weak. Mere insects compared to you humans." Its voice filled with disgust and disdain, the first genuine emotion she'd seen from it. "We believed, at first, that your planet held the genetic key to reversing this...devolution. To restoring us to our former glory."

It paused, those dark eyes gleaming with something that made her want to run again. "Then we discovered something far more... intriguing. Your females...they could carry our young. Not all survived, of course. The process...is taxing. But some did. And one... one female spawned a paired birth. Two young from a single bearer. Unheard of in our kind. Such fecundity...such potential..."

The Tasqal leaned in so close she could see every pulsing boil underneath the hood it wore, every minute detail of its alien features —right before its head snapped sideways with a sickening crack.

Akur growled, his fist still extended from the punch that had sent the Tasqal sprawling across the table. He advanced like a stalking animal, but Constance grabbed his arm, feeling the fever-heat of his skin beneath her fingers.

"Wait!"

"I am ready to end him." The words rumbled from deep in his chest.

"Me too!" Her vehemence made him pause, golden eyes flicking to her face. "But we need to listen to what he's saying."

From the floor where he'd landed, the Tasqal released a wet sound. "It doesn't matter."

There was something in those words—a finality, a weight—that made even Akur hesitate.

"Speak, Tasqal. You have mere moments." Akur's growl held barely contained rage.

"The Restitution has the orb." The Tasqal rose slowly, methodically adjusting its robes as if the blow had been nothing more than an inconvenience. "And it must be destroyed."

Constance stepped closer, ignoring Akur's warning look. "What is this orb? You want us to destroy it? *Why*?" It sounded like another trap. What if the orb was exactly what the Restitution needed to win this war?

"The orb is a device that can traverse worlds. Galaxies." The Tasqal's eyes seemed to expand. "My people plan to take your world. Harvest you...humans. With that device, we can do...anything."

She couldn't breathe. The implications hit her one after another —this was how those gator-guards had appeared past the Restitution's defenses, how they'd caused so much death and destruction without warning. If they could travel to Earth at will...

Her chest constricted as faces flashed through her mind—her family, her friends, her sisters, her nieces, her mother. All the women she knew and loved would be taken to be nothing more than living incubators for these monsters. The pain that lanced through her chest was so real she had to grip the spot over her heart.

She'd rather die right here, right now, if it meant stopping that future.

"That orb will save my people," the Tasqal said. "For a time."

Right, until there were no more humans to harvest. Until they needed to find another civilization to destroy.

"There is no *saving* you." Akur's deep voice resonated through her bones as he positioned himself at her back like a guard.

For the first time, the Tasqal lowered its head. "You are right. We don't deserve salvation."

The admission hung in the air, stilling it.

"What?" Akur's voice had gone dangerous again, quiet. "Playing games again."

He must be right.

"Not games, Shum'ai. Not in this."

For a few moments, the room was silent.

"Explain," she finally said. "And speak clearly." With a jerk of her chin, she motioned to Akur. "My friend here isn't very patient, as you can tell, and even if killing you will cause his death, he doesn't care." Akur grunted in affirmation. "And I don't care about dying either."

She didn't care about dying? Fuck. When had she become someone willing to sacrifice everything? Not a martyr—martyrs died for beliefs, for causes. This was different. This was rage and pain forced into purpose. If she could take even one of these monsters down with her, maybe that would mean one less family torn apart, one less world torn apart.

Besides, what did she have left to lose? The Tasqals had already taken everything else—her home, her family, her entire way of life. All that remained was the chance to make them pay, even if it cost her last breath to do it.

That realization shot home something in her, and suddenly she understood him. Akur. Understood his rage and his stubbornness. Understood why he'd willingly sacrifice it all.

She met the Tasqal's gaze as it lifted its head. "If you think we're afraid, you're sadly mistaken."

Silence again, the air still, and then the Tasqal suddenly threw its head back and laughed, bubbles popping in the air. "It appears your arrival with the Shum'ai was not bad luck after all, human. It appears I might still get what I want out of this."

She grit her teeth. "And what do you want?"

"Some sins cannot be undone. Some crimes cannot be forgiven." The Tasqal's smile faltered. "We have destroyed much. Taken much. Like the Vikteki and the Kyron before us...we have too much power."

Without warning, the Tasqal began to shift out of its flowing robe.

"Qrak, no." Akur's blade was already in motion. When she grabbed his arm again, the heat beneath his skin nearly burned her. He hissed, jerking away from her touch. In all this, she'd almost forgotten about his condition—the heat that seemed to be consuming him from within. He needed more of that medicine, and soon.

"Wait," she whispered, her eyes widening as the Tasqal's garments fell.

The sight stole her breath away. The Tasqal stood naked before them, its toad-like body even more grotesque without the concealing robes. There were so many boils, barely any of its green skin remained untouched. It was taller than her but still appeared squat. Slightly webbed fingers and feet. Humanoid. Alien. But as it turned its back, seemingly indifferent to their horror, she saw something that changed everything. A ridge, a fin, ran down its spine. One that looked horrifyingly familiar.

Did toads have fins? She didn't think so.

"Gods, no." The curse tore from Akur's throat as he stepped forward, his own fin blazing crimson at his nape. The resemblance was undeniable—though the Tasqal's was smaller, less pronounced, almost vestigial, and the same sickly green as its troubled skin.

"Gods..." The word escaped Akur like a prayer, or perhaps another curse.

"The female that took my progenitor's seed," the Tasqal said, its voice carrying an emotion she couldn't quite name, "was Shum'ai."

"Impossible." Akur stumbled back, and for the first time since she'd met him, she saw genuine fear in his eyes. "Your species wipes out all traces of the mor's biological contribution. That is part of your curse."

"Yes," the Tasqal said, reaching for its robe with trembling fingers. "But I am different." It slipped the garment back on in silence, while she and Akur stood frozen, as if witnessing something that shouldn't exist. "There are others like me. Others that bear the evidence of my species' biological deterioration. My bloodline...it is tainted. Diluted. The fin..." Its webbed hand brushed the ridge briefly, "...is a physical manifestation of this...mingling. But the true change...it is within. We, the tainted ones, we wish for how it was before the...the sickness. A time when our people were not driven by conquest and...and breeding."

The Tasqal finished adjusting its robe, and Constance saw something she hadn't noticed before—the way it winced at each movement, how its face tightened with concealed pain.

Despite herself, despite everything these creatures had done, she stepped forward. "It hurts, doesn't it?"

The Tasqal went absolutely still. Behind her, she felt Akur's heat flare as he moved closer, ready to intervene if needed.

"The boils. They hurt."

Those dark eyes studied her. A long moment passed before it

spoke. "If I do not pass on my seed, this existence will have been long and painful for nothing."

She met its gaze steadily, understanding dawning. "And if you do what your species has been doing for centuries to stay alive, you'll only be dooming your young to the same pain."

Something shifted in those alien eyes, a recognition that made them seem almost...human. "Yesss," it hissed, moving closer with unnatural speed until it was mere inches from her face. She could smell its decay, feel the cold seeping from its diseased skin.

"Don't—" She held up a hand to stop Akur's advance, pressing back against his burning chest to keep him in place. Every instinct screamed at her to retreat, but she stood her ground.

"You are more intelligent than my kin realizes..." The Tasqal leaned in closer, inhaling deeply. Every hair on her body stood on end, but she forced herself to remain still. As Akur growled, a sound promising violence, the Tasqal shifted back slightly, blinking those enormous eyes.

"You're telling us all this because of guilt? Pain?" She was surprised her voice remained steady despite her racing heart.

Its huge liquid eyes narrowed slightly. "Perhaps."

She saw its lips twist as Akur wrapped an arm around her waist, pulling her back against his chest. The heat of him was almost unbearable now, but she welcomed it—anything to chase away the chill of the Tasqal's presence.

"Or perhaps it is the Shum'ai in me. And so...I will help you do what must be done. To end this."

Constance stared at the Tasqal, the weight of its words settling like lead in her stomach. "Your entire species...you're asking us to condemn them to death."

"Destroying the orb will not condemn us." The Tasqal's voice grew gentle, almost paternal. "But it will slow us down. Until another faction rises like the Restitution did to fight against us again." Those bottomless eyes studied her, still intense. "Maybe we will die as we should have long ago. Before we destroyed countless civilizations. Before we became monsters."

The silence that followed was deafening. Behind her, Akur cursed violently, releasing her to stalk across the room. His fist connected with the stone wall with enough force to send tremors through the foundation, but she doubted he even felt the impact through his rage.

"You want us to help you? To end your existence? My qrakking pleasure." Akur's voice dripped venom. "We will. But that means we need a way off this cursed rock. You're giving us a ship, scum?"

"The Citadel of Dawn." Urgency crept into the Tasqal's voice. "You must reach it before they find the other human. They only need one."

"What?" The word stuck in her throat. The *other* human. That could only mean they had the silent woman in their grasp. The one who had been taken with her but hadn't spoken a single word since leaving those cryo pods. Constance's stomach churned at the thought. *What had they done to her?*

The Tasqal's focus shifted, and she felt the moment its attention left her, like emerging from deep water.

"What do you mean they need only one?" She stepped forward, fear clawing at her chest.

"One human." Akur's growl resonated through the chamber as he swung his blades, re-sheathing them criss-cross on his back with practiced precision. "I knew I needed to find you for a reason. This was it." His golden eyes blazed with understanding. "Why those foolish Hedgeruds destroyed an entire base and only left with three humans seemed like a failed mission to me. But they left anyway. Hurriedly."

Nausea rose in her throat as she glanced between them. "Will one of you tell me what he meant by that? Only one human? Why?"

"The orb," Akur said.

The Tasqal's posture changed subtly. That slight smile on its lips again. The sight made her blood run cold. Either it was enjoying them piecing the puzzle together or it was delighted they were falling into its trap.

"Speak, Tasqal, or forget about this deal you're trying to forge here." She had no real leverage, nothing to bargain with, but she poured every ounce of authority she possessed into her voice.

"The orb requires...direction," it said, each word precise and measured. "A pilot. A navigator. A being whose lifeblood remembers the way home."

"A human," she whispered, understanding crashing over her like ice water. That weight in her throat grew until she could barely breathe. "But you said you already have one of us."

The Tasqal didn't blink, but its lips pulled back in that slimy almost-smile. "She is broken. Our pilot cannot harness...it will not work."

Her eyes narrowed as pieces clicked into place. "I thought you said you needed a *human* to pilot this thing."

The smile slowly died on the Tasqal's face.

"We have a being who can operate the device," it finally admitted. "But he is...blind. He needs a map. A human consciousness to show him the path." Those terrible eyes fixed on her with burning intensity. "One unbroken human whose mind can be harnessed."

The Tasqal's mouth snapped shut, and something flickered in those intelligent eyes. Some secret. A truth still hidden.

"Go to the Citadel of Dawn. Take the ship there," it said abruptly. "Leave this place."

"Not without the other humans." She hardened her voice, refusing to let fear make her weak. Not now, when the stakes were so impossibly high.

"I'm afraid that is not possible." The Tasqal's words dropped like stones. "One has already been taken to the citadel. The other is lost on the outskirts in the barren lands."

The Tasqal placed something on the table—some kind of device—before adjusting its robes with those methodical movements that seemed too human. Without another word, it turned toward the door.

"Wait—" The word burst from her before she could stop it. "What is your name?"

The Tasqal paused, those liquid eyes finding hers one more time. "I cannot tell you. There are certain things you must not know."

Akur snatched up the device, his gaze shifting between it and the

Tasqal. "If we head to this place, this citadel," he said, voice tight, "what will you do? How do I know this isn't some elaborate ruse?"

The Tasqal's lips curved in that unsettling way. "You do not." Its black eyes met Akur's with crushing honesty. "Kill me if you must, warrior. But know that without my help, you will never leave this world alive. They will retrieve your human, and humankin, like so many others, will fall." They stared each other down, years of hatred crackling between them. "The luck of the Gods be with you Shum'ai. May destiny prevail."

As the Tasqal slipped through the door, she watched it close. The weight of what they had learned pressed down hard. Earth. Humans. Everything was at stake.

She looked at Akur, saw the way his muscles trembled with suppressed rage, the red fin at his nape still blazing. The revelation of his genetic connection to some of these monsters must be tearing him apart. Yet here he was, still fighting, still refusing to give up.

Her gaze dropped to the device, her eyes widening slightly as

Akur activated it and a map appeared in midair, showing a path that would lead them either to salvation or destruction.

"We have to try," she whispered, more to herself than to him. "Even if it's a trap, even if we're walking straight into death—we have to try."

Because the alternative—letting the Tasqals reach Earth, letting them harvest humanity like cattle—was unthinkable.

Akur's golden eyes met hers, and in them she saw the same determination that burned in her chest. The map between them seemed to pulse with possibility and danger. One path. One chance. The fate of her species hanging in the balance.

And somewhere out there, an orb that held the power to either save or doom them all.

15

Akur

The heat was becoming unbearable.

Akur stared at the map the Tasqal had left, but the holo image blurred before his eyes. His skin felt too tight, every breath drawing in air that seemed to scorch his lungs. The metcer cells had helped, but their effect was already fading. Quickly. Far too quickly.

And now this. This new truth that made him want to tear his own skin off.

His gaze shifted to where Constance moved around the room, gathering supplies left by the Tasqal, her movements precise and measured as she sorted through what might be useful. She hadn't looked at him since their "friend" left. Maybe she couldn't. Maybe now that she knew that he—proud as he was, was linked by blood to one of those things—she saw him differently.

Shum'ai and Tasqal. The very thought made bile rise in his throat.

"These could be useful." Her voice cut through his dark thoughts. She held up what looked like compact ration packs. "If we're heading into the barren lands—"

"We're not." The words came out harsher than intended, and he saw her stiffen slightly.

"We have to." She turned to face him fully, and there was steel in her spine. "You heard what he said. One of the others is out there. *Meredith* is out there."

"And the other human is in the citadel," he growled. "The place we actually know how to reach." He gestured at the map with one hand while the other curled into a fist, claws digging into his palm. The pain helped. A little.

"So we just abandon Meredith?" Constance's eyes flashed. "Leave her to die in the wasteland?"

"She won't. E'lot is out there. He will find her." He pushed off from the wall he'd been leaning against, trying to ignore how the room spun slightly.

"Funny you didn't mention this E'lot before. I thought you came alone."

He exhaled, forcing himself to focus on one breath at a time. "It was just the two of us... He and I. I went after you. He...he went after one of the other shuttles."

"And you think he'll find her?"

"He will."

She huffed out a breath. It was clear she wasn't as confident in E'lot as he was. "He will fight for that female, as hard as I have fought for you," he said. He didn't even know why he was trying to soothe her fears. There were greater things at stake here. "The citadel is our priority. That orb—"

"The orb doesn't matter if they get what they want, anyway!" She took a step toward him, either not noticing or not caring how his muscles locked up at her approach. "They only need *one* human, remember? If they can't use the silent woman, they'll use whoever they find first. Including Meredith." She was glaring at him, all fire and spice. Shouldn't that turn him off? It didn't. Qrakking heat. The temptation to lean in and take her lips again almost made him lick his own. "I thought we both knew we weren't taking everything that Tasqal said as truth. He could be leading us into a trap."

Of course, not. But the trouble was— "How do we decide which part is the lie? The citadel...or the barren lands?"

The obvious effect of his words was clear. Constance blinked, her brows furrowing slightly. There it was, that glitch in her spark. The moment she realized just how cunning their foe was.

"You mean he could have baited us with the wastelands, knowing we'd head there in defiance?"

He could praise her, but that would make him look at the other good parts of this female. Her tenacity. Her bravery. *Her.*

Ignoring her was best, especially when he was in this state.

"We are rebels. That is what we do. We rebel."

She turned from him then, pacing as she bit her thumb. The act looked painful, but she didn't wince. "We still have to try. I think he was telling the truth. There was no need for him to save us. No need for him to come here to warn us. It's a lot of trouble to be part of some elaborate ruse. Some game. As you said, that's not really the Tasqals' style."

The sound of his laugh was low in his throat. "You underestimate these brutes, bright eyes."

She swallowed hard, pacing even harder. "They only need *one* human, Akur."

But qrak, she was right. He'd been so focused on getting to the citadel, on leaving this place and finding V'Alen to warn him about that orb, that he wasn't thinking about that crucial detail. They didn't need all the humans. Just one.

Just her.

The thought sent another wave of heat through him, this one having nothing to do with his condition. The idea of them using her, taking her flesh or breaking into her mind to find the path back to her world...

A growl built in his chest, and he had to turn away, had to put distance between him and her before he did something stupid. His nefre burned in protest, sending pulses of awareness down his spine and straight to that organ nestled in his pouch, pulses that were so intense it made his vision blur at the edges.

"Akur?" Her voice was softer now, concerned. "Are you alright?"

"Fine." The word was more snarl than speech. "We need to move soon. The Hedgeruds won't suspend their search of these tunnels forever."

"You're not fine." He heard her step closer and had to fight the urge to spin around, to grab her, to— No. Focus. "That medicine's wearing off, isn't it? There's more—"

"Leave it." He forced himself to breathe slowly, to maintain control. Those metcer cells were useless, and he knew why. He was too far gone already. Never thought he'd fight a war in heat, but he was never one to shy away from a challenge. "We need to plan. The citadel first. Then we can discuss the wastelands."

"The citadel first?" Her voice held a dangerous edge. "And what exactly is your plan once we get there? Walk in through the front door?"

He turned back to her slowly, fighting to keep his expression neutral despite the fire in his blood. "If we have to."

"That's not a plan, Akur. That's suicide." She crossed her arms, and he caught the slight tremor in her hands before she hid them. "We barely survived the tunnels. How are we supposed to fight our way through an entire citadel full of guards?"

"We don't." He forced himself to focus on the map again, on the intricate pathways marked in a script that made his eyes hurt. Anything to keep from staring at the pale length of her throat, exposed when she tilted her head in challenge. "We find another way in."

"There is no other way in. That's why it's called a citadel."

His lips twitched despite everything. "You humans have such limited imagination."

"Oh?" She stepped closer, and he had to lock his muscles to keep from moving. "Please enlighten me about your citadel-infiltrating experience."

The heat was making it hard to think, but he forced his mind to work. To strategize. To remember all his years fighting. "The Tasqals build everything to impress. To dominate. But they're dying." His voice roughened on the last word, memories of their "friend's" revelations burning fresh in his mind. "They can't maintain their grand structures like they used to. So, they let the Hedgeruds do it and those qeffers are mindless drones, numerous but stupid. Expendable." He spat the last word. "There will be weak points. Abandoned sections. Service tunnels they've forgotten about."

"And you know this how?"

"Because—" He cut himself off, bile rising in his throat. Her hand touched his arm and he jerked away, stumbling slightly as another wave of heat crashed through him. "Because of my citadel-infiltrating experience."

"Akur—"

"Don't." The word was torn from his throat. "Don't touch me. Not now."

She withdrew her hand but didn't step back. "How bad is it? And don't tell me you're fine, because we both know that's a lie."

He wanted to laugh, but the sound would have been too close to a sob. How could he explain? How could he tell her that his body was betraying him in the worst possible way? That every breath she took, every movement she made, called to something primal in him that he couldn't control?

"It doesn't matter," he ground out. "We need to—"

"No." She cut him off, voice hard. "Whatever's happening to you is getting worse. That medicine helped for what, an hour? Less? You can barely stand straight, and we haven't even started moving yet. So tell me how to help, or I swear by whatever gods you believe in, I will walk out that door and find my own way to the barren lands."

The threat of her leaving made him freeze. Would she really? His head swam, instincts roaring to protect, to possess, to— No! She was not his. She was not anyone's. He'd jumped into the void of space to save her and make sure of that fact.

"You wouldn't make it ten steps," he snarled, but it was hard to mask this illogical panic with his usual weapon. Anger.

"Try me."

He'd laugh if her voice didn't sound so hard. So serious. Looking at her over his shoulder, they stared at each other in the dim light, neither willing to back down. She was so small compared to him, so seemingly fragile, yet she faced him with a courage that made her seem fierce. Or maybe that was just the heat spreading through him like a curse.

"You want to know what's wrong?" His voice dropped lower. "You want to understand why I can barely think straight? Why every time you come near me, I have to fight not to—" He cut himself off again, digits curling into fists so tight he felt his claws pierce his flesh again.

"Yes." She didn't flinch, didn't retreat. "I want to understand."

"I'm in heat." It was such a disgrace. "But you know that already. My body is...preparing. For mating." To think he'd thought his brother, Ajos, had been careless to let the same thing happen to him. Now he was in the exact situation.

Constance's eyes widened slightly, but she held her ground. "Like...like animals on Earth?"

A harsh laugh escaped him. "Animal..." He laughed again. "Yes, that is exactly what I am. A beast. This shouldn't be happening. Not now. Not here." He began pacing, trying to burn off some of the energy coursing through him. "Shum'ai only experience heat during specific cycles. Every few orbits. It can be triggered by extreme temperature changes, but—"

"The fall," she breathed. "When you followed my shuttle. It was the entry into the atmosphere...wasn't it."

He didn't answer. Shame held his mouth shut.

"I don't remember much. At least, it's not all clear. Whatever that bastard injected me with really did a number on me. But I...your suit couldn't handle it, could it? It was glowing red-hot during the descent."

"Yes...well..." He wanted to hit something. To tear something apart. To channel this burning need into violence instead of...instead of... "The shock rod didn't help either. Neither did whatever that Tasqal did to transport us here. Too much heat, too fast."

"But the medicine helped," she said, taking a step toward him. "There's more—"

"No!" He backed away, hitting the wall hard enough to send tremors through the stone. "The medicine is temporary. A bandage on a wound that needs cauterizing."

"Then what do you *need*?" Her voice had gone soft, gentle in a way that made his blood surge. "There has to be something—"

"What I need," he snarled, "is to rut. To claim. To mark and mate and—" He slammed his fist into the wall, focusing on the pain that shot up his arm. "But I can't. I won't. Not with you. Not like this."

The silence that followed his outburst was deafening. He could hear her heart racing, smell the spike of...something in her scent that made his nefre pulse with want.

"Why not with me?"

The question hit him like soft wind, yet it left him reeling. He looked up slowly, seeing the flush on her cheeks, the way her chest rose and fell with quick breaths. "What?"

"You heard me." She lifted her chin. "Why not with me? If it would help—"

"No!" The word came out as a roar that made her jump. "You don't understand what you're offering. What it would mean."

"Then explain it to me." She took another step closer, and this time he couldn't retreat. The wall was solid at his back, and she was there, so close he could feel her body heat mixing with his own. "Because from where I'm standing, you're suffering. We need to get out of here, need to stop them from reaching Earth, and you can barely function. So if there's something I can do to help...is the thought of you touching a human so bad?"

This must be in jest.

Touching her? Ha. Ha ha ha. He wanted to *devour* her. To taste her skin, to scent the delicate curve of her neck, to lose himself in the depths of those eyes. He wanted to map the constellations of her body with his lips, to learn the rhythm of her life organ against his own. He wanted...everything.

He'd already caught her scent. Qrak, he'd already tasted her. And now, every breath, every movement, every flash of defiance in those blue eyes had carved itself deeper into his mind until he could think of nothing else. Her presence was like a brand against his senses.

"You don't know what you're offering, human." His voice had gone rough. Speaking was almost painful. "Shum'ai mating...it's not like your human coupling. It's not gentle. Not kind."

She moved closer still, close enough that he could see the flecks of gold in her bright eyes, smell the subtle changes in her scent that made his head spin. "I'm not asking for gentle."

A growl built in his chest, rumbling through the small space between them. "You should be. You should be running from this. From me." Had she no sense of self-preservation? Wait. What was he thinking? Of course, she didn't. She turned back to save him when he'd told her to run. Crawled through the dangerous dark tunnel blind, just to save him. This female was reckless. Just like him.

And that's probably why he was starting to like her so much.

His digits scraped against the stone wall, drawing lifeblood. "I am a rebel. A being that has killed more than he's saved. I'm worthy of no female. Especially not you."

That was clear, wasn't it? She was a pretty soft thing. Untainted by the curse that was his existence. Surely she'd abandon her hopes of saving him now.

The blasted female didn't.

"Stop." She pressed a hand to his chest, and he sucked in a harsh breath at the contact. "You're worth more than that. You came to save me. You alone." Her throat moved as she swallowed hard. "*You*, Akur. No one, not here or on Earth, has ever tried so hard for me before. I owe you my life."

He grunted a mirthless laugh, closing his eyes tight as he tried to fight the urges pulsing through him. She was close. She was too close. "I'm a monster. And you, bright eyes—"

"Would willingly fuck a monster."

His eyes flew open as he caught her wrist, meaning to push her away. Instead, he held her there, feeling her pulse race beneath his digits. "This is no joke, Kon-stahns."

"I'm not laughing."

"You don't care?"

She shook her head slightly. "I don't see what you see, Akur."

It was his time to swallow hard. "What about that Tasqal? You saw what he revealed. The fin, the genetic connection. Everything my people fought against, everything we despised...it's part of our lifeblood now. What we are."

"Don't be silly. You're nothing like *them*." Her other hand came up to touch his face, and he had to close his eyes against the tenderness of the gesture. "You know what's right and wrong. They have survived by taking...but you...you're willing to die to protect others. That makes you *nothing* like them."

"You don't understand." His digit tightened on her wrist, not enough to hurt, but enough to make her feel his strength. There was still no fear in those blue eyes. "If we did this...if I lost control...I could hurt you. Break you."

"I trust you."

His eyes snapped open again. Words failed him. "You *shouldn't*."

She had the audacity to smile. "But I do." She stepped closer, eliminating what little space remained between them. "I've seen you fight. Seen you kill. But I've also seen you protect." Her hand slid from his face to his nape, fingers brushing the burning fin there. He inhaled so hard it sounded as if he was taking his last breath. "You're burning up, Akur. Let me help."

A shudder ran through his massive frame at her touch.

"Kon-stahns..." Her name was a warning, a plea.

"Tell me what happens." Her voice remained steady despite the way her heart raced. "Tell me exactly what I'm offering and let me decide. Is this like a bonding thing? Will doing this make us married or something? Is that why you're so afraid?"

He grunted another laugh. Married. Wasn't that the human mating ritual that signaled lifelong mates? "No," he whispered. "Not married."

"Then what? Will I be marked? Claimed?"

He wanted to push her away. Needed to. But the heat was making it hard to think, hard to remember why this was such a terrible idea.

And she was soft. So very soft. And she smelled good, too. So qrakking good. Gods... "No. There are no consequences except..."

"Except what?"

"Pain. For you." His grip on her wrist tightened fractionally. "I would try to make it good for you. If I hurt you, I..." He couldn't finish the thought.

She nodded slowly, processing. "So, you're considering it. Good."

"No," he growled.

She drew in a sharp breath but didn't pull away. "What if we *don't* do this? What happens to you?"

He shook his head, trying to clear it. It wasn't just her proximity now. It was her touch. The sensation of her softness against him. The scent of her—sweet, tantalizing. Even the sound of her voice. It was slowly driving him crazy. Maybe she was right about him being insane—only, he hadn't expected her to be the catalyst of this unfortunate demise.

"The heat will get worse. I'll lose control, eventually. Become dangerous." His jaw clenched. "I've seen it happen to others. They either find release or..." He let the implications hang in the air.

"Take it?"

He froze, easing back as some clarity reached his mind. "*Never.* No Shum'ai would ever do that to you. We are not like those Tasqals."

She leaned in, cradling his head as those blasted digits of hers brushed his nefre again. "I know." His cock jumped, growing so hard beneath his slit that it was torture. "I know," she whispered.

"I would not force you, but I would be in pain. A lot of pain. Until it eventually faded."

"How long?"

He breathed out a hot breath. The questions felt like a hammer against his mind, but he knew he needed to answer them. She needed to know. "Many turns."

Her free hand shifted, thankfully, from his nefre to touch his face again, and this time he couldn't stop himself from leaning into it. "Then we don't have a choice."

"There's always a choice." But even as he said it, his body was responding to her touch. The heat under his skin seemed to thrum in time with her pulse. "I can bear it."

"We don't have time." She pressed closer, and he had to bite back a groan at the feel of her soft body against his. "Those gator-guards are out there and you're my weapon. We need to move, and you need to be able to fight." Her fingers stroked along his fin again, sending sparks of pleasure-pain down his spine. "Let me help you."

Another harsh laugh grunted through him. "Your weapon? So you'll surrender to me just so I can fight for you."

She breathed out a laugh of her own, her cool breath fanning against his skin. "Funny, isn't it? I never thought I'd be fucking an alien to save the universe." Another breath shuddered through her. "Just like you never thought you'd need to fuck a human to fight the war you've been dying to end."

His muscles flexed as he still resisted. Did she truly understand what she was asking of him? But even as he asked himself the question, Kon-stahns looked up at him. She stared into his eyes, unwavering.

"I trust you," she whispered.

Those words again. They broke something in him, some last barrier of resistance. With a growl that shook the walls, he spun them, pressing her against the stone with his body. His hands came up to cage her in, digits scraping against the rock.

"Last chance," he ground out, fighting for control even as his body screamed for release. "Last chance to run."

Instead of answering, she lifted her face to his and pressed her lips to his mouth.

The sensation of her lips was like touching a flame to gunpowder. Heat exploded through him, turning his blood to fire. A sound somewhere between a growl and a roar tore from his throat as he deepened the contact. Tasting her. Claiming her. He couldn't...resist.

The last of his control. It was broken.

His hands moved from the wall to her body, sliding under the thin remnants of her tunic to touch bare skin. Even with his heat clouding his senses, he could feel the lack of hers. Despite the natural warmth of her body, her skin was cold. She was freezing.

As she shuddered against him, he was about to pull back, to check if she was really alright when she gasped into his mouth, arching against him. The movement pressed her more firmly against his hardness, and rational thought fled entirely. With a single tug, he shredded what was left of her tunic, desire coursing through him at the sight and feel of her bareness.

"Akur," she breathed his name against his lips, and the sound drove him wild. He lifted her, pressing her higher against the wall as his mouth moved to her throat. The taste of her skin was intoxicating, making his head spin.

Qef. This was more than need. This was madness.

Opening his mouth, he ran his teeth against her pulse point, not quite breaking skin. Oh, she was so soft. He could bite her here. The urge to do so now was intense. Maybe later? If she allowed him to? When he was buried deep inside her. When she was crying out his name and begging for release.

It wasn't even a mating need. Just an urge. One he'd never had before as bad as he did now.

"Tell me you want this," he growled against her throat. "Tell me you understand what you're offering."

Her legs wrapped around his waist, pulling him closer. "I want this."

Qrak. With another growl that sounded like the beast he was turning into, he carried her to the small table. It creaked under their combined weight as he laid her down, scattering debris across the floor. He couldn't care less about the noise—not with her underneath him, not with her scent flooding his senses.

With another deft movement, he tugged off her lower garments, desperation overriding finesse. Then he froze, caught in the sight of her. Pale skin, soft curves, so different from the sleek, toned forms of Shum'ai females. Nothing like he'd ever seen before. A wave of possessiveness surged through him, hot like molten lava.

She was so small. Fragile. A tuft of brown fur covered her sex, but even that seemed delicate. His gaze fixed there, worry warring with desire. Ajos had taken a human mate, yes, but...

"What is it?" Kon-stahns whispered. Her blue eyes were steady on him, watching his every reaction.

"You're small."

She grunted a laugh, sending vibrations through where their bodies touched. "Come on, big guy. Worried you won't fit?" Her hand slid down his chest, fearless where others would cower. She didn't seem to mind their size difference. But he was forgetting she was partially insane. "Trust me, warrior. Humans are more adaptable than you think."

His answering growl vibrated through her body where they were pressed against the table. "If I break you..." His brow furrowed as he looked between them again.

Gods, she was beautiful. Beautiful in a way he didn't expect she would be. Her nakedness was making it damn near impossible to grab hold of the last few working brain cells he had to think logically in this moment.

"I told you, you won't." She arched up, pressing the mounds on her chest against him. Qrak. Him. "You've been acting like I'm fragile since the moment we met."

His digits pressed into the table's surface beside her head. "Because you *are* fragile."

"Am I?" As if in challenge, she wrapped her legs around his waist, pulling him closer. And that's when he felt it. She wasn't completely cold. The temperature of her cold skin couldn't distract from a sudden heat. Intense sweet heat. Right at the center of her thighs. And it called him like a beacon. "I survived being trapped on a space-ship in stasis. Survived those gator-guards. Survived the tunnels." Her hand reached for him, tracing the line of his jaw. "I'm not as break-able as you think."

Every shift of her body beneath his sent sparks of need through his system. "Kon-stahns..."

"Qrak," he growled, lowering his head to taste one perfect mound, tongue lapping at the teat. Her back arched off the table as he sucked the sensitive peak into his mouth. Gods of the Shum'ai, she tasted like the sweetest nectar. His hands slid over her body and she responded to him. He could feel the moment she relaxed. The moment she opened to him. "Can't resist."

"Then don't," she panted.

16

Akur

HER SKIN WAS like soft fabric under his palm. Every touch drew new sounds from her—little gasps and moans that made his pouch swell with the pressure beneath it. Dragging his mouth from that soft mound on her chest to her throat, he breathed in her scent. The pulse there fluttered against his tongue, fast and strong.

"More," she swallowed, the movement of the word passing through her throat making him nip her lightly, a groan rumbling past his lips. Her digits dug into his shoulders as she said it again. "More."

Little demanding temptation. He rumbled approval at her tone, even as he kept his movements carefully controlled. She might not think he could break her, but even touching her like this, she felt delicate. Precious. His digits traced feather-light patterns down her sides, learning what made her shiver, what made her arch into his touch. The sounds she made were intoxicating—each gasp and whimper feeding the fire in his blood.

When his hand slipped between her thighs, they both groaned. There was wetness there, the scent of her arousal so strong it made his head spin, made the heat in his blood surge to almost unbearable levels. He wanted to take her now, to claim her fully, but some last shred of control made him wait.

"Come on, big guy," she gasped as he slipped a single digit in. Her sheath gripped him like a vise. "Don't stop now."

He'd long passed that barrier of resistance.

Pulling out his digit, he lifted it to the light. It glistened with evidence of her and without an ounce of hesitation, he brought it to his lips.

He shouldn't have.

The taste of her was electric, sending a jolt of energy down his spine and straight to his cock. He extruded with a wet sounding slop, his cock bending unnaturally in his trouse, and even that pain didn't pull him back from the precipice. With a groan, he thrust his digit inside her again, his complete focus on the way she whimpered and shuddered at the intrusion. Every gasp, every arch of her spine, was like a revelation. Her flesh yielded to his touch as if she was made to surrender to him.

"More," she demanded, reaching for him. Her fingers dug into him as she pulled him closer.

"Patience, female of fire." He kept his touch maddeningly gentle, learning her depths, finding spots that made her gasp and curse. His other claw slid up her body to cup one soft mound, circling the peaked nipple. "I won't rush this."

His eyes rolled back as he continued to pierce her with that digit, even as he took that hardened pink peak into his mouth once more. She was like the land of the gods. Often dreamed about. Only, he never thought he'd ever get to experience it.

"More," she panted and oh, what a sweet sound.

Releasing her nipple, he growled against her throat, allowing himself another gentle nip. The urge to claim, to take, burned in his blood—but he wouldn't risk hurting her. Not her.

Kon-stahns huffed out a frustrated breath. "I won't break."

"No," he agreed, because he could feel the stretch. Another digit in and she stretched to take it, even while she still gripped him so tight. "But I want..." What? To study her? To learn every inch of her? What did that matter? It wasn't like she was going to let him do this again.

And that thought shouldn't make him so disappointed. Thrusting his middle digit deep, she stiffened at the intrusion. It was the thickest one. The one that would tell him whether she could really take him.

"You're driving me crazy," she gasped.

A rumbling laugh escaped him. "Good." Because she was driving him crazy, too. But he would make sure she was ready.

"Akur," she breathed his name like a prayer. Her skin was flushed beneath his palm, life organ racing like a trapped creature's wings.

"Not yet." He growled, not recognizing his own voice. "Need you ready. Need you desperate."

"Stop thinking." She reached up, grabbed his nape and the nefre there, and pulled him into her. So close, Constance breathed against his mouth. Her other hand traced the ridges of muscle across his chest. "Fuck me, Akur. I want it."

Well, there went his careful restraint.

With a sound that was pure beast, he captured her mouth again. His free claw tangled in her long filaments, holding her still as he devoured her mouth while his other hand upped the tempo.

Fuhk her? The human wanted him to? Then he would. He fuhked her with his hand, using his digits to stretch and fill her over and over again. But it only made his need worse. Only made his cock strain even harder. He couldn't hold back much longer.

"Oh...oh god..." She was trembling now, on the edge of release, and he pulled back just enough to watch her face. Her eyes were dark with desire, cheeks flushed, lips swollen from his ministrations. Beautiful. Perfect.

His.

No. Not his.

But he wanted her to be.

Whether that was the heat talking, he didn't know.

"Look at me," he commanded. "I want to see your eyes when you come apart." For me.

But he couldn't say that.

This was a transaction. This human didn't want him. Not really. She wanted to be rescued. She wanted freedom. He would give her his cock, and he would give her that freedom, too.

She obeyed, holding his gaze as her breaths staggered. Reaching between them, she began rubbing something within her soft folds. With a growl, he snatched her hand away, replacing it with his own.

He almost missed it. A small little nub. Only obvious because the moment he pressed against it, she shattered. The sight of her pleasure, the scent of her arousal—it all combined to make his vision blur.

Before she could recover from her first climax, he released her, letting her go to move down her body, before he spread her thighs wide. The first taste of her on his tongue made him almost shatter. His shaft spasmed, a generous amount of spend seeping from his tip. She was sweet and salty and something uniquely her that called to the very lifeblood in him.

"Akur!" she cried out, but he couldn't reply. His mouth was over her slit and not even a host of Tasqals could make him remove it now. Her thighs trembled against his shoulders as he brought her to the edge again.

"Fuck!"

Indeed.

Only then did he rise above her, chest heaving as he looked down at her. Her chest was heaving, too, her gaze sliding down him to land on his trouse. The obvious tent only confirmed his cock had extruded without his input. The wetness that seeped through the special fibers even more confirmation that he was at a point of no return. He was already leaking enough spend to fill her womb twice over.

"Come to me," she whispered, leaning back. She was exposing herself to him and he couldn't say no.

Shifting the clasp of his trouse, he let them fall, the same moment he heard her gasp.

"I guess I don't call you 'big guy' for nothing."

She was focused on his cock, the smooth white expanse of him, her gaze falling to his base where his sac hung tight and full.

"Change your mind?" He could hardly grunt the words. And maybe she'd lost her voice, too, because she shook her head. He supposed the gesture meant the negative, because she opened her legs wider for him, one hand sneaking down to distribute her juices to the hidden bud within her folds.

One move and he was positioning himself at her entrance. He couldn't hold back much longer. Even his muscles were shaking with the effort of holding back so long and his nefre burned like living fire.

"Last chance," he ground out. "Once I start...I won't be able to stop."

Instead of answering, she wrapped her legs around his waist and pulled him closer. The tip of him pressed against her slick heat, and rational thought slipped away.

He couldn't— He tried, but his control snapped. In a single thrust, he seated himself halfway within her.

The world ceased to exist. He was suddenly spinning in the void, overwhelming pleasure encasing him as her heat gripped him tight. Every instinct screamed at him to take, to claim, to possess. Digging his digits into the table, he forced himself to still.

"Kon-stahns?" It didn't even sound like her name. More like a tortured cry. "Kon-stahns, say something."

He trembled above her, every muscle locked as he waited for her response. The effort to remain still was agony—but the thought of hurting her was worse. Her body gripped him like a velvet fist, impossibly tight and burning hot. His breath came in harsh pants that turned into condensation around them.

Constance's eyes fluttered open, glazed but aware. She shifted beneath him, testing, and the movement nearly shattered his control. "I'm okay," she breathed. "Just...give me a moment."

She was taking him without fear. Her trust humbled him even as it stoked the possessive fire in his blood. Reaching up, her hands traced patterns on his chest before she shifted higher, those hands caressing his shoulder before she pulled him in. Her lips found his. Softer and more delicate than any other time their mouths touched. Her tongue flicked out, traced his lips before slipping in to meet his.

With a whimper, she pulled him closer, her body shifting on where he pierced her with his cock enough to make him shudder. When her fingers found his nefre again, he growled, hips jerking forward before he could stop himself.

She gasped, but not in pain. "Do that again."

"Dangerous thing to ask," he rumbled, but he couldn't deny her. Not when she looked at him like that, all heat and challenge.

She fondled his nefre as he moved, each careful thrust earning a gasp. The little temptation must have figured out just how sensitive he was there. No one had ever touched him at that place, not like this. The sensation was overwhelming. A signal of trust. Trust that grew with every gentle advance, every restrained withdrawal. He watched her face, memorizing everything, knowing this will never happen again. Every expression, every change in her breathing. Everything catalogued.

"Akur," she whispered. Never thought a single utterance of his name would make him almost release. But here he was. "I want all of you."

He froze. Life organ thundering in his chest.

She didn't know what this meant to him. This wasn't just physical need anymore. Something deeper was taking root, something that terrified him.

Pressing his forehead to hers, he grit his teeth. The gesture was intimate among his people—a sharing of breath, of life. She probably didn't know the significance, but he couldn't help himself.

"More." She slipped her head to the side of his, nibbling on his ear. "I can take it."

"Stubborn female," he rumbled against her throat. Pulling back, his cock slid in her heat and he gave her a single moment to retreat. "Time's up. No running now."

With one powerful thrust, he gave himself over to her completely. His hips snapped forward, burying his length inside her once, twice, again and again, each thrust measured and deep. And her body accepted him. She wrapped him in wet heat and softness. The table groaned beneath them now, but he barely heard it over the sound of their shared breaths, their mingled moans.

Cradling her to him, he hoped his warmth could push back against the cold as he gripped her hips and pummeled into her.

"Aargh..." A growl of fire and sweetness as he grit his teeth. The pressure of his hips was outside his control now. The movement, the rhythm, all instinctual. But if he was hurting her, Kon-stahns had a strange way of showing it.

Her eyes rolled back to the point he could no longer see her pupils, only pure white. Her mouth opened, slack as a high-pitched moan left the depths of her soul. She gripped him hard as she cried out, her entire body shuddering around him.

And so he fuhked her harder. Deeper. Giving her the entire length of him, only to take it away and fill her with it again and again.

When his cock spasmed, grew impossibly hard, he stiffened, held her hips tight, and growled into the air between them.

He could feel his seed pods beginning to swell, pressure building at his base. The knowledge that he would soon fill her, mark her from the inside, made his nefre burn even hotter.

The wet sounds of their joining filled the air as he slid one hand between them to find that sensitive bud within her folds. The moment his fingers made contact, she cried out, the sound making his seed sack swell in response.

He was going to release. He was—

The sensation almost made him go limp. Only the sweetness of her maintained his connection to reality.

"Kon-stahnsssss," he growled, feeling the first seed pod begin its journey. His vision blurred as it traveled up his shaft, the pressure building until it burst at his tip. The moment his seed flooded her, she screamed, her body convulsing around him.

She was jerking, almost as if she was spasming, too.

"Akur," she gasped, her inner walls clenching around him. "Something's...different."

Her entire body began shaking so hard, it seemed she had no control over it at all.

Her reaction was intense—more intense than he'd expected. Her entire body shook as another seed pod made its way up his shaft. When it burst inside her, she practically sobbed with pleasure, her fingers digging into his shoulders as her eyes lost focus.

"Akur, I—" Her head fell back, eyes rolling over again as she spasmed. "Something is—"

Fear pierced through his haze of pleasure. He'd never seen a female react this strongly to the seed pods. His kind had evolved with these mating hormones—their bodies designed to handle the stimulant that made joining more pleasurable and increased the chances of conception. But Kon-stahns was human.

"Too much," she gasped, even as her body clenched around him again. Another pod was already moving up his shaft, and he tried desperately to hold back. But it was too late. The moment it burst, she screamed again, her whole body stiffening as another powerful orgasm rocked through her.

He held her tight against his chest as she shuddered uncontrollably. Panic gripped him. Ajos didn't mention this. What if something was wrong? What if she was having an adverse reaction? What if his seed pods were too much for her to take?

Qrak. This was a bad qrakking idea. He should have borne the pain. Rejected her offer to help.

"Kon-stahns?" He managed to grunt out, trying to check on her even as his own body betrayed him, preparing to release another pod.

She didn't seem capable of answering, lost in another wave of pleasure as the next seed pod burst inside her. Her body jerked against his, walls clamping down so tight he saw stars.

He should pull out, but she was gripping him so tight that was impossible.

"Stay with me," he growled, fighting his own pleasure to focus on her. He couldn't lose her because of this. Where his kind would experience heightened pleasure, Kon-stahns seemed completely overwhelmed by each burst of seed.

Another pod traveled up his shaft, making him grunt with the intensity. The moment it released, she screamed again, her digits drawing blood where they dug into his skin. Her whole body convulsed, caught in what seemed like an endless loop of orgasms.

"Can't...can't stop." Her eyes watered and those waters ran down her cheeks.

He could barely think straight. His seed sack was still swollen and heavy, drawing almost all his mental power. Another pod was already forming, and he tried desperately to hold it back again. But his body had its own agenda, driven by heat and need and something deeper he didn't want to examine too closely.

The next burst had her sobbing his name, her body shaking so hard he had to tighten his grip to keep her from thrashing.

She was going to...she would despise him after this.

"Too much..." she whimpered, even as her hips moved against his, seeking more. The contradictions in her responses worried him, but he couldn't stop now if his life depended on it.

His seed sack pulsed again, and panic gripped him. "Qeffing qrak." Just how many seed pods had he created for her? She was already overwhelmed—how much more could her human body take?

He had to stop this.

But before he could try to pull out, another pod was moving up his shaft. Kon-stahns felt it coming—he could tell by the way her eyes widened just before rolling back again. When it burst inside her, she went completely rigid, a broken cry tearing from her throat.

"Look at me," he commanded, needing to see she was still with him. But her eyes were unfocused, glazed with pleasure as aftershocks continued to wrack her body. Each pulse of his seed triggered fresh tremors, like waves crashing endlessly against shore.

He could feel more pods forming, his body far from done. But watching her come apart like this—beautiful and terrifying all at once—made him question everything he thought he knew about mating. He...didn't want this female to hurt.

This wasn't just about sating his need anymore. Something was happening to him, something that both thrilled and terrified him.

Another pod began its journey, and he growled in frustration.

"Hold on to me," he managed to grunt out as he felt it travel up his shaft. He wrapped his arms around her. Gripped her to him. Encased her in his warmth. "I've got you, bright eyes. Just hold on."

When the next pod burst, her entire body convulsed. Her cries had grown hoarse, reduced to desperate whimpers as pleasure continued to overwhelm her system. He could feel her life organ racing against his chest, her skin burning hot where they touched.

One final pod made its way up his shaft—the last, he could tell from how his seed sack was finally beginning to soften. When it burst inside her, Kon-stahns went completely limp in his arms, only small tremors betraying that she was still conscious.

"Breathe," he murmured, pressing his forehead to hers as their bodies slowly calmed. She was still shaking, little aftershocks making her clench around him periodically. His shaft remained hard inside her, but no more pods would come. Thank the gods.

Qrak. He'd really made a mess of this mission.

"That was..." Kon-stahns tried to speak, but trailed off instead. Her eyes finally focused on his, and what he saw there made his chest tight. Trust, wonder, and something deeper. Something that must be the heat still messing with his head.

"Rest now," he rumbled, gathering her closer.

They shouldn't have done this. It had changed everything. He could feel it. But those were thoughts for later.

For now, he just held her as her breathing slowly steadied, her body occasionally shuddering with residual pleasure as his seed continued to pulse within her. The mating hormones would take time to work through her system, but the worst—or best—was over.

Pressing her head against him, he kept her there. Maybe because he couldn't bear meeting her gaze now. Didn't want to see the eventual blame and disgust that would rise in her eyes.

So he held her there, silently giving her his warmth, as she drifted into an exhausted sleep against him. A breath shuddered in his chest.

Even now, when she was unconscious, he didn't want to let her go. Qrak him.

He was in trouble and there was nothing he could do about it.

17

Constance

CONSCIOUSNESS RETURNED SLOWLY, as if her mind had been scattered, all semblance of self displaced in the moments before she fell asleep. The first thing she noticed was the warmth—she was enveloped in it, cocooned against the chill of the room. The second was the steady thrum of a heartbeat against her ear.

Akur. He was holding her.

Akur held her cradled against his chest, one arm supporting her while his other hand traced patterns on the map projected in front of them. Immediately, her breath stilled in her nose.

He was holding her...and before he'd been holding her...they'd had mind-blowing sex. Mind-*bending* sex. Oh God, did she really do it? She remembered begging him, unable to stop once they started. Almost as if the very scent of him had been intoxicating.

And his climaxes...what the hell happened there? She was pretty sure his cum had sent her into orbit. Like some sort of aphrodisiac that forced *her* body to climax again and again. Such a thing was so wild, she didn't think it was possible.

And yet, she was sure it had happened.

Keeping her breathing even, she took a moment to gather herself. She felt different—stronger somehow, more alive, despite that she was still exhausted.

"I know you're awake," the alien suddenly rumbled. The depth of his voice vibrated through her, sending tingles through her skin.

Well, guess the pretense was over. Releasing a slow breath, she opened her eyes fully, only to find his golden gaze already on her. He was looking at her strangely. A careful neutrality in his expression that made her chest tight. "How long was I out?"

"Not long..." He paused, looking as if he was about to say something else, but his throat moved as if he swallowed it back.

"Oof," she grunted as she tried to sit up. They were still on the table, as if he'd just pulled her into him and hadn't moved after...

As his arms disentangled from around her, the chill caught her again. She shivered, wincing slightly as she tried to stretch. She almost toppled off the table, but he was there. Those warm arms enclosed around her again in a split second.

"Constance..." He said her name in that way he usually did, all strange, the syllables unfamiliar yet somehow...right. "I am..." He paused again. His heart was thundering against her spine now. "I did not know it would affect you the way it did."

There was something in his voice. Something that sounded like regret. A sound so distinct it made a pit open up in her stomach.

So, he regretted it. Well...she didn't.

Digging down inside her, she tried to find an ounce of the same emotion. She'd mated with an alien and that wasn't so strange now after living on the Restitution's base and seeing all the happily mated humans there. Only, you know, this wasn't a *true* mating. It was just sex. Like a one-night stand. Sex for survival, that's all it was. And she was a big girl. She'd made the decision. She'd gone through with it. He may regret it, but...she didn't.

When she turned in his arms, the motion made her aware of every place they touched, every lingering sensation from what they did just hours before.

"You mean the..." She gestured vaguely, feeling heat rise in her cheeks. "The multiple..."

"The seed pods." His voice was rough. "They contain a mating hormone that enhances pleasure, increases chances of..." His jaw tightened. "Ajos did not mention...qrak," he cursed under his breath. "I should have warned you."

"Hey." She pressed a hand to his chest, feeling his heart racing beneath her palm. The thumps felt massive, almost as if his heart was twice the size of hers. "I'm okay. Better than okay, actually." And she was. Despite the lingering exhaustion, she felt...good.

God, she'd forgotten how good the aftermath could feel. It had been a while since she last—

"You were...overwhelmed. Out of control. I thought for a moment that I had..." His hands tightened on her arms, then quickly loosened as if he was afraid of hurting her.

"Akur." She waited until he met her gaze again. "What happened between us...I've never experienced anything like that. But not in a bad way."

He made a sound low in his throat, his lips pulling back ever so slightly in a snarl. "I saw your eyes release water—"

"From pleasure," she interrupted. "Just pleasure. Nothing else."

"Your temperature has risen." His voice dropped lower.

"Oh." Now that he mentioned it, the room didn't have that same biting cold as it had before. It was still cold, yes, but she could bear it better. "Well," she smiled. "That's good."

He growled again. "You do not seem to care. You could barely take my length and then my seed...Constance...you nearly died."

She choked on a laugh that made her cough. Chest heaving, Akur's brow descended as she directed him to knock her back, as she tried to catch her breath again. "I assure you, what you saw was not me nearly dying. It was quite the opposite."

When she looked at him, that neutrality was gone. He was glaring at her now.

She sighed. "Would it have mattered?" He glared even more. "You needed help. I wanted to help. You have to get out of here and warn the others about that orb. Everything else…" She shrugged, trying to ignore how his proximity still affected her, how her body seemed to remember every touch, every moment of their joining. "We deal with it. Like everything else."

He stared at her for a long moment, something unreadable in those alien eyes. Finally, he released her and hopped off the table. The loss of his warmth was like someone had just turned off the furnace she'd been sitting beside.

"We need to move," he said. It wasn't lost on her that his voice was carefully neutral again. "The Hedgeruds will be here soon."

She nodded, reaching for her scattered clothes, only to remember they were in shreds. Akur made that sound again—the one that seemed caught between desire and regret. Digging in one pocket of his trousers, he took out a little circular thing and thrust it in her direction.

"What's this?" She took the little packet, turning it over in her hand. It was wrapped in something like plastic, a little brown circle. "When I checked your pockets, I found nothing."

"Clothing," Akur grunted. "Shum'ai technology. Unfold it."

She did as he instructed, biting the packet with her teeth to break the film. As soon as she did that, the disc grew; the material transforming from a thin film into a soft, pliable fabric. Within seconds, it had unfolded into a simple tunic, large enough to cover her. "It… grows?" she said, amazed.

"Nanofiber weave." He turned away again, running a hand over his head. It was then she noticed the fin at the back of his head wasn't that raging red it was before. It was more like a muted pink now. She'd high-five her pussy if it wouldn't hurt. She was pretty sure she was sore down there.

"It's adaptable. Durable." Akur turned around again, his gaze lingering on her. "…Practical."

It was more like a large t-shirt, but as she shrugged it on, she supposed it covered her completely, hiding away her nakedness.

"It's thermal-regulated," he continued. "Should help with the…" He gestured at her trembling limbs.

"The aftermath?" She supplied with a small smile, trying to ease some of the tension. It didn't help. His only response was a grunt as he moved back to the map, but she caught the way his fin seemed to throb again, the way his hands clenched at his sides.

Damn. She hadn't considered this when she'd made him that offer, but things felt tense now. Like things had changed. Damnit. She opened her mouth, wanting to dispel the tension, but found she couldn't. They had a mission to complete, a world to save. *Her* world. Everything else would have to wait.

"Thanks." She hopped off the table, testing her balance. Glancing back his way, she found him watching her with those intense golden eyes, and she could see him struggling with something. Before she could ask, he turned back to the map.

"The citadel first," he said, voice gruff. "Then we take that ship and find your friend in the wastelands."

She moved to stand beside him, studying the glowing pathways. She couldn't understand a thing on the map. It was in a language she couldn't read. Worse yet, it was 3D, but with only the pathways shown. Kind of like an architectural drawing of a subway network.

"Your heat…is it better?" she whispered after a few moments.

His muscles tensed, but he nodded once, sharply. "It's managed. For now."

There was something in his tone that made her want to reach for him, but she held back. What was his problem? Had he really hated it so much? Had sex with her really been that bad? This couldn't just be about his concern for her wellbeing. This was something else. But it was obvious pushing now would only make him retreat further.

"Then let's go save the universe," she said instead, keeping her voice light. "Or at least stop it from ending."

His lips twitched slightly—not quite a smile, but close. "Finding the maintenance tunnels will be our best route. If we can reach the power center without being detected, I can shut the lights off, give us more cover, and then—"

A distant boom cut him off, the sound reverberating through the surrounding stone. Dust sifted down from the ceiling as tremors shook the foundation.

"What was that?" She automatically moved closer to him, scanning the ceiling for signs of collapse.

"Hedgeruds." His expression darkened.

"Then we need to hurry." She gathered the remaining supplies—one of those medical vials Akur needed (the other had broken), and the meal bars the Tasqal left them. There was nowhere to put them. She had no bags, but there was something else. Spotting the single bra she had in this universe, she picked up the ripped fabric. The clasp was gone, but the C cups worked great. Stuffing the items into the cups, she wrapped the strap around them to secure them before sliding it up her arm. It was tight, was hardly a bag, but it worked. "Let's go."

THEY MOVED through the narrow maintenance tunnel in silence, Akur leading with that predatory grace that made her wonder how someone so massive could move so quietly. The passageway was barely wide enough for his shoulders, forcing him to angle sideways at certain points. Despite the thermal properties of the tunic he'd given her and the new warmth from her body buzzing from all that pleasure, she could feel the temperature drop the deeper they went.

Another explosion rocked somewhere in the tunnels, closer this time. Small debris rained down from above, pattering against their shoulders like rain. She watched Akur pause briefly at the sound, jaw ticking, before he pushed on again. Apart from the sound of their breaths, everywhere else was silent.

"Think those monster mole rats are gone?" she whispered, glancing up to look around. The map Akur carried cast a dim glow, and it was the only light they were willing to risk.

"The tunnel dwellers? Negative. But there is too much noise in the tunnels. The explosions will send them into hiding."

"Good."

Akur grunted, shifting sideways to go through a particularly narrow section.

She squeezed through too, panting slightly as she paused to take a breath. Looking around again, she tried not to let her fear rise. Everywhere looked identical, each passageway a copy of the other. "I can't believe we're here. That above us is a host of the very beings we both hate...and that we have to trust one of them with this. That map could be leading us anywhere."

Akur grunted again, glancing at her only briefly. They'd been walking for maybe an hour and a half, and he hadn't looked at her properly in that entire time. "It hasn't led us into their clutches yet... but you are right, human."

"So I am, *alien.*"

He grunted again, and she could see the ghost of a smile when he glanced back at her this time. "Constance."

"Akur."

He started walking again, his own gaze scanning upward at a roof she couldn't see.

"How much longer do you think?" He reached back almost instinctively, not really paying attention as he helped her over a large fallen stone. The warmth of his touch shot up her arm. He was heating up again.

Somewhere far behind them, another boom rocked the stone walls.

"What do you think those explosions are?" Heat left her as he released her and kept on moving.

"I do not know, but they know we're down here. They know we haven't left."

She swallowed hard. "So they're hunting us. Do you think that Tasqal—"

"No. They would have found us already."

She nodded, even though he probably didn't see it as she was walking behind him. For the next few minutes, they trod in silence. Climbing over exposed bedrock, squeezing through areas that seemed impossible to traverse. And they kept on going.

The tunnels seemed endless. Whenever she caught a glimpse of it, Constance tried to keep track of their progress using the map, but even if she could read it, the markings were difficult to decipher in the dim light. More concerning was the way Akur's temperature was rising again. She could feel the heat radiating from him even several feet away.

"These tunnels," she said, breaking the tense silence between them, "they all look the same. Are you sure we're heading the right way?"

Akur's pace didn't slow, but she caught the slight tension in his shoulders. "The markings change. Each section has its own designation." He gestured to the wall. When she frowned at the spot, he brought the map closer, shedding light on the old stone. There were faded symbols etched in the rock. "We're nearing the central hub, about halfway to that citadel."

Another explosion rocked the tunnels, sending tremors through the stone beneath their feet. She was in his arms, scorching heat enveloping her as Akur pressed her against his chest before she even knew what was happening. He shielded her as debris rained down.

Every breath she took was like humid air. Akur. His heat...

Should she even mention it?

"You're getting hot again," she whispered. "Is it...is what we did wearing off already?"

He growled low in his throat, the sound echoing in the narrow space as he almost reluctantly released her. "No."

That was a lie if she ever heard one. She was opening her mouth to point that out when he went still.

"Something about these tunnels..." He shook his head as if trying to clear it. He was back to not being able to think straight. His heat was affecting him, and he was lying about it. "The air feels wrong."

"Wrong how?" She stumbled over some loose stones, and his hand shot out to catch her again. The heat of his touch sent tingles up her arm. Images of what they did in that room came shooting back like missiles through her memory.

"Like we're being herded again." His golden eyes scanned the darkness ahead. "The explosions…they're too precise. Too calculated."

"Herded again? You think someone's directing us? That Tasqal said—"

"What that Tasqal said means nothing." His voice had gone harsh. "They are manipulators. Masters of deception. Even the truth they speak is shaped to serve their purposes."

He turned, pushing through the darkness, and she caught up to walk beside him as the tunnel marginally opened up. "But you believed him about some things. About the orb, about what they plan to do to Earth."

"Because those things align with what we already know." Another explosion shook the tunnel, closer this time. "But his motivations… those I trust less than a starving umu in a nursery."

"A what in a what?"

A sound that might have been a laugh rumbled through his chest. "Never mind. The point is—" He stopped abruptly, head tilting slightly. "Do you hear that?"

She strained her ears. It was hard trying to listen through complete silence. You'd think any sound would be harsh, grating, and loud, but that wasn't the case when her mind was creating phantom sounds in the back of her head.

"Wait," she whispered, grabbing Akur's arm. He froze instantly, and she pressed closer to hear what had caught his attention. There was…nothing…and then there was. A faint humming sound coming from somewhere ahead.

"Maintenance drones?" she asked, hoping beyond hope. Akur shook his head.

"Worse." His voice was barely a breath. "Gragmars, I'm sure. Scavenger creatures the Tasqals use to clean their waste systems. They hunt in packs."

As if in response to his words, the humming sound grew louder. It wasn't pleasant. Not like a humming sound should be. Instead, it was like a too-deep vibration that threatened to render her eardrums useless. It raised every hair on her body. It was a sound that triggered

something wild in her brain, something that recognized apex preda-
tors on an instinctual level.

"How bad?"

"Bad." He drew one of his blades silently. "They're drawn to heat
signatures. And right now..." He groaned as he rolled his shoulders.

She understood immediately. She was warmer than she was
before, thanks to the tunic she was wearing. But him? He was probably lighting up like a beacon to any heat-sensitive creatures.

The Tasqals were using the creatures to find them. What better
way than to turn the tables and hunt in a way they couldn't escape
from.

"Options?"

Another explosion shook the tunnel, more debris raining down,
and this time she heard something else. Beneath the humming, a
distinct snapping sound. Multiple snapping sounds.

"We can't go back," Akur growled, scanning the passage ahead.
"The Hedgeruds will have reached our previous position by now."

"And we can't stay here." She could hear more of them gathering,
the snapping growing louder. "How many do you think?"

"Too many." His free hand found hers in the darkness, squeezing
once, and the simple motion made something ache inside her.
"When I say run, run. Don't stop this time. Don't look back. There's a
junction ahead—take the right path. I'll hold them."

"Like hell you will." She gripped his hand harder. "We do this
together or not at all, warrior."

A sound that might have been a laugh rumbled through his chest
again. "Stubborn female."

"You've known that from the start. And you still stayed to
help me."

The snapping sounds were getting closer. Like the claws of a crab?
Snap, snap, snap. She could deal with crab creatures...maybe. Possibly. If it looked like an Earth thing, then it would be easier to
fight...right?

Her mind flew back to the giant molerats...well, maybe not.

"There might be another way." Akur was looking around now and she wished her eyesight was better to pierce the unending dark. "But you won't like it."

"I like being eaten alive even less." The tremor in her voice betrayed her fear. "What's the plan?"

"Gragmars hate light. They dwell in darkness, hunting by heat signature, but they're easily confused by multiple sources." His free hand moved to his blade's hilt. "If I can generate enough heat..."

She caught his meaning immediately. "You'll draw them to you instead of me."

"Yes."

"That's the same shit plan as before, warrior. I'm not leaving you. You're hurt, too, and your heat—"

"Is managed." His tone brooked no argument. "The joining helped. I can control it now."

Liar. But before she could argue, another explosion rocked the tunnel, close enough that the wall to her right shook. The shock wave sent her tumbling against Akur who stumbled back, and kept moving backward. The light from the map disappeared as he pressed the device to her chest in his haste to move, and it took her a moment to realize why.

There, as the last of the light died away, she saw one of the huge blocks shift and fall from the wall, and there, a creature from her nightmares.

18

Constance

"Fuck!" Akur's use of the human word seemed apt as he broke into a run with her gripped to his chest. "You should have taken the moment to run, human. These things will be attracted to me first, before they think to go after you."

Gripping the thick muscle of his arm that was pressed into her midsection as he ran, she squeezed her eyes tight for a moment, her stomach contents heaving as he went airborne in a leap over something she couldn't see.

She just had to trust his eyesight was as good as she thought it was in this darkness, because she still couldn't see shit.

But she could hear. She could hear oh so well, and behind them, that humming, snapping sound was almost deafening.

"Have you stopped to think that maybe that's exactly what they want? For these creatures to take your attention while they come and snatch me in the dark? I'm fucking useless out here. I can't see a thing, Akur."

"Useless?" he grunted. "No. Take this."

Something pressed against her breasts and she realized it was one of his swords. Trembling hands found the hilt as there was a keening sound directly behind them.

"Now, bright eyes," Akur panted. "Run."

He let her go suddenly, and she fell the short distance to the ground. Something clattered and skidded away, the light from the map blinking in and out as the device skated across the stone floor, illuminating the tunnel as she turned to see the creature chasing after them.

Fuck, indeed. It was a writhing mass of segmented limbs and chitinous armor, each segment lined with what looked like sensory organs. It moved like a centipede, but faster, more erratic. As Akur stopped short, it reared up, snappers at what must be its mouth orifice going snap snap snap.

Akur's blade moved like solid lightning, catching the creature mid-lunge as the dim light from the map died. A shriek echoed through the tunnel, but the sound only seemed to excite the others she couldn't see.

The map. She had to find the map.

Knees scraped on stone, palms being scratched to bring blood to the surface as she searched for the device. Without the map, they were blind. Without it, they were lost. Terror clawed at her throat, choking off her breath. She crawled forward, her hands sweeping blindly through the darkness, praying for the touch of metal, the faintest flicker of light. Somehow, her carefully packed bra bag dislodged, its contents tumbling out. She shrugged out of it with a stressed grunt.

"Run!" Akur shouted. "Right tunnel, go!"

"Not without you!" She blindly searched for the device still. But even as she said it, she could hear his plan working. The gragmars were focusing on him, drawn by the waves of heat now pouring off his massive frame.

"Constance." Her name was a growl. "Run. *Now.*"

The command in his voice triggered something in her—not fear, but recognition. Trust. He had a plan, and she needed to trust him to execute it.

With a curse that would have made her mother faint, she rose. At the same time, her foot hit something that skirted off in the darkness. The map. It flickered alive for a moment, enough for her to see it and dive for it, before it died again.

"Constance!!"

Rising, she sprinted for the junction. Behind her, she heard Akur roar—a sound of challenge that made the very air vibrate. The gragmars responded with shrieks of their own. Shrieks that told her once they were done with him, she would be their next meal. And despite everything within her telling her to stay and fight, she had to do the thing that made her fear the most.

She had to leave him. She had to trust him with this.

She reached the junction and took the right path without slowing, ignoring every instinct that screamed at her to go back, to help him. The tunnel ahead sloped upward sharply, making her legs burn as she pushed herself harder.

Another explosion rocked the tunnels, closer than ever. This one was strong enough to create aftershocks that made her sway, Akur's sword clanging on the walls around her as she tried to keep her footing. The sound of combat behind her began fading, replaced by an ominous rumbling that seemed to come from everywhere at once.

"Come on," she whispered, though she wasn't sure if she was talking to herself or to Akur. "Come on, come on…"

The tunnel curved sharply, and she nearly crashed into a wall. A dead end? No. Not again. Tucking the map device under her arm, she used both hands, searching for a secret access point. Maybe it's just another door.

There were symbols here. Etched into the rock. She could feel them underneath her palm. If she could just figure them out…

She was still trying to decipher them when she heard it—the sound of something large moving fast, heading her way.

Pressing herself against the wall, her heart thundered in her chest. If it was one of those creatures, she was dead. Akur's sword was heavy. She could swing it, but she'd need the creature to be distracted enough that her blow could harm it. She had no other weapons, no way to defend herself. Nothing except...the map.

It had a light. Akur said these creatures hunted in the dark. That they didn't like the light. It wasn't much; it was a dim light, but maybe...

Her hand went to the device. If she was about to die, she could at least try this.

The sound grew closer, and she tensed, fingers working desperately across the device's surface, trying to activate it again. But it wouldn't. There were no buttons to press. No display screen or anything.

"Shit."

It fell, so maybe it was broken. Or maybe it was just one of those things that you had to smash to make it work. She didn't frickin' want to do that.

Fuck.

FUCK!

But it wasn't turning on.

Lifting the device, she bit her lip hard as she heard the thing coming closer.

"If you break that map, bright eyes, we're both dead."

Relief hit her so hard her knees almost buckled. "Akur!"

He emerged from the darkness like a warrior god at the same moment that she must have activated something and the map flickered to life.

Akur's chest heaved as he stood a few feet away, covered in blood that looked luminescent in the dim light but very much alive. And he was smiling. Grinning more like.

Constance's shoulders slumped. He really did like the bloodshed and killing, didn't he. And she wouldn't admit it out loud, but it suited him. All barbaric and filled with bloodlust. It only made her remember...

Her cheeks heated just a moment before Akur fell to his knees.

She rushed forward. "You're hurt."

"Not in the way you think, bright eyes." He was scorching hot as she tried to help him up. His heat. He was in trouble again.

"Those creatures…"

"Won't be following." His grin was all teeth again. "But we need to move. That last explosion wasn't random—the Hedgeruds are targeting the structural supports."

As if to emphasize his point, another boom shook the tunnel. This one was accompanied by the distinct sound of stone cracking.

The tunnel rocked again, debris raining down enough that the dust choked the air. She stumbled, catching herself against the wall as Akur struggled to rise.

"Are they trying to bring the whole tunnel system down?" she breathed, watching in horror as more fissures appeared in the rock. "They'd rather bury us than let us escape?"

"Not you." Akur's voice was strained. "They wish to end me, not you."

"Yea, well I'm with you. I won't be much use to them dead, will I."

Akur grunted. "You put much faith in these scum." He got to his feet, but it looked like it took a lot of effort. "They only need you barely alive, female. You would serve their purpose, anyway."

His words made a lump form in her throat, even as their bodies swayed with the shifting ground beneath them.

"The map," Akur grunted. "What does it show ahead?"

With shaking hands, she held up the device, squinting at the holographic display. The symbols were still incomprehensible. "There's…there's a wall here." She traced the glowing lines with her finger. "I can't tell if it's another hidden passage or—"

Another explosion cut her off, this one close enough to send them both stumbling. The crack that followed was deafening—the sound of tons of rock giving way.

"No time." Akur grabbed her arm, practically dragging her into him as he stumbled forward, just as the walls began collapsing around them. When he grunted, more debris falling down as he thrust his shoulder into the dead end before them, she realized exactly what he was doing.

Rearing back, he hunched himself over her before he threw his shoulder forward again. The impact would have rendered any normal man unconscious, but Akur merely grunted again. Dust and debris choked the air, but he didn't relent. Again and again, he pulled back before slamming his shoulder into the wall, each impact reverberating through her like a shockwave that made her teeth rattle in her skull.

He was like a machine, not caring about how he was breaking apart because he had no feelings. At least, that's what it seemed he'd like her to think. But back then in that room, and right now, she could see it. The male who was practically giving his life just so she could survive this. Because he was right. The Tasqals only needed her breathing. No matter if she was broken, near death, hardly alive, once she was still breathing, they'd still get their way.

The light flickered in and out as Akur continued to batter the wall. Behind them, the sound of falling rock grew louder, closer, a cascade of destruction racing to consume them.

"There!" Akur's voice cut through the din. "A chamber. I can see the other side!"

She caught glimpses of it too. He really was a machine, using his body like a hammer to break through the wall before them. There, in the flickering light, was an opening into what looked like a vast cavern. But that little hole, that glimmer of hope amidst the rain of debris, seemed impossibly small.

"Akur," she gasped as the map blinked on long enough for her to see the billowing dust heading their way.

They were going to die here. Both of them. The alien rebel with a death wish and the human he was stubborn enough to save.

"*We'll make it.*" Akur's arm tightened around her as he continued pummeling the rock. "By the gods of Tonvuhiri, we will."

Something swelled in her heart that made her almost choke, made it hard to breathe. The light blinked out before coming on again as she watched the tunnel collapse.

Oh, God...this was really it.

His growl was all she heard before they were tumbling forward.

They burst through the wall just as the tunnel behind them gave way completely. It was gravity against the chase of certain death. Akur tumbled forward, the force of the collapse sending them both sprawling. Twisting his frame, Akur took the brunt of the impact as they hit the ground. Dust and debris rained down around them as the last of the tunnel crumbled, sealing off the way they'd come.

For several long moments, they lay there in the darkness, gasping for breath. He'd done it. He'd really done it. And they were both still alive.

She could feel his heart thundering against her back, his skin burning as hot as ever.

"You," she panted, out of breath. "You did it. You brilliant, brilliant—"

"Of course I did." Akur's chest rumbled with a laugh that she felt through every point of contact between them. "Did you doubt me, bright eyes?"

"Someone has to keep that ego of yours in check." But she was smiling in the darkness, hyperaware of how his arm was still wrapped around her, how solid he felt beneath her.

"And you volunteered for the task?" His voice had dropped lower, rougher. "How...generous of you."

"Someone has to." She shifted, turning on his chest and using her hands to find her way. His chest was still heaving and wet—whether it was his blood or the creatures', she didn't know, but something told her it wasn't only his enemies' the moment her fingers brushed against his shoulder and he jerked at the contact.

"Akur," she whispered, both hands trembling as they found his face. She grasped his jaw, staring down at him even though the darkness hid everything. "You can't keep doing this. Even with your magic healing alien shit, you can't—"

"I promised to get you out of here alive, human."

She swallowed that lump that had risen in her throat again. "Stop calling me that."

He didn't respond. Under her hands, she felt his jaw clench.

"Call me by my name, Akur."

His jaw clenched again. "Constance," he finally said, the word coming from his lips so roughly, with so much restrained emotion, that she choked on what might be a sob.

She shook her head. "We can't keep doing this. If we continue like this, you'll..."

"Die?" he ground out.

She sniffled, looking away even though she wasn't sure he was looking at her. And why did she care, anyway? He was an alien rebel, a killer... If he wanted to die, that was none of her business. So why did the thought make her chest ache?

The harsh laugh that made his chest rise and fall echoed in the darkness. "All these turns, and death has eluded me still, sweet one." He paused. "I promised..."

"To who? Who did you promise to?"

He huffed a soft laugh through his nose. "To you, bright eyes."

She sniffled. "Well, you take back your promise. It's getting worse. They're not letting me go easy so...so if it's a matter of life or death...if it's a matter of leaving me to save yourself," she turned back to face him, putting a little pressure where her hands clasped his jaw, "you save yourself."

For a moment, he was silent, and then it was as if the heat surged within him, spreading through her skin and into her being. He grunted and suddenly she was pressed against him again as both his arms came across her, one across her back, the other gripping her behind with a possession that almost snapped her out of her grief.

"Never," he whispered, his breath so hot and close across her lips. "I don't make promises I can't keep."

His heat seared through her. But instead of burning, it felt like being wrapped in liquid fire that caressed rather than consumed. One of his massive hands slid up her spine to cradle the back of her head, fingers threading through her hair.

"Constance...my human..." he breathed against her lips, and she felt rather than saw him smile. "You think too much."

Then his mouth claimed hers, hot and demanding. The kiss ignited something primal within her, making her gasp against his lips. His other hand tightened possessively at her waist, drawing her closer as she melted against the solid wall of his chest. Time seemed to stop, the darkness around them fading into insignificance as her world narrowed to the points where they connected.

When he finally broke away, they were both panting. His forehead rested against hers, his skin still blazing with that otherworldly heat.

"Akur, your heat…"

He groaned. "We should move." He said this, though he made no attempt to release her. "The Hedgeruds will find another way."

"Let them try," she whispered back, smiling now. "I won't let them take you either."

A laugh rumbled in his chest. "Now who's making promises they shouldn't keep?"

"I learned from the best." Her retort made him chuckle for real this time.

The ground beneath them shuddered, a distant reminder that they weren't safe. Not yet. Maybe never. But for this moment, suspended in darkness with his heat wrapping around her like a shield, she couldn't bring herself to move.

"We need to go," Akur rumbled again.

"I know." As she shifted up on his chest, the wet sensation of blood made her stomach clench. "But you're hurt."

"I heal fast."

"Not fast enough." Her fingers traced what felt like mangled flesh and bone on his shoulder, making him hiss. "And you're burning up again."

A light flickered to life by her side, the same little device he'd used before, and it cast an eerie glow across Akur's blood-streaked face. The sight made her breath catch. His normally teal skin was ashen, and fresh cuts marred his features. But it was his eyes that scared her the most—they were almost completely black, only a thin ring of amber visible around his pupils.

"Your eyes," she breathed, reaching up to touch his face. "They're different."

He caught her wrist before she could make contact. "Don't. Just holding you like this..." His jaw clenched again. He caught her wrist before she could make contact. "The heat...it's progressing faster than it should." He said it almost as if it was his life's greatest failure.

"Because you keep pushing yourself too hard...for me." The words burst out of her before she could stop them. "You're going to kill yourself, and for what? To save one human who's probably going to end up dead, anyway?"

His grip on her wrist tightened to the point of pain. "You are not going to die."

She yanked her hand free, anger and fear making her voice shake. "You can barely stand, you're bleeding everywhere, and your body temperature is high enough to cook your brain! And for what? Some promise you made to protect me? I never asked for that."

"No," he snarled. "You didn't ask. But I gave it anyway. And I will keep giving it until there is nothing left of me to give. And you...you're special."

"Special enough to die for?" The words came out bitter.

His eyes flashed, that ring of amber briefly flaring. "Special enough to *live* for."

The raw conviction in his voice struck her silent.

He meant it. This stubborn, infuriating alien warrior truly believed she was worth dying for. A bitter laugh escaped her lips.

"You're insane," she whispered, voice thick with unshed tears.

He didn't argue, didn't defend himself. He just looked at her, his eyes burning with an intensity that made her heart ache. They were trapped, surrounded by enemies, his body ravaged by injuries and consumed by an alien heat she couldn't comprehend. And yet, in that moment, all he seemed to care about was *her*.

Something snapped inside her. All the fear, the grief, the frustration—everything. Leaning forward, she didn't think. Didn't give herself a moment to pause. She kissed him again, pouring all of that fear, her gratitude, and something else burgeoning deep inside her into that single contact. It was a fierce, demanding claim, a silent plea for him to live.

For them both to survive this.

Akur groaned into her mouth, the sound a mixture of pain and surprise, just as his arms tightened around her. He held her like he was afraid to let go. She could feel the tremors running through him, even as he gripped her like she was the rock that could steady him.

Pulling back slightly, her gaze searched his. "We don't have to do that again, if you don't want to."

His teeth bared. "You have no idea what I want. What's quickly growing deep within me. You should run now, Constance, but not because there are enemies chasing us."

She swallowed, watching his features in the light's glow. "No."

"Stubborn."

"Yes." She leaned forward again. "There's another way. A way to… to ease your heat."

His eyes seemed to dilate even more, and she took a deep breath, ignoring the warmth rising in her cheeks.

"Let me help you."

A complex mix of emotions seemed to flit across his eyes—relief, gratitude, and a flicker of something…darker. He didn't speak, didn't need to. The answer was in his gaze, in the way his hand reached out, one finger tracing the line of her jaw. "And how will you help me, bright eyes?"

She took his hand, her fingers intertwining with his, and brought it to her waist, pressing it against the soft curve of her hip. "Help me," she whispered, her voice barely audible. "Please."

He groaned, a low, guttural sound that sent a shiver down her spine. His grip tightened on her hip, his fingers digging into her flesh, a possessive gesture that made her heart race.

She slid her hand lower, her fingers running from his chest to the lower part of his abdomen and then…against the hard ridge of his arousal. It was strange. Something so big shouldn't be able to hide, but it was like his cock appeared out of nowhere. He shuddered as her fingers brushed over him and she swallowed hard, looking up at him, their gazes locking as she traced the curve of his length.

He seemed to surrender. His eyes closed, his head falling back against the floor, his breath coming in ragged gasps. "Constance..."

She moved closer, her body pressing against his, her hand moving to release the clasp of his trouse. The moment it did and her fingers slid beneath the garment to touch his heated flesh, Akur hissed. He stiffened, his eyes flying open again.

"Just let me take care of you," she whispered. His throat moved as he watched her, those eyes consuming her as she wrapped her hand around his thick head. Rhythmically, gently at first, she moved her hand from the tip to as far down as she could go. Fuck, he was massive. Thick, girthy, wide enough that one hand wasn't enough. Grasping him with both, he hissed again, his hips shunting forward in a sharp jab. "That's it, big guy. Let me take care of you."

She whispered his name, and as she continued to touch him, to stroke him, to ease the fire that raged within him, she felt a shift in his energy, a release of tension, a slow, steady descent from the brink of chaos.

His breathing grew deeper, more even. Those eyes locked with hers as a silent gratitude, a silent understanding passed between them.

He reached out, cupping her face, his thumb brushing against her cheek, as his breaths came shorter. Looking into his eyes like this was intense. Almost as if they were sharing something deep. Something special. Something...inevitable.

As her rhythm increased, her touch growing bolder, she could feel him building, the heat radiating from him intensifying; the tremors running through his body growing stronger. A low growl rumbled in his chest, rivalling the shudder that went through the ground beneath them like a jarring reminder of the danger that still lurked.

She pumped harder, trying with all her mind to ignore the flutter that went through her center at just the sight of him, or how touching him like this was making her throb with a rhythm that matched the one she made.

"Akur," she whispered. "Come for me."

His hips bucked against her hands, his body tensing. He was close. So close.

Increasing her pace, her hands moving faster, her touch more insistent, she didn't know what she felt at first. Like a lump, a ridge moving up his smooth white shaft. Small, hard knots of pleasure that reacted under the pressure of her wrists to make him shunt even harder.

"Constance!!!" With a guttural cry, he shattered.

The first seed pod had her staring wide-eyed. It looked like a soft white berry, emerging from his tip a moment before it burst and another took its place. Her chest heaved, heavy breaths leaving her as she came face to face with the things that almost made her catatonic. The things that gave her the most pleasure she'd ever had in her life. The seed pods burst, one after another, spilling onto her hand, her wrist, her arm. A rush of heat, a tingling pleasure spread through her veins, making her gasp, her body arching involuntarily. It was intoxicating, addictive, a primal cocktail of alien hormones no doubt designed to bind mate to mate.

It wasn't even inside her, and she felt her own body react. Could feel her center swell and throb demanding to be touched. But not now. This was for him.

As the last few seed pods released, Akur collapsed, his body still trembling, his breath coming in gasps. The heat radiating from him was still intense, but the feverish edge was gone, replaced by a deep, satisfying warmth.

She continued to stroke him, gently now, soothingly, until no more seed pods emerged, until his body was still, his breathing even. Only then did she shift her gaze to his. His face was still pale, streaked with sweat, but his eyes...there was a tenderness there that made something in her chest spasm.

The ground shuddered again, a more violent tremor that sent dust and debris falling from the collapsed section not far behind them. They couldn't stay here. Not now.

"Akur," she whispered, fingers still gently gliding over his cock.

She tried not to stare at it. He was still hard, but they couldn't go again. Not here. Not now. "We need to go."

Looking up, they were in another tunnel, but this one seemed different. More like a corridor than anything else.

With a grunt, Akur reached down, his hand covering hers. The breath stopped in her nose as his touch sent a jolt of awareness through her. He guided her hand, slowly, deliberately, down the length of him, then back up, his touch firm, possessive. Her breath hitched again as she felt his hardened length press against her palm, the heat of him searing and yet attracting her like a moth to his flame.

He leaned into her touch, his eyes closing, a low groan rumbling in his chest as he pressed her hand harder, his fingers interlacing with hers, guiding her touch. "Constance." He did that guttural thing with her name again. "You tempt me." She could feel him hardening even more against her palm, when, with a groan, he shifted, his hips canting upwards. He guided her hand now, pushing it farther into his trouse to his sac, hung and tight. He shuddered again, as he pressed her hand there and she felt it, the place where his cock must have come from.

Her mouth went dry, her tongue coming out to lick her lips, neither of them looking away as he guided his cock using her hand, pushing himself back within that pouch.

"Thank you, bright eyes," he whispered as the final inch disappeared from her touch. Her throat felt like it was parched. She could only nod.

His throat moved too, before he nodded, pushing himself up, his movements still a little slow, but the feverish urgency was gone.

She helped him to his feet, shaking her head to dispel whatever spell had come over her. They were being chased, near death at every moment. She couldn't get caught up in—she glanced at him as he picked up his swords and re-sheathed them—whatever was growing between them.

"The map?" she shook her head again before her gaze fell on the device where it had landed on the floor. Its light was extinguished. She picked it up anyway.

"Useless now." Even his voice sounded stronger. That was good. Then why was there a strange feeling still at the center of her chest? Something that felt almost like sadness. Regret?

She wasn't sorry she fucked him or gave him a hand job. Heck, she'd give him a blowjob too, if that meant they'd survive this. So why...why was she sad?

"Which way then?" she asked, her voice barely a whisper.

Akur looked up, more like himself than before now. "We go forward." He gestured in front. There was another way to their right, but that was partially blocked off by fallen rocks and she wasn't in the mood to climb, either. The other direction it was then.

19

Akur

THEY WALKED IN SILENCE, him in front and the female who had just made him feel more than he ever had in sols behind. He tried not to glance over his shoulder at her too much, tried not to let his mind wander back to the way her hands had moved over him, sure and gentle despite her fear. But it wasn't just the physical release that haunted him—it was the look in her eyes. The way she'd touched him without revulsion. The way she'd whispered his name like it meant something.

His shoulder still ached, and his body temperature remained higher than normal, but the maddening edge of the heat had dulled to something manageable. Something he could think through. And think he did—too qrakking much. About how she'd known exactly what he needed. About how she'd seen him at his weakest and instead of running, she'd drawn closer.

Clenching his jaw, he forced his attention back to their surroundings. He was a warrior, trained to protect, to fight, to kill if necessary. He wasn't supposed to feel this...vulnerability. He'd thought Ajos a fool to have let something like feelings mar his objectives. But this...

whatever was happening was more than a growing need to protect the female at his back. He wanted to understand her. To know what made her smile despite their desperate circumstances, what gave her the strength to keep going when most would have broken.

It was strength like that which had kept him going at the darkest times. But she was no warrior. She didn't live for bloodshed and death. So...how...

The sound of her footsteps behind him was oddly comforting— steady, determined, trusting him to lead them to safety. That trust was a weight heavier than any battle armor he'd ever worn. Heavier still was the knowledge that he'd die before betraying it.

A particularly loud crunch of gravel under her feet made him glance back again, catching her eyes in the dim light. She offered him a small smile, and something in his chest constricted painfully. In that moment, he realized with stark clarity that his growing feelings for her had nothing to do with what had just happened between them. It wasn't about the heat, or physical release, or even gratitude. It was about her courage, her compassion, her fierce determination to survive without losing her humanity in the process.

His thoughts were so loud he almost didn't notice the moment his senses peaked. The moment he subconsciously stopped short, causing her to step into his back.

"Akur?" There was a note of uncertainty there, as if she expected to look around him and come face to face with another monster. But it wasn't a creature before them. It was something else.

Pods. Hundreds of them. Each one large enough to hold a being, their surfaces clouded with frost. Some were empty, their doors hanging open like dark, gaping pits. Others...

He heard Constance's sharp intake of breath the moment she looked around him.

"Are those..." She couldn't finish the question.

"Stasis chambers." Akur's growl echoed in the vast space. "This is...a storage facility."

Constance took a shaky step forward, drawn despite herself to the nearest occupied pod. She froze as she brushed the frost away to reveal a face.

The twisted remains of what had once been a Frenshuri. A female, from the looks of it. Akur growled, despite himself. His vision picked out details he wished he couldn't see—the surgical precision of the cuts, the missing organs, the look of terror forever frozen on the being's face. He'd seen this before, but never on this scale.

"They're all...dead?" Constance whispered beside him, and the horror in her voice made his protective instincts surge. "How long do you think they've been here?"

"Many many orbits." He moved closer to her, fighting the urge to shield her from the grotesque display with his own body. "That is a Frenshuri. Their world fell a long time ago. Long before mine." The cold emanating from the pods made his skin prickle, and he saw the moment Kon-stahns wrapped her arms around herself. He wanted to replace her arms with his. To pull her into him. Shield her from this sight and the cold. Shield her from everything. Qef. But he couldn't. She was a pretty little human, and he was a grotesque thing that fed on bloodshed and horror. She was only helping him because there was no other choice. She couldn't...didn't...a sweet soft thing like her couldn't want something like him.

"*They* did this. Experimented on these creatures..." She moved to another pod, brushing away the frost to reveal yet another being that was not a Frenshuri. This one he didn't even know, but it was in the same state. Still cut, still operated on, still dead in horror.

"The Tasqals take what they want from their victims, then store the remains. For study. For spare parts." The words came out as a growl, memories of his own people's suffering rising like bile in his throat. "All these females must have birthed Tasqal young."

Being in this room brought it all back—the screams that echoed across worlds where he'd fought against the Tasqals. The sickening efficiency with which they'd collected their "specimens." The way they'd sorted through the females, young ones and elders, like traders selecting produce.

And how he'd once been too young, too powerless to stop them.

Well, he wasn't a youngling anymore.

When she shifted to another pod, wiping away the frost with such reverence, such respect for the poor being lying dead in that tomb, something ached in his chest.

Standing in this massive crypt, the clarity of what would happen to Kon-stahns if he let the Tasqals win was crushing. The thought made his blood boil, made the lingering heat in his system spike dangerously. He wouldn't let them take her. He really would die first.

He watched her move from pod to pod, her small hand clearing away frost with the same gentleness he'd noticed before. But beneath that tenderness, he could see anger building in the rigid line of her spine, in the way her fingers curled into fists between each pod she examined.

"All these beings," she said, and he stood straighter. In all their time together, he'd never heard her voice so low. So dangerous. "All these lives. Mothers, daughters, sisters..." She turned to him, and the fury in her eyes matched the inferno in his blood. "The Tasqals didn't just kill them. They used them. Violated them."

He watched her, cataloging everything. "Yes," he said. "Many species have suffered from their menace. Many worlds have fallen. Many civilizations ruined. Even those that fought back and won."

Kon-stahns turned. "Won? Some people won?"

Qrak, why was he about to tell her this? He didn't talk about this. He had to pause. "When the Tasqals came to Tonvuhiri, they couldn't take us down. So they tried to weaken us. Barred the trade routes. Left us to starve...and the fear spread like a disease."

Constance stepped forward, her hand finding his arm. The touch anchored him, pulled him back from the edge of old nightmares. "But you survived," she whispered. "You grew stronger. And now you're fighting back."

He looked down at her hand on his arm, so small against his scorching skin, yet containing more strength than she knew. "We all fight back," he rumbled. "Or they will never stop."

She pulled away, but not before giving his arm a squeeze that sent warmth through his chest. Moving to the center of the chamber, she surveyed the pods with new purpose. Her shoulders squared, chin lifting in that way he'd come to recognize—the calm before her storm.

A slow smile stretched his lips, even before she turned to face him.

"You know what?" Despite everything, despite the horror and death surrounding them, his lips curved into that smile too. "I think it's time these bastards learned what happens when you piss off the wrong people."

The look in her eyes, the steel in her voice—it stirred something in him. Not the heat-madness from before, but something deeper. Something that made him want to follow her into whatever hell she planned to raise.

"Come on, Mint Man," she said, her smile growing wider. There was hope yet. There was always hope. "Let's go cause some chaos."

20

Akur

AKUR WATCHED Constance move through the chamber. Could almost see the wheels turning in her head. It was entrancing. She was like a hunter now. Scheming. Planning.

Delicious.

It made him wonder what she might have been like on her planet, Er'th. Did humans adapt so easily on their own world? Did they fight wars or were they peaceful? He didn't imagine her kind being nothing more than a herd species living in communal settings that fostered peace and tranquility. But seeing her now, he might have been wrong.

She tilted her head, looking around the dim cavernous room. "Think you can find the door? There must be a way out."

True. But that was the least of his concern. He wasn't worried about getting out. He'd break himself again by slamming through the wall just to set her free. Getting out wasn't a problem. It's what might get in. The Hedgeruds chasing them must know where they ended up.

Flexing the muscles in his back, he ignored the tenderness of his nefre as he rolled his neck. The pressure of his heat, though tempered, was like a constant annoying ache that made him plant his feet into the dusty floor beneath them.

"Only, we don't even know where we are, do we?" Constance bit her lip and his cock throbbed in its pouch where he'd tucked it away —where he'd used *her* hands to tuck it away. He shouldn't have done that. The sensation of her soft flesh touching him there had been torture in itself.

"The map is dead and we could be walking straight into a nest of those assholes." She paced, worrying her lip again as her brow furrowed. His tunic that she wore swayed as she walked. It swallowed her, and still it was as if he could see every line and curve of her body.

Qrak.

She'd helped him twice now and still he wanted more. Only, he wasn't sure it was the heat causing him to watch her so closely...to remember the way she'd felt...

"There has to be a control center." Her words floated to him through the growing haze. She was moving around the pods now, examining them. "There must be something managing the power distribution here. Life support...Well, if they were alive, that is." Her fingers moved over one pod with surprising confidence. "There must be something that's kept these things running."

He almost whimpered, barely kept it silent as he moved. Why the qrak was he ready again so soon? He'd just released. It should be enough to—qrak, it should just be enough.

Forcing himself to move closer, he scanned the chamber with new purpose. She was right. The pods weren't arranged randomly. They followed a pattern, all connected to central conduits that disappeared into the walls. Following one such conduit with his eyes, he spotted something.

"There." He gestured to a recessed door nearly hidden behind a cluster of empty pods. "Must be maintenance access."

The door was sealed, of course, its control panel dark, but that hardly mattered. After what he'd just done to the tunnel wall, a simple door wouldn't stop him. But as he stepped forward to break it down, Kon-stahns caught his arm.

"Wait." She headed over to the panel, studying its dead display. "If the pods have power, this should, too. We just need to..." Her fingers slipped over the display, removing the dirt laden frost. "It's been awfully quiet in here so far, and I don't trust it. We just need to find a way in without destroying the thing and causing an alarm."

Fine. But he really needed to smash something. His shoulder was already stitching itself back and the reducing pain was only making him focus more on that hard, painful thing between his thighs.

"Let me," he growled, stepping in front of Kon-stahns. It took him a few moments to find what he was looking for, and suddenly the display flickered to life.

Kon-stahns stared at him. "How did you—"

"The Restitution uses similar tech in some areas." He was already working the controls, all the while trying not to look down at the female whose face was now lit by the light from the panel. "Different language. Same basic principles. Power routing, emergency protocols..." A smile curved his lips as the door slid open with a soft hiss. "And manual overrides."

She patted him on the back, and he froze. Qrak. Did she have any idea how her touch sent lightning through his veins? "A jack of all trades. I guess I shouldn't be surprised at what you can do anymore."

Well, she should be surprised at what he *wanted* to do. If she knew, she wouldn't be standing so close to him.

Constance peered ahead, and he pushed the thoughts from his mind as best as he could.

The maintenance tunnel beyond was narrow but lit, emergency strips casting everything in harsh shadows. Turning off his light disc, he tucked it back into his pocket as he jerked his chin at the female at his side. "Ready, bright eyes?"

He saw her swallow hard. Saw the moment where she took a deep breath before nodding. "Ready."

Akur took point, moving silently. Every few steps he paused, listening for any sign of others, but the only sounds were their breathing and the distant hum going through the power systems.

The corridor branched ahead, one path sloping up while the other continued level. Without the map, they were flying blind, but his instincts told him to go up. They must be near the citadel now, and that meant civilization was somewhere above them.

They crept forward, taking the upward path. The tunnel grew progressively brighter, emergency lighting giving way to actual illumination panels set into the walls.

"We're getting closer to populated areas," Akur whispered, his voice barely a breath. Every few steps he paused, head tilted as he listened intently.

Constance kept close behind him, and it was clear she was trying to match his silent movements. She was small. Light on her feet. But the brightness was concerning. It meant they were more likely to encounter others.

A distant metallic clang made them both freeze. Without a thought, his hand shot out, pressing the female against the wall as heavy footsteps echoed down an adjoining corridor. Two Hedgerud guards appeared, and his lips immediately pulled back in a snarl.

He hated nothing more than he hated the Tasqals and their minions.

It took everything not to draw his blades, but he was already reaching back for one. If those Hedgeruds looked down the corridor they were in, they were in deep excrement.

But the fools kept on walking.

"...searching the lower levels for that jerkin and the nuisance with her," one was saying. "No sign of them yet."

"Keep looking. The High Ones want the human alive."

He didn't realize he was still pressing Constance back until she touched his arm lightly. That bare touch sent a shiver through his entire being.

"We should keep going," she whispered. "We're like sitting ducks here."

He didn't know what she meant about sitting and ducking, but if she meant they needed to remain low and hidden, then bin-qeffing-go. That was the name of the game. "We need to move faster."

They pressed on, more urgently now, until the corridors began showing signs of regular use—cleaner floors, maintained lighting, occasional doorways leading to what looked like storage areas and machinery rooms.

The air itself smelled tainted. Filled with scents of the species he'd dedicated his existence to eradicating.

Nearing another junction, he suddenly went rigid. Reaching back, he pulled Constance into his spine. There, ahead, was the distinct sound of multiple beings approaching from two directions. He could tell the moment she heard them, too. The slight stiffening of her soft body. The way her breath held.

Qrak. They were right out in the open.

"Akur." A harsh whisper against his back. "We have to go back." He could feel her twisting against the pressure of his arm around her. "There!"

Looking over his shoulder, he saw what she was pointing to. A door set in the wall a few strides down. His jaw ticked. He didn't know if that door opened up to more enemies. Closing his eyes for a moment, he tried to clear his head. To think! But at least this heat wasn't only a hindrance, it enhanced his senses, too. Because he could smell them.

There were probably three Hedgeruds approaching from the corridor to the right. Another four from the corridor to the left. And a —disgust made him snarl—a Tasqal was with them.

"Akur!" Constance whispered at his back. This was urgent. He had to move.

Cursing under his breath, he backtracked, tugging her with him. The door opened, and they slid into the darkness moments before being seen. The room was empty. Small. Used for maintenance, maybe.

Their bodies pressed tight as the heavy footsteps approached. The door was only slightly ajar, a thin crack he could see through. He reached for the hilt of his blade once more.

Wide blue eyes were focused on that crack in the door as Constance's life organ thundered against his chest, but she remained perfectly still, barely breathing. The patrol of Hedgeruds passed within inches of their hiding spot. The fools were so painfully unaware, but he supposed that was working well in their favor.

"The High Ones grow impatient," one guard growled. "If we don't find them soon…"

"We'll find the jekin and the rebel. The tunnels are sealed. They have nowhere to go."

One of the other guards hissed. "We already brought them *one* human. The other in the tunnels should be left to die. It is dark and musty down there. And those tunnel dwellers—oi!"

A sharp crack into his snout made him stumble. The Hedgerud that hit him snarled before walking again. "They don't want that human. I heard my master saying she is useless."

One of the others grunted. "Then maybe they should give her to us. If they don't want the jekin, we could use her…"

His claw tightened even more on his blade when Kon-stahns' breath hitched at their words. The Hedgeruds were annoying pieces of scum that only deserved to be crushed underneath his boot.

Time seemed to still as the fiends took their time walking down the corridor. As their footsteps faded, Constance released a shaky breath, practically melting against him. He bit his tongue in an effort to not wince. Everything hurt, and it wasn't a pain he was used to. "That was close."

"Too close." His eyes narrowed as he scanned the corridor. "They're increasing patrols. We need to move faster."

Slipping from the tight little room, Constance took the lead now, creeping through the corridor.

She was remarkably silent. Remarkably fast, too. Which idiot on the Restitution spread the rumor that these females were soft, prey things that cowered at the least sight of struggle? He watched as her head tilted, catching any sound before she'd peek her head around the corner when they came to a junction. Then she was darting across the gap, confident he'd follow.

And he did.

Soon, he was watching her more than the way ahead.

Soon, she was all he could see.

But this needed to stop. He needed to get her out of this place.

They pressed on, each step bringing them closer to what he hoped was the citadel proper. The maintenance tunnels gave way to wider corridors, the stark utilitarian design replaced by the Tasqals' preference for grandiose architecture. The ceiling soared overhead, support columns carved with the Tasqals' likenesses that seemed to watch their progress.

"I don't like this," Constance whispered. "It feels like we're being herded again."

He grunted in agreement. The lack of resistance was making his battle instincts scream. "Stay alert. They—"

A door hissed open ahead, the sound cutting off the words in his throat. He could hear the breath rush into her nose as he yanked Constance behind a column as three Tasqals emerged, their white robes billowing. Unlike the Tasqal who'd helped them, these ones bore themselves with regal arrogance, their diseased faces proudly displayed.

Pressing into the column, they had no choice but to face the massive window beside them. Below, the citadel's grounds stretched far and wide. A sprawling fountain dominated the courtyard. Hundreds of Tasqals milled around its edges, their white robes matching the white stone. He could tell the moment Kon-stahns saw them and the moment she saw the other thing that had caught his attention.

A sprawling complex dominated the eastern quarter—all sharp angles and gleaming metal. Massive ventilation towers released controlled bursts of steam. Countless Hedgeruds in protective gear moved between buildings, pushing hover carts loaded with sealed containers. Armed Hedgeruds patrolled the perimeter, their weapons trained, ever vigilant. It made his brow tighten. Whatever they manufactured there, they guarded it with paranoid dedication.

"The device is almost ready." The Tasqals in the corridor were speaking. Bubbles popped as one laughed. "Once a human's consciousness is properly connected..."

"And what of the broken one, my pleasure?" That one was female. It always sickened him how they spoke.

"That creature is useless. Her mind is too fractured to provide a path to her kind. Navigation data."

"Then let us put it where it will be most useful, my pleasure. Beneath your strong thighs, fostering a youngling for you and me."

More bubbles popped and he must have tensed because in his arms, Constance looked up at him. She reached up, touching his jaw, her fingers splaying over his heated skin. And in that touch was something he didn't expect to find.

Peace. Calm.

Qrak. Her touch rivaled the thirst for making those fiends bleed.

But even with that, he could feel her muscles coil. She wanted to end these creatures, too and, gods knew, he couldn't believe he was holding her back.

Because they couldn't do anything now. Not yet. Not when they were so exposed.

The Tasqals passed, their conversation fading, but the tension remained. Constance was trembling slightly, whether from rage or fear he couldn't tell.

"We'll find your comrade," he promised quietly. "But we need to be smart about this."

"I know." Her voice was tight as she stared at the strange building with the Hedgeruds guarding it. "This is their world. There are no threats to them here. What could they be guarding like that?"

"Not guarding. Making." His brow tightened more. "That's a manufacturing plant."

He swore she shivered a little.

"Let's go." She was already moving, but he tightened his arms around her. "Even I know the chance of making it out there is next to nil."

"I know," she whispered again. When her gaze shifted to the door the Tasqals just exited from, he felt his life organ wither a little in his chest. "Whatever device they were referring to could be in there. The device that will use the orb." Her gaze shifted back to the window and to that strange building. "Or there. We have to choose and we can't make it out there so…"

Both their breaths were coming tight, strained through their chests, and yet the room beckoned like a trap. As he released her, his gaze slid back to that factory they could see. He'd bet his nefre and his seed sac that whatever was in there would help them win this war. But he wasn't budging when he said they wouldn't make it. His priority right now was getting Kon-stahns off this planet.

"We can't ignore what we just heard." Constance's throat moved even as she took a step toward the door. His hand shot out, gripping her arm. *Where did she find this bravery? This recklessness?* He almost grinned. Gods, she was infuriating. Was this what she meant when she called him stubborn? Or had she been viewing her reflection in a looking glass?

"Wait," he growled softly. "If that device is in there…"

"Then we need to destroy it," she finished. "Before they can use it to hurt more people."

His jaw clenched as he studied her determined expression. She didn't have to tell him twice. If she wasn't here, he wouldn't have been creeping through these corridors. He'd have been loud and proud, letting instinct take over as he bathed himself in their lifeblood.

But that wasn't reality.

Reality was that she was here. And everything in him screamed to get her to safety first. He'd put her on that ship. Get her out of here. He couldn't make a mistake when they were so deep in enemy territory now.

"Five clicks," he conceded. "We look, we assess, we leave. No heroics."

A ghost of a smile touched her lips. "Says the warrior who broke through a wall with nothing but his shoulder."

"That wasn't heroics. That was necessity." Checking the corridor, he tucked her to him as he slipped across the space to the other side, right in front of the door. It opened without protest and he gripped his blades again, ready.

But...inside was silent.

The chamber beyond was vast, its high ceiling lost in shadows despite the harsh lighting below. Cold white slabs filled the space. But it wasn't the sight or the strange coldness in the room that made them freeze.

Before he could even stop her, Kon-stahns was moving. Her shoulders shook as she stared down at the female lying motionless on top of the slab. He didn't need to move closer to see that it was a human. Dead, like all the other females on slabs in this room.

A strangled sob tore from Kon-stahns' throat, and something inside him broke. His grip on his blades tightened, but for the first time in his life, the familiar urge to kill wasn't enough. He lowered the weapons, the tips clinking softly against the smooth floor in their uselessness.

Violence wouldn't fix this. Couldn't erase what they were seeing.

Without conscious thought, he moved toward her. He didn't know how to comfort—he knew how to fight, how to kill, how to conquer. But watching her shoulders shake, hearing those quiet, broken sounds... His body seemed to know what to do, even if his mind didn't. He positioned himself behind her, close enough that she could feel his presence, but not so close as to crowd her grief.

"I'm..." What should he say? "I'm here, bright eyes," he said roughly, the words feeling strange on his tongue. "You don't have to face this alone."

His life organ clenched as she turned to him, waters streaming down her face. The fading bruises on her jaw, the scrapes along her temple, the dried blood at the corner of her mouth—they should have made her look broken. Weak. Instead, they were badges of everything she'd survived. Everything she'd fought through. Even now, with the eye waters cutting tracks through the dirt on her face, she stood straight-backed before horror. Where his people would have channeled grief into rage, she let herself feel it fully while refusing to let it break her.

He'd never seen strength like that before.

As she wrapped her arms around him, pressing her face into his chest, he couldn't help but hold her. She stirred something protective and fierce inside him. Something that made him want to shelter her from more pain, even as he respected her strength in facing it.

It was while holding her, his attention split between her quiet grief and scanning the room for threats, that he saw it. His instincts hadn't abandoned him even in this moment. Because there, across the room, something caught his eye. Something that made his muscles tense, even as he tried not to alert her.

"No," he whispered, but Constance didn't hear. Wiping her eyes, she whispered gratitude before turning back to the slabs. Moving from one to the other, she began checking the bodies for what he assumed was a pulse.

"They're all dead," she whispered, still moving from one to another. "And it's strange...but..." She paused, focusing on one of the bodies as he took a step closer to what had caught his attention. "Their eyes are all open...their irises completely white, Akur. Like marble. Their mouths are all open, too. I've never...I've never seen anything like this before. It's like they were all killed by the same thing in the same way...but there are no wounds. Just...just terror. F-frozen in their eyes."

He was still moving closer to that thing across the room, his own horror mounting. "What about the human the Tasqals brought here? The one that was on the vessel with you. Is she..."

"No." Constance was still moving from slab to slab. "The silent woman...I don't see her. I can't find her, Akur."

But he couldn't even respond. For there, in the corner of the room, suspended in a complex framework of metal and crackling energy, was a being he never expected to see here. Tall and ethereal, the markings that etched all across the being's skin seemed to shimmer with its own inner light. Delicate tendrils of the being's hair floated around its head as if suspended in water, even though he was not.

Kon-stahns was suddenly at his side. "I don't see her. She's not here. But that's good, right? That means..." she trailed off. He could almost sense the alarm go through her as she stood staring at the being before them. "What is that?"

"An Arois," he breathed, his voice tight with recognition and something else. Rage? "They have an Arois."

The male's eyes were closed, his face serene despite the dozens of nodes attached to his body. Each node pulsed with a sickly green light that seemed to draw something from the Arois' body, making his skin fluctuate between brightness and shadow. At the center of his forehead, the gem that all Arois have was dull. Unlit.

"What are they doing to him?" Kon-stahns whispered. The horror was evident in her voice.

Akur swallowed hard, forcing his eyes closed as he tried to temper the rising emotions in him. Fight. Kill. Fuhk. Everything was like a concoction ready to make him drunk.

He forced his gaze to the females dead on the slabs. None of them had swollen bellies. And with Kon-stahns' observations—the white eyes, the open mouths, the lack of wounds or those sickening pustules that plagued the Tasqals... These humans weren't used for breeding. They were used for something else.

The moment his gaze shifted back to the Arois, a horrible feeling developed in his gut.

He only knew one Arois. His name was Yce and the qeffer was a powerful being no one should ever cross.

"The Arois are psychic," Akur explained quietly as they moved closer. "The strongest telepaths in known space. We have one on the Restitution. They're peaceful, but their abilities..." He shook his head. "This is wrong. This is so wrong."

The Arois didn't respond to their presence, but something about his face suggested awareness. Pain, perhaps, or resignation.

"Why would they have a psychic here?" Kon-stahns turned, gaze scanning the room once more. "In this room, with these women. And that device they were talking about..."

He could sense her scanning the room for it, even as his focus remained on the Arois.

"It's him." His utterance was a whisper colder than the room's frigid air. "They're using him." The reality of how much they didn't know was crashing down just as a sudden noise at the door made them both spin.

As the door opened, Akur moved without thought.

A Tasqal stood at the entrance, its bulbous eyes widening in surprise before narrowing with cruel delight.

In one fluid motion, Akur crossed the room, his grip on the creature before the door closed and he slammed the Tasqal against the wall. One hand covering the Tasqal's mouth while the other pressed a blade to its throat.

"Signal for help," Akur growled, "and I'll separate your head from your body."

The Tasqal's eyes darted between them, lingering on Kon-stahns in a way that made his rage rise. There was something possessive in that gaze, something that spoke of intentions that made him want to send his blade home without this stupid hesitation.

But he couldn't be rash. He had to think about her. He had to get her to safety.

"So...this is where you are," the Tasqal gurgled. "Those fools have greatly underestimated you, rebel."

Akur growled. He couldn't even speak. Qrak. He couldn't even see. Rage was blinding him.

The sound of bubbles popping filled the air. "The Restitution is dead. You are too late, rebel."

Kon-stahns appeared by his arm, a snarl on her lips, too. "Too late for *what*? What have you been planning? Why are the women in this room lying dead with no visible wounds? Why do you have a psychic tied up here?"

The Tasqal stared at her. Its black tongue slipped out, running across its lips as it watched her. "You dare speak directly to me, a High Tasqal... I will enjoy seeding you, little one."

A sharp crack echoed through the chamber. The Tasqal's head snapped to the side, its body momentarily frozen. There was a flicker of surprise, quickly masked by a cold fury in its eyes, a dangerous fire ignited by Kon-stahns' audacious slap. The Tasqal lifted a hand to its jaw, its digits tracing the spot, a chilling smile spreading across its lips. "Spirited," it hissed. "I will break you yet, little human. And then...I will seed you."

That's it. Why even let this scum breathe?

Akur's blade slid into skin and he watched the Tasqal's lifeblood coat the metal, his eyes locked with his enemy's before a soft hand stopped his arm.

"Wait," Kon-stahns said. "Don't kill him yet."

A wet sound released from the scum as more bubbles popped.

"My patience has never been more tried than on this mission."

She actually smiled. "And all for me." She squeezed his arm before turning her attention back to the Tasqal. "Where's the machine?" she stepped closer. "The one that controls the orb?"

The Tasqal's eyes widened a fraction, a subtle flicker of surprise it couldn't quite suppress. It recovered quickly, its expression hardening into a mask of disdain. "You seem remarkably well-informed for a... captive," it sneered. "Who told you of our plans?"

Constance's lips pulled back in a snarl that made him proud. "Akur," her eyes narrowed. "Kill him."

The Tasqal winced, its bravado faltering in the face of imminent death.

Qrak, he could press his mouth against Kon-stahns' again. Rejoice in her intelligence. Because if it's one thing these scum didn't like, it was facing death. That was the whole reason they destroyed so many lives. In a desperate bid for their own survival.

"Such a primitive thing, asking such obvious questions," the Tasqal said. "Did you think we needed a machine to bridge the gap between worlds?" Its eyes fixed on Kon-stahns again, that malicious glee returning. "The Arois is our bridge. They are powerful. So powerful, this one's mind spans the gap between dimensions, and through him, we'll reach across the void."

Akur stiffened, as did Kon-stahns. "Reach across space?" she whispered.

Bubbles popped as the Tasqal laughed. It felt like the world slowed down.

How did the Restitution not know? What else did they not know? All this time they had been fighting, thinking they were getting somewhere, and the Tasqals had been leagues ahead.

"The orb," he breathed, the horrifying realization dawning. "They won't use it to go to your world."

Kon-stahns blinked. "I don't understand."

"They'll use it to create some kind of... gateway." He breathed hard, fighting the heat that was qrakking rising again at the worst possible time. "They'll use it to create a gateway," he glanced over his shoulder at the Arois. "Through him."

In the silence, the Tasqal's entire body shook, bubbles popping as it laughed harder. "You Shum'ai aren't as dumb as you look," he said. "You have our orb, but once we retrieve it, you will not stop us." Its eyes glazed over as if it was seeing a pleasant dream in the back of its head. "Soon, thousands of humans will simply...appear. Pulled by the power of the orb and our very own Arois servant. They will come right here in our citadel. Ready for processing, for breeding, for—"

"That's not going to happen."

"Over my dead body."

He and Kon-stahns spoke at the same time, a moment before the Tasqal sobered, a strange look coming into its eyes. When its hand shot out, reaching for a panel on the wall, Akur's blade moved in a flash of silver. The Tasqal slumped, its final breath escaping in a wet bubble.

"Qrak!" Akur snarled, letting the body fall. "We need to—"

A sound from the Arois made them both turn. Though the male's eyes remained closed, his face contorted in obvious distress. The nodes were pulsing faster now, the green light becoming more intense.

"Can we free him?" But he was already moving to examine the framework before Constance's words passed her lips. The complexity of the framework was beyond anything he'd ever seen. "These restraints, the nodes—his gem isn't lit. If I unplug him, I'm not sure what that might do to him."

A new tension filled the air, an electric sensation that made his skin prickle. The Arois' face tightened further, and somewhere in the distance, alarms blared.

Turning to face Kon-stahns, he sheathed his blade. "We need to move." Leaving the Arois felt wrong, but staying meant her capture or death.

Kon-stahns stared at the suffering being. He could see her mind racing. See the moment she realized there was nothing they could do. That they had to run.

As he snatched his blaster from his hip and handed it to her, the door burst open, and chaos erupted.

21

Constance

THE BLASTER FELT heavy in her hand as Hedgeruds poured through
the doorway. Everything happened at once—the thundering of
clawed toes, shouts echoing off cold walls, the sickening whine of
energy weapons charging.

Her body jolted as she dove behind a slab just before blaster shots
seared the air where she'd stood. Her heart slammed against her ribs
as she gripped the weapon, trying to remember how she'd used it the
last time. The sound of metal meeting flesh made her peek around
the edge of the slab.

Akur moved like liquid death.

His blades caught the harsh lighting as he spun, ducked, and
slashed through the first wave of guards. He was poetry in motion,
each movement precise and deadly. Two Hedgeruds fell before they
could even raise their weapons, dark blood spraying across pristine
white floors.

But more were coming.

Forcing down her fear, she squeezed the trigger. The blaster
kicked harder than she remembered, but her shot caught a guard in

the chest just as he was aiming at Akur's back. The Hedgerud went down with a gurgling cry.

"Nice shot!" Akur called out, his voice tight with battle fury as he engaged three more guards at once.

She didn't have time to feel proud. More blaster shots scorched past her position, forcing her to scramble to another slab. The acrid smell of burnt flesh filled her nostrils as shots impacted around her, hitting the bodies of women she had no name for. Women that could have been her, or her mother, her sisters, her friends...

Their sacrifice only made it more important that she survived. Her gaze shot to the Arois in the background. He was silent now. His face an unreadable mask as if he was completely unconscious again.

She made a silent promise that he would be saved, too. One way or the other, this would end.

"We need to get to the door!" she shouted, firing again. This shot went wide, but it made two Hedgeruds dive for cover.

Akur's response was a primal roar as he picked up one guard and threw him into two others. The tangle of bodies crashed into a medical console, sparks flying. But even as they fell, more rushed in to take their place.

The room was too exposed. They needed to move.

Constance's hands were steadier now as she fired again. Fuck this. Fuck the Tasqals. Fuck these gator-guards. Fuck everything. She fired again, trying to keep the guards from completely surrounding them. But her shots were growing more desperate as the enemy pressed closer. There were just too many.

A plasma bolt grazed her arm and she bit back a cry of pain. Before she could even process the injury, a massive hand grabbed her shoulder and yanked her back.

"Stay behind me!" Akur growled, his massive frame shielding her as he parried a guard's blade thrust. The clash of metal on metal rang out as he knocked the weapon aside and drove his own blade up under the Hedgerud's chin.

They were being pushed back toward the corner where the Arois hung suspended. Panic clawed at her throat. They needed an exit. Now.

Her eyes darted around wildly until they landed on a grate on the floor, but it was past a group of those fucking Hedgehogs. Hope flared in her chest, anyway.

"Akur! The vent!" She pointed with her blaster even as she fired again, dropping another guard.

He saw it immediately. Without warning, his arm wrapped around her waist and he practically threw her behind him as he charged the line of guards blocking their path. His blades became silver arcs of death, cutting through armor and flesh with terrifying efficiency.

She provided what cover she could, but her hands were shaking again. Not from fear this time—from awe. Blood sprayed across his chest. Blood hit her too, but he never slowed.

When the path was momentarily clear, she ran for the vent, digging her fingers in as she tugged on it. "Fuck! Come on!" she screamed, just as blaster fire exploded against the wall above her head. At the same moment, the panel came loose, and she looked back to see Akur engaging what had to be six guards at once.

"Now!" he roared.

She dove into the vent shaft headfirst, the metal cool against her palms as she scrambled forward. Behind her, she heard more fighting, more screams.

"Come on," she whispered. He had to make it. He had to make it, too. "Come on!"

A flash of teal made her heart leap. The shaft shuddered as Akur forced his massive frame through the opening.

"Go go go!"

Blaster fire followed them into the shaft, the heat intense enough to make the air so hot it was uncomfortable to breathe. Crawling as fast as she could, she tried to ignore the sounds of pursuit echoing through the metal tunnel. "Just keep swimming. Just keep swimming."

"Your sense of humor evades me, bright eyes."

She choked on a laugh, pushing forward even though her injured arm trembled with each movement. She was bleeding badly. She could even smell it.

"Left at the junction," Akur called from behind her, his voice tight. "We need to get above this level."

How did he even know?

Didn't matter. She trusted him with her life.

She took the turn, grateful for the slope that led upward. The shaft was narrowing though, and she could hear Akur grunting, just to push through.

"Are you okay?" she called back.

"Forget about me. Just keep moving!"

Rich words coming from a male that kissed her breath away in protest of her saying the same thing. But the urgency in his voice made her push harder, ignoring the burning in her muscles. They couldn't get trapped in here. The sound of pursuit was only growing louder.

Blaster fire erupted again. Akur grunted. Pretty sure he'd been hit. The air heated once more, enough to make the metal shaft hot to the touch. She bit back a cry and kept crawling.

"Almost there," Akur growled. "I can smell fresher air ahead."

She wanted to ask how he could smell anything over the scent of blood and burns, but another shot forced her to focus on movement. Up ahead, she could see light filtering through another vent cover.

When she reached it, she paused, breaths coming hard. "Sorry, big guy." There wasn't time to explain. Pressing down, her feet found his shoulders as she braced on him for support. Two hard pushes and the metallic cover gave way with a shriek.

It felt like a truck was pushing her from behind as she tumbled out into a wider corridor. Akur exploded from the shaft behind her, spinning to face the opening with blades ready.

The first guard to emerge got a blade through his throat for his trouble. The second fired his weapon, but Akur was already moving. His other blade found the guard's neck as plasma scorched the wall.

More were coming. They could hear them in the shaft and down the other side of the corridor.

"Run!" Akur grabbed her hand, his touch scorching almost as bad as the blaster fire. Her shoulder ached and her arms felt like she'd put her skin over a flame. But pain could wait.

Turning a bend, her heart stuttered in her chest as they nearly collided with a group of Tasqals gliding down the corridor. Six of them, their robes pristine and faces serene—until they registered what they were seeing.

One opened its mouth, hand rising in indignation. "Halt, you degenerate!"

Akur didn't even pause. His blade flashed out in an arc, nearly taking the Tasqal's head clean off as they charged through. The Tasqal's body hit the floor with a wet thud, but they kept running.

Risking a glance back, she saw the remaining Tasqals pressed against the walls. Their previous composure shattered as they stared at their dead companion.

As they sprinted down the corridor, shouts and heavy footfalls echoed off the walls as guards poured from other passages to come after them.

Her lungs burned as they ran, but she forced herself to keep pace with Akur's longer stride. The corridor seemed endless, branching off in multiple directions. Some had Tasqals down them. Some had gator-guards searching for them. Others were empty. They took turns at random, trying to lose their pursuers, but the sounds of pursuit never faded completely.

"We have to find it," she gasped out between breaths. "We have to find that ship the Tasqal told us about."

Akur's response was cut off by blaster fire from ahead. They'd run right into another patrol.

Without breaking stride, he yanked her behind him and charged. His blades flashed once, twice, and two guards fell. But more were coming from behind.

Constance spun and fired, her shot catching a guard in the leg. As he fell, she saw something that made her blood run cold—a Tasqal gliding down the corridor behind the guards, its white robes billowing.

This one was bigger than any other Tasqal she'd come in close contact with so far. And the look on its face, even with the distance, was clear. Fury. Pure, cold fury. "Get them, you useless fools!" it screamed. "Do not let them leave the citadel!"

"Akur!" The panic in her voice made him turn. His eyes narrowed at the sight of their real enemy approaching.

"This way!" He kicked open a door and pulled her through into what looked like...oh fuck. Her stomach churned. Bile actually rose, and she threw up on the door.

The chamber was stacked with bodies all in various stages of decay, and all covered with the same large pustules that fill the Tasqals' skin. Their abdomens distended where the Tasqal's parasitic offspring incubated. Some victims still had expressions of agony frozen on their faces, a testament to their final moments.

They had barely made it halfway across the room when the door on the far side burst open. More guards poured in, weapons raised.

"Surrender," one of them growled. "You cannot escape."

Akur's only response was a savage laugh that would have sent chills down her spine had she not known him. His blades twirled once, catching the light. "Come then. Let me show you how a Shum'ai warrior dies."

The air crackled as Constance raised her blaster, back-to-back with Akur as they turned in a slow circle. Her hands were steady now, despite the horror surrounding them.

"You got me, warrior?"

"I've always got you, bright eyes."

She grunted a harsh laugh that felt like it scraped against her dry throat. Because they were trapped. There was no getting out of this. And this moment, unlike all the others, this moment might well be their last.

"I won't let them take me alive," she whispered, just loud enough for Akur to hear. "I won't end up like..." Her eyes flicked to the bodies around them.

"You won't," Akur's voice was steel and silk. "Not while I draw breath."

She only knew the first guard lunged because Akur's muscles flexed at her back. He met them with a brutal efficiency that would have been beautiful if it wasn't so deadly. In the corner of her eye, another moved and her finger depressed the trigger, firing into the group at her side. Everything slowed down. The movement of Akur's blades, the blaster fire as she gritted her teeth and pumped out shot after shot.

Blaster fire filled the air as more guards poured in through both doors. They had no choice but to break apart. Losing Akur's warmth feeling like it took a piece of her heart along with it. Time still moved in milliseconds as she spun and rolled out of the way of a lunging gator-guard. Her injured arm screamed in protest as she pumped the trigger till the blaster began burning.

There were too many of them.

For a moment, in all the chaos, she looked up and saw Akur fighting in a sea of enemies. Fighting for them all. Fighting for *her*.

"Constance!" His wild eyes darted to where he'd seen her last, and she saw the moment he realized she wasn't there.

In that fleeting moment, she saw something in his eyes that made her breath catch in her throat. It wasn't just concern. Not just protectiveness. It was...fear. Raw, unadulterated fear. Fear for *her*.

He'd been so careful, so guarded. But now, she could see it as clear as day. The thought of her lost, of her taken, had shattered his mask, revealing the depth of his...caring. The male she saw now was the male that had jumped out of a ship in space and come after her. This wasn't just a job or some mission he had to complete.

It went past that.

Akur cared.

He cared more than he'd ever let on.

The moment passed, his gaze shifting as his head lowered.

And then he changed.

The controlled, efficient warrior vanished, replaced by something wild, something...feral. His movements became a blur of motion, his blades flashing like lightning, a whirlwind of death and destruction.

He roared, a guttural sound that echoed through the chamber, a challenge to any who dared to stand in his way. He was a force of nature, a whirlwind of Shum'ai fury unleashed. A beast, driven by instinct, by a primal need to protect what was his. And in that moment, she knew, with a certainty that defied logic, that she was... she was his.

When three guards rushed him at once, he caught the first one's blade on his own, kicked the second in the chest with enough force to collapse his ribs, but the third sliced across his chest. Dark blood spattered the floor.

Constance's heart nearly stopped.

"No!" The word tore from her throat as she broke cover, firing rapidly. Her shots caught the third guard in the back of the head just as he was raising his blade for another strike.

"Constance." The way Akur uttered her name, almost like a whisper, was so soft she didn't know how she heard it. Her eyes filled with tears as their gazes locked.

Akur's roar of rage echoed off the walls as he fought his way toward her. But there were too many. The gator-guards kept pouring in like an infestation. Blood ran freely down his chest now, like someone had opened a spigot and refused to shut it off.

"Akur," her throat felt choked, even though she refused to let the tears fall. But she couldn't even say it. Couldn't even tell him to forget about her, because she didn't want him to. Didn't want to die here. Was that selfish? Maybe. But when Akur's golden gaze found her, it was clear all those other times he'd told her he wasn't leaving her in this place, he'd spoken the truth.

He fought despite the blood, despite the unending stream of gator-guards coming their way.

Pressing the trigger now was useless. No more shots rang out from the weapon and it burned in her hand. When a guard snarled next to her, she didn't even look his way. Slamming the butt of the weapon into his snout as he stretched for her, she couldn't take her eyes off the rebel heading her way.

Reaching out, she screamed Akur's name and watched as he did the same, his arm stretching in her direction. Their fingers touched and her heart did a big walloping thing, moments before the door behind them burst open again. This time, a Tasqal glided through, its white robes pristine despite the carnage around it. Its lipless mouth curved into what might have been a sneer.

"Enough of this," it said, its voice calm. Too calm. "Take them."

Something hit Constance's neck. A needle—no, a dart maybe. The world immediately began to spin. She tried to grab hold of Akur, but her arm suddenly went dead. Through blurring vision, she saw Akur stagger as multiple darts struck him, too.

"No…" The word came out slurred. She tried to reach for him again, but her legs gave out.

The last thing she saw before darkness took her was Akur fighting even as he fell to his knees, still trying to reach her.

22

Constance

CONSCIOUSNESS RETURNED SLOWLY, painfully. Every muscle ached as if she'd been beaten. Maybe she had been.

Akur?

It felt like his name only echoed in her mind. As if her tongue was too heavy to form speech, her throat too parched.

Agh. A groan as she tried to move. Only the cold metal floor beneath her cheek helped clear some of the fog from her mind.

Constance forced her eyes open. She was in a cell, maybe ten feet square, with energy barriers forming the walls. Beyond them, she could see other cells, all empty.

"Akur?" Her voice was barely a whisper. Fear clawed at her throat as she pushed herself to her knees. "Akur?!"

Swaying, she almost face-planted before she settled back on her haunches.

Where the hell were they?

Blurred vision made her head swim before she stabilized herself.

That's when she saw him.

They had him chained to the far wall, arms spread wide, feet barely touching the ground. His head hung limply, blood still dripping from various wounds.

"Akur!" She scrambled to the barrier, despite the warning tingles of energy against her skin. A zap sent her flying back. Pain rocketed down her spine. Stars made her vision cloud again.

It took her a moment to rise to her knees once more, and then to stand. "Akur." Her gaze found him across the way. "Akur, wake up! Please wake up!"

His head lifted slightly, eyes finding hers through a face that looked bruised, bloody and swollen. "Constance." His voice was rough, pained. "Are you hurt?"

A laugh that was half a sob escaped her. Of course, he was asking if she was alright. "Oh, Akur. What did they do to you?" The more she looked at him, the more trauma she could see. One of his arms was even set strangely, as if the bone was only being held together by skin.

"I've had worse." He tried to grin, but it turned into a grimace.

"Where are we?" It looked like cells similar to those that had been on that ship. The one she and Meredith had escaped from. But she was sure she couldn't get out of this the same way she did then. All her cards were played.

But there was no hum of an engine. They weren't on a ship this time.

Before Akur could respond, a door hissed open. Constance's shoulders tightened, her heart thudding a little harder as she turned toward the sound. She saw the white robes before the large figure entered. A Tasqal, followed by two guards flanking him on each side. He stopped the moment he noticed she was awake.

"So...you finally join us, human."

Constance moved up to the barrier, ignoring the warning tingles of energy that ran along her skin. "Let him go."

The Tasqal merely stared at her, its face unreadable.

"Let him go. You've got what you wanted. You've got me."

The Tasqal blinked slowly, its eyes disappearing under its skin. This one had more pustules than she'd seen on any of the others. Almost as if it had an advanced form of whatever disease was plaguing their kind. One pustule at the corner of its eye popped, oozing yellow pus down its nose ridge. "What I want?" It said calmly. "You presume much, human. Your companion refused to provide the information we seek. Perhaps you will be more...cooperative."

"Don't tell them anything, Constance," Akur rasped, chains rattling as he tried to straighten.

The Tasqal raised a hand.

"Yes, High One," the gator-guard to his right said, right before that same guard pressed a control. Her gaze snapped to Akur a moment before she saw the chains hum with energy, making him jerk and grit his teeth.

"Stop it!" Constance gritted her teeth. "What do you want to know?"

The energy ceased, and the Tasqal stepped closer to her cell, dark eyes reflecting the barrier's glow. It studied her for a long moment.

"What. Do. You. Want from us?"

The Tasqal hardly moved, just stared at her in a way that made her feel small enough that if the barrier wasn't there, he would swallow her whole.

"The location of the orb," it finally said. "Where is the Kyron that retrieved it?"

Her blood ran cold. "I don't know what you're talking about," she said, stepping back from the barrier.

"No?" The Tasqal did a clicking sound in its throat. "Then perhaps we should continue our earlier discussion with your comrade. He's proven quite resilient, but every being has their breaking point."

"Don't," Akur growled. "Constance, whatever happens—"

The chains hummed again, cutting off his words with a choked sound of pain.

"Time is short, human," the Tasqal said softly. "And my patience wears thin." The Tasqal motioned again and the chains holding Akur hummed with energy once more. His grunt of pain made her heart shatter.

"Stop! I'll tell you!"

Fuck, what would she tell them? She didn't know where Alaina and the cyborg went. She had no idea where they were. But she could lie. She could buy them time...even though that might be useless at this point.

The Tasqal stepped closer, eyes gleaming. "Speak." A single command that seemed to crackle the air.

"They're..." she swallowed, taking a deep breath. Come on. Buy some time. "They're keeping it safe."

The Tasqal's eyes narrowed almost unnoticeably. Before she could react, one of the gator-guards at his side stepped forward and thrust one of those energy rods through the bars. It crackled a moment before it reached her belly. The pain was white hot, immediate, and fast.

Her knees buckled as she lost sense of time and space.

The pain. It was unlike anything she'd ever experienced before. As if her skin, muscle and bone were separating cell from cell. The ravaged, torn sound that escaped her lips didn't even sound like herself.

"Piece of scum!" Akur snarled. "I will tear you apart with my bare hands!"

"Bold words from one in chains." She heard the Tasqal say. Through fluttering eyelids that didn't seem to know what to do with the light, she caught glimpses of the Tasqal as he glided closer to Akur. "But your defiance will fade, as it always does. You will break, as they all do. And she will watch."

Akur spat blood at the creature. "Touch her, and I'll—"

The Tasqal backhanded him, the sound echoing off the walls. One guard provided something for him to wipe away the blood Akur spat. "Filthy Shum'ai *pest*," the Tasqal growled. "We should have ravaged your world when we had the chance. You can do nothing but watch as we take everything from you. Starting now. You and the other rebels are a nuisance we should have eradicated eons ago. Always thwarting our plans. Always in our way. This time, Shum'ai, you have gone too far. Taken something that belongs to usss."

It gestured and one guard stepped forward, pressing the same shock rod against Akur's side. Electricity ran across his body. His back arched as he tried to bite back a roar, but the sound escaped anyway, tearing at her heart one more time.

"Stop it!" She crawled toward the barrier. "Stop!" Her body spasmed in the aftershock of what the weapon did to her. She pushed herself to speak, to fight against the lingering pain, anyway. "Can't you see you're killing him? Why? What the *fuck* is wrong with you? Can't you see what you're doing? Can't you see what you've *done*?"

The Tasqal turned to her, those black eyes swallowing her. "Wrong? Survival is not *wrong*, little human. It is...necessary. Any species, faced with the extinction of their kind, would do the same."

"No." She shook her head, voice trembling with anger. "No, they would not. Not every species resorts to abduction, to torture, to...to breeding other sentient beings like...like they're nothing! There are other ways to survive. Ways that don't involve destroying other civilizations!"

The Tasqal grunted. "Foolish. But I cannot expect a lower species like yourself to understand. That is why we, the High Tasqals, must preserve ourselves for the betterment of this universe." He lifted his chin, exposing a yellow wetness in the folds of skin where the pustules had popped and leaked. "This is only the beginning, human. You will watch the Shum'ai suffer, watch him break, and know that it's all because of you. Because he chose to help you. And then you will know our power. You will kneel and know that we are to be revered. That your existence means nothing without usss."

"Don't listen," Akur gasped out. "Not your fault...Constance."

The guard pressed the device into him again. This time, Akur couldn't hold back his roar. The sound ripped through Constance like the pain was hers.

"You see?" The Tasqal's voice was almost gentle. "This is the price of defiance. The price of hope. Resistance is..."

"Futile?" Constance choked on a laugh, her gaze burning into the Tasqal. "Do you know what your problem is?" She forced herself to her feet. "You think you're so superior, but you're just afraid. Afraid of dying out. Afraid of change. Afraid that maybe, just maybe, you're not the masters of the universe you pretend to be."

The Tasqal's eyes narrowed to slits. "Fear? We do not fear. We control. We dominate. As we always have."

"Really?" She lifted her chin higher, refusing to tremble. "Then why are your people dying? Why can't you fix what's happening to your own bodies? For all your supposed superiority, you can't even save yourselves."

Another pustule burst on the Tasqal's face. It wiped the seepage away with deliberate slowness. "You dare—"

"I dare because you're proving my point right now. Look at you— you're falling apart. And instead of working with other species who might help you, you torture them. Experiment on them. Make them hate you. How's that working out?"

"Silence!" The Tasqal's calm facade cracked. It gestured sharply, and the guard moved toward her cell with the shock rod.

"She's right," Akur's voice was weak but carried clearly. "Your empire is crumbling, Tasqal. More systems declare independence every cycle. Your grip is failing."

The Tasqal spun toward him. "Our grip never fails. We merely allow temporary rebellion to identify the troublemakers. Like *you*. Have you forgotten how your people begged? How the great Tonvuhiri fell?" It nodded to the guard. "Again."

The guard changed course, returning to Akur to press the rod into his side.

"Stop." Constance forced through gritted teeth. Again, the rod was pressed into Akur's side. "*Stop.*"

Tears streamed down her face now, even though she was trying to hold them back. She watched Akur convulse in agony. His muscles spasmed, veins standing out in his neck as he fought against the pain. Blood ran freely from where the chains cut into his wrists, from that gaping wound in his chest, and from all the other abrasions across his frame.

"He's only fighting for survival, just like you are," she whispered. "Just like all of us are."

The Tasqal raised a hand, and the guard stepped back. Akur sagged in his chains, chest heaving as he gasped for air.

"This can end," the Tasqal said. "Simply tell us what we wish to know. We want the location." The Tasqal stepped closer. "Surely, the Shum'ai told you where the orb was while he was filling you with his seed."

She stiffened and the Tasqal's upper lip curled.

"*Disgusting*," it said. "I can scent his spend on you." He walked a few paces and she tracked him, not exactly sure what he was going to do or say next. "We know your humankind enjoys such soft things. Such...sharing. You dislike our rough mating practices."

Her hands clenched into fists. "Go *fuck* yourself."

The Tasqal's expression didn't change, but something in its eyes grew colder. "As you wish." It gestured again.

This time, when the guard stepped forward, he had a different device. Something with blades.

Akur's gaze found hers through the barrier. Even though he could hardly open his eyes, she could see that he was only focused on her. "Don't look, bright eyes."

But she couldn't look away as the guard began his work. Each cut was precise, calculated to cause maximum pain without fatal damage. Dark blood welled up in precise lines across Akur's chest. He didn't shout out this time, but his jaw clenched so tight she could hear his teeth grinding.

"The cellular structure of the Shum'ai is...fascinating," the Tasqal said conversationally, as if discussing the weather. "So resilient. They can endure so much more than most races before their bodies give out." It stepped closer again. "It was a pity when your world did not yield, Shum'ai. We once thought Tonvuhiri, that you Shum'ai, might be the key we were waiting for in all these orbits. That your regeneration could spark ours."

"Once?" Constance croaked.

The Tasqal moved its shoulders like it shrugged. "Useless. We couldn't get a serum to actualize." Then it hummed in its throat, that definite sneer on its face once more. "But that regeneration." She could have sworn it groaned. "It made your females perfect for our purposes."

Now, that made Akur grunt, lips pulling back in a snarl.

The guard switched to a different blade, this one glowing with heat. The smell of burning flesh filled the air as he pressed it against Akur's wounds, cauterizing them even as he cut new ones.

Constance retched, bile burning her throat. But she forced herself to keep watching. She owed him that much, at least. To witness his suffering, to share it in the only way she could.

"Your deaths will have meaning," the Tasqal continued. "Your bodies will nurture the next generation of *my* kind. Is that not a noble end?"

"I'll show you a noble end," Akur growled, then spat blood in the creature's face again. He faced the Tasqal, staring at him with eyes that blazed violence and thunder.

The Tasqal wiped the blood away almost delicately. Then it plunged its hand into one of Akur's open wounds, twisting its fingers. This time, Akur couldn't hold back his roar. And she screamed with him. The sound tore through her, ignited something desperate and dark. Her hands slammed against the floor, again and again, the impact jarring up her arms. She barely felt the skin splitting on her knuckles, barely noticed the smears of red she was leaving on the pristine surface. All she knew was Akur's pain, and her complete inability to stop it.

"Fascinating," the Tasqal mused, withdrawing its bloody hand. "Such loyalty between species. Such devotion. It makes breaking you so much more...satisfying."

"You want satisfaction?" Akur's voice was raw, but his eyes still blazed with hatred. "Come closer. I'll show you satisfaction when I rip your spine out through your throat."

The Tasqal's lipless mouth curved. "Still so much fight. Good. It will make this last longer." It turned to face her. "Remember, human. I do not expect the Shum'ai to reveal the secrets we want." He sneered a little. "His kind is frustratingly loyal. Often known to take secrets to the end. Even to death. But you..." He sneered wider. "Your kind is weak. Emotional. Every moment of his pain is because of you. Every drop of lifeblood, every breath of agony—you could end it all with a few simple words."

"She doesn't know," Akur gritted through the pain. "And even if she did, she would not tell you, *scum*."

Constance met his gaze. Despite everything, despite the blood and pain, she saw the same strength there that had drawn her to him from the start. The same unwavering spirit.

"Shum'ai aren't the only ones who can keep their promises," she whispered.

Pride flickered in Akur's eyes before another shock rod was pressed into him.

Time lost meaning after that. Minutes or hours passed in a haze of blood and screams. The Tasqal tried different methods, different tools, but always with the same detachment. As if Akur was dirt in the street rather than a living being.

Through it all, Akur never broke. Never begged. Even when they brought in devices that made his muscles seize and his back arch until she thought his spine would snap, he kept his defiance. But she could see him weakening, see the light in his eyes growing dimmer.

He was going to die. And there was nothing she could do about it.

Finally, the Tasqal stepped back, regarding its handiwork with those cold black eyes. "Enough for now. Let them rest. Consider what awaits you on the next sol." Bubbles popped as it laughed, and with the sound came the stench of rot. "After all, you have no power here, rebel." It glided to the door, then paused. "Oh, and so you don't get too comfortable—"

It gestured and the gator-guard activated a control panel set into the wall. The chains holding Akur suddenly retracted upward and stretched farther apart, pulling him higher along the wall and stretching his limbs. His shoulders made a horrible grinding sound as they bore his full weight.

"Rest well." The Tasqal's words dripped with mock concern as it left.

When they were alone, Constance pressed as close to the barrier as she could without touching it. "Akur?"

He lifted his head with obvious effort. "Still here, bright eyes."

"I'm sorry. I'm so sorry."

"Don't." Despite everything, his voice was firm. "This isn't your fault."

"They're hurting you because of me."

"They're hurting me because they're monsters." He tried to shift position but could only manage a slight swing of his body. "This was always a possibility when I chose to come after you."

"You must regret it." The words whispered from her. "You must regret it all."

"No."

A part of her wanted to believe that was true. But there was only so much a single soul could take.

For a long moment, Akur was silent. When he finally spoke, his voice was softer than she'd ever heard it. "I don't regret it. Because you've proven, bright eyes...that you are worth the price."

Tears spilled down her cheeks as she pressed her forehead against the floor. "You'd have done this for any human? I'm going to be honest here. Some of us aren't worth this, Akur."

"Not *any* human." His chains rattled as he tried to lean toward her. "But you. You have been worth it all."

A sob tore from her throat. "I can't watch them hurt you anymore. I can't—"

"You can. You will. Because you're stronger than them. Stronger than their pain. Stronger than their fear." His voice grew fiercer with each word. "You're a warrior, Constance. You will make it through this. *Somehow*. After all," he chuckled, but it sounded like even his throat bled, "you learned from the best. Akur the...Akur the..." He trailed off, going silent.

"Akur the Undefeated," she whispered. But he didn't repeat the words. It was clear he saw this moment as his true defeat.

She looked up, meeting his gaze through the barrier and her

tears. Despite his wounds, despite hanging helpless in chains, he looked at her like she was the most precious thing in the universe.

"We're getting out of here," she whispered. "I don't know how, but we are. And then we're going to burn this whole place to the ground."

A ghost of his old smile crossed his bloody lips. "That's my bright eyes."

23

Akur

HE HUNG FROM HIS CHAINS, each breath a struggle against broken ribs and the weight of his own body pulling at his dislocated shoulders. The cell block's artificial lighting had dimmed to simulate night, but time held little meaning here. Only pain marked the passing hours—sharp spikes when he shifted wrong, dull throbs from his countless wounds, and the constant burning in his overtaxed muscles.

But worse than his own pain was watching Kon-stahns. She hadn't slept, hadn't moved from her vigil near the barrier separating them. Even in the dim light, he could see the tracks of dried eye waters on her face. The way her hands still trembled from the shock rod's effects. The determined set of her jaw as she refused to look away from him, sharing his suffering.

"Rest," he rasped, the word catching in his raw throat. "You need strength."

"So do you." Her voice sounded hoarse.

He wanted to laugh, but knew it would hurt too much. Resting was impossible in this position. The Tasqal knew that—it was part of their torture method. Keep the prisoner weakened, exhausted, vulnerable to questioning. He'd seen it before. He'd even survived it before.

But he'd been younger then. Stronger.

And he hadn't had someone he cared about being forced to watch.

"Tell me about your world," he said. Maybe he could distract her. "The places you loved there."

She gave him a look that said she knew exactly what he was doing, but played along. "I used to go hiking in these mountains called the Rockies. There was this one trail that led to an alpine lake. The water was so clear you could see straight to the bottom, and in the morning, the surface would be like glass. You could see the reflection of everything around it. Like a painting..."

Akur let her voice wash over him, painting pictures of a world he'd never see. It helped him focus on something besides the agony wracking his frame. Helped him pretend he didn't notice how his vision was greying at the edges, how each breath came a little harder than the last.

The internal damage was worse than he was letting on. He could feel it—the slow seep of lifeblood into places it shouldn't be, the grinding of bone fragments with every movement.

He wouldn't survive another session with the Tasqal's implements.

The thought didn't frighten him. He'd made his peace with death long ago. But the idea of Kon-stahns being left alone here, at their mercy...

His claws clenched into fists above the chains, sending fresh rivulets of blood running down his arms.

"Akur?" Kon-stahns had stopped talking. She was watching him now.

"Just adjusting," he lied. "Tell me more about these mountains of rocks."

Her upper lip disappeared into her mouth and something swelled in her eyes. Sadness. Such visible sorrow. But before she could say anything, a faint sound caught his attention. He stiffened, and she did, too. Footsteps, but lighter than the heavy tread of the guard patrols. Coming closer.

"Someone's coming," he warned in a whisper. "Stay back from the barrier."

The footsteps stopped just by the door. There were muffled voices before two heavy thumps that made Kon-stahns jerk. Her wide eyes flew to him. Something was happening.

The door hissed open, but it wasn't the Tasqal and its guards returning. Instead, a single robed figure slipped inside.

"Be silent," it whispered, moving quickly to the control panel. "We have little time."

Akur's eyes narrowed as he recognized the voice. The same Tasqal who had helped them before; the one who had given them the map.

"You," Kon-stahns breathed. "From the tunnels."

The Tasqal made a soft hissing sound. "Quickly. The guards will change rotation soon. I can only give you moments to escape. Make them count."

The energy barrier of Kon-stahns' cell flickered and died. At the same moment, the chains holding him retracted into the wall, and they retracted too quickly. He crashed to the floor, unable to catch himself, a grunt of pain escaping before he could stop it.

Something soft was under him in an instant—Kon-stahns, her small frame straining under his weight, supporting him despite her own injuries. She shouldn't be doing this. Shouldn't have to. He needed to be stronger, needed to protect her, not the other way around. Red hot shame washed over him, mingling with the pain. He swayed, his vision blurring. Just...keep moving. Don't...don't fall.

"Can you walk?" she asked.

Even trying not to lean on her was creating agony in his bones.

"Have to," he growled, forcing his arms under him. Everything screamed in protest as he pushed himself up. The room spun like a ship caught in a vortex.

"The way to the landing bays will be cleared for exactly seven clicks," the Tasqal said, still working at the controls. "After that, you're on your own. There's a ship waiting in bay twelve. The codes are already loaded."

Constance got her shoulder under Akur's arm, obviously trying to take some of his weight. And he leaned on her more heavily than he wanted to. Even then, his legs didn't seem to want to hold him.

"You're helping us again." She said to the Tasqal. "When they could find you here, with us."

The Tasqal's hands stilled on the controls, his head lowering slightly underneath his hooded garment. "Because change must begin somewhere. Even if it begins with treason." He turned to face them. "Now. Quickly."

They stumbled into the corridor. Each step sent daggers of pain through his chest. Breathing felt like the air was filled with shards.

The Tasqal beckoned as he slid out the door. "This way. Hurry."

They followed, Akur fighting to keep his feet under him with each step. His body threatened to fail him, but he pushed through it. They had one chance. He wouldn't waste it.

Just outside the door, they had to step over the bodies of two fallen Hedgeruds.

"I had no choice. They would have raised an alarm," the Tasqal said, head tilting lower under the hood he wore. "Come."

The corridors were mercifully empty as they made their way through the citadel. Eerily empty.

Was this another trap?

No. That didn't make sense.

"Where are your minions? Your people?" Akur hissed.

The Tasqal tilted his head slightly in a way that made Akur know he was looking over his shoulder. "You have been captured, but the other, your comrade, has been found in the barren lands. Much of the High Guard has been diverted there as you pose no threat now."

Gods. E'lot was in trouble.

"And your kin?" Akur asked.

The Tasqal faced forward again, robes shuffling as he hurried on. "A gathering has been called. We have a human now...or so they think. The next steps to retrieve that orb are being discussed."

Akur snarled, grunting as he forced his body to go on.

"You didn't tell us you had an Arois."

The Tasqal didn't pause. "You cannot know too much. Not about me. Not about anything. The Arois might seem unresponsive, but his mind can still reach far."

Kon-stahns glanced up at him, eyes searching his, and the worry within hers was clear, even though she didn't say anything. But he understood what the Tasqal meant. If the Arois was working for the Tasqals, even being forced to, any information that passed through these walls would get back to them.

They pushed on, the Tasqal leading them through what seemed like endless identical hallways, occasionally pausing to check for guards or his kin.

"How much farther?" Kon-stahns whispered. "Akur is bleeding out."

"Not far," the Tasqal replied. "The ship is waiting in a landing bay two levels up."

The corridor ahead stretched endlessly, each step an eternity of pain. Worse, his vision kept fading in and out. Only Kon-stahns' grip kept him upright, her determination flowing into him, giving him the strength he needed. Even when his legs trembled with each step. Blood dripped steadily from his wounds, leaving a trail he knew would eventually betray them. But he kept moving, one foot in front of the other.

They reached a junction and the Tasqal froze, lifting a hand in warning. Voices echoed from around the corner.

He could feel Kon-stahns stiffen even as he looked for somewhere to hide. But they were in a stark white corridor. There was nowhere to go.

The Tasqal's four-fingered hand tightened into a fist. "Stay here," he whispered. "And be silent."

Before they could protest, he straightened his robes and strode purposefully around the corner. His voice, when it came, held all the imperious authority of his high station. "What are you doing in this sector?"

"High One!" The Hedgeruds' response was immediate. "We are to relieve the ones guarding the jekin and the rebel."

"They are locked away. They are no longer a priority." There was a pause and Akur could almost feel Kon-stahns' pulse pick up. "Every moment you waste here is a moment that other rebel draws closer to escape. Head to the barren lands immediately!"

"Yes, High One! At once!"

The sound of heavy footsteps heading in the other direction made Akur release a breath. Kon-stahns sagged underneath him.

"Come," the Tasqal whispered. "The lift is ahead."

They carried on. Turning another corner, the doors to the lift finally came into view. Even seeing it now, so close, it felt like a million leagues away.

Come on. You can do it. Don't give up now.

The words filtered into his mind like a comforting mantra. One that didn't sound like his inner voice till he realized it was the female beneath him saying the words over and over again.

"Come on, Akur. You can do it."

And for her, he would.

Just as they neared the lift, an alarm began to wail. Only, it didn't sound like it was coming from the walls or even above. It was coming from the Tasqal's arm.

"What's that sound?" Kon-stahns asked.

"Nothing good." Akur forced his legs to move faster, ignoring the way his wounds reopened, the warm trickle of fresh lifeblood down his chest. Ignored the way his one arm hung limp and useless. He wasn't healing. Not fast enough. Didn't feel like he was regenerating at all. "Have to reach...the bay...before things get worse."

The Tasqal lifted his arm, looking at a device strapped there.

"Citizen alert," the Tasqal said. "They must have realized you're missing. Hurry!"

They crowded into the lift; the Tasqal putting in a code that caused the lift to rise as Akur sagged against the wall, his legs finally giving out. Only Kon-stahns' grip kept him from collapsing entirely.

"Stay with me," she whispered. She was so close now, those bright eyes searching his face. "We're almost there."

Qrak.

For the first time in his existence, he didn't want to die. Not while she still breathed.

The lift hummed as it carried them upward, each click stretching into eternity.

"Almost there," Constance whispered, her grip on him tightening. He could feel her trembling with the effort of holding him up, but her voice remained steady. Strong. Like she always was.

The lift slowed, then stopped. The doors opened onto a vast chamber that made Kon-stahn inhale. The landing bay stretched before them, a massive space too big for what it was used for. Ships of various sizes dotted the space—some sleek and brand new, a few captured rebel craft, and...

"There." The Tasqal pointed to a small shuttle near the far wall. "That one is prepared for you."

Akur studied the vessel through blurring vision. A C-class transport—old, but reliable. Fast enough to break atmosphere, small enough to slip past orbital defenses. If they could reach it.

They stepped out of the lift, each movement igniting fresh waves of agony. Eyes focused on the transport, he still didn't miss the slight gasp that came from Kon-stahns' lips as she looked behind them and saw the pool of lifeblood he'd left behind. Too much. He was running out of time.

"I've input all necessary codes," the Tasqal said as they made their slow way across the bay. "Forget about my original plan. This ship will take you to Hudo III. You will be safe there. It is beyond Tasqal space." Then he looked up from under the hood of his robe. "And you find that orb. And you destroy it. By any means necessary."

They were halfway to the ship when Akur's legs buckled. He caught himself against a support pillar, breath coming in ragged gasps. Kon-stahns' small hands pressed against his chest, trying to steady him.

"Just a little further," she pleaded. "Please, Akur. Don't you dare leave me now. We're so close."

He forced himself upright, leaning heavily on her. One step. Another. The ship grew closer, its promise of freedom almost tangible now.

"Thank you," Kon-stahns said to the Tasqal. "For everything."

She was thanking the fiend when it was his kind that put them in this situation in the first place. His mortal enemies.

Akur's jaw clenched, decades of hatred and suspicion warring with the undeniable truth before him—this enemy had risked everything to help them escape. The same race that had imprisoned him, tortured him, was now offering salvation. His pride demanded rejection, but Kon-stahns' warmth against his side grounded him in the present moment.

Looking at the hooded Tasqal, he forced his throat to work. "You..." The word came out rough, guttural. Every instinct screamed against what he was about to say. "You have done us a service this day." Each word felt like he was being forced to swallow his own intestines.

The Tasqal tilted his head, perhaps sensing the monumental effort behind that simple acknowledgment.

"My people...the Shum'ai..." Akur continued, his good hand tightening into a fist. "They would call me a traitor for this. But honor demands..." He drew in a ragged breath. "I owe you a debt."

Kon-stahns' hold on him tightened, almost as if she was supporting him emotionally, too. As if she understood what this admission cost him—generations of hatred, the weight of his people's suffering, all things he'd had to set aside.

"Save your strength, Shum'ai," the Tasqal said. "You will need it for what lies ahead."

Akur gave a slight nod, relief and shame mingling in his chest. The galaxy, it seemed, was not as black and white as he'd believed. Even as his body failed him, this realization shook the foundations of everything, *everything* he'd known.

They were almost at the ship's boarding ramp when the massive lift doors exploded inward.

Hedgeruds. They poured through the breach like a flood of pestilence, and behind them, the lumbering forms of several High Tasqals.

Qrak.

He should have known this wasn't going to be easy.

"Traitor!" The lead Tasqal's voice rang out across the bay. "You dare betray your own kind?"

Here it was. The moment this wretched Tasqal would turn on them.

Again, he was wrong.

"Run!" their ally shouted. "Get to the ship!"

Blaster fire filled the air. The Tasqal who had helped them went down immediately, his pained cry hitting something within Akur that shouldn't be possible. Regret? Care?

Time stopped for a split click as dark blood spread beneath the Tasqal's robes.

"Come on!" Kon-stahns was tugging him now, straining toward the ship before them, but his legs locked up. Looking at the female before him, the panic in her eyes, the hope, he knew they wouldn't make it. He was too wounded; too slow. Already, the Hedgeruds were closing in.

They wouldn't make it.

Not both of them, at least.

But she could.

Gathering every bit of strength he had left, he knew what he had to do. "Forgive me," he whispered.

With one powerful move, he shifted out of her grasp and lifted her with his one good arm.

"Forgive me, bright eyes."

Her body went airborne as he threw her toward the ship with all his remaining strength. The landing wasn't gracious. She caught herself on the boarding ramp. When she spun back toward him, her eyes were wide with horror.

"No!" she screamed. "Akur!"

Throwing himself toward the ship, he aimed for the external hatch control. He barely managed to hit it. The ramp began rising.

"Go!" he roared, even as blaster fire sizzled past him. "Live!"

The last thing he saw was her face, tears streaming down her cheeks as she scrambled toward him, gravity working against her now as the hatch sealed shut. Then pain exploded in his back.

24

Constance

THE WORLD SLOWED to a nightmare crawl as she watched Akur fall.
Blaster fire sizzled through the air where he'd been standing like a
rainbow of death. Slamming her good shoulder against the closing
hatch, her fingers scrabbled uselessly at the sealed edges.

"No!" The scream tore from her throat. "No! You can't do this! You
fool! You fool! Open!"

The ship's systems hummed to life around her, auto-sequence
initiating. Lights flickered across unfamiliar control panels as engines
began their startup cycle. Through the narrowing gap, she could see
Akur on his knees, blood pouring from fresh wounds in his back. Yet
somehow he was still fighting; his massive frame between her and the
advancing Hedgeruds.

He looked up then, and they locked eyes.

There the world seemed to spin on its axis, between them both.

Her heart thundered in her chest, fueled by either anger or something else she didn't quite know. She wasn't sure. All she knew was
that she was moving.

Through the ship's viewscreen, the terror out there made her heart fall. The landing bay had become a killing field. Dozens of those gator-guards swarmed forward, weapons drawn, long snouts opened in identical snarls, yellow eyes gleaming, and their long armored tails swaying. Behind them, about thirty High Tasqals stood, simply observing with little interest.

The odds were beyond impossible.

But if the rebel fighting below her had taught her one thing in this whole ordeal, it was that there was always a choice. She could give up now. Truly surrender. Or she could fight.

She spun, searching the controls. Most were incomprehensible—surfaces that glowed with strange symbols, panels that seemed to respond to even the slightest touch. But there, rising from the main console, was something startlingly familiar.

A control yoke. Not exactly like the ones in aircraft or video games, but similar enough that her hands knew what to do. It was slightly warm to the touch when she grabbed it, the material somewhere between something like plastic and living tissue. When her fingers closed around it, she felt a subtle vibration, as if the ship itself was waking up.

"NEURAL INTERFACE ACTIVATED." The ship's computer announced. "CALIBRATING."

The holographic display that materialized in front of her was like nothing she'd seen before, but the concepts weren't. There were targeting reticles and power levels. Like the universe itself had decided some things were too fundamental to change.

Point. Shoot. Destroy.

Her grip tightened as her heart hammered. Even within the ship, she could hear the shouts and roars from outside. She had to help Akur.

"WEAPONS SYSTEM ONLINE," the ship announced as the yoke hummed beneath her palms. Two targeting reticles appeared in the holo-display and when she moved the yoke, they tracked.

There was no time for manuals, no time for training. But she didn't need them. Right now, she just needed to make something go away. Preferably in pieces.

Through the viewscreen, she could see Akur still fighting. Even wounded, even dying, he was magnificent. His remaining good arm caught a Hedgerud by the throat, hurling the creature into its companions. But there were so many, and more kept coming.

"Come on, come on," she muttered as she pushed the yoke. It wasn't perfect. The targeting reticles didn't pick up the lifeforms below. Maybe because they weren't designed to fire on living beings.

"Fuck." Her heart was hammering so hard she couldn't think straight over the sound of her own pulse in her ears. "Fuck!" It took her a moment to realize that though the cannons weren't picking up the damned gator-guards or the Tasqals, they were picking up the other ships.

Glancing up, she mapped two of the closest ships and dragged the yoke to target between them.

"LIFTOFF UNDERWAY."

"Cancel." Her heart thudded even harder as she watched Akur fall on one knee, a Hedgerud's blade stuck in his side. Way off, still near the lift, the High Tasqals still stood watching the show. Some were even looking at the ship slowly rising with her inside. She saw the moment one gestured toward it. The moment when several of those gator-guards changed focus and headed her way.

"Cancel! Cancel liftoff and fire!"

The targeting system responded sluggishly. Too slow. Too slow! A warning sound blared—and the damned launch sequence began counting down. No! If she didn't override it soon, the ship would take off without him.

Finally, the weapons came online. Twin cannons, it seemed. She doubted they were meant for firing indoors. That would only matter if she cared. Pushing the yoke, she grunted at the pain in her hands. The targeting display landed between the two ships in front. "Yes!" But the Hedgeruds were so close to Akur...

She hesitated for a split second, terrified of hitting him.

In that moment, she saw him look up at the ship. Hardly recognizable except for those golden eyes. Even through the wounds, the blood, the exhaustion, his eyes found hers. And in them she saw everything—strength, determination, and something else. Something that made her heart clench with sudden understanding.

This warrior from another world who'd protected her, fought for her, been willing to die for her...she couldn't lose him. Not like this.

Her finger stabbed the firing control.

The cannons roared to life, their blue-white beams cutting through the air. Immediately, it was clear as day that this wasn't a weapon to be used in such an enclosed space. The first set of gator-guards it hit exploded in a rain of guts and blood.

Her brows dove, teeth grit as she stabbed the controls again. Bodies flew as explosions rocked the landing bay. The yoke vibrated as she pulled back, sweeping the beams in arcs, creating a perimeter around Akur while desperately trying to avoid him.

The auto-launch sequence blared another warning as the ship swayed, destabilizing her. The cannon fire swerved, eating up the wall as the High Tasqals tried to run for cover.

"No! You don't get to run! *Fuck you!*" She regained her footing and targeted them next.

"Override!" she shouted at the computer. "Cancel launch!"

Time slowed down. All her fear, all her anger, all her hatred came gushing right through her. Blue-white fire lit up the Tasqals' elaborate robes as they scattered like insects. Their bodies popped like mighty fluid-filled bags. Several didn't make it to cover in time. Good. Let them feel what it was like to be hunted.

The ship lurched again, rising higher. Through the chaos of smoke and weapons fire, she saw Akur stagger as two gator-guards threw themselves on him.

Come on. Something had to work!

"Lower landing ramp!" The command came out in a desperate shout as she kept firing, cutting down everything that was moving.

"RAMP DESCENDING."

The ramp began descending agonizingly slowly, but the ship was still rising.

Shit.

The ship lurched higher, metal groaning as the ramp opened.

There was a heavy thump and when she looked back, all she could see was a dark claw as it dug into the metal. A gator-guard was trying to pull himself up on the ramp. Yellow eyes met hers as his snout appeared, a hateful smile. Through the smoke-filled chaos below, a teal arm appeared over the snout a moment before the guard was suddenly ripped backward. Akur. His body seemed to buckle as two guards threw themselves on him, golden eyes meeting hers one last time before disappearing under their weight.

The scream that tore from her throat felt like it drew blood as the ship spun and she fired wildly, but the ship's movement threw off her aim. Energy beams carved molten streaks across the hangar walls.

A grinding shriek of metal cut through the din. Emergency lights flashed as something massive struck the ship's hull. The entire vessel listed sideways, sending her sprawling across the console. Warning alarms blared.

"HULL INTEGRITY AT SEVENTY-ONE PERCENT. EMER-GENCY PROTOCOLS ENGAGED."

She scrambled up, blood trickling from where she'd split her lip. Through the half-open ramp door, she saw what had happened. A column had fallen, its massive width pinning the ship against the wall. That accident halted its ascent.

But the ship's systems fought to compensate, thrusters whining as they tried to break free. But they were caught, suspended halfway between ground and ceiling. The landing ramp hung open like a tongue, still within jumping distance of the floor.

Below, the scene had devolved into pure carnage. Bodies littered the ground, some still moving, others terrifyingly still. The air was thick with smoke and the acrid stench of burned flesh. Through it all, she couldn't see Akur.

He wasn't fighting anymore...and if he wasn't fighting...

The lump in her throat made breathing hard.

He couldn't be dead. He couldn't...

But then she spotted it. A bit of teal buried under bodies of gator-guards. Akur's arm...unmoving.

Time seemed to still, her heart cracking into a thousand unmendable pieces.

And in the aftermath of it all, through the corner of her eye, there they still were.

"Enough, human." The voice reached her loud and clear. Through the corner of her eye, she saw them—the surviving High Tasqals rising from behind their shelter of docked ships. Some of their robes were singed, but their arrogance remained intact.

Turning to face them, she stared through the viewscreen at the beings that had started all this. Dark, soulless eyes stared back at her. A ripple of pure evil. A host of pure malevolence.

"Look what your resistance has brought, human." She couldn't even tell which one was speaking. Didn't care. All that was building inside her was something she'd never felt before. Something she couldn't name.

"The Shum'ai is dead." Another voice, colder than the first. "Your protector lies broken. Submit now, and we may yet show mercy."

Mercy.

Ha.

Something wet fell on her hands where they gripped the yoke. She stared at the droplets, uncomprehending at first. Tears. She was crying. The realization came distantly, as if happening to someone else. Her chest burned with each breath, vision blurring even as her teeth bared in a snarl.

"You see now...this is the natural order," one of the High Tasqals moved forward, robes rustling against the debris-strewn floor. It stepped over fallen gator-guards as if they meant nothing. "Your species, like all the others, exists to serve us. To sustain us."

Another Tasqal glided toward what was visible of Akur's still form. His foot connected with the teal arm, shoving it aside with casual disdain. "Even the mighty Shum'ai fell before us. They were never meant to rise above their station as warriors."

A series of bubble popping sounds only made her spine tighten.

More tears fell silently on her hands, but her jaw clenched until pain shot through her temples. Each breath came shorter, harder, as if the air itself was turning to fire in her lungs.

"How many worlds have we conquered?" The first one spoke again, spreading his arms wide. "How many species now exist only to ensure our continuation? Your human colonies will make excellent additions. Already, the females we had in our facilities proved...suitable."

Her fingers whitened on the yoke. That thing building inside her? It was something beyond rage, beyond grief. Something primitive and terrifying.

"The strong survive. The weak submit. This is the way of the universe." The first Tasqal's voice dripped with superiority. "Your rebellion was amusing, but ultimately futile. Like all the others who dared to resist. Now come. Kneel before us...and you can be mine." He tilted his head, studying her through the viewscreen. "I will treat you well, little human. After all, I will not breed you immediately. You can be the first to see your human colonies transformed into breeding grounds. To watch your people learn their proper place in our empire."

Through tear-blurred eyes, she watched them as they all stood unmoving now. Their dark eyes reflected nothing—no conscience, no mercy, no soul.

Another tear landed on the control panel. Then another. But these weren't tears of sadness anymore. These were tears of pure, distilled hatred.

The liquid spread and the yoke suddenly pulsed warm beneath her hands.

"ORGANIC MATERIAL DETECTED. DNA ANALYSIS COMPLETE. HUMAN GENETIC MARKER IDENTIFIED."

There was a single moment when the lead Tasqal's face shifted. Surprise. The ship's systems suddenly hummed to life with new purpose. Holographic symbols scattered across the display, then reformed into new patterns. Different. Alive.

"TACTICAL ASSISTANCE INITIATED."

"Enough, human!"

Tactical assistance? What did that even mean?

She stared at the group of Tasqals before her. There was no winning. Either way she took it, only death was at the end of this line. "Can you assist me?"

The ship responded. "VOICE COMMANDS ONLINE."

"Good." Her gaze locked with the Tasqal in front. "Then target everything," she whispered. "Everything that moves."

The Tasqals froze, their expressions shifting from smug superiority to confusion. When the first energy beam slammed into the group, vaporizing the lead Tasqal in a flash of blue-white light, his scream was cut short. It echoed through the hangar.

The other Tasqals scattered, their robes billowing as they scrambled for cover. But the ship's targeting system was too fast, too precise. Energy beams lanced out, cutting them down one by one, their bodies exploding in showers of gore and bone fragments.

When a group of fresh gator-guards suddenly swept in, they were taken down, too.

Constance gripped the yoke, her knuckles white, her eyes fixed on the carnage unfolding below. She didn't flinch, didn't hesitate. She fired again and again, each blast a testament to her rage, her grief, her unwavering determination to do exactly what he wanted from the start.

To kill them all.

The air became thick with the stench of burning flesh and rot. The screams of the dying echoed through the chamber. She watched impassively as the last of them fell, their bodies reduced to smoking heaps of charred flesh.

There was no satisfaction; not exactly. Just...emptiness. A hollow ache where her heart used to be.

It took moments before she realized pressing the trigger no longer did anything. The ship was out of ammo.

And so was she.

She stood there for a moment, chest heaving, hands trembling on the controls. The tears had dried on her cheeks, leaving salty tracks through the blood and grime. Nothing moved in the carnage below.

Her body screamed in protest as she pushed away from the console. She had to find him. Had to know for sure.

The drop from the ramp jarred every bone in her body. She stumbled, fell, pushed herself up again. Her feet slipped in pools of blood as she made her way across the battlefield that had been a hangar.

"Akur..." Her voice cracked as she reached the pile of dead guards. Her hands shook as she grabbed the first body, straining to push it aside. "Akur."

One by one, she pushed the massive corpses away, each one straining her body so much it felt like she would break. Her muscles burned. Fresh tears blurred her vision. It took forever before she uncovered him.

Constance froze.

He lay still, so still. His teal skin was darker in places, bruised or worse. She fell to her knees beside him, hands hovering over his chest, afraid to touch, afraid to confirm what she already knew.

"You weren't supposed to die," she whispered. "We were supposed to leave this place together."

Her fingers finally found the courage to brush across his face. Over the ridges that defined his skull. Over his brow, the bridge of his nose, his eyes that would dance with humor when he was being cocky.

"You promised me." Her voice broke.

But what exactly did he promise? Not that he wouldn't die. No. He'd simply promised that he'd get her out of here. He promised he'd get her home—wherever that place may be.

Her shoulders shuddered with silent cries as she leaned down on him.

"You promised," she whispered again.

When a wet cough pierced through her grief, Constance whirled around. Through the remaining smoke, she spotted movement near a fallen support beam. A High Tasqal. Her spine stiffened, hand reaching for a weapon that wasn't there. But it wasn't just any Tasqal. As the Tasqal shifted, she spotted the fin on his back before he fixed his robes to cover himself.

It was him. The one that had helped them before. His chest heaved, his usually pristine robes now soaked in blood.

"Human…" His voice was barely audible. "You must…go. Now."

No words came to her mouth. Leave? Nothing seemed to matter anymore.

"More will come." Blood bubbled at the corners of the Tasqal's mouth. "The bay will be swarming soon. Leave while…while you can."

Constance turned back to Akur. *Leave?*

The word echoed, strange and hollow in her mind. She'd never considered leaving without him. Not once in all their struggle had she imagined walking away alone. They were supposed to escape together, find freedom together. Ever since he jumped in the void after her shuttle, the future had always been "we," never "I."

Her gaze fixed on Akur's still form. No. She wasn't leaving—not without him. She didn't care if it was stupid or impossible or if the entire Tasqal army was bearing down on them. She wouldn't abandon him here, wouldn't leave him to be desecrated by the ones who had hunted them.

Staggering to her feet, she grabbed his shoulders and pulled. Muscles screaming in protest, but his massive frame barely moved. Sweat mixed with tears on her face as she tried again.

"Leave him!" The Tasqal wheezed. "Save yourself."

Funny, Akur would have said the same thing. He'd said it before, many times. Just how many times had he tried to sacrifice himself for her? The least she could do was take his body away from this place.

She could bring him to a place where his soul could find peace.

"I won't leave him here for them to…" Her breaths came hard and fast. "Help me. Please."

She didn't think he would. After all, there must be a limit to his generosity. But as she tugged and pulled, she heard a shuffling movement. Glancing over her shoulder, she saw the Tasqal push himself up agonizingly slowly. Blood seemed to swell from a wound in his side, soaking his robes some more as he stumbled toward her.

"You humans," he muttered, making his way over. He seemed

annoyed. Angry even, but as he reached her side, together they grabbed Akur's shoulders. Every movement was torture, but inch by inch, they dragged the Shum'ai's body across the gore-slicked floor.

"We're almost there," Constance gasped. "Just...a little...farther."

The ramp seemed impossibly steep. With the ship off the ground, thrusters still fighting for it to rise, there was a gap between the floor and the ship that forced them to lift his body completely. Somehow, they did it. With another grunt, the Tasqal helped her up, too.

They heaved Akur's body next. She pulled while the Tasqal pushed, both of them trembling with exhaustion. Her arms felt like lead, her legs threatening to give out. But she wouldn't let go. Couldn't let go.

Finally, they got him inside. Constance collapsed beside his still form, her chest heaving. The Tasqal collapsed to the floor below.

"Thank you," Constance said. She couldn't see him now, his body practically hidden by the ramp. "You've proven you're not all bad. Your people—there's hope."

The Tasqal made a gurgling sound. "The orb," he whispered. "Must be destroyed. Save...both our peoples."

She nodded, even though he might not have been able to see it.

"Come with me," she suddenly said. "You don't have to die here, too."

The Tasqal made another gurgling sound. "There is more to do here."

Sounds came up through the open lift. Shouts that sounded like an army of Hedgeruds coming.

"Go!" The Tasqal shouted. "Divert energy to the rear thrusters. It should wrench you free."

"Computer!" Leaving Akur lying on the ground tore at her as she hurried to the controls. "Close ramp! Divert all power to rear thrusters!"

The ramp began rising with that agonizing slowness. Through the narrowing gap, she caught a final glimpse of the Tasqal's blood-soaked robes before the metal sealed with a hiss.

"POWER DIVERTED. WARNING: STRUCTURAL INTEGRITY AT RISK."

The ship screamed. There was no other word for it. Metal groaned and twisted, the hull vibrating so violently she thought it might tear apart. Warning lights flashed across every console, bathing the cargo hold in pulses of angry red and blue.

"WARNING: STRESS LEVELS CRITICAL."

Something snapped overhead as the ship suddenly lurched forward before righting itself and turning vertical. Another tremendous groan of protest from the ship. The deck plates beneath her feet began buckling. Just when she thought the hull would rupture, there was a final, terrible shriek of metal—and they broke free.

"Come on," she whispered. "Come on!"

The sudden acceleration threw her backward. She slammed into Akur's body, the impact driving the air from her lungs. As she gasped for breath, a massive cloud of dust billowed up from below where the ship had been anchored.

Rolling onto her side, she crawled to the nearest viewport. The dust was already beginning to settle, revealing the scene below like a curtain being drawn back. Dozens of Hedgeruds were pouring into the hangar, their reptilian forms making them look like a riverside of swarming crocodiles. They converged on the fallen Tasqal, some already reaching for medical supplies.

The ship gave another violent lurch as it headed upward. This time, she didn't fight it. Instead, she let herself fall back against Akur's chest the way she had so many times before. But there was no warmth there now. No steady rise and fall of breathing. No strong arms to wrap around her.

She turned her face into his shoulder, breathing in his familiar scent one last time before it faded forever. Her fingers curled into his chest, holding tight as if she could keep some part of him with her through sheer force of will.

"I'm sorry," she whispered against his cold skin. "I'm so sorry."

The ship's computer chimed softly. "ENTERING AUTOMATED FLIGHT PATH. CHANGE DESTINATION?"

The words felt like hearing a strange language. She couldn't react. She just lay there in the cargo hold, clinging to the body of the one she...cared for. She cared for him more than anything. The computer could wait. The mission could wait. The whole damn universe could wait.

For just a little while longer, she just needed to hold him. To remember.

To grieve.

25

Constance

THE SHIP HUMMED QUIETLY AROUND her as she lay motionless against Akur's chest, feeling the coldness seeping through his skin. Her tears had long since dried, leaving salty tracks on his teal flesh. She couldn't bring herself to move, to face what came next. Not yet.

"Computer. Status?" Her voice came out hoarse, barely a whisper.

"CURRENT TRAJECTORY MAINTAINING. ALL SYSTEMS NORMAL."

The emotionless response echoed through the cargo hold. She almost laughed at how absurd it was—systems normal, everything fine — while her world had shattered into pieces.

Her fingers traced absent patterns on his chest, remembering how it used to rise and fall with each breath. "You were so stubborn," she whispered against his skin. "So determined to protect me." Her throat felt raw from screaming. From crying. "But you did it, didn't you? You got me out of there. Just like you promised."

The ship's gentle vibration continued beneath them as the endless darkness of space surrounded the ship. She didn't even know how far they had to go or how long it would take to get there.

It didn't matter.

Nothing mattered.

Her mind drifted to the other women—Meredith and the silent one. She'd left them behind. The thought made her stomach clench.

"I couldn't even help them. Couldn't save anyone. Some hero I turned out to be." Her voice cracked. "But you...you never stopped trying. Never gave up."

"You know what's funny?" she continued softly. "I used to think you were just another one of those rebels back on the Restitution camp. Just another alien that I shouldn't trust, even if you were helping me. But you weren't like that at all, were you?"

She shifted slightly, her lips whispering against his cooling skin. The familiar scent of him was already fading. Fresh tears threatened to well up. "I never told you...about when you were in heat. I never... we never talked about what we did...or why I did it." She swallowed hard, tucking her face more into his neck. "It wasn't just about surviving. I mean, at first maybe it was, but..." She swallowed hard. "I liked being with you. Liked how you made me feel safe. Protected. Like I mattered."

A bitter laugh escaped her. "Guess that makes me pretty pathetic, huh? Falling for the alien warrior who was just doing his duty."

"But...if you'd claimed me then...told me I *had* to be your mate...I wouldn't have fought it. Wouldn't have wanted to." Her voice dropped even lower, barely audible even to herself. "No one's ever fought for me like you did. No one's ever...cared that much." The admission made a tremor go through her. All those times she'd told herself he was insane, bound by his warrior's code that made him protect her. Just his sense of duty. She'd been such a fool.

The tears were flowing freely again now. God, she really was pathetic. But she couldn't help it. "I never got to tell you. Never got to say that I..." She choked on the words, unable to voice them even now. As if speaking them aloud would make this reality permanent. Would cement the fact that he'd never hear them.

She curled closer, trying to share what little warmth she had left with his too-still form. The ship's dim lighting cast shadows across his features, making the proud warrior look carved from stone. She'd seen him endure so much. No matter what they'd been through, he'd always pushed through. But this was different.

Hours seemed to pass as she lay there, drifting in and out of consciousness. She didn't rise to eat. Didn't rise to find a place to sleep. She just...couldn't.

The ship's computer occasionally announced course corrections or system updates, but she barely heard them. She just remained there. Unmoving. Shivering in the cold but unable to rise.

She spoke to him, words spilling out in broken whispers. Stories she'd never told him. Things she'd always meant to ask. "Remember that first time? When that gator-guard broke into my and Alaina's room? I was so terrified, and then suddenly you were there." A ghost of a smile touched her lips. "This huge alien warrior, fighting like something out of a nightmare. You were ruthless."

Her fingers absently traced the scars on his chest. "I thought all hope was lost when that tractor beam pulled me away from you. Funny how things work out—here I was, terrified of being taken onto an alien ship, and now..." She swallowed hard. "Now I can't imagine being anywhere else. Watching you dive through space toward me, like some crazy guardian angel...that's when I first started thinking maybe you were different."

The silence that answered her was deafening.

She stared at one of the deeper scars crossing his chest—a reminder of all the battles he'd fought. How many had been against the Tasqals? How many others would fall trying to stop them? Her chest ached as she imagined them spreading across the universe like a plague. Imagining them bringing humans through that psychic rift they wanted to create. Many more would suffer. Many more would die.

"They've won, haven't they?" she whispered. "In the end, they will win. Even if we destroy that orb...they'll find another way...I can just feel it. And then more will fall. More good people will die. Like you."

Her fingers curled against Akur's chest in helpless anger. "It's not fair. You deserved better than this. Better than dying for some worthless human who couldn't even tell you—"

The ship shuddered slightly as it made another course correction.

"I don't know how to do this without you," she whispered. "How to keep fighting when it all seems so pointless. You were the one who believed in retribution. I just wanted to survive." She paused. "But maybe that was your point all along, wasn't it? That just surviving isn't enough. That we have to stand for something. Fight for something." A bitter laugh left her throat. "Took you dying for me to finally understand that. Guess I'm a slow learner."

More time passed. Or maybe it didn't. Everything was like a dream. The silence seemed to press in around her, broken only by the soft beeping of the console and the distant hum of the ship's engines. Her body ached from lying in one position for so long, but she couldn't bring herself to leave him. Not while some irrational part of her mind still hoped that if she just stayed there long enough, somehow...

She didn't feel it at first. Too numb from everything that happened. But when her eyes fluttered open, consciousness returning, she realized she had drifted off. Her head was pressed against his chest, despite the wounds there, despite the evidence of all he'd done for her.

A slow breath released from her nose as she stared ahead, seeing nothing through vision that was blurred. Deep inside her chest, her heart was cracked into pieces, a pain in her chest that wasn't there before growing so intense it was like she'd been shot.

Swallowing hard, she closed her eyes again...and that's when she felt it.

There, beneath her ear, so faint she could barely hear it, was a flutter. The slightest movement.

Constance froze, even her breath stilling.

She didn't dare move, too scared to hope and hoping all the same as she kept her ear pressed to the spot. Seconds stretched into eternity as she waited, praying she hadn't finally lost her mind.

There it was again. A flutter. No. Not just a flutter. A *heartbeat*. Weak, but unmistakably there.

"Akur?" Her voice shook as she pushed herself up, staring at his face. "Akur!"

He looked as still as ever. There was no indication she hadn't just imagined the sound.

Pressing her ear to his chest once more, she strained to hear. The sound was barely there, like a distant drum, but it was real.

Her voice cracked. "Computer, scan for life signs!"

"SCANNING...ONE LIFE SIGN DETECTED."

Her heart plummeted. Had she imagined it? Fuck. Was she really going insane?

But no. She'd felt it. That flutter. That impossible, beautiful flutter.

"Scan again!"

"ONE LIFE SIGN DETECTED."

No.

Pressing her ear to his chest once more, she kept her wide eyes on his face, her heart beating impossibly fast. Fast enough that it might have been sending too much blood to her brain.

"No," she said, pushing herself up. "I know what I felt."

Positioning herself over him, her heart thundered more as she stared at his cold, lifeless form. But she'd felt it. She'd felt the flutter. Clenching her jaw, she remembered the emergency medical training from what felt like a lifetime ago. "You never gave up on me," she whispered, as she positioned her hands over his chest. "Not once. So I'm not giving up on you."

The first chest compression made her wince, afraid she'd hurt him somehow, but she forced herself to continue. Each push against his chest was precise, rhythmic, desperate.

"ONE LIFE SIGN DETECTED," the computer repeated, almost mocking.

"Shut up!" she snapped, continuing the compressions. "He's still in there. I felt it."

Sweat blossomed and grew cold on her forehead as she worked.

Her arms burned, but she wouldn't stop. Couldn't stop. After thirty compressions, she tilted his head back, pinched his nose, and breathed into his mouth. His skin was so cold against her lips.

"Come on, Akur," she demanded between breaths. "Don't stop fighting now." Another set of compressions. Another breath. "I need you to fight."

Compression after compression, breath after breath, she fought for him like he'd always fought for her.

Because somewhere beneath her hands, so faint it defied detection, a warrior's heart was fighting to beat again.

And this time, she would be the one who saved him.

26

Akur

PAIN. Endless, crushing pain.

That was his first awareness as consciousness flickered at the edges of his mind. Every breath felt like molten metal in his chest. His body was heavy, unresponsive, as if trapped beneath the weight of an ocean.

"Computer, where are the medical supplies in this thing?"

Kon-stahns?

No. She shouldn't be here. She should be far away from this place. Safe on a ship, heading away from this nightmare.

Had he failed? Had he failed in the one thing he'd been so hell-bent on doing?

The thought clawed at him, dragging him deeper into the darkness. He couldn't protect her. He couldn't even open his qrakking eyes.

But her voice kept pulling him back, a rope thrown into the abyss.

"There must be a medical bay or something here *somewhere*."

"THERE IS NO MEDICAL BAY ON THIS SHIP."

Who was that? The voice was mechanical. Kind of like the standard artificial voices used on vessels.

But...that couldn't be. How was he on the ship with Kon-stahns?

"What do you mean?!" Her voice rose. "There has to be *something!*"

"THIS IS A CARGO VESSEL. BASIC MEDICAL SUPPLIES ARE LOCATED IN STORAGE UNIT 2-B."

He tried to move, to speak, but his body refused to respond. The darkness kept pulling him under.

Kon-stahns let out a low, exasperated growl, and he could hear her footsteps pacing. Then a pause.

"Unit 2-B. Unit 2-B. Which one is unit 2-B?!?"

"AFT SECTION, PORT SIDE."

"Okay, port side. Port side."

Her footsteps faded, leaving him alone with the oppressive silence. He tried to force his body to move again, but it was as if his limbs were submerged in bonding agent. His mind screamed at his muscles to obey, but they didn't even twitch.

He wanted to open his eyes. Just so he could see her.

Instead, he slipped into the void again.

WHEN CONSCIOUSNESS FLICKERED BACK, it was to the sound of rummaging. Containers being opened, items shuffled and discarded. Her voice was closer now, muttering under her breath.

"None of these things make sense." There was a sharp clatter as something hit the floor.

"These will have to do," she muttered, her voice tight but resolute.

Her scent reached him first—warm. Sweet. *Her.* It grounded him in a way nothing else could.

He felt her presence next. The heat of her body radiated near his side as she knelt beside him. The sensation was faint, muted by the haze of pain, but it was enough to make him want to shift closer. Only he couldn't.

His body was useless.

"Alright," she murmured, and he could feel her hands on him now, hesitant at first but growing surer as she worked. "I can do this."

There was a sharp, tearing sound—fabric being ripped. Her clothes? His mind was too sluggish to process fully.

Oh, Kon-stahns.

It wouldn't be the first time she ripped her own garments just to save him. Wouldn't be the first time she worked hard just to keep him living.

"God, Akur." She muttered. Her hand shuddered as she worked. "I don't know how you're still breathing, but I'm glad. I'm so glad." Her hands trembled again as she began tending to the largest wound on his chest.

Her hands were gentle. He felt a cool cloth on his skin, wiping away the stickiness of blood and grime. The pressure stung, but it was distant, as though the pain belonged to someone else.

"You're going to be fine," she whispered, almost as if trying to convince herself. "You've been through worse. Right? You can handle this. You always handle this."

Time blurred, but her voice was a constant in the haze, alternating between muttered curses and soothing reassurances.

"Where's the antiseptic? Computer?"

"ANTISEPTIC IS LOCATED IN..."

He drifted.

～

"Sorry," she whispered, her voice closer now. He felt her fingers brushing against his skin as she worked. "I know this hurts. I'm trying to be careful."

Her touch was feather-light, but even so, the pain flared, dragging him closer to the surface of awareness. He tried to speak, to tell her it was alright, that he could take it, but his throat felt like sandpaper, and no sound came out.

"Shhh," she murmured. "Don't talk. Just...just stay with me, okay? Stay."

The cloth returned, wiping at another wound. Then the faint tug of bandages being wrapped.

"You're never doing this again," she muttered, her voice breaking slightly. "You hear me? You're never doing this again. Not for me. Not for anyone. It's about time you realized your life isn't expendable. That people don't want to see you dead. That I don't—"

She stopped herself; took a shaky breath.

"It doesn't matter. We'll talk about it later. When you're better."

At some point, the weight of his trouse disappeared.

He felt the cool air against his skin, the rough tug of fabric being pulled away.

"Sorry," she said again, softer this time. "I need to get to all of it. I —" She hesitated, and he could hear the faint hitch in her breath. "It's not like I haven't seen your nakedness before. This is just...different."

Her hands worked quickly, efficiently, though he could feel the slight tremor in her touch. She cleaned his wounds, applied bandages, her touch a strange mix of careful efficiency and...something else. Something softer, something that made his life organ beat a little faster despite the pain.

Then, her fingers brushed against his groin, against the sensitive pouch where his shaft was hidden. A jolt of electricity shot through him. Hot enough, he almost gasped. His hips instinctively tilted upwards.

"Oh," she breathed, the word a soft exhale against his skin. He could feel the heat radiating from her hand, the warmth spreading through his groin, igniting a flicker of desire amidst the pain. He wanted her touch, craved it with a desperation that surprised him. He wanted...he wanted... He wasn't sure what he wanted, only that he wanted it with *her*.

"Sorry," she repeated, voice barely audible. "Didn't mean to...Just trying to...make sure everything's...alright." Her fingers moved away, continuing their ministrations, but the memory of her touch lingered, a phantom sensation that made his lifeblood sing. He was acutely aware of her now, of her every movement, her every breath, her every whispered word. She was saving his life, patching him up, piece by piece. And he...he wanted her. With a fierceness, a desperation that both terrified and exhilarated him.

He wanted her. More than he'd allowed himself to admit before this point.

Time stretched on. He drifted in and out, each time waking to the sound of her voice or the gentle press of her hands on his skin.

At one point, he felt her fingers brushing across his jaw.

"You're doing great," she whispered. "Just keep fighting, okay? You're too damn stubborn to give up now."

Her lips brushed his temple—a fleeting, delicate touch that sent a ripple of warmth through the cold haze.

When he finally opened his eyes, the dim light pierced his pupils like narrow shards.

Where...where were they?

His gaze found the beeping console up ahead, focus shifting over the ship. It was the same one he'd put her on. How he managed to be on the same vessel, he didn't know. It didn't make sense.

Turning his head slightly, he found her slumped beside him, her head resting on her folded arms where she slept atop what looked like a soft sleeping cushion she must have found.

She looked exhausted, her hair a tangled mess, dark smudges beneath her eyes. One hand was still resting on his chest, her fingers curled loosely against his skin.

Guilt twisted in his gut. She'd been taking care of him all this time, pouring everything she had into keeping him alive, and he'd done nothing but lie there like dead weight.

"Kon-stahns..." His voice was a cracked whisper, barely audible.

Her head jerked up anyway, eyes unfocused at first, as if waking from a deep sleep. For a moment, she just stared at him, uncomprehending. Then her eyes went wide.

"Akur?" The word came out rough, uncertain. "Akur!" She pushed herself up, swaying slightly as blood rushed to her head. "You're...." She blinked hard, steadying herself against the wall. "You're awake!"

She half-stumbled to a flask nearby, nearly dropping it in her haste. When she returned, her smile was trembling, exhausted. "Thank God. I wasn't sure if..." She trailed off, her throat working as she swallowed hard.

She pressed the flask to his lips, making water trickle in.

"I'm sorry, bright eyes," he rasped.

A sound cracked in her throat. "Don't. Don't you apologize. Just... don't scare me like that again, okay?"

He managed a faint smile, though it felt like it took all the energy he had.

"I mean it," she said, her tone firm despite the tremor in her voice. "You're not allowed to die on me. Not now. Not ever."

Her hand cupped his jaw, her thumb brushing lightly against his skin. Then, before he could process what was happening, she leaned in and pressed her lips to his.

The mouth touching was soft, lingering, filled with something that made his chest ache more than the wounds ever had.

When she pulled back, her eyes glistened with unshed waters.

"You scared the hell out of me," she whispered.

"I'm sorry, bright eyes," he said again, voice stronger this time.

She gave a watery laugh, shaking her head. But there was no anger in her voice. Only relief. It took everything in him to reach up, claw trembling as he brushed away a lock of her filaments from her face.

"Thank you," he murmured.

For the first time since the citadel, the crushing weight of pain and exhaustion seemed to lessen. He was alive. *They* were alive. And somehow, miraculously, they were together.

Kon-stahns sat back, her hand still resting on his jaw. She was looking at him like he would the stars. As if looking at something wonderful. Something mesmerizing. Something beautiful.

He wanted to say something, anything that could convey the depth of his gratitude, the guilt that she'd been the one to tend to him when it should've been the other way around. But as her thumb brushed against his lips, silencing him, he realized words might not be enough.

"You're impossible," she murmured, her voice soft. "Do you know that? You drive me out of my mind, Akur."

Her hand drifted down, her fingers lightly tracing the edge of the bandages she'd wrapped around his chest. The touch was delicate, cautious, but it stirred something inside him—a warmth that spread out from her fingertips and settled low in his gut.

He swallowed hard, the dryness in his throat fading as her scent filled the air. Sweet and warm, like her—like *home*.

"Kon-stahns," he rasped, catching her wrist. His digits curled around her pulse. It was fast, erratic, matching the rhythm of his own.

Kon-stahns' eyes widened as she looked at him, her lips parting as though to question him, but the words never came.

He tugged her closer, not with strength—he didn't have much of that left—but with intent. She shifted, her knees coming to the edge of the makeshift bedding beneath her.

"You should rest," she whispered, voice faltering even as she leaned in. Her hand pressed lightly against his shoulder as though she was trying to keep him still. "You're not—"

"I'm not letting you go." The more she touched him, the stronger he felt.

"Akur..."

His claw slid up, trembling but determined, until his palm rested against her jaw. The barest touch he wasn't even sure she could feel. "I am here because of you," he whispered. "You, female of fire, are impossible. You fought for me." His gaze studied hers. "You...saved me."

Her lips trembled, and she turned her face slightly into his palm. "Of course, I did. What else was I supposed to do? Leave you there? Let you die?"

"I was prepared to die if it meant you got off that rock alive."

Her brows drew together. "And what about me, Akur?"

He didn't understand her question.

"Do you think I want a world without you in it?" Her throat moved. "Akur, I—. Don't you realize I—" She stopped herself, her voice cracking. Then she leaned down, her forehead brushing against his as her breath mingled with his own.

"You stubborn fool," she whispered, but there was something tender in the way she said it.

He smiled faintly, the corners of his lips tugging upward despite the pain that still lingered.

Her lips brushed against his again, tentative at first, as though she were afraid he might break. But when he returned the contact, slow and deliberate, Kon-stahns melted into him. Her hands cradled his face as though it were the only thing anchoring her.

The ache of his injuries was momentarily forgotten as her weight settled against him. She was cautious, careful not to press too hard against the bandages, but he could feel the heat of her through the thin barrier of the fabric she still wore.

Her fingers ran down his jaw, then his neck, tracing his frame as though memorizing him. He reveled in it. Each touch, each point of contact, was like electricity going straight through him.

"You were so cold. Freezing, Akur. But you're getting warm again," she murmured against his lips, before she paused. "Your heat..."

He shook his head, his forehead brushing hers. "It's not the heat."

She pulled back slightly to look at him, confusion mingling with something else in her gaze. "Then..."

"This has nothing to do with my heat cycle." The words came out rough. "Qrak..." He hesitated. Wondered if he should say it out loud. "I've been fighting this since the tunnels, Kon-stahns. Telling myself it was just instinct, just biology. But lying here, feeling your hands put me back together piece by piece..." One digit traced her cheekbone. "I can't lie to myself anymore."

Her breath caught, her eyes searching his.

"Every time you touch me, every time you say my name—it's not hormones driving this need. It's you. Just you. The way you fight, the way you care, the way you see right through me..." His voice dropped lower. "I need you to be mine, Kon-stahns. Not for a heat cycle. Not for now. For always."

His breath stilled.

There. He'd said it out loud. This was the part where she rejected him. The part where she made it clear that what happened in those tunnels was a one-off thing. That he was getting ahead of himself. His growing obsession with her like all his other obsessions. Something that would consume him. Something he'd never be rid of.

Because she was in his lifeblood now. In his soul. Even if she wanted nothing to do with him, she was the female he wanted. There was no other.

And yet, even though he was sure it was coming, even though she hadn't yet responded, his tongue still spilled words as if trying to convince her. As if his rambling thoughts would make her say yes.

"I cannot offer you much. My life is dangerous, my world harsh. I am not..." His claws flexed against her skin. "I am not what most would consider a worthy mate. But if you would have me, everything I am is yours."

She pressed her fingers against his lips, stopping his words.

"Everything you are?" Her voice was barely a whisper. "Your honor? Your strength? Your stubbornness that drives me absolutely mad?" A soft laugh escaped her, watery but real. "Akur, don't you understand? That's exactly what I want. I...I want you, Akur. Scars, dangers, harsh world and all. I want your strength, your determination, your..." Her voice caught. "Your way of looking at me like I'm the only being in the universe. Like I'm..."

"Special?" He breathed. "Important?" He'd known she was both of those things, but he hadn't known she was both those things for *him*. Not till it had been almost too late.

He tugged her closer, his hands finding her hips despite the tremble in his digits, and she shuddered against him, lips finding his once more. He was never good with words. Action was his sort of thing. "I don't have much strength left." A faint smile tugged at his mouth. "So if you're going to stop me, do it now."

Her answer came as a giggle against his lips. "We can't do that," she whispered, her lips brushing against his jaw. "I don't want to hurt you."

"You won't." His claws slipped beneath the fabric of her tunic to rest against her bare skin. "Just...slow."

27

Akur

Kon-stahns inhaled deeply, nuzzling into him before a delicious shiver went through her frame. When she began peeling away the barriers between them, his lifeblood pumped so hard he swore he soaked the bandages. As the fabric slipped over her head, the sight of her left him breathless.

"Stars...you're beautiful," he rasped, drinking her in.

Her cheeks flushed, but she didn't look away. Instead, she reached for him, her hands gentle as they explored the planes of his chest, careful to avoid the bandages.

"You're...hurting," she murmured, her brow furrowed with concern as her fingers brushed against a particularly nasty gash near his ribs.

He chuckled, a low rumble in his chest. "Nothing I can't handle."

She looked up then. A genuine smile crossed her face. Then her eyes went thoughtful. "I know what might make you feel better."

"What?" he almost growled. He could already tell whatever it was would drive him to the edge of sanity.

"A blowjob."

Akur paused. She'd mentioned that before. He remembered.

"You have promised this job of blows before."

Kon-stahns giggled. "A what now?"

"I must admit, bright eyes. Getting blows of any nature wasn't exactly what I was imagining…"

She chuckled this time before lifting a hand to wipe at her eyes. "I can't believe I'm laughing. Days ago, I thought you were dead. The sun stopped shining."

"Days?" He eased up slightly, wincing with the effort. "We have been on this vessel for many turns?"

Her mirth disappeared and she dipped her chin to her chest a few times.

And all that time, she'd been trying to keep him alive. "Kon-stahns…"

Her hand slid lower, her fingers tracing the line of his abdomen. Despite himself, his hips tilted upward into her touch.

"Maybe I need this more than you," she whispered, gaze dropping to his hips. They were covered with a thin sheet of film he couldn't name. Something she'd obviously spread there to give him some decency. "Let me show you what I mean."

Her fingers dipped underneath the film and brushed against the sensitive slit of his pouch. He shuddered immediately, a wave of heat washing over him. He'd been so focused on her, on the feel of her hands on his skin, that he hadn't realized how near to the edge he was already.

Kon-stahns slid down, gaze on his as she lowered her head. Her lips brushed against the sensitive skin of his inner thigh, sending shivers of pleasure radiating through him. He groaned, his hands tangling in her hair, his fingers tightening as she continued her exploration, her touch growing bolder, more confident.

She pressed her lips there, a soft, lingering contact that made him arch his back, a low growl rumbling in his chest. Then, the film barrier disappeared. Her lips found the slit of his pouch, her tongue tracing the sensitive line.

"Gods," he gasped, his body tensing. Not even that stopped it from happening. He extruded immediately, his cock emerging in a wet slop as his seed sac plopped out beneath it, swollen and heavy.

He'd never experienced anything like this. The feel of her mouth on him, the warmth of her breath, the delicate flick of her tongue against his most vulnerable point—it was exquisite torture, a delicious agony that made him want to both scream and surrender.

"Oh!" Constance didn't hesitate. She kissed him there, her lips soft and warm against his sensitive skin. He groaned, arching into her touch, his hands tangling in her mane, holding her close as she explored him with her mouth, her tongue tracing the ridge of his slit, the curve of his engorged cock, the heavy weight of his seed sac. Each touch sent shivers of pleasure radiating through him, a fire spreading through his veins, consuming him from the inside out.

He whispered her name, a plea, a prayer, lost in the haze of sensation. She continued her ministrations, her touch growing bolder, more confident, her rhythm increasing, drawing him closer and closer to the edge...until she did what he somehow didn't expect. She took him into her mouth.

His entire body stiffened, pain forgotten.

"Kons—"

"Mm." She sucked on him, bobbing her head over his length, obscene sloppy sounds leaving her throat as she sucked and swallowed him.

He couldn't take it. He couldn't last much longer. He could feel the seed pods already swelling and rising, the pressure building within him, a delicious torment that made him writhe beneath her touch.

If he'd known this was what a job of blows was, he'd have been more excited about it from the start.

"Kon-stahns..." A deep rumbling growl as she dipped her head and tried to take him in all his entirety. She failed, choked, and kept on it.

The sight, the sensations, it only made him shatter.

The first seed pod rose and burst in her mouth. She pulled off him, breathing hard as her eyes rolled back in her head. Another rose and spilled from him, running over her fists that were clenched around him.

"Kon-stahns..."

She dipped her head again and tasted him, her tongue lapping at the spilled seed, her eyes meeting his just a moment before they rolled back in her head again. The sight of her, her lips glistening with his essence, her cheeks flushed with a combination of desire and...something else...something that looked like wonder...it sent a wave of emotion through him, so intense it made him shatter again.

Qrak. He was going to drown her in it.

Reaching for her, his grip was stronger than it had been since he woke up. He pulled her up, his hands shaking as he cupped her face, his thumb brushing against her swollen lips, glistening with his seed. He knew the look in his eyes was fierce; the look of a male driven to the edge of control.

She gasped as he claimed her mouth, his tongue sweeping in, tasting himself on her. He groaned, the sound feral, hungry. His hands slid down to her hips, gripping her tightly, his fingers digging into her soft flesh. She whimpered into his mouth, her body melting against his as he deepened the contact, consuming her as if he were a starving male and she his first meal in days.

He shifted beneath her, his cock still hard, still spilling seed, and still wanting more. His body forgot about the pain and fatigue as raw instinct took over. He needed her. Needed to claim her, to make her his in every way possible.

His hands moved to her thighs, urging her to straddle him. She complied, her breath hitching as she felt his hard length press against her core. He swallowed her gasp, his tongue never leaving hers, never breaking the contact of their lips.

He rocked his hips upwards, his cock sliding against her, coating itself in her wetness and coating her with his. She moaned, her hands clinging to his shoulders, her nails digging into his skin. It was a different kind of pain. One that made him growl at the sensation, mixing with his pleasure, driving him closer to the edge.

He broke the contact of their lips, his mouth moving to her jaw, her neck, his teeth grazing against her skin. She shivered, her head falling back, giving him more access. He took advantage, his mouth latching onto the sensitive spot where her neck met her shoulder, sucking hard, marking her.

She cried out, her hips grinding against his, her body begging for more. He could feel her heat, her wetness, her desire. He could *scent* it. And it was *intoxicating*, driving him mad with need.

His hands moved to her ass, gripping her tightly, guiding her as she moved against him. Moved against his cock as it slid back and forth, the friction exquisite, the sensation overwhelming. He could feel her trembling, her breath coming in ragged gasps, her heart pounding against his chest. She was just as affected as he was. But he was going to give her more.

Her breath hitched as he lifted her, positioning her so that his cock pressed against her entrance. He could feel her tension, her anticipation, her need. He wanted to draw this out, to savor every moment, every touch, every gasp. But his body was impatient, desperate for her, desperate to claim her fully.

"Akur..." His name was a whisper, a plea on her lips. Her eyes met his, wide and full of desire; full of him.

"You are mine, Kon-stahns," he growled again, his voice low and possessive. "Mine."

With that, he thrust upward, sheathing himself inside her in one smooth motion. She cried out, her body tensing around him, her inner walls clamping down on his shaft. He groaned, the sensation overwhelming, the pleasure intense.

He stilled for a moment, giving her time to adjust, giving himself time to regain some semblance of control. But she was having none of it. Her hips began moving, slowly at first, then with increasing urgency. He matched her rhythm, his hands guiding her, his body meeting hers with each thrust.

Their breaths mingled, their gazes locked, their bodies moving in sync. She really was a part of him, as necessary as the air he breathed, the lifeblood in his veins.

Her moans grew louder, her movements more erratic. He could

feel her climax building, her body tightening around him. So he slipped a hand between them, his fingers finding that sensitive nub at the apex of her thighs. He stroked it, his touch feather-light, designed to tease, to torment, to push her over the edge.

"Akur...I...I can't..." Her words were a jumbled mess, her body trembling, her breath coming in sharp gasps.

"You can," he growled. "With me, Kon-stahns. Come with me."

He increased the pressure on her little nub, his hardness driving into her with more force, more urgency.

"Yes..." she whimpered, her gaze locked onto his. Her body was taut, balanced on the precipice of release. He could feel the tremors running through her, her inner muscles fluttering around him, gripping him as if they wanted to strangle him. And qrak, it felt good.

"Now, Kon-stahns," he commanded, his voice a deep rumble. He pinched her nub gently, and she shattered.

Her cry echoed around them, her body convulsing as waves of pleasure crashed over her. He felt her climax, her body pulsing, drawing him deeper, milking him. It was too much, too intense. With a final, powerful thrust, he joined her.

His release exploded from him, seed pods filling her with his essence. He roared her name, his body shaking with the force of his climax. Lights danced behind his eyes, his heart pounded in his chest, and for a moment, he was lost, drowning in a sea of sensation.

For a moment, he truly died and came back again.

Kon-stahns collapsed onto him, her body seizing with peak after peak, and he held her there, refusing to let go. He wasn't ever letting her go.

They lay like that for a long time, their bodies entwined, their breaths mingling, life-organs beating as one. He stroked her filaments gently, his digits combing through the soft strands as she nuzzled into him, as if, like him, she didn't want to move.

As the ship continued on and they lay there together, one thing became clear.

Death and retribution were no longer the goal.

"Before you," he whispered, "my existence was a battlefield. An endless cycle of violence and loss. I was a weapon, forged in fire, honed for destruction. I knew nothing but duty, nothing but pain. But you...you have shown me something new. You have shown me...hope. You have shown me...life." His hand tightened on her waist, pulling her closer, his voice dropping to a husky whisper. "You are not just mine, Kon-stahns. You are...my salvation."

She looked up at him then.

"Forever."

She smiled. "I like the sound of that."

28

Akur

KON-STAHNS LAY DRAPED OVER HIM, her breathing soft and steady against his chest. For the first time since they met, he allowed himself to feel the weight of her—not just her physical presence, but the meaning behind it.

She was exhausted, her body limp and utterly spent. He could feel the subtle tremors in her muscles from their earlier union, the way her hands had gripped him, the way she had clung to him as if he was the only thing tethering her to this world. And now, she slept —deep and unbroken, the kind of sleep that could only come after days of relentless vigilance and fear.

She'd been afraid. But oh so very brave.

Glancing around the ship, his gaze narrowed as he took in their surroundings. The dim light from the console flickered, casting eerie shadows across the bulkheads. The air smelled faintly of lifeblood, metal, and antiseptic—a reminder of the state he'd been in when she'd fought to save him.

Shifting slightly, he tested his limbs. Pain flared in his chest, the bandages tight against his ribs, but it was manageable now. Slowly, carefully, he slid his arms around her, lifting her from his chest. His muscles protested, but he ignored the strain. Kon-stahns murmured something unintelligible, her head lolling against his shoulder as he carried her to the sleeping cushion she'd fashioned for herself.

"You're safe," he whispered, voice rough but low. "Sleep, bright eyes."

She didn't stir. For a moment, he couldn't move. Couldn't leave her side. His life organ thumped hard as he watched her, concern growing in his gut. Her body was so completely relaxed that it unnerved him. She had been running on nothing but adrenaline, her will to keep him alive carrying her far beyond her limits. Now, she had nothing left, and it showed in the way her body had just... stopped. Almost like she'd gone into some kind of hibernation. It showed too in the pallor of her skin, the way her breathing hitched faintly even in sleep.

Frowning, he leaned closer, rubbing his nose into her throat.

"I am sorry," he whispered. "Sweet, soft things like you don't deserve an existence like this."

Her mane was a tangled mess, strands clinging to her damp forehead. There were minor cuts on her arms, bruises along her wrists, the bloody bandages on her shoulder. Guilt twisted in his gut like a blade.

The old Akur would have called this a failure.

He ran a hand down his face, exhaling slowly. No. That life was gone. The male he had been—the weapon, the killer—he had no place here. Kon-stahns had saved him, not just from death, but from himself.

If Kon-stahns hadn't been there...if she hadn't saved him...he'd have been completely blinded by nothing but bloodlust.

And that wasn't the way to end this war.

Rising on unsteady legs, he began searching the small vessel. His steps were silent, instincts taking over, but the ship was quiet, the hum of its engines the only sound. He checked the trajectory on the console, sharp eyes scanning the navigation display.

They were on course, heading toward a neutral zone—one of the few places where they might find refuge. Relief washed over him, but it was fleeting. Neutral zone or not, the Tasqals weren't going to simply let Kon-stahns go. They wouldn't stop till they had what they wanted.

And what they wanted was her.

This wasn't over yet.

Turning his attention back to the ship's interior, he began searching for supplies. They were sparse—medical kits, water flasks, and a few ration packs stored in a compartment near the cockpit. He grabbed a flask, his gaze darting back to Kon-stahns. She hadn't moved.

He crouched beside her again. Dipping a strip of cloth into the water, he began cleaning her wounds. She didn't stir, not even when he pressed the damp cloth against the cut on her temple or the one on her shoulder.

"You've done enough," he murmured, his voice barely audible. "It's my turn now."

Her lips parted slightly, a soft breath escaping her, and he froze. But she remained asleep. Slowly, he resumed his work, his hands steady despite the tremor of exhaustion in his limbs.

She looked so small, so fragile, but he knew better. She was the strongest being he'd ever encountered. Stronger than him, in many ways.

This wasn't weakness—to care so deeply, to let some other being become a part of him. It was strength. A different kind of strength. The strength to fight for something more than revenge or survival.

Easing up from where he crouched watching her, his gaze shifted to the viewscreen. He didn't know why he stared at the void. Wasn't sure what had twigged his awareness.

Standing now, his brow tightened.

This was just a small cargo ship. Old. Worn. Without the usual instruments of more modern vessels. All he had was the path toward Hudo III. One the ally Tasqal had plotted and set the vessel on. But something was...different.

His nefre twitched as he moved over to the controls, peering through the viewscreen at the void beyond. There was no way to check exactly *what* had changed. All he had to rely on was his instincts. Instincts that had kept him alive for so long and would keep *her* alive, too.

The sharp chirp of an incoming transmission shattered the silence. Akur's head snapped up, muscles tensing as the console's warning light pulsed an angry red. A message.

Heavily encrypted, but with a signature that was unmistakable.

The Restitution.

But that was impossible. He and Constance were essentially off the grid. No one knew where they were. No one knew they were even alive.

Unless...

His fingers flew across the controls, decoding protocols on a vessel not meant to receive such a message. It took forever, each click like an eternity as the message decrypted. When the text finally resolved, his blood ran cold.

TASQAL PURSUIT VESSELS DETECTED. THREE WARSHIPS, HEADING 2.7.4. ENTERING YOUR SECTOR. GET OUT. NOW.

Frowning at the message, he stared at it.

Below the warning were coordinates, a location deep in the dark reaches—completely in the opposite direction to where they were heading now.

Was this some kind of trick?

No. How would the Tasqals know the Restitution's signature?

He stared at the message longer, uncertainty making him pause.

After encountering that rogue Tasqal, something he'd have thought impossible if he hadn't been there in the flesh, he wasn't so sure what to believe anymore.

Apparently, everything was possible.

Glancing over his shoulder, his gaze settled on the female still resting on the sleeping cushion. Yes. Everything was possible.

For even he had a mate.

Pulling up the ship's scanners proved useless. The equipment wasn't enough for long-range detection. The Tasqals could be right on top of them and they wouldn't know until—

The ship shuddered, lights blinking in and out.

Oh, qrak.

His digits scraped against the console as he braced himself. A low, ominous hum coursed through the ship—a sound that hadn't been there before.

Behind him, Kon-stahns bolted upright, her eyes wild, her breath coming in short, panicked gasps.

"What—" she started, voice hoarse.

"Stay down!" He didn't mean to snarl, but his instincts were screaming, his nefre twitching uncontrollably. His fingers flew over the controls, trying to stabilize the ship.

"What's happening?" she demanded, her voice stronger now. Closer, too, as if she'd risen.

"Pursuit vessels," he muttered. "Tasqal warships. They're here."

"Oh, shit." She was by his side now, peering out the viewscreen, wild eyes shifting but seeing nothing—just like he couldn't see them but *knew* they were there. "How did they find us?"

"Not sure. Maybe they were tracking this vessel all along." The ship bucked again, a low boom resonating through the hull. His gaze flicked to the scanner, narrowing.

"That...what was that? That wasn't a hit, was it?" Kon-stahns' digits clenched into fists.

"Proximity charges." His brow tightened. "They're trying to slow us down."

"To catch us," Kon-stahns whispered. Her gaze skipped to the readouts on the console nearby her. "They're not firing because they don't want to blow us out into space. They want us alive."

He grunted, shook his head. "No, bright eyes. They want you alive. It's always been you. I'll die before—"

Her jaw tightened. "Not an option. And they're not getting me either."

Grunting, his lips shifted into a grin. "Right. You're mine."

Their gazes locked as her cheeks changed color, almost going red like when he was in heat and his nefre burned with the fire of a thousand suns.

"I'm not letting them take you."

Gaze not shifting from his, she jerked her chin to her chest in silent affirmation.

This vessel wasn't built for combat or speed—it was a cargo ship, stripped down and barely functional. The shields were minimal, the weapons nonexistent or completely drained. They were as vulnerable as hatchlings.

"Can we jump?" she asked.

"No such luck, bright eyes. This ship isn't made for that."

"Fuck." She ran a hand through her brown filaments. "We have to lose them somehow."

As another pulse hit the ship, his jaw clenched. "There is a way."

"Do it."

He grunted a laugh in his throat. "You do not know—"

"I trust you."

Something swelled in his throat. It wasn't the first time he'd heard her say that, and something told him it wouldn't be the last.

"Buckle in, bright eyes. We're not heading to the neutral zone anymore," he said, pulling up the coordinates from the encrypted message. "We're taking a detour."

She didn't even pause. Dropping into the seat beside him, the restraints pulled themselves across her at the same moment that one of the Tasqal ships finally came into view. His entire frame tingled as Kon-stahns reached for him, gripping his arm almost on instinct.

The Tasqal ships were beasts. Black. Sleek. A symbol of their wealth, power, and status.

"Shit, Akur, take that detour."

"CHANGING DESTINATION," the ship communicated. "MANUAL CONTROLS ENGAGED."

"Manual?" Kon-stahns' gaze slid to him.

"The only way." His gaze shifted to the viewscreen. "The only way for us to get through that."

He could tell the moment she noticed what they were swerving toward. The moment it became clear their chances of survival had once again dimmed.

"Um...Akur..."

Before them was a massive expanse of wreckage, the blurred forms of dead vessels and tiny parts becoming clearer the closer they went.

"This detour..." Kon-stahns gripped his arm tighter.

"It came in a comm. I don't know who sent it...But it's the only chance we have. If we stay on this course, they'll catch us in clicks. We have to trust it."

Kon-stahns jerked her chin to her chest, squeezing his arm tighter, her warmth flooding through him like a salve. "Do it. I trust you. They'll have to slow down to follow us. We can use the debris for cover."

"It's a risk," he said, not bothering to hide the warning in his tone. But he should already know this female was as insane as he was. After all, she'd accepted him inside her not once, but twice. She'd even accepted his seed in her mouth. She was his, and maybe that insanity was what bound them.

"Everything's a risk," she shot back, her eyes blazing as she met his gaze. "But if we stay out here, we're dead."

For a moment, neither of them spoke. Then he gave a sharp nod, his claws moving to adjust their course.

"Hold on," he said.

The ship banked sharply, diving toward the sprawling field of twisted metal and shattered shipwrecks. The proximity alarms screamed in protest as the debris loomed closer, jagged fragments spinning in the void.

Kon-stahns gripped his arm tighter; so tight he could feel her life-organ pounding through her veins. He could almost feel her stomach sink at the sight of the Tasqal ships closing in. Their sleek, predatory forms moved with terrifying precision, their engines flaring as they adjusted their trajectory to follow.

"Akur, they're not slowing down."

"They don't need to," he growled. "They're faster, stronger. Better shields. They'll tear through the debris like it's nothing."

"Then—" Her wide eyes flew to him. "Why the fuck are we doing this?!"

His gaze slipped over her. Over her thin brows, the way her pert little nose tilted to the air, the way her lips were full... "Because I'm going to do something insane."

She didn't even flinch. Instead, her eyes narrowed as she faced the debris field before them. Her shoulders set. In that moment, he knew, whatever he decided, she was with him. "What are you thinking?"

He grinned, a flash of teeth in the dim light. "Something even you might think is crazy."

"Try me," she challenged, her grip tightening on his arm. She sent him a small grin, too.

The sight sent a tingle down his spine. He met her gaze, a spark of shared recklessness passing between them. They were partners in this madness, two rebels against the universe, a warrior and his human taking on an empire.

"Hold on tight, bright eyes," he said, shifting the controls. "This is going to get...interesting."

The ship plunged deeper into the debris field, alarms screaming. Jagged fragments spun past the viewscreen, some cutting into the tiny ship's hull.

"They're right behind us," Kon-stahns whispered, eyes locked on the scanner now. But her voice was calm, almost detached, as if she was 'therapying' the disaster rather than facing imminent death.

He glanced at the scanner, too, his jaw tightening. The Tasqal ships were closing fast. "I know," he muttered, directing the small ship as it weaved through the chaos. The same wreckage slowly stripping the ship's armor was the only thing they could use as a shield. Each near miss, each jarring impact, bathed the small cockpit in red.

"There," Kon-stahns said, pointing to a hulking derelict. "What's that? Can we use it?"

He followed her gaze. The derelict ship was massive, a twisted monument to some forgotten disaster, but it offered a sliver of a chance. It was an old Class-4 power station. The kind that used unstable reactor cores to fuel entire colonies.

"Risky," he said, his voice a low growl, "but it might work. The space is tiny."

"Like threading a needle. But you can do it. You're the best space pilot I know."

He grunted a laugh, warmth flooding through him. "I am the *only* pilot you know."

Kon-stahns laughed, the sound so rich it momentarily deleted everything around him. In that single moment, all he could see was her.

"They're going to fire, Kon-stahns." He broke the truth. The peace of her laughter was immediately shattered.

"We'll make it." Her gaze locked with his.

Her trust in him was indescribable. And she had no idea what it did to him.

"After this..." he said, watching her face as the derelict ship came closer. "After this...when it's over...will you...will you let me show you my homeworld? Tonvuhiri. When it's safe. You could meet my... what's left of my clan..."

He didn't know why his life organ stopped beating as he waited for her response, even as they flew toward something even more dangerous than any answer that could come from her lips.

Kon-stahns' gaze flashed to him and she shifted her hand from where she was gripping his arm. As the derelict vessel became so large it was all they could see before them, she leaned over, her lips closing over his.

"Of course," she whispered. "Of course, I will."

Moments before their ship was to slip through the jagged hole in the derelict's side, the scanner screamed. The qrakking Hedgeruds had locked weapons.

"Hold on!" he roared, banking the ship hard as they entered the hole. The first plasma bolt streaked past their starboard side, close enough that the heat sensors wailed. The second struck the derelict exactly where he wanted it to.

The hidden reactor core.

As they flew out the other side, Akur held his breath. For a click, nothing happened, and he wondered whether the core had been stripped. Gods knew how long the ship had been floating in this debris field. Scavengers could have taken every and anything worth a few credits.

But then the readings on the console before them exploded.

Raw energy erupted from the derelict's spine, a tsunami of radiation and plasma that lit up the void brighter than a star. The Tasqal ships' superior shields meant nothing against that kind of power. They were too close, too committed to their pursuit.

"Holy shit," Kon-stahns breathed, gripping his arm tighter.

But they weren't safe. The blast wave was coming.

He yanked the controls, trying to outrun the destruction they'd unleashed. The little ship groaned, metal shrieking as if it was being torn apart. Warning lights flooded the cockpit. The heat inside spiked.

Something exploded behind them and their ship lurched, spinning. Kon-stahns screamed as she fought to stay in her seat.

"We've lost an engine!" His claws flew over the controls, fighting to stabilize them.

The blast wave hit them full force. The entire ship shuddered. For a moment, he thought the hull would crack open like an egg.

"Akur..." Kon-stahns' voice was tight. "That doesn't sound good."

He grunted, still wrestling with the controls. "Ship's dying around us."

More alerts screamed for attention. Hull breach. Life support failing. Power fluctuating. The console in front of Kon-stahns sparked and went dark. She jerked back with a curse, smoke curling from the dead panel.

"How long?"

"Two hors. Maybe three." His jaw clenched as another system failed.

"If we're lucky."

A distinct hiss cut through his words. They were losing air.

Scrambling, he sealed off the rear of the little vessel. Two hors? Now they only had one, if the gods decided to spare them.

Pulling back on the controls, the remaining engine struggled as the little vessel clawed its way out of the debris field.

Beside him, Kon-stahns' chest heaved as she studied the scanner. Her cheeks were flushed, her eyes wide. "Are-are they following us?"

The remaining sensors picked up nothing but scattered debris. "Negative."

Her chest heaved, breaths puffing from her lips before she collapsed in her seat. "You...you did it."

His chest heaved as he checked the readouts. "Told you it was insane."

"Insanely brilliant," she corrected. But there was something underneath her smile. A fear he could feel, too. "You're a goddamn genius, Mint Man."

He could only gaze at her. He had a mate. A human mate. And she was...magnificent. He would get her out of this.

Pulling up the new coordinates, the ship lurched as he turned, the damaged hull groaning. They were still bleeding atmosphere some-where, and their remaining engine wouldn't last forever. As Kon-stahns tugged out of the restraints, his arms opened as she climbed into his lap, wrapping her thighs around him.

Maybe it was because she could feel the danger they were in. Maybe it was because she wanted him to keep her safe. It didn't matter why she sought his touch. Tugging her to his chest, he stared out the viewscreen.

Through willpower alone, he'd make sure she made it.

"That was amazing. *You* are amazing. You know that?" she whispered, breath tickling his skin.

He forced his voice to stay light, despite the warning lights still flashing around them. "I *am* amazing. That is a known fact."

She slapped him playfully. "Cocky."

He growled. "What's this about my cock now?"

Kon-stahns laughed. But her chest was still heaving. The threat of what just occurred still pushing adrenaline through her being.

And they weren't done.

"They'll come again, you know," she whispered.

"Yes." He did know. He was now in constant awareness of that fact. "Hopefully we get there before more arrive." They *had* to.

"There?" Kon-stahns lifted her head, gaze searching his. "There where?"

He wished he could answer.

Looking at the coordinates he just punched in, he couldn't.

Because the truth was, he had no idea.

29

Constance

SHE WAS STILL on his lap. She'd have let him go. Allowed him to pilot the ship better, but he didn't seem to want her to move. One arm wrapped around her, he kept her seated as he focused on the controls.

He'd gone silent, and the silence in the ship was almost deafening. From the near-death experience of a moment before, it felt only natural. She couldn't talk either.

Maybe because her heart was still beating too hard. Or maybe because where they headed next had her spine set in a hard line, so much so that even though she was pressed against him, she could hardly relax.

The coordinates they were following had come from someone... and neither of them knew who.

As she wrapped her hands around his neck, the fin along Akur's nape twitched—a sure sign he was sensing something she couldn't.

"Akur," she whispered, rubbing her jaw against his in a move that was both comforting and grounding. "What's wrong?"

His jaw tightened against hers. "There's something..." He trailed off, frowning at the viewscreen. "The scanner is picking up intermittent signals, but I can't see anything."

Glancing over her shoulder, she stared into the darkness of space. "More Tasqal ships?"

He shook his head. "No. This is different. Almost like—"

The ship suddenly lurched, throwing her forward against him, and Akur's arm wrapped tighter, steadying her.

"What the—"

Right in front of them, seeming to emerge from the void itself, a massive vessel was materializing.

Her breath caught. The ship was unlike anything she'd ever seen—sleek, impossibly white, with lines that seemed to defy physics. It hung in space like a work of art, beautiful and terrifying in its sudden appearance.

"Oh my God. Is that the Tasqals?"

Akur's entire body tensed. "No. That's...the Elysium," he breathed.

"You know this ship?"

"I know its captain." His eyes narrowed.

Before she could ask more, a transmission cut through their comms—or, at least she thought it did, before she realized the sound wasn't coming from their ship. It was within her head.

"Akur...human female." The voice was melodic, almost ethereal. Her eyes widened as she stared at Akur. "We have been waiting for you." The words were smooth, almost as if she was hearing an inner voice that wasn't hers.

"What the..." she breathed. But it seemed Akur had heard the voice too, and it wasn't freaking him out.

He straightened, staring at the massive ship before them. "Yce. You sent the coordinates."

"Yes," the voice said, still tickling her mind. "Now dock before more Tasqal ships arrive. We have much to discuss."

She stiffened slightly, glancing at Akur. "You heard it too, didn't you?"

His gaze shifted from the large ship to hers before his hand moved to her back, steadying. "It's Yce. He is Arois."

Her brows furrowed. That name sounded familiar. And then it dinged. "Arois. Like that male. The one we saw tied up back in that citadel?" Something like unease threaded along her spine.

Akur didn't respond. Instead, he watched her. "Yce rarely invades a being's mind like this. Especially one who has never encountered or felt his mind speak before." His fingers moved up to her temple, brushing away some of her hair. "We do not have to go in if you don't want to."

"He's psychic," she whispered.

"A powerful one."

She swallowed hard. Back on Earth, these things didn't exist. The psychics she knew couldn't do this. But then again, they couldn't use orbs to breach reality, either.

"The Elysium is one of the most advanced ships the Restitution has," Akur went on. "I thought he had lost it on a mission, but..." His gaze shifted back to the large ship floating before them. "We will be safe here."

But despite his confidence, Constance couldn't shake her unease. The telepathic voice, the ship appearing from nowhere—it was all so far beyond her experience. She watched as their small craft was smoothly drawn into the pristine bay, the massive ship vanishing around them like a ghost swallowing them whole.

As the airlock began cycling open with a soft hiss, Akur stood, keeping his hand at her back as they moved toward the now open ramp.

They weren't alone.

Her breath stilled in her throat as Akur moved in front of her, his stance protective as they emerged into the Elysium's pristine interior.

Four figures waited for them. At the front stood a being Constance assumed must be Yce—tall, ethereally beautiful, with skin that glowed with light as if lighting threaded through his veins. His eyes shone white. The gem in his forehead shone the same. He was exactly like the male imprisoned in that Tasqal citadel, only, he looked alive. She realized now that without his inner light, that other Arois looked nothing like he should. The gravity of his imprisonment was even greater.

Beside the Arois was a tall human woman with striking ice-blue eyes and red hair. She stood with her legs apart, arms folded across her chest. The sleek black leather that she wore made her look like some kind of superhero or something. Behind them stood the cyborg. V'Alen. The one that had helped Akur that night when the gator-guards had come and taken her away. But it was the fourth figure that made Constance stop dead in her tracks.

"Alaina." Her heart stopped. Everything stopped.

The human woman was the closest thing she'd had to a friend back on the Restitution base. And she was standing there. Alive! Just like their Tasqal ally had said.

Only, she was so different.

Constance couldn't move. Her feet felt rooted to the pristine white floor of the Elysium's docking bay. Her lungs seemed to have forgotten how to function. The world narrowed to just Alaina—this new, changed version of her friend.

Gone was the wild mane of dark curls that Alaina had always been so proud of. Her head was completely bare, and in the bright light of the bay, Constance could see the faintest trace of a surgical scar running from ear to ear across her crown. But it was her right arm that drew and held Constance's attention. It was encased in what looked like metal—sleek, too.

"Alaina?" Her voice cracked as she stepped forward. For the first time, Akur stayed back. He was allowing her to find her words on her own. Allowing her some space as she came to terms with all of this.

"Constance." Alaina moved forward and the cyborg, V'Alen, followed right behind her.

"You're really alive." Before she knew it, she was hugging the woman. There were so many questions, so much she wanted to say, but the words wouldn't come. Just holding her, knowing she was truly alive, was enough for now.

"Meredith and the silent woman...I couldn't..."

Alaina made a shushing sound. "It's alright. Constance...it's alright."

When they finally pulled apart, she noticed the tears in Alaina's eyes matched her own.

"I thought..." Alaina's voice wavered. "When we found Yce, he told us Akur and E'lot had gone after you. We hoped for the best. But then everything went silent...I thought—"

"I'm okay," she said, even though 'okay' was relative after everything that had happened. Her gaze dropped to Alaina's transformed arm. "Are you?"

"Better than okay." Alaina smiled. "V'Alen saved my life. He..." She glanced at the cyborg who stood at her back. "He took care of me."

The cyborg inclined his head. "You were strong enough to save yourself," he said, his voice carrying a gentleness she didn't expect. "I merely provided the means."

The red-haired woman stepped forward then, her ice-blue eyes assessing Constance with careful scrutiny. "I'm Diana," she thrust her hand forward for a handshake.

Taking her hand, Constance nodded. She remembered her. This woman was one of the original five. The ones that weren't in stasis pods. The females who were spoken about in whispers, revered by humans and aliens alike back on the Restitution base.

"Welcome," Diana said. "We're happy to have you here."

Constance could feel Akur's presence as he stepped up behind her. "Diana," he said. "Still keeping Yce out of trouble?"

"Trying to," Diana replied with a slight smile, before turning serious again. "Though trouble seems to have found us, anyway."

The Arois captain stepped forward then, and Constance fought the urge to step back. His presence was overwhelming—not just physically, but mentally. She could feel him at the edges of her consciousness, like standing too close to a powerful electrical field.

"Forgive my earlier intrusion," Yce said, his voice deeper than it had been in her mind, as if he'd purposely tried to speak softer so as not to scare her. "Time was of the essence, and I needed to ensure you would trust us enough to dock." The lightning bolts beneath his skin pulsed gently as he spoke. "I am Yce, captain of the Elysium and..." he paused, his glowing white eyes meeting hers, "an ally of your mate."

Mate.

Her cheeks grew warm.

So he knew.

"You knew where we were," Akur said, moving closer to Constance. "How?"

Diana huffed a small laugh. "Yce keeps surveillance of all the Restitution's leading minds. Mine. Yours. Your brothers and all of his unit." She shifted slightly, her smile growing warmer. "After what happened on the Restitution's base, we got word you'd left on a ship with E'lot."

"And I found you..." Yce tilted his head. "But not him."

Glancing up, she could see Akur's jaw clench.

They hadn't had time to speak about what happened to his friend *or* hers. E'lot, Meredith, that silent woman, and that strange Arois guy were still trapped on that horrid planet.

"You need to rest," Diana suddenly said, glancing between her and Akur. Their disheveled state must be obvious—clothes torn and dirty. The bandages. The wounds. "We've prepared quarters for you both."

"We don't have time—" Akur started, but Yce raised a hand, the lightning beneath his skin pulsing stronger.

"A few moments to collect yourselves won't change anything," the Arois said softly. "And what we need to discuss..." His gaze shifted to her and all the hairs along her arms stood on end. There was a tickling sensation in her head. She could almost feel him there, hovering just above her brain but not making contact. "It requires clear minds."

Alaina touched her arm. "Come on. I'll show you to your room. We have fresh clothes waiting."

She hesitated, glancing at Akur. He nodded slightly, his hand brushing her lower back one last time before letting her go. "Take all the time you need, bright eyes. I'll meet you on the observation deck."

V'Alen stepped forward. "I will show Akur to his quarters."

As they separated, Alaina led Constance through the pristine corridors of the Elysium. The ship was unlike anything she'd ever seen—even the Restitution base seemed primitive in comparison. The walls seemed to glow with an inner light, similar to Yce's skin.

"It's beautiful, isn't it?" Alaina said, noticing her wonder. "Arois technology."

Her gaze scanned around as they continued on. "Just...who are they?"

Alaina shrugged. "I wish I knew. Turns out, we humans are really far behind on...well, everything."

They reached a door that slid open silently at their approach. Inside was a spacious room with a large viewport. Clean clothes were laid out on a bed. Leather. Like Diana's.

"The shower is through there," Alaina gestured to another door. "Take your time."

Constance nodded, but as she moved toward the bathroom, Alaina caught her arm.

"Constance..." Alaina's voice was tight. "What happened to you out there? *Where* were you? We searched everywhere."

Looking at her friend, it felt like she'd shifted realities. Everything that happened in the past few days felt like a horrible dream. "We were...on a planet. With them." She swallowed hard. "We were on a planet with the Tasqals."

"The Tasqals?" Alaina's voice hardened, her hand tightening slightly.

"They have a world, Alaina." Constance swallowed hard. "And they have plans. Plans for some orb. We found out exactly what they're going to do."

Alaina's face went pale before she nodded. "Get cleaned up. We need to tell the others about this." She stepped back, composing herself. "I'll wait outside."

The shower was heavenly—hot and cleansing. Constance stood

under it until her skin turned pink, trying to wash away the memory of the Tasqal citadel, the grime of the tunnels and those horrible creatures they fought. The stench of death and decay.

When she emerged, Alaina was waiting, as promised. They walked in silence to the observation deck, where the others had already gathered. The room was circular, with floor-to-ceiling windows showing the vast expanse of space. Seating was arranged in a semicircle, and in the center stood a holographic display currently showing star charts.

Akur was there, cleaned and changed as well, wearing a fresh tunic and trouse. For a moment, she could only stare at him. He didn't look like a male that had died and resurrected. As a matter of fact, he looked exactly like the proud male she'd seen walking around the Restitution base before it all went to shit. And there was that glint in his eye again. The one when he was thinking about bloodshed and murder.

"I sensed your distress," Yce was saying, his voice almost quiet. "But the signal was...strange. I could not locate you. It wasn't until you crossed some kind of threshold that I could lock on to you precisely."

Akur eased back in his seat, gaze sliding to her immediately. He didn't even have to beckon. Her feet took her over to him as he pulled out the seat for her by his side.

"It's a planet that exists on no star chart," he said as she sat. "Hidden. I only found it because of her."

He gestured to her, and Constance realized they were all looking at her now.

"Their base?" Yce asked.

"Yes." Akur's words made a hush go through the room. They were all silent before V'Alen seemed to sit up straighter.

"And you escaped," he said.

Akur grunted a laugh. "I didn't. But she did. She saved me."

They were all looking at her now.

"I had help." She cleared her throat. Somehow, she just knew what she was about to say was going to turn this meeting into a glacier. "A Tasqal. He helped us."

The silence that followed her words was deafening. Diana was the first to react, shooting to her feet with such force her chair floated away.

"A *Tasqal*?" Her voice dripped with venom. "You trusted a Tasqal?"

"Diana, my mate." Yce's calm voice cut through the tension, but the lightning beneath his skin pulsed faster, betraying his own unease.

"No." Diana's eyes blazed. "This is...incomprehensible!" She slammed her palms down on the table, an echoing thud going through the room.

"Enough." Akur moved between Diana and her, his massive frame blocking Diana completely. His voice carried the weight of someone who'd seen too much to suffer prejudice. "Despite how it tastes like excrement in my mouth to say this...that Tasqal risked everything. Without him, we'd both be dead or worse. I've fought their kind for many moons, but I know honor when I see it."

"Honor..." Alaina shook her head. "From a Tasqal?"

Yce leaned forward as Akur settled back. "He speaks the truth. They both do."

That tickling in her head grew more intense, and she met his gaze. "He's part of a faction within their society that wants change. They're sick—dying—"

"Yes," Diana spat. "Let them all die."

"You're right." Constance took a deep breath. "I don't want them to live either. But he helped us. They're not...they're not all as bad as we think."

For several heavy minutes, the silence in the room felt like lead.

She took another deep breath. "I believe there are those who are truly sorry, truly tired of all their species has done. But they are afraid. Their leaders—the High Tasqals—they're planning something big. Something bad. They have an Arois prisoner."

At this, Yce's entire body grew more tense, the lightning beneath his skin flaring bright enough to make her squint. "Yes," he breathed.

"I have felt him through the void. But his signal was...wrong. Twisted."

"They're using him," Akur spoke up. "They've found a way to harness his power, to combine it with an orb. They plan to use it to create a massive portal—to transport humans to their world."

Alaina's head snapped up from where she'd been resting it against her arms. "What?" She and Diana said together.

Yce's light flickered violently. The temperature in the room seemed to drop.

"Describe him," he demanded, his voice suddenly carrying an edge she hadn't heard before.

"Tall, like you," Constance said. "But his light was...gone. Like... dim. The gem in his forehead wasn't shining like yours, either. He looked—"

"Dead," Akur finished. "But still breathing."

Yce turned away sharply, his hands clenched. Diana was at his side immediately. She pulled him into her. "Yce...do you know him?"

"No," he said, his voice barely a whisper. "But he is suffering...and if they plan to do this...to use that orb to create a gateway..."

Constance looked around, gaze shifting from one person at the table to another. "Can they really do that? Are these psychic powers that...well...could one being be that powerful?"

The lights in the room flickered and dimmed, and an icy wind swept through the sealed chamber. Yce turned back to them, his entire body now crackling with energy. The lightning beneath his skin wasn't just pulsing anymore—it was racing, streaming across his form in violent arcs that made the air taste like metal. His eyes blazed white-hot.

"You have no idea what we are capable of." His voice resonated oddly, as if coming from everywhere at once. Small objects on the table began vibrating. "The void speaks through us, shapes us, fills us. And if they have found a way to corrupt that connection, to twist it..." The temperature plummeted further, their breath now visible in clouds before their faces.

Diana's hand on his arm seemed to ground him somewhat. The

intense display of power ebbed, though the lightning still danced beneath his skin at a frenzied pace. "One being? No. But a being forced beyond their limits, their power stripped raw and connected to something like that orb..." His eyes shone again. "They could tear reality apart trying."

"We can't let that happen," Alaina said.

Constance swallowed again. "Where is this orb?"

"Safe," the cyborg said.

"We have to destroy it."

"I'm with her. We destroy it," Diana said.

"No." V'Alen's voice was so calm, it was like he was talking about something mundane. "The orb cannot simply be destroyed. Its power must be contained, controlled. Destruction could tear reality apart."

"And leaving it intact could give the Tasqals exactly what they want!" Diana countered.

"We might have another solution," Alaina whispered.

Constance's gaze shot to her a moment before there was a soft sound from the center of the table. A circular depression suddenly created itself before turning into a hole where two vials emerged from. The contents swirled within them.

"What you're looking at," Alaina said, "is the Tasqals' salvation... or their destruction."

She reached for the two small vials—one filled with a clear liquid, the other a murky green. "125, one of V'Alen's brother clones, gave us these before we left V'Alen's world. One contains the cure for the Tasqals' disease. The other..." She swallowed hard. "The other could wipe them out completely."

The room went completely still. Even Yce seemed frozen, his ethereal glow dimming slightly.

"A genocide in a bottle," Diana whispered, but there was no triumph in her voice now, only weight.

"We can't make that decision." Constance shook her head. She couldn't believe what she was saying, but it was the truth. "Not alone. Not without consulting, I don't know, the rest of the Restitution! We're talking about *genocide* here. And they're not all...not all of them are assholes. Killing them all is a decision we need to think about. Properly."

For a few long minutes, silence filled the table. They knew she was right.

V'Alen suddenly straightened. "That is not a weight you beings would like to bear." Her brow furrowed slightly. He spoke like he had firsthand experience in that regard, which was troubling. "Akur," he said, "your communications device. May I see it?"

Akur frowned but reached up to his ear, removing a tiny disk. V'Alen took it, his cybernetic components whirring as his chest opened and he slipped the device in.

Suddenly, a voice filled the room—scratchy, distorted, but unmistakable.

"—anyone receiving? This is E'lot. We're stranded in...qrak...some barren wasteland. Hedgeruds at every turn. The human—" Another voice cut in. Female. Unmistakable. "Meredith, you big lump!" E'lot groaned, stressing her name unnecessarily. "*Meredith* is injured, but alive. I lost the other shuttles carrying the other humans and Akur... he went after one. Only gods know if he still breathes. My coordinates are..." He listed off a string of coordinates. "A planet that shouldn't exist. If anyone receives this—we have found the Tasqal base."

The transmission cut off. Constance felt her heart in her throat as she looked at Akur, saw the raw emotion in his eyes at hearing his friend's voice.

"That transmission," V'Alen said, "was saved in your comm's buffer."

Akur's brow tightened. "I didn't hear it."

The cyborg handed him back the device. "The magnetic interference...whatever is hiding that planet...must have interfered with the signal."

"How long ago was that sent?" Akur rested his arms on the table, his focus on the two vials in Alaina's hands.

"On the same turn that you went silent," V'Alen said.

"If they're still alive," Constance stood. "We can't just leave them there."

"No," Akur agreed, his voice hard with determination. "We can't."

Alaina shook her head. "You would go back? To that place?"

Constance's hands formed into fists. "I will do whatever it takes to end this."

Alaina gripped the vials, gaze shifting to them. "So will I."

Easing back, Constance's shoulders squared. "So what's the plan?"

They spent hours arguing. Hours coming up with ways to spin their next move. Hours dissecting every possible approach, each plan bearing a devastating cost. The holographic display in the center of the table became a graveyard of failed strategies, each one marked with an angry red block.

"If we go in with a full assault," Diana traced her finger along one trajectory, "they'll see us coming. They have more firepower than us. We lose both our people and our element of surprise."

"How many rebels are left?" Akur asked. "How many escaped? Regrouped?"

"Enough," Alaina replied. "Several ships made it out. Commander Xul has a few with him. They are ready to fight. Plan is to find those brutes, take down the hostiles, then...use one of these vials."

"You'd have to get in the base first to do that," Constance said.

"Stealth approach." Alaina glanced from one to the other. "Small team, under their sensors—"

"There is no going under their sensors. Not after E'lot and I got in. They'd see them coming. And if they catch them..." Akur's face was grim. "They'll have everything they need. They'd have a cure...and no guarantee they would end this war. They would still be a pain in our seed sacs. Only, they wouldn't be diseased anymore. We'd be handing them the keys to your planet and so many others."

Constance watched each plan crumble, each strategy dissolve into impossible choices. Save their people but risk Earth. Protect

Earth, but kill an entire species. Strike hard and fast, but lose their only advantage. Wait too long and lose everything.

The weight of it all pressed down on her shoulders like a physical thing. Every path seemed to lead to sacrifice—the only question was what they could bear to lose.

30

Akur

HE COULDN'T STOP WATCHING Kon-stahns. Each time an idea fizzled into nothing, outwardly, it seemed she was still holding strong. But he could see the way her jaw tightened. The slight furrow of her worried brow. How her fingers curled into fists when another plan proved impossible. Her determination both filled him with pride and terror. She would go back there—he could see it in her eyes. She would walk right back into that hell to save the others.

His chest tightened. After everything they'd been through, after finally finding her, the thought of losing her again made his blood run cold. He'd waited so long for this moment, dreamed of bringing down the Tasqals, but not like this. Not at the cost of her.

When she squeezed his hand in response, he knew she understood his unspoken fears. That was the thing about Kon-stahns—she could read him like no one else ever could. Even now, as the others around the table debated strategies, her thumb traced soothing circles on his palm, silently reassuring him she wasn't going anywhere.

He stood abruptly, startling the others. "No." The word came out like a growl. "The females stay. They are too precious to send back there." Even as he said it, he caught Kon-stahns' slight head shake. It was futile, but he still needed to try.

The one named Alaina looked at the one named Diana a moment before V'Alen spoke. "It is not our choice, Akur. We would have to chain them."

"I'm not risking losing Yce," Diana spoke up, chin lifting. "If he goes, I go, too."

"The same with V'Alen," Alaina said.

"And I'm with you," Kon-stahns crossed her arms, a challenging look in her eyes.

A hot breath huffed from his nostrils. Qrakking crukks, were all human females this stubborn? Glancing at Kon-stahns, he saw the small smile twisting the corners of her lips. She knew exactly what he was thinking, and her amusement at his frustration only made him adore her more.

"They only need *one* human," he stressed.

Diana squared her shoulders. "I guess that means we better not fail."

Qrak.

He must have cursed under his breath because Kon-stahns huffed out a laugh beside him. Her hand found the small of his back, a gentle touch that somehow managed to both soothe and strengthen him.

"She has a point, hon."

Hon? That was a term of endearment. See, this was why he couldn't risk losing her. She meant too much to him. Had become essential to his very existence in a way he never thought possible.

There was only one thing to do. The plan that gave them the best odds.

"How do the vials work?" he asked, turning his attention to the dark-skinned female.

Alaina shook her head. "We can't release it into the atmosphere, if that's what you're thinking."

V'Alen spoke up. "It must be delivered to the Tasqal lifeblood."

"Only putting the odds against us even more." Diana leaned on the table. "What if we synthesize it? Attach it to our blaster fire."

"That's what we were thinking," Alaina nodded. "But there's no way for us to target them all. It's not efficient. Not effective. And most of all, they'd shoot us from the skies before we even land to start."

"Their central treatment facility," V'Alen spoke up.

"Their what now?" Diana sat up.

"The Tasqals manufacture all their treatments there," V'Alen replied. "The Restitution has been searching long and hard to find it, to no avail. I have no doubt it is on that planet."

Diana jerked her chin to her chest a few times, wheels obviously turning in her head. "Yes, because those assholes probably don't trust anyone else to do it." Her gaze slid to his. "Akur, did you see anything there? Anything that might suggest a large facility like this?"

He thought for a moment. He hadn't been looking. But then Konstahns spoke up.

"Yes." Her throat moved. "Before we saw that Arois...we saw something else. It looked like a factory. The gator-guards there were walking in protective suits. I remember because I've never seen them wearing clothes before. It must have been the plant."

Silence filled the table; everyone caught in their thoughts as they mulled over the next steps.

"If we could get the vial's contents into their next production run..." Alaina finally spoke, her eyes widening at the possibilities. "Every Tasqal in existence receives these treatments?"

"Affirmative," V'Alen replied.

"They have to," he affirmed, too. "Without them, their deterioration accelerates."

Diana shook her head. "That only puts the odds against us even more," she said, leaning on the table. "Getting into that facility—*if* it's even the one you saw—won't be easy. Security will be extreme."

"But once we're in," Yce's eyes glowed a little, "their own distribution network becomes our weapon. They'll deliver it themselves, to every outpost, every ship, every colony."

"The vial's contents won't activate immediately," Alaina warned.

"We'd have a small window before whatever effect—death or salvation—becomes evident."

"Long enough for the shipments to reach their territories." Diana seemed to perk up. "By the time they realize something is wrong..."

"It will already be everywhere..." he murmured.

Qrak him. He knew exactly what they needed to do. Gaze shifting to Kon-stahns, he saw her smile, too. He knew that look. Trust. Her unwavering trust in him.

"E'lot," he said. "We need to get those vials to E'lot."

Confusion was evident across the table, but Kon-stahns' hand tightened on his arm. Whatever risks he was about to take, he could see the fear in her eyes. But there was also unwavering support.

"Yce." He turned to the Arois. "You can reach minds across space. Find E'lot through me. Send him a message."

"What?" Kon-stahns stood now, alarm clear in her voice. "Is that even possible?" Her protective instincts were as strong as his own, he realized with a surge of affection.

Yce's eyes glowed slightly. "The Tasqals have defenses in place. Barriers even I struggle to breach. It is why I could not find you in the first place, Akur. Why that base of theirs is so elusive. And if they're using one of my kind..." He trailed off, the implications hanging heavy in the air.

"Try." He moved closer to the Arois, but Constance's hand remained firmly on his arm. "Through me. I was the last one with him. I saw the planet. I was there. Perhaps that will be enough."

Yce stood slowly. They all watched as he moved around the table to stand right in front of him.

"Akur..." Kon-stahns' voice carried a wealth of emotion—fear, something warm and deep that felt like a cloak around him, and concern.

He turned to face her fully, cupping her face in his hands. "I won't die, bright eyes."

"So you've been telling me...but you've sure as hell come close to it one too many times."

His lips twisted into a smile as he pressed his forehead to hers. "I'm tougher than you think."

She scoffed, but her hands came up to grip his wrists, holding him there for a moment longer. "You better be."

The others tactfully looked away, giving them this small moment of privacy. When he finally pulled back, Kon-stahns moved to stand beside him, her hand finding his claw again.

Yce barely gave him a nod before his eyes began glowing. Immediately, it felt like ice-cold needles pierced his skin. The sensation quickly transformed into white-hot agony that seared through his skull, setting every nerve ending aflame. Behind his eyes, colors burst and swirled—violent purples and sickening greens that shouldn't exist.

His mind became a battlefield of sensations—memories ripped loose, thoughts scattered like leaves in a storm. The barrier between self and other dissolved, leaving him raw and exposed. Static filled his ears, rising to a deafening crescendo that threatened to shatter his sanity.

Through it all, he clung to one anchor—Kon-stahns' presence beside him, her hand gripping his claw, her voice calling his name through the chaos. Even as the darkness rushed in, even as his consciousness splintered like unhooked threads, he held on to that connection.

Thoughts. So many thoughts. He could no longer tell which memories belonged to him and which were echoes of someone else's pain.

Until, suddenly, he heard it—E'lot's voice, distant and strained.

"—coming from all sides! Meredith, behind you!"

The sound of blaster fire filled his mind, along with bestial shrieks that didn't sound like Hedgeruds.

"E'lot," Akur said.

"What in the seven realms?" E'lot's confusion was clear, even through the chaos. "Akur? How—"

"Listen carefully, brother. We're coming. With an army. But first —" He felt Yce pushing the rest of the message through, explaining about the vials they would send, about what needed to be done if they didn't arrive on time.

"Understood." E'lot's voice was growing fainter. "But hurry. They're—" The connection snapped, leaving Akur gasping as he returned to himself.

He found himself on his knees, Kon-stahns' arms around him, her face tight with worry. She was murmuring softly to him, words of comfort that helped ground him back in reality. "I'm here, bright eyes," he managed, his voice rough. "I'm here."

"Did it work?" Diana asked, already half-risen from her chair. Alaina's hand was pressed against her chest while V'Alen had moved closer.

Akur nodded, allowing his mate to help him to his feet. "They're alive. Fighting. But alive."

The collective exhale was almost audible. Diana sank back into her chair, shoulders sagging with relief, and Alaina closed her eyes briefly, a silent prayer or thanks perhaps, before straightening with renewed determination.

"We need to move fast," Yce said, his own voice strained from the effort. "Gather our forces. And pray we reach them in time."

The others began to move, discussing next steps and preparations, but Akur held Kon-stahns back for a moment. In the controlled chaos that followed, they created their own small bubble of calm.

"I know what you're thinking," she whispered, reaching up to trace the line of his jaw. "And you're not leaving me behind."

He caught her hand, pressing his lips to her palm. Even in this situation, when his body shouldn't respond, it did. Maybe because it knew this may be the last peaceful night they spent together. "I wouldn't dream of it, bright eyes. Not anymore." The admission cost him something, but her brilliant smile was worth it.

She was in his arms in a split click, her legs wrapping around him as he stumbled backward, her lips pressed to his. He didn't know how or when he staggered back to his quarters or when the door shut.

All he knew was the heat of her skin, the way her fingers splayed across his skull, pulling him closer, as if she couldn't bear even the smallest distance between them.

Kon-stahns didn't wait for him to take the lead—she never did. She tugged at his tunic, dragging it over his head with a ferocity that made his pulse thunder. He let her strip him, let her hands roam over the hard planes of his chest, the scars she had once patched and bandaged. Her touch was electric, igniting every nerve in his body as she explored him like she was memorizing every inch all over again.

He wasn't gentle when he stripped her bare. He couldn't be. He was careful, but his movements were fast, desperate. He needed her skin against his, needed to feel her warmth, her life, her everything pressed to him. When her garments were gone, he pulled her close, their bodies colliding in a tangle of limbs and heated breaths.

Her nails raked down his back, leaving faint trails of fire in their wake. He growled low in his throat, a sound that came from somewhere primal, somewhere raw. She answered the sound with a gasp, her lips finding his neck, his jaw, his mouth again.

"Kiss me," she panted.

Kees? But then he knew what she meant. Knew, because she kissed him like they might never have the chance again, and he kissed her back just as fiercely.

When he lifted her, pinning her against the wall, she didn't hesitate. Her legs tightened around his waist, her arms locking around his shoulders as their bodies aligned perfectly. He could feel her heartbeat against his chest, fast and wild, matching his own. The heat between them was unbearable, consuming, and he didn't want it to stop.

In that moment, there was no war, no pursuit, no danger waiting for them outside the thin walls of the ship. There was only her—her breath in his ear, her body against his, her voice whispering his name like it was the only thing that mattered.

And when they finally came together, it was with a ferocity that stole the breath from his lungs. It wasn't slow or careful—it was raw, unrelenting, a collision of two souls who had been through hell and refused to let go of each other. Her body moved with his in perfect rhythm, every gasp, every cry, every whispered word driving him closer to the edge.

In the end, they didn't just come together—they shattered. The tension that had been building between them for so long broke like a dam, and in its place was a release so powerful it left them both trembling. He collapsed against her, his breathing ragged, his body spent, but he didn't let her go. He couldn't. He pulled her against his chest, stumbling backward onto the sleeping slab, his arms wrapping around her as if to shield her from the universe itself.

For a long time, they lay there in silence, their bodies tangled together, life organs pounding in unison. Kon-stahns rested her head on his chest, her fingers tracing lazy patterns over his skin.

"Akur..." she murmured, her voice soft, almost hesitant.

He tilted her chin up, forcing her to meet his gaze. Her eyes were luminous. Shining with something he couldn't quite name. "What is it, bright eyes?"

She hesitated for a moment, then smiled—a small, tender smile that made his chest ache. "We're going to make it, you know. You and me. All of us."

He didn't respond right away, didn't trust himself to speak. Instead, he pulled her closer, pressing his lips to her forehead. He wanted to believe her, wanted to hold on to the fragile hope she was offering him. But the weight of what lay ahead was heavy, and he couldn't ignore it.

"I love you."

He froze. "Love?"

She smiled, her thumb brushing against his cheek. "It's...hard to explain. It's...it's like...when you feel safe. Protected. Like nothing can hurt you. Like...like you're wrapped in a warm cloak, even when it's cold and dark all around." She paused, her gaze searching his. "It's... it's wanting to be with someone. Always. Wanting them to be happy. Even if it means...sacrificing everything."

Ah yes. That was exactly the description of something he'd felt but never named. The warmth that spread through him whenever she was near, the fierce protectiveness that consumed him, the bone-deep sense of connection, of belonging. The feeling of being wrapped in star light even when surrounded by shadows.

"Ah," he murmured. He could almost choke on the heavy emotion filling his throat. "That feeling." He leaned closer, his forehead brushing against hers, their breaths mingling. "I...love you too, Kon-stahns."

It was a moment of peace. A moment to believe that maybe, just maybe, they could survive this. That they could fight for something more than revenge—for love, for family, for a future worth living.

They had a chance. A small one, but sometimes that was all you needed to change everything. He knew, with a certainty that defied logic, that they would face whatever came next. And they would win. They always did.

Because some things were worth fighting for. Worth dying for. And as he looked at Kon-stahns, saw the love and determination burning in her eyes, he knew she was worth everything. Together, they would save their friends, defeat the Tasqals, and forge a future worth having.

The path ahead was dangerous, but for the first time since this all began, he felt truly hopeful. Because he wasn't just fighting for revenge anymore. He was fighting for love. For family. For a future with the female who had changed everything.

And that made all the difference in the universe.

AFTERWORD
❋☆✿☆❋

A.G.: Well, that was intense.

Akur *<growling>*: You made me drop her.

Constance: Technically, the gravity beam made you drop me.

A.G.: Hey, don't blame me! I just write what happens!

Akur *<nefre pulsing>*: And what happens next?

A.G. *<nervously>*: Um...you'll have to wait and see?

Constance: At least tell us if we're going to win this!

A.G.: And spoil the fun? Besides, Akur might break my keyboard if I say too much.

Akur: *slams fist on nearest surface*

A.G. *<jumping>*: See what I mean? Anyway, this marks the end of Constance and Akur's story, though obviously there's much more to come.

Akur: Then stop talking and write it.

A.G.: Fine! Fine! *muttering under breath* Someone needs more anger management classes...

If you've reached this far, thank you so much!

Ready for the next book in the series? <u>Join my mailing list for New Release updates!</u> I can tell you that it will star **E'lot and Meredith**, if that wasn't obvious. I cannot wait!

It's taken a while to finish this series because...well...the plot thickens. Quite literally. But there are two books left, and the story is coming to a close. Thank you for coming with me on this ride into a universe where the Tasqals rule (*shakes fist* I created them but I truly do not like the bastards).

What will happen next? Will the Tasqals win? Will we kill them all? Having the death of an entire race on your shoulders is a burden I'm sure none of us really want. But...it's the qrakking *Tasqals*.

Constance: Hey! Don't forget one of them helped us! That means

317

they're not all as wretched as we think. Sometimes even the worst behaviors come from pain or fear. A species that's caused so much destruction might be acting out of desperation. If we understood that—
A.G.: You're still here?
Akur: You cannot therapy the evil that is the Tasqals. You cannot seek to understand such *SCUM.*
Constance: Babe—
A.G.: Oh my God! Get out of my office!

Anyway, what do you think our rebels will choose?

If you've enjoyed this story, please take a moment to leave a review! I truly appreciate it.
Once again, thank you so much for being such great readers!

♥ A.G.

ALSO BY

Captured by Aliens

Xul

Crex

Yce

Kyris

Kyro

Riv's Sanctuary

Riv's Sanctuary

Sohut's Protection

Ka'Cit's Haven

The Restitution

Ajos

V'Alen

A New Home

An Alien for the Farm

An Alien for Her Heart

An Alien for the Future

Captured Earth

Arrival

Base Zero

Cataclysm

War

Rebirth

Fated Mates of the Atari

Claiming His Mate

Craving His Mate

Fighting for His Mate

Guarding His Mate

The Midnight Seven

<u>Outlaw</u>

Scan the QR code to view all books

ABOUT THE AUTHOR

A. G. Wilde is an avid reader, a gamer, a lover of all things space, alien, and sci-fi.

She is addicted to intense romance, irresistible heroes, and deliciously naughty things.

patreon.com/agwilde
facebook.com/agwilde
x.com/authoragwilde
instagram.com/authoragwilde
amazon.com/author/agwilde